Skate It Till You Make It

Also by Rufaro Faith Mazarura

Let the Games Begin

Early Praise for
Skate It Till You Make It

"Ari and Drew heat up the Winter Olympics in this gorgeous fake-dating hockey romance. Rufaro deftly (stick)handles the couple's emotional journey with each other, friends, and family to a beautiful, heartwarming, and absolutely satisfying conclusion."

—Lily Chu, author of *The Stand-In* and *Drop Dead*

"I've never read a hockey romance like this before—it's vulnerable, gritty, and emotional. Rufaro Faith Mazarura has skillfully weaved together a cast of authentic and lovable characters that kept me turning the pages. When you're not rooting for the heartwarming romance, you'll be cheering for Ari as she unexpectedly steps into the role of captain of her hockey team at the Olympics. *Skate It Till You Make It* is a must-read for fans of the Olympics, sports romance, fake dating, and love stories that are impossible to put down."

—Aurora Palit, author of *Sunshine and Spice* and *Honey and Heat*

"*Skate It Till You Make It* hit me straight in the heart. Reading about a woman fighting to carve her place in a male-dominated sport—especially in the high-stakes backdrop of the Winter Olympics—was as inspiring as it was exhilarating. Mazarura has crafted a captivating story that's fierce, romantic, and full of hope. It's the perfect read to kick off the Winter Games."

—Kanitha P., author of *All You Need Is Gloves*
and the Full Throttle series

"*Skate It Till You Make It* is a brilliant, heartwarming story about love, friendship, and believing in your dreams. Fake dating has never felt so atmospheric and riveting. Mazarura expertly weaves feminist social commentary into her writing, and it will have you rooting hard for every sportswoman in the story. This is the deep, layered, dreamy sports romance I've been waiting for my entire life!"

—Anam Iqbal, author of *The Exes*

"I savored every delicious page of *Skate It Till You Make It*. Rufaro Faith Mazarura pulls off a hat trick in her expert balancing of Ari and Drew's bewitching love story, the lush tension-filled backdrop of the Winter Games, and the question of what it really means to follow your dreams. This is a second gold medal–worthy book from Mazarura."

—Pyae Moe Thet War, author of *Here for a Good Time*

"Rufaro Faith Mazarura expertly weaves humor, conflict, and charm to write the gold standard of sports romance. Prepare to fall in love with Ari and Drew; their palpable tension had me swooning through this addictive page-turner. It was impossible to put down! Heartwarming, relatable, and compelling; loving this book is the ultimate green flag!"

—Annabelle Slator, author of *The Launch Date* and *Risky Business*

"*Skate It Till You Make It* balances fake dating, family drama, and above all, the sizzling tension between Ari and Drew, with effortless charm. A fun, fantastic read."

—Grace Reilly, *USA Today* bestselling author of *Wicked Serve*

"*Skate It Till You Make It* is a tender, grounded story that will warm your heart, even with its wintery setting. Ari and Drew's chemistry jumps off the page, as does the world that Mazarura has built. Prepare to follow the leads through their own journeys of self-discovery, packed with plenty of hijinks and an equally enticing supporting cast. Mazarura has expertly crafted a world full of beautifully complex characters that you can't help but root for, all the way through the Winter Games."

—Jasmine Burke, author of *Quarter-Love Crisis*

Skate It Till You Make It

A NOVEL

Rufaro Faith Mazarura

FLATIRON BOOKS
NEW YORK

SKATE IT TILL YOU MAKE IT. Copyright © 2026 by Rufaro Faith Mazarura. All rights reserved. Printed in the United States of America. For information, address Flatiron Books, 120 Broadway, New York, NY 10271. EU Representative: Macmillan Publishers Ireland Ltd., 1st Floor, The Liffey Trust Centre, 117–126 Sheriff Street Upper, Dublin 1, D01 YC43

www.flatironbooks.com

The Library of Congress Cataloging-in-Publication Data is available upon request.

ISBN 978-1-250-42525-6 (paperback)
ISBN 978-1-250-42526-3 (ebook)

Our books may be purchased in bulk for specialty retail/wholesale, literacy, corporate/premium, educational, and subscription box use. Please contact MacmillanSpecialMarkets@macmillan.com.

First Edition: 2026

10 9 8 7 6 5 4 3 2 1

*For the person who's always wanted to tell stories,
this is your sign to start.*

London, UK

December 2025

1

Ari

Arikoishe Shumba was on her way to becoming a legend. By the age of twenty-one, she'd won an international Ice Hockey World Championship, received two Player of the Year Awards, and scored the majestic winning goal against the Netherlands that had led Team GB's women's ice hockey team to qualify for their first-ever Winter Olympics. Which was why she and her teammates were sequestered at a secret boot camp to train for the Games. They had spent the past five days in rigorous preparation for the competition that awaited them. But for some reason, the first question Ari's favorite teammate asked her when they got back into the locker room that day was:

"Can I set you up? I promise it won't be as bad as last time." Izzy's smile that signaled trouble. Izzy wasn't just Team GB's star goaltender. She was also the team's resident matchmaker and one of Ari's best friends.

"The last guy you set me up with found my Wikipedia page

halfway through dinner, read out my stats, and still spent the whole date saying he could deadlift heavier weights than me," Ari said, shivering at the memory. She took off her helmet and sat on the bench in front of her locker.

"But you didn't have to take him to the gym in the middle of the night to prove you were stronger than him," said Izzy in her warm Welsh accent, laughing as she undid her ponytail and let her red hair tumble down.

Ari smiled at the memory. She had ubered Overconfident Connor to the closest open gym and challenged him to a bench press "lift off." Ari won, setting a new personal record of 225 pounds. Her prize was . . . never hearing from Connor again. But it was for the best. He was the last in a long string of bad dates that had made her ponder a vow of celibacy. But her friends were determined to set her up before the start of the Winter Olympics.

Izzy, ever the hopeless romantic, pressed even further. "This guy's different. He's on the Canadian men's ice hockey team, and they're in London for a couple days before they fly to the Olympics. It would be so cute! You could train together, take romantic winter holidays, and bond over skates."

Ari smiled and shook her head as she dipped a sponge in warm water and used it to wipe her hockey helmet clean. Ever since qualifying, her friends had spent every locker room session coming up with grand plans for St. Moritz. Her dating life was just the next bullet point on their Winter 2026 agenda.

Yasmeen folded her jersey then shuffled over in the silk-lined slippers she'd gifted each of her teammates for Christmas last year.

"Ari, think about it from a business standpoint." Yasmeen was as strategic on social media as she was on the ice rink in her role on defense. Her Persian parents had promised to be supportive of her athletic career as long as she made sure to diversify her income. Because athletics careers are short, and none of the girls on the team got paid enough to dedicate their entire lives to hockey. So Yasmeen was constantly reminding her teammates to make a plan for their lives beyond ice hockey, too.

"You already have a decent following, and romance sells," Izzy insisted. "If you get together and post coupley content, your followers will eat it up. It might even you get another brand deal."

Sienna, who played right forward, shook her head as she changed into an oversized Team GB hoodie. "Or . . . you could get him to use his clout to convince one of the big sports magazines to actually feature a women's team for once?"

Izzy shook her head. "We're supposed to be setting her up for love, not a PR campaign."

"Dating men is miserable," Sienna replied with a shrug. "You've got to get *something* out of it."

"Which is why I don't date men, but this guy . . ." Izzy said, scrolling through her phone for photos. "Seems sweet."

"Iz, the last guy you tried to set me up with didn't even have a bed frame," said Yasmeen, who had also been a victim of Izzy's matchmaking services. "He slept on a mattress, on the ground. Why did you think we'd be a good match?"

"Well, you got as far as seeing the mattress, so he had to have *something* going for him," Izzy joked, then wiggled her tongue.

"Hot guy, but too much of a hot mess to last beyond the night." Yasmeen laughed. All at once, everyone started chiming in, revealing the worst dates they'd been on and all the guys with obvious red flags they'd gone on a second date with anyway.

Ari loved hearing stories about her friends' love lives. They spent so much time talking strategy, fundraising, and logistics that she craved conversations that failed the Bechdel test. So, she folded up her uniform and joined in, sharing her worst anecdotes. That afternoon, the locker room was filled with light conversation because, as demanding as their coaches, schedule, and practice matches were, the first few days of precompetition boot camp were always the most fun. Ari and the twenty-two other girls on her team had left their families on Boxing Day to travel to a secret Team GB training facility just outside London. They'd launched straight into an intense training regimen and spent the week after Christmas on a strict meal plan to prepare for the most important competition of their lives, the 2026 Winter Olympics. But despite the stakes of the two months ahead of them and the constant reminders of just how close they'd been to not making it this far, their postmatch conversations always ended up dissolving into locker-room talk.

"So, you want me to date this guy . . . so we get more funding and press coverage?" Ari asked.

"Exactly," said Yasmeen with a grin. "Have you seen Yara and Ezra?" she asked, reminding them of a famous tennis doubles team who were obviously in a PR relationship. The buzz around them as a couple was generating enough hype for them to sign a multimillion-dollar joint sponsorship deal with the sportswear brand For Athena. Yasmeen shrugged. "I'm just saying, it pays to be strategic."

"Maybe we should channel all of that strategic thinking into *training* instead of planning a fake romance?" asked Sienna. "What would Gracie think?"

Their team captain's flight to boot camp was delayed, and Ari knew Sienna enjoyed being the default voice of reason in her absence. But Sienna was right, so Ari nodded in agreement.

"We're going to the Olympics. I'm way too busy to meet someone new, so I don't know why you're so focused on setting me up."

Her friends went quiet, glancing back and forth at one another as if they were in the middle of a silent meeting she hadn't been invited to.

"Am I missing something?" Ari asked as the energy in the room shifted. Izzy, Sienna, and Yasmeen were her best friends. They were the only ones close enough to tell her the truth. But they were avoiding her gaze.

Izzy suddenly became deeply interested in her phone, and Yasmeen began to fold her uniform piece by piece. In the end it was Sienna who finally sighed and sat beside her.

"When we get to St. Moritz you'll be too busy to meet someone new, but . . . you might see someone from the past," Sienna said softly. And just like that, their attempts at setting her up made sense. She should have known.

"Come on, are we still talking about this? I told you, it's over," Ari said, suddenly defensive.

"It's just . . . we know you still like him and he's obviously going to be at the Olympics. We just don't want you to get—" began Izzy.

But Ari put her hands up to stop the suffocating protectiveness that came over her friends whenever they broached the topic of her ex-boyfriend Harrison. Mentions of him always soured conversations among Ari and her teammates. But they were right, it was inevitable that she was going to bump into Harrison at the Games because he was a gold medal–winning snowboarder on Team GB. They would all be flying out to Switzerland together and staying in the same athletes' accommodation block. But unlike her friends, Ari knew that her on-again-off-again relationship with her ex was *truly* over this time.

"Me and Harrison aren't getting back together, if that's what you're worried about," she snapped. Yasmeen and Sienna exchanged knowing glances, as if they'd heard her say the same thing a dozen times. She had. Which was why she knew her friends didn't believe her. So, instead of trying to convince them she was sure this time, she took a deep breath, softened her tone, and decided to play along with their matchmaking scheme. Anything to bring some levity back into their conversation.

"If you're trying to set me up to stop me from sneaking up the stairs of GB House to find Harrison, I don't want to hear it. But . . . I'm not opposed to having a bit of fun before the opening ceremony *if* this hockey player is as great as you say he is," Ari said. "Pass me the phone, let me see Mr. Canada," she relented. Izzy grinned and shuffled across the locker room, dangling her phone from her fingers like a carrot.

Ari turned her attention to the screen in front of her. Chad Thompson was the alternate goalie of the Canadian men's ice hockey team. He was six foot four with a sweet, crooked smile. Judging by the photo of Big Ben on his Instagram story, he was in London with his teammates to celebrate New Year's Eve before they flew to Switzerland. He didn't have the face of a could-be serial killer, but you could never be too sure.

"I don't know about this," Ari said as she scrolled through photos of Chad. She had a long, messy history when it came to dating other athletes. They either feigned disinterest if they thought she was more successful than them, tried to downplay her achievements if they were further along, or, like Harrison, got strangely competitive the minute her success began to eclipse theirs. "I think I'm done with athletes."

"Ari, you've got to date *at least* one hot hockey player in your lifetime," said Yasmeen.

"I don't need to date a hot hockey player. I *am* a hot hockey player," said Ari with a wicked smile, a comment that was met with a wave of agreement from the rest of the girls on the team.

Ari and the other girls had started playing the sport as children. Their parents had ferried them to the local ice rink every weekend and cheered them on from behind the glass-lined stands. But no one had ever *really* thought they would get that far.

While hockey was one of the biggest winter sports and the UK was home to some of the most successful athletes in the world, their women's ice hockey team had never qualified for an Olympic tournament.

Until a couple of years ago, when their team had signed a game-changing new player, Gracie Walters. The twenty-six-year-old, London-born, Montreal-raised ice hockey champion had moved to Canada when she was three years old, and she'd become one of the top players in North America. But to everyone's surprise, she'd moved back to the UK in 2022 to study for her master's. She'd given up her prestigious North American career and used her dual citizenship to join Team GB. A decision that shook up the entire International Ice Hockey Federation.

The months after Gracie joined the team had been a beautiful blur. Gracie pushed Ari and her teammates to believe in themselves, train harder, and play better than ever before. She took a vested interest in each one of them, spending hours studying the way they played to amplify their strengths and improve their weaknesses. For some reason, she'd taken Ari under her wing, taking her out for coffee to talk strategy and giving her advice on how to be a better leader on and off the rink. It was inspiring for Ari to have a captain who genuinely believed they could win and forced the rest of the ice hockey community to take notice of them.

The uninspired coach they'd been stuck with for the past few years was replaced by Niall McLaughlin, the legendary former head coach of the men's ice hockey team. And then, after years of being warned that they would never see an international win in their lifetimes, Ari and her newly thriving team won their nail-bitingly tense qualifier match against the Netherlands. With that, they'd secured their place at the 2026 Winter Olympic Games. Which was why they were spending the days after Christmas at a high-intensity, six-week-long boot camp.

But it was New Year's Eve. At the end of their afternoon training session, Coach McLaughlin had given them an unofficial pass to celebrate the most successful year of their careers before their schedules filled up with more training sessions, uniform fittings, and travel plans. But Ari and her team were still split on whether to do the responsible thing and spend the night in the boot-camp hotel or throw caution to the wind and head into the city.

"Why don't we just stay in and relax? We could watch a movie or something," said Sienna. She'd spent the better part of her teenage years sneaking into clubs she was too young to be in and was too tired to go out-out now.

Ari agreed. "Coach isn't going to give us this much time off again for the rest of the winter." She was salivating at the prospect of a sleeping in after an intense day on the ice.

"It's New Year's! We're not staying here all night," said Izzy, who loved a good party. "I heard the hockey boys are going to the—"

But Sienna cut her off. "There's nothing I'd rather do less than sit in a random countryside pub and talk about training regimens with the *hockey boys*," said Sienna.

Ari didn't want to go, either. Harrison was friends with them, and she didn't want bumping into him to ruin the last night of her year. But the rest of the team was determined to go out.

"Shall we get a train into London? I think I could get us into a good party," said Yasmeen, pulling her phone out. Yasmeen was the most well-connected person Ari knew. She'd spent her early twenties as a firm fixture on the London party scene, and her contacts were filled with the kind of musicians, DJs, and celebrities who threw star-studded parties every week. But before Ari could try to convince them that they would have just as much fun watching the New Year's Eve scene of *When Harry Met Sally* as they would at an actual party, she heard a muffled voice calling her name through the locker room speakers.

"Arikoishe, could you please come to my office once you've finished getting ready? Thank you," the voice said. The whole team *ooh*ed as Ari finished putting on her tracksuit. Coach McLaughlin only asked people to go to his office when they were in trouble, and Ari *never* got in trouble.

She got up, slung her duffle bag over her shoulder, and promised she'd be back to finish making New Year's plans. Then she walked out of the locker room, curious to hear what Coach McLaughlin wanted to talk about. As she did, she clasped her black-leather-and-gold watch around her wrist. It made a quiet, reassuring ticking sound each second, as if it was excitedly counting down to the new year with her.

Ari couldn't help but walk with a spring in her step as she made her way through the corridors of the ice hockey building. She looked up at the walls decorated with old, framed team photos and vintage posters from matches played decades before she was born. There were barely any Black players in those photos, and beyond her group of friends, Ari had never quite felt like she belonged to the ice hockey community. She'd answered, "Yes, there are Black ice hockey players" and "No, the cold doesn't bother *people like me*" more times than she could count. But random people's preconceptions mattered way less to her than the fact that she got to play her favorite sport with her best friends. Because one day her face would be in the photos up on those walls, and there would be countless more after her. While it was daunting to be one of the first, she knew it meant she wouldn't be the last.

Coach McLaughlin was a Northern Irish man in his mid-sixties who spent every single match pulling at his hair and indirectly shouting at the referee until he was red in the face. But off the rink, he was a quiet, easygoing guy who spent training sessions carefully choosing his words, as if one wrong move might cause the team to turn against him. He didn't tell them anything more than they needed to know, which was why the immediacy of what he said as she walked into his office sent a chill down her spine.

"I have bad news," he began as Ari took a seat. Coach McLaughlin looked nervous as he fidgeted in his seat and glanced over at the clear glass door.

"If it's that we have six a.m. training on New Year's Day, Coach, I can't be the messenger," Ari joked.

"It's not that," he said, his voice solemn.

"Are the uniforms arriving late?" Ari frowned. "Yasmeen made a whole list of video ideas for the team TikTok account, and she'll be devastated if we can't film those this weekend."

"Arikoishe."

"Coach," she replied, concerned by the seriousness of his tone.

"Have you heard from Gracie?"

"Yeah, her flight kept getting canceled because of the storm. But she should get here by tomorrow though, right?"

"She's not going to be here tomorrow; there's been an accident," Coach said. Ari's stomach dropped. He quickly clarified. "Don't worry, she's okay, she's already out of hospital."

But Ari was already imagining worst-case scenarios. "What happened?" she asked.

Coach sighed. "She fell, badly, and tore her ACL." He began pacing around the room as he explained what happened. "She's too injured to play, so she won't be joining us these next few weeks . . . or competing at the Olympics."

Ari froze. A part of her reasoned that if she sat completely still and didn't make a sound, she could convince herself that this wasn't happening. Trick her brain into believing this was a bad dream and rewind her watch by a week to change the course of time. Maybe that way she could stop Gracie from going ice skating after Christmas and return her life to a timeline that made sense.

But sitting still wasn't enough to stop the next fifteen seconds from happening. Or stop the next sentence Coach McLaughlin said from altering her team's future. She watched as Coach walked around the room before returning to his desk.

"This isn't the way things were supposed to happen, so we won't tell the rest of the team until after New Year's. You all deserve a break before things heat up. But Arikoishe, I'm telling you first because I'm making you the new team captain."

Ari's mouth dropped open.

"What?" she asked. Coach gave her what was supposed to be a reassuring look. But it didn't do anything to stop the wave of doom from washing over her.

Ari was a player, not a captain. She didn't know how to stop her teammates from going to a misjudged New Year's Eve party, never mind how to lead them to anything that resembled victory at their first Olympics. But before she could protest, reason, or try to convince Coach McLaughlin to change his mind, his head turned toward the noise outside his door. She turned in her seat and glanced through the glass office door to see that her teammates had left the locker room and were walking down the hallway. She could hear the sounds of laughter and twenty-two pairs of trainers hitting the freshly waxed wooden floors as they made their way through the building. Blissfully unaware that their dreams were at risk.

"Coach, I don't think I'm ready," she said, scrambling to get him to change his mind.

"I wouldn't give you the responsibility if I didn't think you could handle it," he said as he opened the door and walked toward the water fountain in the hallway. Ari got up from her seat and followed him out. She had a dozen questions. But before she could ask him anything, her teammates flooded the corridor. Abuzz with chatter about some party.

"Let's talk about it tomorrow, okay?" he said.

"Talk about what?" asked Sienna.

"Nothing to worry about," said Coach. But Ari could see the apprehension in his eyes. "Anyway, it's four p.m. on New Year's Eve. What are you still doing here? Enjoy your last night of freedom," he said, waving them a cheerful goodbye.

"Come on, Ari. We have a party to get ready for," said Yasmeen.

The winter chill washed over her as soon as they stepped outside. It was already dark out, and the uneasy feeling that always found her in the week between Christmas and New Year's Eve felt stronger than ever. But tonight was supposed to be a celebration, so Ari let her friends drag her across the boot-camp grounds. She did her best not to let her feelings show, but Sienna noticed her trailing behind and linked arms with her, pulling her in as the icy winter air blew against their skin.

"Next year, which is in less than twenty-four hours, we're going to be Olympians," said Sienna, her eyes twinkling as their footsteps crunched against a frosty patch of grass.

"Everything's about to change," said Izzy, looking up at the stars beginning to appear in the dark blue sky.

Ari just nodded. Everything *was* about to change. But the watch on her wrist didn't feel like it was counting down to the new year anymore. It felt like a doomsday clock ticking down until the moment the team's fate was put into her uncertain hands.

2

Drew

Drew Dlamini had been a college dropout for twenty-three days.

Twenty-three days, four hours, and twelve minutes, to be exact.

He'd woken up on December 9 in a cold sweat. Shaken by a nightmare he couldn't remember once the lights were on. So, he'd gotten out of bed, opened his laptop, and typed up an email with the subject line: WITHDRAWING FROM MY STUDIES.

Drew had sent the email first thing in the morning, so he couldn't call it a late-night mistake. He'd edited it in the library on a Tuesday, so he couldn't blame it on the Sunday Scaries. And he'd spent hours drafting and redrafting it until he was sure it wasn't just a spur-of-the-moment decision.

So, Drew had nobody but himself to blame for why the first thing his grandma said to him when he walked into a London restaurant three weeks later was:

"It's your right to throw your education away, Andrew, but I draw the line at being late for lunch." She was teasing him about lunch, but the education part? He knew he'd be hearing about that for the rest of his life.

The Dlaminis were staying in London for the holidays and his grandparents had planned their itinerary around all the restaurants on their must-try list. Today's reservation was Akoko, a place in Fitzrovia they'd picked for its West African food and Michelin star. It was too upscale to be the setting for another family argument. So, when Drew walked into the warm, dimly lit restaurant, he headed straight to his family's table. He hugged his grandma, an elegant woman in her seventies who wore her Sunday best on every occasion. Then he accepted a customary nod from his grandpa, a man who was technically retired but visited the accountancy firm he owned once a week and never left the house without a suit and a business proposal.

"So, I spoke to the guys at the firm, and they said they could find a place for you in January," his grandpa said before Drew could even reach for a menu. He was trying to be supportive and use his connections to get Drew a job. But the pained expression on his face made it clear that, while he'd taken the advice he'd read in all the *My grandchild is throwing his life away. What should I do?* articles he found on the internet, he was still reckoning with Drew's newfound status as a dropout.

"A job and some structure will be good for you. You're smart, so you'll adjust quickly," Grandpa said, reaching out to pat Drew's back. Affection didn't come easily to him, but ever since Drew had dropped the news that he wouldn't be returning to USC or California after winter break, everyone had been treating him with kid gloves.

"Just don't make any more rash decisions," his grandma pitched in, running her hands through the silk press she'd been wearing since the seventies. She took a sip of her wine, gave him her classic *I have an idea* smile, and aimed her lifelong commitment to fixing things at her grandson. There was no issue she couldn't solve with a good plan.

"I have a friend on the board of your university. Do you remember Betsy? The sweet lady you met at your cousin's graduation? Well, Betsy still owes me a favor from nineteen eighty-two. I'm sure she could help you reenroll by the spring."

Drew's grandpa enthusiastically nodded. "I was looking up the guidelines last night, and I think you still have thirty days before the decision is finalized, so it's not the end of the world, Andrew."

But it *was* the end of that chapter of Drew's life, because he wasn't going to change his mind. He'd reeled off a list of fake excuses to explain himself. Said he wasn't enjoying his time at USC, argued that he didn't need a degree to become a professional photographer, even went as far as to say that he missed Wisconsin. But his reason for dropping out was simple.

His grandma had Alzheimer's.

He'd found out on Thanksgiving. It was his favorite holiday, so he always left college for the weekend to take the trip back home. Usually, he woke up on Thursday to the smell of a roasting turkey, the sound of old gospel music, and the sight of the expensive plates and cutlery she reserved for special occasions. But when he'd woken up, the only sound in the house had been the voice of his panicked grandpa calling up everyone they knew. Because Grandma had disappeared.

Her shoes were gone, her phone left behind. The turkey was prepped and the oven was on, but the door was left ajar, the heat filling up the kitchen in a way that made it clear it had been like that for hours.

His sister, Thandie, wasn't due to come home until the evening. So, he and his grandpa spent the morning and afternoon driving around town. Trawling the streets and calling up friends and family to ask if they'd seen her—with no success.

When a police car rolled up to their front porch at around four p.m., the time she'd usually be making the final touches to dinner, Drew ran outside. Two officers got out and opened the back door to reveal their passenger: Grandma. She was shaken but indignant, determined to tell them she'd taken a walk on purpose, even though they all knew she'd gotten lost. It was only then that Grandpa sat him down and explained everything he'd missed out on while he was at school. The diagnosis, the symptoms. How things were progressing faster than either of them had anticipated. He allowed Drew to ask a flurry of questions under one condition: He couldn't tell Thandie. She'd just come out of recovery, was in the midst of a stressful season at work, and nobody wanted to make it worse. So, the three of them decided to keep it a secret from her until the spring.

So, they drove to the grocery store and made a meal of freezer-aisle dishes. When Thandie finally got home that night, they blamed their not-so-traditional meal on a faulty oven. They couldn't afford to let her know the truth.

At the end of the weekend, Drew took his scheduled flight back to USC, where he spent days trying to come up with a list of reasons to stick it out until graduation. The cost of tuition, the two and a half years he'd already invested, and the fact that all the best career opportunities were in California. But in the end, it came down to a simple question: What was the point of staying at college when his favorite person in the world needed him?

So Drew decided to go back home and spend as much time with her as he possibly could. Even if that meant leaving college in the middle of his junior year. So, he'd dropped out of USC, packed his things, and moved back to his hometown in time for Christmas. Madison, Wisconsin, was smaller than he'd remembered; the walls of his bedroom were still covered in posters from high school, and he'd long outgrown his twin-sized bed. But he'd felt an immediate sense of relief to be back home.

"We just want you to know that it's never too late to go back," his grandma said now, looking over at her husband and tapping his shoulder. The two of them exchanged a look that made it obvious that they'd already talked about this and, after a moment, his grandpa's tense expression gave way to softness.

"We just want the best for you," his grandpa said, his voice stilted like the line was rehearsed. It definitely was, because his grandma was not so subtly mouthing the words along with him. Drew stifled a laugh. His grandparents had been doing this tag-team parenting since he was a little kid. But as pure as their intentions were, Drew was too far gone.

"I'm not changing my mind," he said, opening his menu as his grandpa gave him a look. His grandpa had reassured Drew that he could take care of his grandma without his help. Drew didn't believe him. They'd gone back and forth for hours, disagreeing about pretty much everything except the fact that his grandma couldn't know that she was the reason why Drew had left college behind.

"But you worked so hard, Andrew. I just can't believe you would throw it all away." His grandpa was now using the *not angry, just disappointed* voice.

"I worry about you, you know," his grandma said, looking at him like he was a little kid. Her affection was almost too much to bear. "We're not going to be around forever. So, we need to know you'll be stable and secure when we're gone."

Drew studied the lines around her mouth earned by years of laughter, the proud grays in her hair, and the warmth in her eyes. He *knew* she wasn't going to be around forever. There wasn't a single day he didn't think about it. But he couldn't tell her that.

It was easier to let her think he was throwing his life away than admit he'd moved back home to help take care of her. So, he tried to change the conversation.

"Think of it this way: Me being back home for a while means I'll finally get around to putting together all those albums you've been asking about," Drew said. His grandma lit up at that, and began a monologue about the family photos she wanted to print out while his grandpa quizzed an unsuspecting waiter about the origins of all the items on the menu. Drew was about to decide between a Domoda stew and a jollof rice bowl when his phone rang.

He looked down at the caller ID and sighed in relief. *Thandie.* He excused himself from the table, answered the phone, and walked as far away from his grandparents' table as he possibly could.

"I can't believe you left me to handle family dinner by myself," he said as soon as he stepped out of the restaurant. Thandie appeared on the screen, power-walking through the streets with her hair pulled into a tightly braided ponytail.

"How badly is it going? Do you need me to run over and provide some comedic relief?" she asked as she crossed a tree-lined street Drew recognized from his own walk to the restaurant.

"It's . . . not going well," Drew admitted.

"Has Grandpa offered you a job at the firm yet?" Thandie asked knowingly. He'd been trying and failing to get one of his grandkids to become an accountant since they were kids.

"Yeah, we've already had the *we can pull strings to get you in* conversation."

"It's because you spend too much time with them," Thandie laughed. She was right, they'd both moved out of state to stop their grandparents from getting too involved with their lives. "Love them, but you need to get some distance or else every conversation becomes about the life they think you should be living," she said with the easy detachment of a youngest child.

"Is that why you're late for dinner? You're decentering your grandparents?"

"No, I just got lost on the Tube. But that's not why I'm here. I called to tell you that *we* have New Year's Eve plans."

Drew and Thandie were only a year apart, so Drew could automatically tell when his little sister was about to try to convince him to do something she knew he wouldn't want to do.

"I already have New Year's Eve plans," he said flimsily.

"What? Are you tagging along to the retirees' river cruise?" she asked, raising an eyebrow. His grandma *had* invited him. But as strong as the pitch was, ringing in the new year with a boatful of senior citizens would have taken his week to a new low.

"I have . . . other plans," Drew lied. He paced back and forth down the sidewalk, the December air making him wish he'd worn a coat.

"Sitting in a sad hotel room, staring up at the ceiling, and questioning every decision you've ever made while watching your college friends' Instagram stories as the clock strikes midnight isn't a New Year's Eve plan," Thandie said.

"Actually, I was going to take a walk through the city, listening to sad songs and watching the fireworks as I questioned every decision I've ever made," he said, only half joking. "Isn't an existential crisis the whole point of December thirty-first?"

"Drew, you're in London, and it's New Year's Eve. I'm not letting you waste it because you're *sad* or whatever," she said, pointing around at her surroundings.

"I don't really want to go to a random party—"

"You wouldn't just be *going* to the party. I got you a gig . . . to take photos."

Drew's ears perked up at that. He'd left his photography

classes at USC behind, but his passion for taking photos hadn't faded away. Fleeing LA to move back to Wisconsin left him with fewer opportunities to get his camera out. So, he was desperate to get behind the lens again.

"I'm listening," he said, curious to know how she'd found an opportunity on the other side of the world.

"Do you know Klaus Lindberg?" Thandie asked.

Everyone knew Klaus Lindberg; his family owned the biggest sportswear brand in the world.

"The son of the Zeus Athletics guy?"

"Not just *the son*," she said. "The second-born son, the one who's trying to push his older brother Lars out and take over his dad's company."

"Yeah, I've heard of him. But what do they have to do with New Year's?"

"Well, Klaus is hosting Zeus's annual blowout New Year's Eve party tonight, and he wants to make it bigger than ever. Every single famous, influential person under the age of thirty is going to be there, and as of ten minutes ago, so are you."

"What?" Drew asked, confused.

"I have connections." She shrugged. "Klaus is old friends with a girl I went to college with who lives in London. We all went to breakfast together and he invited me to his party and said that I could bring you as my plus-one."

Drew didn't know what was more surprising. That his sister was casually friends with a twenty-two-year-old billionaire or that she'd gotten him an invite to photograph one of the most exclusive parties of the year.

"He was supposed to have two photographers for his party, but one of them has food poisoning. He mentioned that he was looking for someone else last minute, so I suggested . . ."

"Me?"

"Yes, you. I showed him your work, and he really liked it. It took some convincing and maybe I exaggerated a little to convince him you'd be the right fit, but he said you can come along and bring your camera. There's going to be an official party photographer all night to get the most important shots, but Klaus wants someone who can run around and get some extra photos for socials. I said you'd be perfect."

"I don't know about this," he said. He'd gotten a few good gigs back in California: a student press pass for a few Dodgers games, a spring internship with the Lakers, and a fall internship with a local football team. But those were all structured opportunities that he'd spent weeks planning for. "Zeus is a big deal, and I'm not sure I—"

"Stop trying to talk yourself out of a good thing," she said firmly. "Plus, it's not like you have anything else going on since you—"

"Dropped out and threw two and a half years of my life away?"

"You said it, not me," she teased. "But it's a great opportunity and it will be good for you. You need to leave the hotel and pick up your camera again."

"But . . ."

"Drew. When January third comes around, you'll be back home with absolutely nothing to do. Driving around Wisconsin and letting Grandma send you on errands."

"Oh, that really is my future," Drew said, letting the realization sink in.

"It doesn't have to be," she said, her voice softening. "Come to the party."

Drew could already imagine all the ways his life was going to shrink when he flew back home. The nights he was going to spend questioning his decision and the days he was going to spend longing for a type of certainty he wasn't sure he'd ever feel again. When January came, he'd probably be working at his grandpa's accounting firm, reckoning with his grandma's deterioration, and spending hours at a time watching the lives of his college friends unfolding online.

Maybe one last party was exactly what he needed to mark the end of his hellish year.

"Are you in?" Thandie asked.

"Send me the address."

3

Ari

DECEMBER 31, 2025

If her dad hadn't skipped out on her family when she was a kid to run away with a new woman to a different country, Ari would have never become an Olympian. The money he'd sent to assuage his guilt sent her to an elite private school where everybody's parents were wealthy and well connected. She'd gone into it expecting to feel out of place. After all, she'd gone to a state school from the ages of five to eleven and was one of the only Black girls joining her private school in the middle of the year. But she hadn't expected to feel so lonely.

However, after a few weeks of roaming the halls alone, she'd met a half-Trinidadian girl with braces and a halo of brown hair, named Sienna, who had invited her to tag along to the after-school ice hockey club. At that point, Ari's only experience of ice skating was the time her mom had taken her and her younger sister to a pop-up ice rink at an annual Christmas market. But to everybody's surprise, Ari took to the ice like a duck to water. Playing ice hockey for the first time with Sienna and her new school friends felt like finding the missing piece to a jigsaw puzzle she'd spent her whole childhood trying to assemble. And Ari almost immediately excelled. She skated faster than any of the other girls on her team, plotted out each move to set her teammates up for success, and played with the kind of strategy that made her one of the most valuable players on her team. Ari lived for the thrill of scoring the winning goal and loved each second she spent on the ice.

But being a great player at eleven and a great captain at twenty-one were two entirely different things. Only one of which she felt equipped to do.

She needed to cast that to the back of her mind, though, because she'd promised Coach McLaughlin that she wouldn't tell any of her teammates about Gracie's injury or her new role as captain yet. The bad news could wait until January 1 because tonight was her and her teammates' last chance to celebrate before they flew to Switzerland. So, Ari forced herself to succumb to the heady atmosphere taking over the seventh floor of their boot-camp hotel.

Every single door in the hallway was wide open as music blared out from speakers in different bedrooms. There were old-school R&B tracks, 2000s club classics, sad girl pop bops, and house anthems playing under the sound of her teammates laughing, talking, and getting ready for the night ahead. Freshly sprayed perfume merged with the smell of hot hair curlers as they ran back and forth between rooms to swap jewelry and borrow bobby pins. Their beds were covered with glamorous dresses and mismatched sparkles. The dressing tables were laid out with tiny bags and twinkling necklaces. The bathroom sinks were adorned with hairbrushes, overflowing makeup bags, and boxes of fake eyelashes. Ari and her teammates spent most of their lives in oversized jerseys, ice skates, and protective helmets, but tonight they were going all out. Half of the team was going to a spontaneous Team GB party at the pub down the road from boot camp, and a handful of the others were staying at the hotel to ring in the new year with a movie marathon. But Ari had agreed to join Sienna, Yasmeen, and Izzy at the blowout New Year's Eve party Zeus Athletics was throwing in central London.

"Could somebody help me zip up the back of my dress?" asked Ari as she walked out of the bathroom and into the hotel suite she was sharing with Izzy, Sienna, and Yasmeen. Yasmeen was sitting on the floor surrounded by the emptied-out contents of her makeup bag, applying a perfectly sharp winged eyeliner. Sienna was half dressed, singing along to an old Sugababes song while she decided between two equally sparkly tops. And Izzy was slowly taking her bright red hair out of rollers and marveling at how each perfectly formed curl fell onto her shoulders. But when Ari walked in, all the girls looked up at her in delight.

"Ari! You look gorgeous," said Sienna, getting her phone out to take a picture of their New Year's Eve looks.

"I am going to steal that dress from you the minute you take it off," said Yasmeen as she walked over, zipped up Ari's dress, and gave her a YSL Black Opium–scented hug.

Ari studied her reflection in the mirror and concluded that while she hadn't dressed up to meet the guy her friends were trying to set her up with, or the ex-boyfriend they were trying to keep her away from, she did look really good. She was wearing a midnight-blue dress with sparkly silver detailing. Her hair was blown out into big, bouncy, seventies-style curls and she was wearing glamorous diamond-cased earrings that twinkled each time she tilted her head.

"Chad is gonna—" began Izzy, but Ari shook her head and decided to put an end to the New Year's romance plot. The Zeus party was going to be filled with athletes and famous people their age, so she didn't want to spend the whole night letting Izzy play a game of matchmaker.

"Izzy, I love you. I appreciate your efforts, but I don't want to meet *Chad*," she said, looking around at the women she'd been friends with since she was a teenager. "In fact, I don't need you guys to set me up with anybody." To mark the moment, she picked up a nearby glass of sparkling water and raised it in the air for a toast. "To focusing on our matches. Swearing off men, especially Harrison. And spending the rest of the night dancing with you." She could tell by the looks on her friends' faces that they didn't really believe the Harrison part. Still, they smiled, clinked their glasses, and launched into a conversation about all the athletes taking pit stops in London before they flew to Switzerland for the Winter Games.

But Ari couldn't distract herself enough to shake off the dread she'd been feeling ever since Coach McLaughlin had broken the Gracie news. She'd never been a team captain and was daunted by the prospect of stepping into it for the first time, just weeks before the Olympics. Because being a good captain wasn't just about being a good player, it was about being an excellent leader, keeping her teammates in line, and getting them to respect her, specifically, on a professional level. And as much as she loved her best friends, they could be a bit of a nightmare.

"Who's taking shots?" said Izzy as she pulled a bottle of tequila out of her suitcase, seeming to forget that alcohol was banned from their strict pretournament diet and that none of them could afford to take risks in the first week of boot camp.

"Should I go with black, or white?" asked Sienna, lifting two pairs of shoes. Ari shuddered at the height of the six-inch heels; Sienna was one mistimed dance move away from a twisted ankle. If anything happened, the team would be without one of their best shooters.

"I love Gracie, but I'm kind of glad her flight was delayed. Because if she was here doing up team captain, we definitely wouldn't be going to a party right now," said Yasmeen. The other girls began to laugh along with her, blissfully unaware that Gracie wasn't coming to boot camp. And that their new team captain, Ari, was right there in front of them. Noticing every small choice that could jeopardize their futures.

Ari was usually easygoing. Joked around with her teammates, danced on every occasion, and gave herself the freedom to occasionally indulge in small bursts of recklessness. But now that she was their team captain, it was up to her to get them to the party, through the party, and back from the party without any injuries, runaways, or dumb decisions that could affect their performance. The responsibilities that came with being the team captain now rested on her glitter-covered shoulders.

But one hour, three mocktails, and a ridiculously expensive Uber ride later, Ari's worries were slowly, temporarily, beginning to retreat. She and her friends spent the journey passing the aux cord around, convincing the driver to sing along to their favorite songs. They drove into London with the windows down, playing Raye and Jorja Smith on full blast. Laughing, gossiping, and dancing their way into the final hours of the year. The car sped past a skyline of tall, spectacular buildings, big groups of late-night revelers, and city lights that pointed them in the direction of the party. But when they arrived, Ari began to question if they'd typed in the right address. The building they pulled up in front of was in one of the strange dystopian parts of Canary Wharf where all the skyscrapers were tall, expensive, and seemingly empty. The kind of apartments you knew belonged to mysterious oligarchs who bought a London postcode for *business purposes* but didn't pay taxes. The buildings were glossy, the streets were eerie, and there wasn't a parked car in sight. But their Uber driver needed to pick up his next round of passengers, so they got out and followed Yasmeen.

"Yas, are you sure that this is the right place?" Ari asked as they stepped into the lobby. The building was silent except for the sound of their footsteps. Yasmeen turned around and led them to the other side.

"This is the right place," she said as they stepped into the elevator. Yasmeen pressed the button for the fifty-first floor. Ari looked out of the window as they went up. From this height, they could see the entire city. She liked imagining the lives of people who lived in buildings like these. Tall, multimillion-pound apartment buildings that stretched out into the sky like private hands reaching out to the heavens. The girls were quiet by the time the doors opened, in silent awe of the view that welcomed them on the top floor. Yasmeen led them down the corridor until they reached an unassuming door marked by two men with headsets and iPad guest lists. Yasmeen walked over and said a few words to them, and then the guards instructed them to hand their bags over for a search.

"Have a lovely evening, ladies," one of the security guards said with a nod once he was done.

Yasmeen walked down the corridor, pushed the door open, and led them into a room where they were instantly engulfed by colors, lights, and sounds. The room was packed with some of the most beautiful people Ari had ever seen, and they were all swaying along to an intoxicating beat. Ari stood mesmerized as she watched them under the light of a mirror ball that was slowly spinning around the room, reflecting specks of light that looked like stardust. Eyelids glittered, dresses twirled, and a perfectly curated soundtrack lifted backs from the dark shadows and out onto the dance floor.

"Where are we?" Ari asked, locking eyes with a handsome server as he offered her a tall, shimmering glass of champagne and winked before turning his back.

Yasmeen turned to her with a glint in her eyes.

"The best party of the year."

4

Drew

The best photographers knew how to be invisible. How to step into a party filled with glamorous people letting go of their inhibitions and fade into the background enough to capture them at their most honest. How to roam around a crowd with a camera in hand and blend into the scenery so that each image they captured felt raw and unstaged. And for a few moments that night, with his black blazer, silver press lanyard, and unassuming camera, Drew was practically invisible. A shadow among the beautiful people in dazzling dresses and expensive suits.

Drew was pretty good at spotting stories in a crowd, so when he arrived, he immediately began taking photos with his Fujifilm X100V. As he walked past the dance floor, he saw a trio of tall, stunning models dancing offbeat to the biggest song of the year, their dresses a glittery blur. He aimed his camera and took a photo. As he turned the corner, he spotted a crowd of A-list actors congregated around a table of untouched canapes exchanging passive-aggressive barbs. So, he took a picture and captured them, too.

Drew weaved his way through the party and watched it unfold with quiet awe. He took photos of the champagne tower and then the DJ dancing behind the booth. There was a Premier League football player on her right and a Grammy Award–winning rapper on her left. They were both drunkenly bobbing their heads and shouting song requests Drew knew she would never play. But the juxtaposition between their polished outfits and messy demeanor felt so stark that he had to capture it. The party was a visual feast, and Drew wanted his camera to devour every second.

Unlike his sister, who'd always thrived at parties and immediately got lost in the crowd, Drew was more comfortable standing on the sidelines. Which is why his grandmother had given him a green disposable Fujifilm camera for his seventh birthday. Drew was a shy kid, so at first the camera became something to hide behind. A barrier between him and everybody else. But as the years went on, it became his favorite way of seeing the world. In high school, he'd taken his camera with him every day to take photos of his friends. He'd spent his freshman year of college taking portraits of the most interesting people on campus, and, after deciding to major in photography, he'd spent his sophomore nights doing freelance gigs for local newspapers and popular websites.

But his real dream was to become a sports photographer. There was something about the atmosphere of a game, both on the field and in the stands, that always pulled him in. He loved watching the crowds' reactions and following the small melodramas that unfolded as supporters celebrated, fought, and channeled all of their energy into their favorite game. Which is how he'd met his ex-girlfriend, Sade. Her dad was a senior exec at the football team he'd interned at last summer, and they'd met at a preseason celebration. As Drew looked around at the New Year's event, he couldn't help but notice the same out-of-place feeling he'd felt in LA creeping up on him.

"Drew, you promised me you wouldn't get all weird and existential in the middle of the party," said Thandie, materializing from the crowd in a purple jumpsuit and passing him a Negroni that immediately pulled him out of his thoughts.

"Who said I was getting weird and existential?" he asked, taking a sip before shaking his head. As much as he wanted to loosen up, he couldn't afford to drink on the job.

"Your face? You look miserable," she said, shaking her head and then examining him. "Are you thinking about Sade again?"

"I *wasn't*," he said. But now that she'd brought his ex-girlfriend up, he was. Wondering if she was spending her New Year's Eve in LA with all their college friends and whether or not they missed him. He wasn't heartbroken about the breakup, but he still felt blindsided by the ending.

"I just don't understand how . . ." Drew began. His sister sighed and put her hand out as if to give him permission to talk it out.

"I just don't understand how something that meant everything to me meant so little to her that she would just hook up with some random football player? His performance last season was below average, and he's holding a fish in pretty much every photo he's ever posted. He has nothing going for him," Drew said, voicing the thoughts he'd been suppressing all week.

"Except being a professional football player," his sister teased.

"He's just a basic bro," Drew said dismissively.

"And being a photographer, whose dream job is to follow professional athletes around the world, makes you . . . less basic?"

"I have a personality; it's different," Drew said, knowing how ridiculous he sounded. But he couldn't help it. His ex-girlfriend had cheated on him. And now, she and her new boyfriend were moving on while his life fell apart.

"Well, I don't know the guy. But on your behalf, I'll hate him too." Thandie nodded in solidarity.

"And another thing." Drew wasn't done. "When I took photos at the stadium, I got to know all the players, and he was the only one who never said thank you to the team staff at the end of the day. Nobody in the stadium liked him, he was such an asshole. Sade *used* to think so, too, so it's wild that they somehow just *accidentally* ended up together. She didn't even have the decency to—"

"What if we just hatch a plan to break them up, hmm? Get him kicked off the team and her kicked out of USC?" Thandie said, as if genuinely thinking it through. "You were *never* in love with her and admitted that the breakup just bruised your ego. But if getting in the way of their happiness is what it takes to make you feel okay again, I can make it happen," she continued, turning to face him. "In fact, I know a guy who could just completely get rid of them . . . if that would stop you from whining about your ex-girlfriend in the middle of the coolest party of the year!"

"Okay, okay, I get it, I'm killing—"

"You're killing the vibe. Yes, you are, Drew," she said, but he knew she didn't mean any harm. Tough love was just the way his sister took care of the people around her. Drew had been wallowing in the aftermath of his breakup for months and he knew she was the only one who would try and kick him out of his funk.

"Alright, alright. No more Sade talk for the rest of the night," he promised, knowing that rehashing the breakup wouldn't change a thing. It was California he missed the most, anyway.

"Trust me, you'll enjoy yourself more if you stop thinking about her, at least for the next couple of hours, okay? Drink your drink, take some photos, and live a little!" she said, shaking him by the shoulders until he lightened up. "It's New Year's Eve. I'm going to go and dance for a bit, but I better not see you sulking when I come back."

"I can't guarantee it."

Thandie rolled her eyes.

"At least *try* to look like you're having fun," she said, giving him a pointed look and then heading back to the dance floor to find her friends.

But Drew couldn't help himself. It was only a matter of minutes before he was reaching for his phone, going onto Instagram, and subjecting himself to the quiet torture of seeing his college friends move on without him. As soon as he pressed PLAY on Sade's Instagram story, he was hit with a photo of her new boyfriend and a bunch of their friends by the beach. They'd rented out a place in Big Sur and were having a party without him. It stung because that trip was Drew's idea. He'd been the one to want to spend New Year's Eve with all their friends in California. But they'd broken up and he'd left so abruptly that they'd gone ahead and went without him. It stung to know that their lives were moving on while his stagnated.

So, he put his phone away, tossed his drink back, and focused on his assignment. He held his camera up and tried to lose himself in the visual potential of the crowd. When he found a group of Formula One drivers popping bottles by the bar, he angled his camera to get a shot of them from above. Then he adjusted the exposure settings to capture the way the disco ball reflected shards of light onto a pop star being thrust into the middle of a dance circle. As he watched the people around him let loose, Drew tried his best to convince himself he was having fun.

But he couldn't spend the entire night surrounded by people having the time of their lives when his own felt like such a mess. The contrast between their joy and his melancholy was too great.

It was 11:44 p.m., sixteen minutes before midnight. He knew it was too early to go back to the hotel. He had a job to do after all. But he figured that there was just enough time to make a quick, temporary escape. If he left now, he could be back on the dance floor by midnight. So, he walked down the hallway and opened a door that looked like an exit. There, he saw a set of stairs labeled ROOF ACCESS. Some time alone would do him good. So, Drew buttoned up his blazer, left the party, and braced himself for the winter air.

5

Ari

DECEMBER 31, 2025

Ari was in the middle of the dance floor, moving like the world would end at midnight. Laughing with her best friends like this was the last time they would ever be this carefree. Because once Coach broke the news to the rest of the team, and they made their way to Switzerland, everything *would* be different.

"Sip this," said Izzy, passing Ari her glass. After a misguided round of shots, Izzy had befriended one of the bartenders and convinced him to make the team complicated but delicious mocktails for the rest of the night. They wanted to celebrate, but they were athletes with training the next day. So, Ari drank a sip and immediately started dancing to "Rush" by Troye Sivan with Sienna by her side. The song had been on their warm-up playlist for years, but it sounded extra special under a disco ball.

"How did things go with Hot Hockey Chad?" asked Sienna. Ari shook her head. Somehow Izzy had wrangled her into a conversation with him.

"Hot Hockey Chad spent ten minutes mansplaining the rules of ice hockey to me before I told him that I was on Team GB and scored more goals in my last match than he did in his entire last season," Ari said.

"So, you're sticking with the no-men rule?" asked Sienna.

"I think I'd rather die alone than speak to another—" began Ari, but she stopped midsentence. Because the man she really didn't want to see that night had just walked in.

Harrison Cavendish.

He was tall, devastatingly handsome, and exuded a level of confidence that instantly made him the most attractive person in the room. He was wearing a white shirt with just enough buttons undone to reveal the kind of build you could only get from years of being a professional athlete. He'd clearly just run his hands through his gorgeous brown hair, and his eyes were flicking around the party as he saw old friends and pulled people he'd just met into his orbit. But then his gray eyes landed on Ari, and for a moment it felt like they were the only two people in the room.

Ari had watched hundreds of romcoms and was well accustomed to the scenes when the romantic interest walked in. To the moments when time stilled as the two characters in the love story saw each other for the first time. The meet cute.

But despite how attractive the man crossing the room to walk toward her was, Ari's breathless reaction wasn't a symptom of love at first sight. It was a feeling that triggered the sensation of sharp-winged moths in her stomach and made her want to end the night before it could even really begin.

Sienna looked at Harrison, then Ari, and sighed before walking back over to the other girls. Ari opened her mouth to make some sort of excuse or promise that she would be back in a moment, but they knew how these things always ended.

Ari knew who Harrison was after the charm faded. The way

his demeanor changed when he didn't get his way, and how much smaller she felt when she was around him. But she couldn't shake off the hold he had on her. A part of her still wanted to run her fingers through his hair, tuck herself into the crook of his shoulder, and spend the night letting herself get lost in his eyes.

But she couldn't. After the last incident, she'd promised to never let herself fall again.

They were in the middle of the dance floor, where the music was so loud that everyone needed to shout to be heard above the noise. But when he approached her, Harrison took it one step further and leaned over to talk directly into her ear. His lips brushing against her skin. "If I knew you'd be here, I would have come sooner," he said, laying his hand on her bare shoulder.

A tingle went down her spine. She could always feel herself getting pulled back in by his gravity. It was an unholy mix of dread and desire. Because men like Harrison Cavendish had a way of pulling you in with the very best of who they could be. Or pretend to be. When she'd met him at a Team GB induction event two years ago, she'd been swept off her feet. He was a smooth talker and complimented her on both her ice hockey performance and the new hairstyle she'd shown up with that day. During their first two weeks together, he'd hand-delivered flowers to her front door, gifted her a signed copy of her favorite athlete's autobiography, and taken her on a date to one of the most exclusive restaurants in London. So, when he'd asked her to be his girlfriend, she'd accepted without hesitation. It was Ari's first real relationship, and so she found herself completely mesmerized by the charming, seemingly faultless man before her. Harrison was a few years older than she was, already had two gold Olympic medals for snowboarding, and had the kind of face that only the heavens could have formed. Within weeks, she'd been reduced to a giggly schoolgirl who couldn't stop telling all her friends about "Harry."

How Harry held her hand when they crossed the road, how Harry said *I love you* first, how Harry always picked her up after training, and how Harry always wanted to know every single detail of her day. Who she hung out with, where they went, what she wore, when she was coming home, why she wanted to spend time with her friends instead of him, why she kept wearing dresses like that when there were other men around, why she didn't answer on the first ring when he called. Why was she so hell-bent on making him jealous? Why couldn't she just be a good girlfriend? Why didn't she thank him for loving her more than anyone else ever had? And anyone else ever would?

She didn't realize how bad things were until a year in, when she found herself crying on the phone in a restaurant bathroom. Apologizing for "ruining" Harry's weekend by going to a birthday dinner with her team instead of spending Saturday night with him. The control started so subtly, masquerading as care, until it slowly crept into every area of her life. Her friends noticed and pulled her aside. Told her that it wasn't normal to constantly walk on eggshells with someone she loved. The intervention was the wake-up call she needed to break up with him. But a few weeks later, they were back together and well on their way into a two-year cycle of breakups and makeups instigated by his overreactions and her willingness to forgive. Her friends hated him, and Ari had gone a week without speaking to them after their second intervention. So, they'd learned to bite their tongues and just be there for her in the fallout.

Until September.

Ari had spent the day running around London on her own. Listening to an audiobook as she ran errands on one of her rare free weekends. She'd gone to the supermarket to pick up ingredients to bake a cake for her teammates, an apology for missing out on a team dinner to spend the night with Harrison. But when she'd gotten back to her flat, she'd found Harrison standing over the garbage can as he threw her favorite hockey skates away. She hadn't given him a spare set of keys, so his being in her room was strange enough. But throwing away her favorite skates? He shrugged it off and then presented her with a box of new skates, telling her he'd bought them as a surprise to replace the old ones. But the experience was strange enough for her to start seeing him differently. In that moment, she thought back to all the other things he'd thrown away and replaced. All the subtle ways she'd let him change her into who he wanted her to be. The risk of losing herself in the relationship didn't alarm her, but the risk of Harrison getting in the way of doing what she loved was the thing that finally rang her alarm bells. So, the next day, she broke up with him and promised herself that this time it was for good.

But Harrison was a professional snowboarder and, like her, he was going to Switzerland to compete as part of Team GB. They would be eating in the same canteens, training in the same gyms, and sleeping in the same building for three weeks. It made her feel uneasy because she couldn't figure out if the heightened awareness she felt around him was some strange remnant of attraction or her fight-or-flight telling her to run. Luckily, her phone started vibrating before she had to find out. She pulled it out of her pocket and glanced down at the caller ID. It was her sister, Anesu. Harrison glanced down, too, reading the screen as if it was his own.

"I'll let you deal with that," he said quickly. Ari's family made him uncomfortable to the point where he left as soon as they came up. It had bothered her when they were together. But now, it was the perfect way to get him to leave her alone. For once, she was grateful for her family drama.

"But I'll find you at midnight," Harrison said, his voice deep and slow.

Ari unconsciously glanced down at his lips before shaking her head and reminding herself of the promises she'd made. She couldn't go back, never again.

She clutched her phone, left the dance floor, and walked down the hallway until she found somewhere quiet enough to call her sister back.

"What happened? Are you okay? Aren't you supposed to be at Auntie Vimbo's party?"

"I should be, but Mom's decided to ruin everything," her sixteen-year-old sister said. Ari let out a sigh.

"She's just disappointed," said Ari, realizing that she'd left the party to rehash the same conversation they'd been having since Christmas.

"That doesn't mean she can control my life! Or stop me from getting to know the rest of our family. I have two parents. I know you don't like him, and neither does Mom, but he's our dad. I can talk to him if I want to."

"But did you have to bring it up at Christmas?" Ari said, slightly irritated as she scanned the doors down the hallway for an exit that would take her somewhere quieter. "You know how she gets." Ari always found herself trying to convince Anesu to be nicer to their mom.

But Anesu was adamant. "I don't care how *she gets*. Mom doesn't get to decide whether I see him. I'm sixteen, so I can fly by myself. And since I have dual citizenship, I can go to Dad's whenever I want to."

Ari had given up on her dad a decade ago. He'd left when she was eleven, old enough to see him for who he was: unreliable and disappointing. But Anesu had only been six years old. So, despite everything, she still thought he hung the stars. Their mother spent years watching both father-daughter relationships unfold with pained resignation. That was until Anesu announced, first thing on Christmas Day, that, on her request, their dad had not only gifted her plane tickets to spend the February holidays with him in Zimbabwe, but also that he was inviting her there to attend his wedding to the woman he'd cheated on their mom with.

Ari declined the invite, but Anesu accepted it, announcing that she'd be flying out during the half-term holidays. Their mother, unsurprisingly, saw Anesu's plan to attend the wedding as a grand act of betrayal. Anesu tried to defend herself as she peeled Brussels sprouts, but their mom was already crying by the time she sliced the turkey. The two of them tried to hash it out over roasted potatoes, but Anesu got so upset that she left the table before the gravy could get cold. Ari and her mom spent the rest of the night on the sofa, watching bad Christmas films in a deeply unfestive silence.

Ari knew how to mediate arguments, but with the Olympics around the corner, she'd been forced to pack her bags and leave for boot camp before she could fix things. However, her physical absence hadn't stopped her family from getting her involved. She'd been fielding calls all week, her sister complaining about their mom and her mom asking what she'd done for her younger daughter to *betray me like this*. It was supposed to be her last night of freedom. She was supposed to be celebrating with her friends. But Ari was the reliable one, the fixer, the mediator. The one who stepped in when things went wrong. So, instead of enjoying the New Year's Eve party, she walked toward the ROOF ACCESS sign, pushed the door, and carefully climbed up a set of stairs that led outside. The cool winter air immediately engulfed her.

"All she does is try to guilt-trip me for 'betraying' her. But what she forgets is that I didn't get to grow up with my dad because she couldn't get over things and move on. Isn't that the bigger betrayal?" asked Anesu, making Ari wince. Her sister was only six years younger, but they seemed a whole generation apart when it came to how they saw their parents. Ari was about to interject in defense of their mother when she heard their mom's voice on the other end of the call.

"Anesu Shumba, was I a bad mother?" said their mom, who, from the sounds of it, had just walked into the room. Ari knew her family well; this wasn't the kind of conversation that would end quickly. So, she searched around for somewhere to sit before deciding on a metal step. They were having a mild winter; she hadn't seen snowfall yet. But the step felt as cold as ice. She knew that in a few minutes, her body would lose all the heat absorbed from being in a packed room full of dancing bodies. So, she promised herself to end the call after five minutes.

Her mother continued, "Who went to all your parents' evenings? Who nursed you back to health whenever you got sick? Who read you stories, bathed you, took you to swimming class, and made you dinner every day? Me. And your reward is to abandon me . . . for *him*?"

Ari felt a sharp pang of sadness. She hated hearing her mother like this.

"Mama, I'm not abandoning you! I'm just going to a wedding."

"To the wedding of the man who skipped the country with *that woman* when he should have been looking after his own family," she said, enraged.

"But we're still his family; someone should be there to support him," Anesu shot back.

"Support him? Support him? That man doesn't even come to your birthday parties. He posts a check, sends a text, then calls it a day."

"It's really not that deep," said Anesu, who was immune to their father's small betrayals.

"Arikoishe, your sister clearly wants to kill me, but you don't need to be a witness to that. So, go and enjoy your party. At least one of us should have a good time tonight," said their mom, no stranger to exaggeration.

"Why can't you just be normal about this one thing? All the kids at school with divorced parents get to see both," said Anesu. Ari already knew where their mother would take that.

"*Mwari, ndibatsirei,*" their mom said with a weary voice. "Anesu, all the kids at school's parents live in the same country because their fathers are not good-for-nothing—" But then Anesu, or their mom, or a bad phone signal ended the call.

Ari closed her eyes for a second and then let out a large exhale. "*Thank God,*" she muttered under her breath as she put her phone back into her bag and stood up, smoothing her dress down, then feeling the goosebumps that were starting to pop on her skin. It was way too cold to be outside in the middle of the night. She was supposed to be downstairs, celebrating with her friends. But Ari wasn't ready to go back inside, not yet. So, to prolong her return, she decided to get off the stairs and explore the rooftop. It was bigger than she'd expected. It spanned the entire stretch of the building. Part of it was gated off, likely reserved for some private resident. But the rest of it looked communal, with outdoor chairs, winter shrubbery, and a small string of lantern-shaped fairy lights. Her heels tapped the roof as she walked toward the far right end, making her way toward a mesmerizing view.

The sky was black, deep into a winter's night. But there were thousands of brightly lit buildings, sparkling against the skyline. She could see cars whizzing across the bridges, tiny boats leaving ripples across the inky Thames, and hear the distant sounds of millions of people waiting to ring in the new year. It was 11:44 p.m., but she had no desire to go back to the party in time for the countdown to midnight. Not when she knew that Harrison was lurking around the dance floor, no doubt trying to find her.

If she went back downstairs, all her worries would come rushing back. The pressure of becoming responsible for the team's Olympic dreams. The fact that she'd soon be stuck in St. Moritz with her ex-boyfriend. And the persistent feeling of carrying more than she could handle or shake off.

Eventually, Ari would have to face reality. But if she stayed up here, maybe she could avoid it for the night? So, she sat on the rooftop and watched the skyline twinkle, taking in every single glimmering angle of the night. Alone, but content.

Until she heard footsteps and the click of a camera shutter.

6

Drew

Drew couldn't stop taking photos. Every element of the party had caught his eye. Elegant dresses shimmering under the disco ball. The early glimpse of laughter in someone's eye. He'd learned that the best shots were taken a few seconds before he realized a moment was worth capturing. Which is why he reached for the camera around his neck as soon as he walked onto the roof.

The view of London felt like something out of a movie scene. He could hear the faint sounds of cars fifty floors below, and there was a strangely charged stillness in the air that felt almost otherworldly. Like he was in a realm that opened only in the final moments between one year and the next. He couldn't capture a feeling, but he could frame a memory. So, as he took in the skyline and thought about the moments that had led him to this point in the year, he readied his camera to take a photo.

But then he noticed a person walking across the rooftop. They were perfectly framed by the night sky, their dress and hair gently blowing in the wind. So, he adjusted the focus on his camera to blur the background a little and focus on the silhouette.

"Taking photos of strangers is kind of creepy, you know?" the person said. "Especially in the middle of the night . . . on a roof . . . when we're the only two people around." It was a woman with a British accent.

Drew stepped out of his photo-induced haze and back into reality. He looked down at his camera, suddenly self-conscious of his impulse to capture every moment. When he stepped back and assessed the situation, it *did* seem kind of creepy. He stepped into the light so the woman could see him, then put his hands up to show he meant no harm.

"Sorry, force of habit," he said.

"So, this is just a regular Wednesday-night activity for you?" He could hear the smile in her voice.

"Every *other* Wednesday," he joked. "Don't worry, I was brought in to take photos of the party. I'm not just some creepy guy who lurks on rooftops."

"Who says you can't be both?" she asked, a playful lilt in her voice. "But if you are the latter, just know I have enough upper-body strength to dangle you off the edge of the roof until you cry and throw up. So . . . no funny business." It wasn't until she turned away from the skyline that he finally saw her face. She had deep brown skin and a halo of curly hair. She wore a blue dress with silver details that shimmered under the twinkly lights strewn around the rooftop. There was a glint of curiosity in her eyes. As if she was trying to figure him out.

"Well, I only have enough upper-body strength to carry a camera bag and a few spare batteries, so I'll keep my distance," he joked in response to her threat. She laughed. It was a warm, genuine laugh that instantly made him feel at ease.

"I'm Drew," he said by way of introduction.

"Ari," she replied.

Ari took a seat on a bench with a perfect view of the skyline. Then she gestured to the space beside her. Drew walked over, put his camera in his pocket, and sat down.

"Do you know how many New Year's Eve parties there are in London every year?" she asked.

"Nineteen thousand two hundred and forty-six," he said, not missing a beat.

"Really?"

"I made that up." He shrugged.

"Well, let's say there *were* nineteen thousand two hundred and forty-six. What do you think the chances are that out of all the New Year's Eve parties I could have gone to tonight, the one I agreed to is the same one that my least favorite person in the world showed up to?"

"I knew I shouldn't have come."

"You could have at least brought flowers to make up for ruining my night," she teased.

"Damn it, I had one job."

Ari was smiling, but it didn't reach her eyes. Drew didn't know her, but she seemed distant, burdened. He wanted to stop and ask her if everything was alright, but he was on assignment. He was supposed to be downstairs taking photos of the last ten minutes of the year. Putting his all into the kind of freelance gig that could give him the connections he so desperately needed. But he couldn't leave a stranger on the roof by herself. Not when she seemed this sad on what was supposed to be one of the best nights of the year.

"Do you want to see the photo I took of you?" he asked. He was always inclined to make people feel better by showing them beautiful things. So, he picked up his camera and scrolled through until he landed on the photo of her silhouette framed by the night sky. She examined it for a moment, swiping through a few more from the party, before studying him.

"You're good at this. So why are you lurking on the roof instead of taking photos?"

Drew paused for a moment. Thinking about his grandma, college, and the life he'd just left behind was a part of it. But the truth was, he'd started to feel like he was intruding on the party.

"People stop enjoying themselves when they see a lens," he said. Because as hard as he tried to blend into the scenery, eventually, the actors put their glasses down, and the athletes stopped dancing. He'd gotten a few good candid photos, but the moment he'd felt his camera making people self-conscious, he put it away. "They put on their best selves when there's a camera involved."

"But isn't that what this is all about?" she asked, gently tapping his camera. "Capturing people at their best?"

"Their most honest," he said. "If I take the photo before people realize, I get them when they're being themselves."

"It's kind of like you're trying to figure out their secrets," she said.

He'd never looked at it that way but she was right.

There was a gleam in her eyes. "So now that you've taken a photo of *me*, what do you think *my* secret is?"

He paused and reached down to look at the photo on his camera again. But she gently put her hand out to stop him. Their fingers touched, his skin tingled. For a moment, time stood still. He met her gaze and held it.

"You can't check your notes," she said softly. "That would be cheating."

"If I knew this would be a closed-book exam, I would have studied you longer," he said. Her mouth twitched up.

"Well, time's up. I need an answer," she said, playful.

"Your secret? I think that you'd rather be anywhere else than at this party."

"That's hardly a secret. I'm on the roof less than ten minutes before midnight. Try again. Actually, no . . . I'll try it this time."

"You want to guess my secret? Go ahead." He was curious to hear how a stranger perceived him.

"I think . . . you hide behind your camera and observe people from a distance so they can't guess your secrets," she said.

His eyes widened.

"That easy, huh?"

"I'm easy to read," he admitted. "My turn."

"You better get it right. If not, I'm stealing your job," she teased.

Drew studied her and thought about it for a moment, trying to find a story through her face alone.

"Okay, I think . . . you came to this party even though you didn't want to because it's New Year's, and your friends dragged you along. But now you're up on the roof avoiding someone downstairs instead of just going home and enjoying the last few minutes of the year . . . because it's easier to hide out than feel like you're letting people down by leaving early."

He immediately worried that he'd gone too far. But she seemed completely unbothered.

"Correct. But *so* specific that it could only be said by someone who feels the same way."

She said it like a compliment.

"Well, we're both sitting on the roof avoiding *the best—*" Drew began.

"*Party of the year,*" Ari finished.

Based on his observations, the only people truly having fun were the people too famous to care. Everybody else was exchanging contacts, talking about their latest projects, and trying to work the room as if each conversation was a potential opportunity. Thandie had a bunch of famous friends, and he'd been Sade's plus-one to his fair share of parties like this back in California. So, he'd developed a habit of trying to guess what social status someone carried to get an invite to a thing like this. But Ari's appearance didn't give anything away. She was beautiful, but not tall enough to be a model. Dressed well, but didn't carry herself with the confidence of an actress. Maybe she was a musician, an athlete, or the founder of some buzzy tech start-up. As he tried to figure her out, he found himself drawn to her eyes. They were such a dark shade of brown that he could see the whole city reflected in them. But when she looked away, he looked away, too. They sat in silence for a moment before returning to the topic of the party.

"It feels like a networking event disguised as a party down there," he said after a moment.

"It's a glorified business mixer," Ari said, nodding. But her tone wasn't judgmental. "People have been asking me, 'Where do I know you from?' all night."

"Where *do* I know you from?" he joked.

"Nowhere," she said. "But parties like this are for people who stick around just in case *you are* somebody."

"Even if I was a somebody—"

"Are you?" she joked.

"Do I look like a somebody?"

"Not in the slightest. I was just asking to be polite," she said.

Drew laughed. "Well, I'm not. But even if I was, I have at least twenty red flags that would make them want to run for the hills as soon as they got to know me."

"Oh, me too," Ari said. "But it's a party. You've got to show your best side. It's kind of like a first date. I tell guys I'm a foodie, but the only thing I can cook is pesto pasta, and I order the same meal from the same restaurant whenever I go out. You embellish the good and hide the bad."

"My profile on the apps says I care about climate change. But I always end up buying plastic bags, and I'm too lazy to recycle," he admitted.

"Oh, so you hate the planet. You're the worst kind of person," she teased. "But my deepest, darkest secret is that I skip to the last ten minutes of a film before I decide to watch it from the start."

Drew gasped in mock horror. "That's not a red flag. It's a siren."

"But imagine if people were this honest on every first date."

"Are you saying this is a first date?" he asked, lowering his voice.

"Hypothetically speaking," she said, meeting his eye. "If everyone shared their red flags on a first date, we would all know what we were getting ourselves into from the start. It would save a lot of disappointment."

"But would you still like me if I told you all my flaws?" he asked.

"Who said I liked you?"

"You did, when you said this was our first date."

"*You* said that, Drew. I was just speaking in hypotheticals."

He was about to reply when he noticed her shivering. So, he wordlessly took off his blazer and handed it over to her. She hesitated for a moment before taking it, but they both knew she needed it more than he did.

"So, hypothetically speaking, would you stay on the roof if I told you all my secrets?" he asked.

"Honestly, if I knew them, I'd probably enjoy the rest of the night more."

"Why?"

"Because then I could just talk to you without trying to figure out if you're flirting with me or if there's a spark." She shrugged.

"I'm *definitely* flirting with you."

"I know," she said as their eyes met.

"And I'm pretty sure there's a spark," he said, surprising himself.

"Yeah, but if I knew all of your flaws and you knew mine, then we'd quickly realize that this"—she gestured between them—"me and you? It would never work out. So, the end of the party would mark a clear ending, and nobody would leave disappointed."

Drew understood what she meant.

"If it's doomed from the start, there's nothing to lose." He nodded.

"Exactly."

Their eyes locked. They were in the middle of one of the busiest cities in the world on the loudest night of the year. But for a moment, the world fell silent. All he could hear was his heartbeat and the gentle winter breeze.

"So where do we go from here?" he said. Her mouth twitched into a small, knowing smile.

"How about . . . you show me your worst parts, and I'll show you mine."

7

Ari

Ari didn't have anyone to confide in. Gracie, the one person who could give her advice on how to be the new team captain, had sustained a career-altering injury, and Ari didn't want to call her to fret about being handed the kind of job that people spent their whole lives dreaming of. Her teammates were her best friends, but she played the role of the stable, responsible one and rarely told them what she was worried about. And because her family was always in the middle of some sort of conflict, she never told her mom, dad, or sister anything meaningful.

Ari only allowed people to see the most polished version of herself. She refused to be anybody's burden. But even she could admit that silently sifting through the messy details of her life got exhausting. Sometimes, all she wanted to do was talk it out.

The cute American guy on the roof couldn't solve her problems, but she reasoned that maybe telling a stranger the truth would take some weight off her shoulders. They'd met randomly enough that she knew she was never going to see him again. So there was no harm in opening up. As long as he went first.

"So, what's the big one?" Ari asked. "Your whistle-blaring siren of a red flag."

"You'll judge me," he said, shaking his head.

"I would silently judge you if you told me three months down the line, but we only have . . . ten minutes left until the new year. I don't have time to judge you," she said.

He smiled at that—it was a good smile. Infectious. The side of his face was lit up by the moonlight, and a small dimple appeared on his right cheek.

"Okay." He took a breath. "I dropped out of college a couple of weeks ago, and I'm pretty sure it's the worst decision I've ever made."

She could hear the heaviness in his voice, so she decided to lighten the tone.

"Oh, this would never work out then," she teased. "I graduated first in my class, so I only date guys who finish their degrees."

Drew didn't miss a beat. "If I knew I was going to meet you, I would have stayed in school."

"But if I'm honest, I peaked in secondary school," she admitted. "And I got a degree in sports science, so . . ." She shrugged.

"Your destiny is to become a high-school gym teacher clinging on to your glory days?"

"Something like that," she said, thinking about the Team GB Olympic Kit that awaited her back at Bootcamp.

"Okay, your turn. Anything worse than throwing your career away on a whim?" he asked.

Ari thought about it for a moment, flipping through her rolodex of regrets. Ari was all for sharing secrets with a stranger, but this was still a Zeus party. She couldn't risk telling him too much too soon. It was a small world where reputations were tarnished overnight. She couldn't risk it all for someone she didn't know.

"Hmm, what will make you judge me . . . ? Oh, I have a good one," she said. She kept her voice light, but her first secret had been weighing down on her for years. "I once got into a *competition* with one of my rivals at . . . *work* . . ."

"The long pauses make me feel like you're not being honest," he said.

"I'm not lying. I'm just being evasive."

"Oh, that is something I could get a degree in." He laughed.

She cupped her hand to her ear. "I think I can hear . . . alarm bells?"

"If I can admit I'm evasive, then you can hide the details of your story. No judgment if we're on the same page," he said.

If this had been a real first date, Ari would have run for the hills. But she was never going to see Drew again, so what was the harm in opening up?

"Okay, so I was in a competition at work. And I wanted to win. So, I did my very best and put all my energy into the . . . game. But in the process, I accidentally hurt someone. Physically. It could have left her injured for life," she admitted, thinking back to a fateful hockey match from years ago that troubled her to this day.

"But it was an accident, right?" he said, looking over at her.

"A complete accident. Nobody was supposed to get hurt," she said, recalling the moment she'd tried her best to forget.

"So, there's nothing to feel bad about."

"Oh, but it gets worse," she said before he could try to make her feel better about it. "It almost ended the other person's career but it did wonders for mine. In fact, that accident changed my life." Ari felt simultaneously exposed and unburdened. She'd been thinking about that match ever since she'd heard the news about

Gracie. What were the chances that two injuries four years apart would have such a significant impact on her career? She searched Drew's expression, expecting to find judgment in his eyes. But instead, he just nodded.

"Her loss was your gain. I've been there before," he admitted. "I once told a girl that . . . wait, no. That's too far," he said, stopping himself.

But Ari was curious. She glanced down at her watch to check the time.

"Why hold back? There's only a few minutes left until midnight, and after that, we'll never see each other again," she said. "Imagine we're in a confession booth. If you tell me your secrets, I'll absolve you."

He hesitated for a moment before he spoke again.

"I once told a girl, who in my defense I did really like—"

"Said every fuckboy ever. No judgment, of course." She teased as she watched him shake his head and look up at the sky.

"I dated this girl, Sade . . . whose dad just happened to be one of the top execs of a football team I was interning at. For the record, that isn't *why* I dated her—"

"The gentleman doth protest too much, methinks."

"We were friends for a while before we started dating. I was an intern in their marketing department, and she worked on the social media team. I knew she had a crush on me, so we started dating. But I realized pretty early on that I didn't like her as much as she liked me. So, I was about to end things because I respected her too much to waste her time. But . . . her dad ran the internship program. And knew the powerful executives of all of the sports teams in LA," he said, looking guilt-ridden.

"Oh, this is *really* bad," she said.

He looked mortified, but he carried on speaking. As if it was too late to turn back.

"So, I decided to postpone breaking up with her until *after* I got a reference from him. But then she said I love you . . ."

"Oh no," Ari said, her eyes widening. Drew's face was a portrait of regret. But he couldn't stop talking.

"I didn't want to hurt her feelings, so I said . . . I love you, too." He grimaced and held his head in his hands.

"Then what happened?" she asked, grimly curious.

"We were together for a year."

"Wow." It wasn't nearly as bad as her secret, but it wasn't great, either. "You *were* together, as in you no longer are?"

Drew shook his head and looked back up at the stars.

"She cheated on me with a football player. According to Instagram, they're in love."

Ari put her hand over her mouth.

"I know. It *is* kind of funny," he chuckled sadly. "What goes around comes around, I guess. . . . Wow, this is a terrible first date."

"Our first and last," she laughed. "You can't stop thinking about Sade, and I can't seem to avoid Harrison."

"Harrison?" he asked gently.

She debated telling him about her ex-boyfriend, but she didn't want Harrison to take up any more of her night than he already had, so she changed the conversation. "Okay, my turn to share a secret."

"Do your worst. But I think I might have set the bar too low."

"Oh, I can go lower," Ari said. She hadn't told her next secret to a single soul. "My dad broke up with my mom when my sister and I were kids. And then he started a new family on the other side of the world, so I kind of hated him."

Drew looked over at her and nodded. Encouraging her to carry on.

"He knew that I was never going to forgive him, so he stopped making an effort with me. Which is fine." She shrugged, even though it wasn't fine. "He kept sending my little sister birthday cards. But I didn't want to let him keep getting her hopes up, because I knew he wasn't going to stick around long enough to make things right . . . so I hid every birthday card he sent her from the time I was thirteen until I turned eighteen." She was a little shocked at her own honesty.

"That's . . ." he said, rubbing his temple, momentarily lost for words.

"A little messed up?" she suggested. Still feeling guilty about it.

"Yeah. But I think I'd probably do the same," he said. "My grandma has Alzheimer's and it's getting worse, way faster than we thought it would. But my sister, who lives on the other side of the country most of the year, doesn't know. Me and my grandparents are hiding it from her."

"Why?" Ari asked softly, noticing him tensing up.

Drew took a deep breath. "Because my sister is about to have the most important few months of her life. She's under so much pressure that I can't risk making it worse."

"But?" she asked, sensing there was more.

"But we've always been really close, so it feels strange to be hiding the truth from her."

Ari wanted to ask whether Drew thought he might be denying his sister's right to make her own decisions. But she couldn't ask that without sounding like a hypocrite. So, she just nodded. Tonight was about sharing secrets, not giving advice.

"I guess we all do things to protect the people we love," she said after a moment.

"You don't have to pretend my red flags are orange to protect my feelings."

She laughed. "Don't worry, I'm definitely still judging you for lying about loving someone to get a reference from their dad."

"I'm making a terrible first impression," he said.

"Me too."

A gust of wind blew across the rooftop. Ari buttoned up the blazer he'd given her to try and warm herself up. It smelled like fresh laundry and firewood, homey. Drew's secrets were flags too bright to ignore. But he was attractive. She liked talking to him, and the look in his eyes made her want to lean a little closer.

"We should trademark this and put it on a set of cards," she joked. "*Worst Foot Forward.* The game to play to ensure you *never* fall in love with someone."

"So, what I'm hearing is that if I hadn't told you my secrets, you would have fallen in love with me, Ari?" His mouth curved up into an expression that made her feel like the two of them were in on a secret. It was dangerously alluring, so she shook her head and used all her strength to hold his gaze, instead of melting under it.

"It's not me who's in trouble, babe."

"Yet I can feel you getting lost in my eyes," he said. She hated that he was right.

"Well, it's a good thing we both already know that this would never work out."

"Why?" There was a gleam in his eyes.

She bit the inside of her mouth and tried to remember her reasons.

"Well, we both have complicated exes."

"And you could never just be a rebound." His voice was low, and flirty, as if speaking like this came naturally to him. Ari saw right through it, but was having too much fun not to play along.

"More importantly, you don't sound like you live in London."

He nodded. "I fly back to the States next week. But there are five days before then."

She shook her head and tried not to get pulled in.

"Even if you *were* staying, as of an hour ago I've officially sworn off men. At least until the spring."

"But if we saw each other again in April and all those reasons disappeared . . ." he said, raising an eyebrow.

"It still wouldn't work out. In fact, I can already predict the breakup."

He leaned closer and looked her in the eyes. "How would it end?"

60! 59! 58! came the distant sound of a shouted countdown.

"Well, you would try to sweep me off my feet, but I know I wouldn't let you."

"Why?" he asked.

"Because I don't trust charming men," she said simply. "You could be the perfect guy, and I'd still hold you at a distance."

He looked away for a moment, as if trying to find his own reasons.

"If we were together, I think you'd eventually get frustrated by me," he said.

"Why?"

47! 46! 45!

"Because I'd rather become distant than risk hurting your feelings, which kind of makes me a coward," he admitted, looking into her eyes.

"Well, I would rather orchestrate a situation to push you away than have a difficult conversation. Which makes me a coward, too," she said. But she could feel the strange tension in the air.

34! 33! 32!

"I'd keep you at arm's length," she confessed, "then run at the first sight of trouble."

"I'd hang on even when it's too far gone." He shrugged. "I can't help it, I'm a fixer."

"I've learned to be a bolter."

"Then," he whispered, "I guess we'd be a match made in hell."
21! 20! 19!

Yet there they were, knees pressed against each other, faces so close she could feel his breath. She wanted to sink her teeth into the tension. But then, to her relief, he made the first move.

Drew gently ran his finger down the side of her cheek, the friction on her skin sliding toward a spark. He found a loose curl, caught it between his fingers, and gently brushed it behind her ear. His touch slowly lit up every nerve in her body. So, she let her hand find his arm, slowly drifting up as she felt the firm muscle beneath his shirt. He watched her hand rise until it settled on his shoulder, tightening as his finger traced small circles on the soft skin between her neck and jaw. When she spoke, her words landed so softly he had no choice but to lean closer.

8! 7! 6!

"The breakup would be awful," she whispered, biting her lip. But she could feel the warmth spreading across her body as he glanced down at her mouth and then back into her eyes.

"But maybe it would be worth it?" he said, lips twitching upward, like a man willing to risk it all.

"Which is why . . . we should *never* see each other again."
3! 2! 1!

But when they collided, all her worries and reasons faded. He kissed her, soft and slow. The gentle pressure of it sending a streak of heat across her body, like a match gliding until the friction turned into a flame. Before she knew it, she was leaning in. He was wrapping his hands around her waist. And their lips were moving in rhythm, achingly slow and sensual like two lovers on a dance floor. Her body was begging her to lose her senses. But she couldn't give in. He was handsome and honest, and in so many ways, the exact kind of escape she needed that night.

But Drew knew her secrets, and Ari knew his. So, she pulled away, ignored the fireworks lighting up the sky, and ran down the stairs. She left the party before the taste of his lips could change her mind.

St. Moritz, Switzerland

February 2026

8

Drew

Drew had been in the Village for less than forty-eight hours but was already responsible for a casualty. Because he was the kind of person who would do *anything* to get the perfect photo, he'd climbed onto a slippery bench to take a portrait of a Finnish speed skater practicing her routine on the outdoor ice rink. Then dangled himself from a tree to capture a shot of a group of Ecuadorian ski mountaineers huddled around a fire after a walk. He'd balanced on bridge handrails, run down icy steps, and even gone as far as to ride a bike with no hands in pursuit of the perfect photo. But in the end, it was a patch of grass hiding a layer of black ice that brought him to his knees.

He'd slipped and watched in horror as his camera flew into the air, crashed into a tree, and landed on the ground. He'd escaped the scene with just a couple of bruises, but the shattered glass he'd heard on his fall looked as ominous as it sounded. He sat on the icy ground for a moment, devastated to see the shattered remains of his new telephoto lens. As he headed to the press office to see if he could order a replacement to arrive in time for the opening ceremony, he wondered whether breaking his new professional camera within twenty-four hours of arriving at the Winter Games was as bad an omen as it felt.

"You can use this, but don't tell a soul that I helped you," said Luiz, handing him a replacement lens that worked perfectly on the Canon EOS he was using that day.

Luiz Souza was a press liaison assistant from Brazil who'd moved to Switzerland to work for the Olympics. His job was to make sure that everything ran smoothly when it came to the journalists, photographers, and media teams working in the Village. His short brown hair was smartly swooped back, he was wearing a crisp tailored suit under his PRESS TEAM jacket, and he always seemed to be running an hour ahead of schedule. Which is why he'd immediately noticed Drew's . . . haphazard approach. But rather than getting annoyed, Luiz took Drew under his wing and helped him find a replacement for his broken lens.

"Thanks, man. You've saved my life. I can't afford to mess things up on the first day," said Drew. He attached the loaned lens to his camera and thanked the universe for protecting his SD card.

"Well, lifesaving is a onetime thing. From now on, you and your bad luck need to stay fifty meters away from me *at all times*," said Luiz, his foot impatiently tapping the floor as he waited for Drew to collect his things.

"If you ever need a favor, just know I owe you one."

"The best thing you could do for me is get to the closing ceremony without breaking a body part. I'm way too busy to take you to the emergency room and file an incident report," Luiz joked. "*Out there?* It's every man for himself." Luiz pushed open the door at the end of the hallway and they stepped out into the truest representation of organized chaos.

The press office was an ultrahigh-tech building that housed over ten thousand journalists, seven hundred accredited photographers, and more laptops, phones, and camera screens than Drew could possibly count. It was filled with people at the peak of their careers. Legendary photographers who had captured some of the most important stories of the twenty-first century and Pulitzer Prize–winning journalists who'd covered wars and landmark elections. That winter's press office was a who's who of some of the most acclaimed storytellers in the world, and among the crowd of serious journalistic icons was . . . Drew.

Because his sister was right: One night could change everything.

After kissing the girl who'd disappeared at midnight, Drew had gone downstairs to take enough photos of the party to make up for missing the countdown. Emboldened by the magical first few minutes of the year, he'd gone around and captured everything that caught his eye. People tearing it up on the dance floor, sneaking up onto the roof and celebrating with strangers as if they'd known one another all their lives. After a tough couple of months, the party was exactly what Drew had needed to usher in the new year—a temporary escape from his everyday life. He'd reconnected with his love for photography that night. Filled his camera roll with strikingly rich photos, and kissed a gorgeous girl at midnight. Yes, she'd disappeared before he could get her number, but Drew had still left the party with the kind of hope reserved for the first day of the year.

As soon as he'd arrived back at the hotel that night, he'd opened his laptop and gotten to work. Curated the best photos from the party and edited them until they resembled a digital version of a nostalgic photo diary. When he sent it to the team at Zeus that had organized the New Year's Eve party, they were so impressed that they shared his behind-the-scenes photo diary across their social channels. The collection gave viewers what felt like a secret glimpse into one of the biggest and most exclusive parties of the year. And so, within a couple of hours, his photos went viral. People across the internet shared the hazy, dreamlike moments he'd captured, and rumors of the party spread like wildfire. It turned out that Drew had photographed the kind of moments that ordinary people craved to be part of. The photos were reposted and shared thousands of times within the span of a day, leaving the bigwigs at Zeus Athletics thrilled.

Which was how he'd ended up in St. Moritz with a press accreditation and an assignment to take photos for one of the biggest companies in the world.

Stories from the Village had dominated everyone's feeds during the 2024 Summer Olympics, and Zeus wanted their brand to be all over the 2026 Winter Games. So, they'd sent a team of seasoned photographers and social media managers to Switzerland three weeks before the Winter Games, and Drew had gotten a call offering him a last-minute accreditation pass to take photos as part of their online campaign. He had mentally prepared himself to spend February questioning his life choices while sleepwalking around his childhood home in Wisconsin. So, when the opportunity came, he accepted it without hesitation. His family was already scheduled to fly to Switzerland to watch the Winter Olympics, so he figured that there was no harm in hitting pause on his quarter-life crisis and heading to St. Moritz to follow his dream.

The start of his year was working out better than he could have ever imagined. But despite his best efforts, he hadn't been able to find the girl that had set it all off. He knew her secrets, but he didn't know her last name or any facts to help him find her online. So, after a few days of scrolling Instagram for leads, he'd decided to take her abrupt departure as a sign that she didn't want to be found. A part of him couldn't help but wonder if her new year was off to as good a start as his was.

However, there wasn't time to think too hard about that as he walked through the hectic atmosphere of the press office and listened to Luiz's sage advice.

"Just make sure you have your accreditation on you at all times. They won't let you into any of the buildings without it," said Luiz as they meandered through the crowds of journalists frantically typing emails, taking loud calls, and grabbing extra battery packs. There was so much going on that Drew could barely take it all in. So, he just nodded, followed Luiz's lead, and tried to absorb as much of his surroundings as possible. This was the opportunity of a lifetime, he couldn't mess it up.

"Take this," said Luiz, handing Drew a piece of paper as they walked past two news producers having a hushed argument. "Study this map like your career depends on it. If you think two ice rinks are ten minutes away from each other, assume it's a twenty-minute walk," he said. Drew nodded emphatically, taking a photo of the map and mentally planning out his routes. Luiz had been working for the Olympics since 2022, so Drew took each piece of advice he gave as gold.

"Arrive early, stay late, and take exceptional photos. Then maybe, eventually, they'll stop thinking you got lost and went to the wrong building," he said, making a joke of the fact that when Drew had shown up that morning, someone assumed he was a tourist who'd taken the wrong turn.

Now Drew watched as a film crew walked into the press office. He hadn't felt this out of his depth since his first week of college. "When do you start feeling like you're supposed to be here?"

Luiz went over to his desk and grabbed his walkie-talkie.

"There are natural talents, and then there are people like us," he said.

"Are you saying I'm not a natural talent?" Drew joked, knowing just as well as Luiz did that he'd gotten into the Village by sheer luck.

"Neither of us are." Luiz shrugged. "Success is mostly about ending up in the right place at the right time with *just enough* skill to pull it off. But look around."

"We're in the room now," Drew said, the reality of the situation sinking in.

"Exactly. One day your work will be so good that you won't walk in each day feeling like an imposter. But up until then, buy the assistants coffee, befriend the volunteers, and get the security guards on your side. That way, they'll be more likely to help you when you lose your accreditation . . . again." Luiz picked up the lanyard Drew didn't even realize he'd dropped. Before he could say anything else, Luiz waved him goodbye and ran up the stairs to help a live news broadcast team hunt down five extra extension cords.

The press office was buzzing with activity. Drew could hear an Al Jazeera journalist preparing for an interview with one of that year's top speed skaters, and he could smell the drip coffee an ESPN reporter was drinking as he typed an article about an upcoming ice hockey game. Busy journalists flitted around the press office as they prepared for the busiest two weeks of the winter sports calendar. All against the backdrop of the large world clocks on the wall. Each time zone was counting down the hours, minutes, and seconds until the opening ceremony began.

Drew wanted to just sit in the middle of the press office and soak it all in. To observe the journalists around him and absorb all their wisdom. But if he was going to be ready for the two weeks ahead of him, he needed to get to know the Village map like the back of his hand. So, he zipped up his coat, hung his camera around his neck, and pushed the front door open until he finally stepped out into the blistering, icy cold of the Winter Olympics.

9

Ari

Ari had been born on June 21, the day of the summer solstice. But despite her summer birthday, she was, to her very core, a winter girl. She loved being wrapped up in a thick coat and feeling the icy air against her cheeks when she stepped outside, but she'd never experienced a winter's day as perfect as that early February morning in St. Moritz. It was minus eleven degrees Celsius, and Ari's eyes widened as she saw the untouched white blanket outside GB House. She put one foot out and smiled as she felt her boot connect with the snow. The quiet crunch filled her with a childlike sense of delight.

A moment later Yasmeen, Izzy, and Sienna bounded out into the snow wearing the coziest iteration of the uniform they'd been given on New Year's Day. Puffy red winter coats embroidered with the Team GB logo and cozy blue beanies that Yasmeen had hand-sewn silk lining into on the plane to Switzerland.

"It's so beautiful," said Izzy as she ran across the snow to pull

Ari into a bear hug. "Can you believe we're here?" Ari and her teammates looked around. The sky was a bright shade of blue; the sun was hanging low, its rays lighting up a fresh layer of brilliant white snow.

"We've got to go and see the frozen lake, take a ride on the Glacier Express, go to that spa I sent you a link to, and take a few pictures before we ruin our uniforms," said Yasmeen, excitedly scrolling through the list on her phone.

"More importantly, we've got to get our strategy together and figure out how to make it past the preliminary round, which seems pretty damn impossible to me," said Sienna.

"Ah, it's good to hear you're feeling optimistic," sighed Izzy, already tired of Sienna's catastrophic thinking.

"How are you *not* panicking right now? Everything we've been working toward could fall apart before the end of the week."

Sienna had been freaking out three times a day, every single day, since New Year's morning. When they'd woken up after the party, Coach McLaughlin called the whole team into his office and broke the news that their superstar team captain wouldn't be joining them at the Winter Games. Despite Ari's attempts at encouragement, the team didn't take the news well. Sienna was the most worried of them all.

"I can't understand why everyone is so calm," said Sienna, shaking her head as she nervously gritted her teeth. All the girls glanced over at Ari, as if looking to her for reassurance as they walked out of the athletes' quarter, through the training area, and down toward the hockey rink.

"We've been training nonstop for weeks. We know our strengths, we're working on our weaknesses, and we earned our way here. There's no need to panic, because we're prepared," said Ari with practiced composure. It was the line she'd been telling herself every day for the past six weeks, the mantra she'd been repeating whenever she woke up in a cold sweat or the team's nerves manifested on the ice rink.

Because something fundamental had shifted in the dynamic Ari had with her friends the minute Coach announced that she was their new team captain. There were twenty-three girls on the team, but Sienna, Izzy, and Yasmeen had always been her closest friends. They'd seen each other through breakups, birthdays, deadlines, and injuries. They genuinely loved spending time together, and in an emergency, they were the ones she would call. But overnight, Ari went from being their friend to becoming the leader who was supposed to be ten steps ahead.

So, instead of ending the nights after boot camp making tea and chatting to Ari about the girls she fancied, Izzy drank hot cups of lemon water and asked Ari for tips on improving her game and saving more goals. Rather than asking Ari to help her film videos for their team's social accounts, Yasmeen sent her links to hockey analysis podcasts. And instead of spending hours on the phone sharing industry gossip and speculating about other ice hockey teams like she usually did, Sienna spent each boot-camp breakfast sharing her worries about what lay ahead of them. The girls were looking to Ari for reassurance, so she couldn't let her doubts show. They'd landed in the Village by the skin of their teeth, but they hadn't worked this hard to only come this far.

So, Ari was going to lead her team to victory.

However, when they walked into the hockey stadium and saw the ice rink, Ari was reminded of just how many hurdles they would have to jump to get to the other side. Because right there, speeding across the ice with enough focus, skill, and excellence that it sent a chill down her spine, was the one team they'd never won a match against in their lives. The winners of the International Ice Hockey Federation Championships and the team with the second-most Olympic ice hockey medals in the world.

Team USA.

They were so brilliant that it was annoying.

Ari and the other girls walked down the stadium's steps and sat in the bleachers. Amelia, who played on defense, studied every move intently. Orla, one of the left wingers, gritted her teeth as she saw just how precisely their opposition scored. As Ari watched the Americans practice, the reality of the dream she was chasing came into focus. As did the sheer improbability that her team would achieve it.

When Team USA finished training, they skated out of the rink and looked up at the stadium. A few of them smiled and waved as they headed back to the locker room. But one player stayed on the rink and skated a final loop around the perimeter before gliding off the ice and taking off her helmet. Her dark brown hair tumbled down her back, and her face lit up with an expression that Ari could only interpret as twisted delight. Ari's shoulders tensed, her mouth dried up, and her heart began to beat a little faster. Because the girl looking up at her from the ice was no ordinary Team USA hockey player. She was Thandie Dlamini—one of the best players in the league. And ever since Ari misjudged a tackle that had broken Thandie's leg and stopped her from competing in the 2022 Winter Olympics, Thandie had been harboring a long and fraught personal vendetta against her.

It was an accident. Ari had only ever intended to take possession of the ice puck to win the game. She would have never gone out of her way to injure someone on purpose. But the match that almost ruined Thandie's career had catapulted Ari's team up the rankings. Team GB became the curious underdogs of the season, and the attention they'd gained for almost winning against one of the best teams in the world had boosted their visibility and won them an unexpected Zeus Athletics sponsorship. It wasn't enough to take them to Beijing 2022, but it was enough to capture the attention and investment of some of the more senior figures who ran Team GB. In short: Thandie's loss was Ari's gain. And from the look on Thandie's face as she stared up at the stands, it was clear that she still hadn't forgiven her. In fact, Ari knew that Thandie had spent the past four years learning her weaknesses and getting into her head before every match to plot her downfall. What started as a friendly rivalry had become a one-sided feud. And now that they were both at the Winter Games, Thandie was finally in the position to get her revenge.

"See you on the ice, *Captain*," Thandie said, her words laced with venom as she followed the rest of her team out.

Ari sighed and shook her head. Every decision she'd ever made came back to haunt her as her team stared blankly at the ice.

"We're screwed, aren't we?" said Sienna, rubbing her temples and closing her eyes.

Ari didn't need to reply for them to know her answer: *Yes. Yes, we are.*

10

Drew

Drew liked to delude himself into thinking he could gain people's respect with talent and hard work. But Luiz *knew* that the quickest way to win over the other journalists in the press office was through good coffee and free pastries. So, when he mentioned that he was going to the café to pick up snacks for them, Drew immediately decided to tag along. He'd spent that morning out on the slopes with a group of Ukrainian snowboarders, taking photos of them midair, then sitting in the snow as they shared the moments that had led them to the Olympics. So, by the time he took his final photo, he was more than ready to get his freezing cold hands around a hot cup of coffee.

He spent the walk to the café quizzing Luiz about that evening's opening ceremony and asking him about all the people he'd worked with in the press office. Luiz was in the middle of telling him a story about how he'd accidentally ended up as a guest on a Tanzanian news channel when Drew saw a familiar face in the crowd.

"Wait, is that Hans Leitner?" said Drew, turning his head at the man who'd just walked into the café. The seventy-two-year-old documentarian had an old Olympus film camera around his neck, a notebook in his hand, and a vintage Lake Placid 1980 Winter Games jacket resting on his shoulders.

"The man himself," said Luiz with a nod. They watched as he ordered a flat white.

Hans Leitner had spent decades making Academy Award–winning documentaries about athletes, politicians, and public figures, including one of Drew's favorites: an early 2000s film about one of the first Black Winter Olympic medalists.

"Should I go up to him?" he asked, thinking about how bizarre it was to see someone he idolized waiting in line for coffee like a regular person.

Luiz looked horrified at the suggestion. "Why would you do that?"

"Because I love his work."

"Don't meet your heroes. It never ends well."

Drew knew that Luiz was probably right. But he couldn't help but glance over at Hans and the film crew surrounding him with cameras, microphones, and matching LEITNER PRODUCTIONS coats. Drew had always been drawn to taking photos, not videos, but there was something about the way Hans made his films that inspired Drew. He never took the obvious route when it came to the stories he told. When he'd made a film tracking the activity behind the scenes of the Oscars, he'd told the story through the walkie-talkie radio communications between the staff instead of filming regular camera interviews. When he'd made a documentary about a famous restaurant in the final week before its closure, he made the film from the point of view of regular diners. Telling the restaurant's story through its most loyal customers and their favorite meals.

"You want to meet someone like that when you have something to show him, a conversation starter," said Luiz knowingly.

"And all I have now are standard press shots," Drew agreed, knowing that there wasn't anything close to spectacular on his camera's memory card.

He was grateful for his assignment at Zeus. Working with a brand as big as theirs was the kind of opportunity that his freshman-year self would have dreamed of. But he didn't want to just send Zeus folders of competition photos. With the right technique, anybody could get a shot of a snowboarder midair or a figure skater midspin. It was the intimacy of his New Year's Eve photos that had made them so special. People craved the chance to get a behind-the-scenes look from the perspective of an insider. It's what made celeb mirror selfies at the Met Gala and biopics of elusive musicians so compelling. Drew needed to fulfill his assignment and get the photos the team at Zeus had asked for. But he knew he would have to capture something more impressive if he wanted his temporary press pass to resemble anything that looked like a job. So, after he and Luiz collected the coffees and dropped pastries off at the press office, Drew grabbed his headphones and pressed PLAY on *Songs in the Key of Life*. It was his favorite album, the one he played whenever he needed to get out of a creative rut.

He'd gone to college with nothing but creative excitement and blind ambition, striving to make the kind of art that filled the walls of his favorite galleries. But as the semesters went on, he became acutely aware of the gap between the kind of work he wanted to make and the level of skill he actually had.

He could take a good photo, but he struggled to truly capture the character, emotion, and tension of a moment. He'd struck gold a few times. A candid photo of a local hero that won a campus photography prize, a photo diary of a ballerina in recovery featured in a citywide newspaper, and the NYE photos for Zeus that had led him to the Olympics. But he still didn't think his track record was impressive enough to be capable of the kind of work Hans made. However, if he was going to be back in Wisconsin in a few weeks scrambling for opportunities, he needed to come up with a way to impress the team at Zeus. It would take something big to stay on their radar and be at the front of their minds the next time an opportunity came up.

So, he spent the journey from the press office over to the hotel his grandparents were staying at trying to come up with photo diary ideas compelling enough to stand out. When he walked into the lobby, he immediately noticed a girl wearing a blue winter coat embroidered with stars. She turned around and waved at him. It was his sister, Thandie.

"How does it feel to officially be an Olympian?" Drew asked, giving her a hug.

"Exciting and terrifying," she said, thumbing the Team USA logo on the sleeve of her coat. "It's been such a long time coming."

Drew smiled. There was nobody who deserved a moment like this more than his sister. Thandie had been playing ice hockey her whole life and was one of the best players in the world. So, when the 2022 Winter Olympics had come around, she was automatically placed on the Team USA roster. But a few months before she was due to fly to Beijing, an injury had left her bedridden in Wisconsin. The heartbreak of missing out on something she'd spent her whole life working toward had been devastating. But Thandie was one of the most resilient people he knew, and she leaped straight back into action the minute her doctor signed her off.

"But how about you: Are you ready for your weekly interrogation?" she asked knowingly.

"I guess I don't have any other choice." Drew grimaced, bracing himself for their pre–opening ceremony family lunch. As they turned the corner of the lobby, they spotted their grandparents walking in, their grandpa in his standard three-piece suit and their grandma wearing a glamorous deep red coat.

"Look at my baby! All grown up," Grandma said as she and Thandie ran toward each other and into a hug. Thandie had been so busy with hockey training that they'd only seen her for a few days in December before she was off to pre-Olympic training camp.

"Grandma, you have to let me borrow that necklace," Thandie said, squeezing her tight. They'd always been close, but with Thandie spending the majority of her year training in Colorado, Drew knew they hadn't spoken much. He was grateful for the temporary distance between them, because if Thandie had been present enough to spend time with their grandma, she might have noticed some of the signs, started asking questions, and figured out that something was wrong. Finding out about their grandma's Alzheimer's this close to the most important tournament of her life would have distracted her from her number-one focus: ice hockey. So, Drew and Grandpa had decided to do what they could to make sure that Thandie and Grandma didn't spend enough alone time together for Thandie to connect the dots.

"And my favorite grandson, come over here," Grandma said, hugging Drew as if she was seeing him for the first time in months, even though he'd been living with them since December.

"This is so much nicer than USA House," said Thandie, glancing at the luxurious furniture and chandeliers. Their grandma believed the most important part of a vacation was where you slept, so she'd booked a gorgeous mountainside hotel in St. Moritz.

"I don't know why you're not just staying with us, Drew," Grandpa said as they walked from the lobby into the restaurant. It had floor-to-ceiling windows that gave them the perfect view of the snow-coated mountains of St. Moritz, dazzlingly white against the bright blue winter sky. Grandpa gave the name of their reservation and then the four of them made their way across the restaurant to a beautifully laid-out table in the center of the room. As they ordered their drinks, a pianist on the other side of the room began playing a slow, gorgeous jazz medley.

When Drew's grandparents had found out that he would be taking photos for Zeus and traveling to the Games on his own terms, they'd immediately offered to include him in their booking. But Drew didn't want to stay in a fancy hotel room paid for by his grandparents or be spotted with his Olympian sister in the middle of the Village. He didn't want the other journalists and photographers to think his family connections were the only reason he'd gotten the job. Even if they kind of were.

"That's the issue with you kids," began his grandpa as he leafed through the menu. Drew glanced over at Thandie, who was covertly holding three fingers up as she counted down to their grandpa's infamous origin speech.

"When I moved to Wisconsin in the seventies, all I had was a bag and a few hard-won school qualifications. But I worked hard, built the firm from the ground up, and fought every day to keep us afloat." His grandpa wasn't a man of many words in his everyday life, but since Drew left college, every family dinner had become a lecture. "I put my blood, sweat, and tears into making sure that you could have a good life without having to struggle as much as we did. But here you are, Andrew, throwing away your—"

Grandma gave Grandpa a look that made him pause mid-sentence.

"Why won't you just accept our help, Drew?" Grandpa said, softening his tone. Drew knew he was talking about work and college, but it was easier to just focus on the hotel room.

"Because I don't want to stay in a grand hotel like some trust-fund baby," Drew said, ignoring how incompatible the prices on the menu were with his desire to feel like a self-made man.

"But you do have a trust fund, Drew"—his grandma smiled—"and you're *my* baby. There's nothing to be ashamed about."

Thandie, who was sitting next to him, stifled a laugh. Drew shot her a sharp look. She made a show of pretending to zip her lips before picking up her phone and pretending to look busy.

"Andrew, it's not even about the hotel. It's about your future. What comes next?" Grandpa asked.

"Don't worry, I have a plan," said Drew. He did not have a plan.

"You're a terrible liar, son," Grandpa said, shaking his head and leaning back in his chair, clearly over the conversation.

"But you would have made a brilliant doctor, Caleb. . . ." Grandma said, her gaze far away as her sentence trailed off.

Drew stilled, his heartbeat quickening.

Grandpa squeezed his wife's hand and whispered something only the two of them could hear. She looked confused and then embarrassed, unable to make eye contact with anyone in the room. Drew didn't know anyone called Caleb. Or a man who would have made a brilliant doctor. But his grandma had said it with complete confidence. He wanted to correct her but knew it was easier not to. Her lapses in memory and confusion were becoming more and more frequent, and Drew was powerless to the illness he could see unfolding. He glanced over at his sister to see her reaction, but she was tapping away at her phone, no doubt texting her team group chat about their plans for the opening ceremony. Drew sighed in relief, grateful that she hadn't noticed anything. He knew it was better to keep Thandie in the dark. But he couldn't help but wish he could talk to his sister about it.

Drew glanced over at his grandma, noticing the bags under her eyes that she'd tried to cover up with makeup, the layers of clothing that didn't quite hide how much weight she'd lost, and the gentle looks his grandpa kept giving her. Silent reassurances that everything would be okay. But Drew knew it wasn't true.

"You wanted this your entire life," Grandma said, back on the topic of his dropping out of college. "I just . . . I just don't believe you woke up one morning and randomly changed your mind."

She was right. But he couldn't admit it was because he knew she was sick. Thandie still didn't know, and with the biggest competition of her life just around the corner, telling her the full story just wasn't worth the risk. So, he changed the conversation to stop any further interrogation.

"What we should *really* be focusing on is that Thandie's probably going home with her first Olympic medal this year," he said, beaming at his sister as she put her phone down. He knew that their grandparents would leave him alone once the topic turned to ice hockey.

"How did practice go, Sugar? Are you ready for the opening ceremony?" Grandma asked, her face lighting up as their drinks arrived. Drew thanked the waiter as he placed a hot Americano on the table. Drew picked it up and sat back, glad to no longer be the focus of attention.

"More than ready," Thandie said, radiating confidence as she took a sip of her hot lemon-and-ginger tea. "The girls are killing it. We're all on top of our game and that gold medal is ours."

"How about the competition?" their grandpa asked, his eyes lighting up as he doted on Thandie. He was a die-hard ice hockey fan, always excited to hear the inside scoop.

"Weaker than ever," Thandie said, smiling mischievously

before her face darkened. "And guess who I saw watching us from the stands yesterday, looking like she'd seen a ghost?"

"Who?" Grandpa asked. He loved the behind-the-scenes drama as much as the sport.

"The girl who almost ruined my career," Thandie said. Drew tried to trace his memory back to 2022, to remember the exact match that led to her injury. But his sister had been playing ice hockey since they were kids, so all the dramatic tournaments blurred into one.

"Were you okay seeing her?" Drew asked, concerned. He didn't like knowing that anyone could have the ability to throw her off her game. Because he knew just how hard Thandie had worked to get here. The months of physical therapy, years of self-doubt, and countless days spent training to get back to her pre-injury form. She deserved this more than anyone, so he refused to let anything get in his sister's way.

"More than okay. It kind of lit a fire in me. Reminded me what I almost lost and how determined I am to make it right this year," Thandie said, tapping the table in excitement. "We're going to *crush* her team. And I'm going to enjoy it more than anything I've ever done."

"Be nice," their grandma said reflexively as she lifted her teacup. But Thandie wasn't fazed.

"Nice doesn't win medals"—she grinned—"and I'm going home with gold."

11

Ari

"I feel like I'm exactly three steps away from making an international embarrassment of myself," said Ari as she and her teammates stood outside in the cold, waiting to go into the stadium with the rest of Team GB.

"Just put one foot in front of the other and stay focused on what's in front of you," said Izzy as she walked alongside Ari in her matching blue-and-white ceremony coat.

"And if your arms get tired, we'll help you carry it," Sienna said, tying a bright red woolly scarf around her neck.

Ari nodded as she stretched her arms out to accept the ten-foot flagpole the official was giving her. For reasons beyond her understanding, someone had decided to store them outside, meaning that by the time she clasped her gloved hands around it, the metal pole was freezing cold.

Months of planning went into deciding who would carry the flag for each competing country. There were short lists, votes, and secret discussions to decide each flagbearer. Flags were carried by multimedal-winning athletes, legendary coaches, and famous stars. And that year, Team GB had awarded the honor to two people: a legendary ski jumper competing for the last time and Gracie. But with Gracie back home in Canada, recovering from her accident, the officials were forced to find a quick replacement. When Ari got a call from an unknown number in the second week of January, she'd assumed it was some telemarketing scam. But the call had ended with an invite to become one of that year's flagbearers: a symbol to celebrate their team making it to the Olympics for the first time. She'd accepted it with a stunned thank-you, as honored as she was terrified.

It was a strange flag. One that had been used countless times to divide the country and make people like her feel unwelcome in their own home. It was a physical reminder of all the ways the country had wreaked havoc on the other nations competing in the Games. And she got the sense that her ancestors were rolling in their graves as they watched her carry something they'd spent their lives trying to fight against. But as complicated as her relationship with it was, the Union Jack was a symbol of the place she called home. The flag belonged to her just as much as it belonged to everyone else on the team. So in spite of all its contradictions, she clutched it extra tight.

"I can't believe this is really happening," Ari said as she and her friends looked up. The flag was billowing in the early-evening wind, and above the flag was a bright night sky filled with more stars than she'd ever seen all at once. She could already feel the moment forming into the kind of memory she'd spend the rest of her life playing back. She wanted to pause and take it all in, but the ceremony was running on a tight schedule. So, with the help of her friends, she shifted the flagpole and carried it through the crowd, passing by a dozen photographers and journalists as they hurried along.

She was taking in each detail of the stadium when she spotted a flicker of something familiar. Someone familiar. She vaguely recognized a photographer in the crowd but she was too far away from the stands to make out the details of his face. Maybe he was a photographer that covered the ice hockey circuit? Or a sports journalist she'd met at a match in the past? He walked away before she could get a closer look. So, she shook her head, refocusing her attention on carrying the flag to the stadium gates where she was met by the other flagbearer, a kind man in his early forties competing for the final time. He'd spent the past hour caught up in doing a news interview, but now that he was done, he reached over to take turns carrying the flagpole as they walked to the entrance together. When they reached the entrance, they were met by the rest of the athletes on Team GB—a crowd of people Ari had known for years. She waved at a bobsledder from Edinburgh who she'd met at the gym, hugged a figure skater from Sheffield who'd taught her how to do an Axel jump a few summers ago, and gathered alongside her friends to take a photo with the men's ice hockey team. At one point, she briefly spotted Harrison trying to make his way toward her in the crowd, so her friends put a twenty-something-person barrier between them to stop him from getting in the way of a perfect night. But Ari knew that even he couldn't ruin this moment for her, because, after hundreds of matches and early-morning training sessions, she was finally at the Olympics.

When the volunteers finally opened the gates and the announcer called out "Great Britain," the audience roared. The intensity of it caught her by surprise, so much so that she momentarily lost her grip on the flag. Her eyes widened as she watched it fall; but before it could hit the ground, Sienna caught it and handed it back. The two of them laughed as the rest of their team cheered. Izzy squeezed her shoulder, and Yasmeen recorded a video of them walking around the stadium with over two hundred other athletes in matching uniforms, living out their childhood dreams.

Ari had no idea what would happen over the next two weeks. The odds of their Gracie-less team winning even one preliminary game were practically impossible. Ari knew it, the rest of the team knew it, and the pundits back home had so little faith in them that they'd likened their arrival in St. Moritz to watching lambs skating over to a slaughterhouse. But moments like this only came around once in a lifetime. So, as the crowd cheered and confetti fell on their shoulders, Ari decided to just enjoy this magical moment with her best friends. The stadium was filled with people wearing bright coats, colorful scarves, and flag-themed hats. The crowd was dancing, waving their hands from side to side and cheering them on with every step. It felt like something out of a dream. Ari looked around and tried to take it all in. But she couldn't stop staring up at the sky.

Bright, dazzling fireworks were shooting out of the stadium, brightening the dark winter night and sending bursts of light against every surface in her line of sight. It reminded her of New Year's Eve. Ari had tried her best to push the memory of that night to the side and, thanks to the long days she'd spent in hockey practice, there'd barely been time to think about anything other than the next match. But as a bright dot shot up and burst into a brilliant explosion of white-and-gold lights, she couldn't help but wonder where the guy she'd met on the roof that night was right now. Whether he was somewhere else in the world, watching the opening ceremony on TV, or staring up at another firework-lit sky.

She carried on walking, her team cheering behind her. When she looked out at the crowd, her eyes zeroed in on the press pit again. They were closer now, and she could make out the details of people's faces. There were a few photographers and journalists she knew from past international games, but that's not where her focus landed. When she'd first spotted a familiar face in the crowd, her thoughts had been so far away from New Year's that she hadn't even thought to make the connection. But when her eyes landed on a boy aiming his camera up at the sky, she realized that her mind wasn't playing tricks on her. She knew exactly who she was looking at. The memory of the last time she'd seen him came back to her with startling clarity.

It was the boy from the roof. Drew.

But what on earth was *he* doing *here*?

12

Drew

THE OPENING CEREMONY

MESSAGE FROM: Zeus BTS team
Key people: First-time Olympians
Assignment: Capture the energy behind the scenes of tonight's opening ceremony celebrations. Put a special emphasis on photos of first-time Olympians.

Drew had never witnessed a moment as jubilant or wholesome as the sight of the athletes leaving the stadium at the end of the opening ceremony. There was something magical about watching Olympians clothed in uniforms from all around the world taking photos, celebrating, and forming friendships under a firework-lit sky.

But the Olympians weren't the only people on the cusp of the two most important weeks of their lives. A few yards away, a group of journalists and photographers were hunched over their chairs with laptops and external hard drives, uploading photos, sending them to their editors, and posting them online. Drew knew they were working fast to ensure that the photos they'd taken would be on newspaper front covers in the morning and in website headlines before the end of the night. Because soon he would be doing the same. But first he needed to run across the stadium and take photos of all the Zeus-sponsored athletes.

He showed the security guard his press credentials, left the press pit, and weaved his way through the crowd.

The team at Zeus had sent him a long list of athletes to photograph over the course of the Games. In the few days he'd been in the Village, Drew had already begun to notice the difference between the various people on his list. They could broadly be split into two groups. First, there were the world-famous athletes who politely declined to do anything beyond their contractually obligated photo ops. And second, there were the new and upcoming athletes who would answer all of Drew's questions and let him take his time behind the camera because of how excited they were to be there. Once Drew snapped shots of the top stars on the list, he went into the crowd to find the newbies he could get quotes from. He knew the easy option would be to find his sister and talk to her team, but he wanted to push himself. So, he photographed a Slovenian snowboarder who told him about the childhood sledding that inspired him to learn how to snowboard. And then he talked to a speed skater on the Refugee Olympic Team who told him the advice her childhood sports teacher gave her to become completely fearless on the ice.

By the time he'd tallied up enough athletes to complete his assignment, the crowd was thinning out. But then he spotted his sister, running toward him in her Team USA uniform. He immediately pulled her into a hug.

"You made it!" he said, immensely proud of all the work she'd done to get to this moment.

"Can you believe it? We're heading to a postceremony after-party to celebrate. Do you want to come?"

A part of him did. He was sure he'd probably get some good behind-the-scenes shots at a party. But he had a bunch of photos to edit and send to Zeus before the morning. So, he waved her away, promising to join her at the closing ceremony parties, then began to make his way home.

He was walking out of the stadium when he spotted a crowd of red-and-blue uniforms that didn't belong to Team USA. He did a double take when he saw the person standing at the center of it.

It couldn't be her, right? he thought to himself as he cast his eyes back to the face that had caught his attention.

He looked closer and realized that, no, he wasn't seeing things. Because right there in the middle of a crowd of British athletes was a face that had been coming back to him in flashes ever since New Year's Day. Among the striped hats and woolly scarves was a girl with big, bouncy curls, a world-stopping smile, and eyes Drew would have recognized in any crowd.

She was way too deep into the conversations she was having to notice him, but Drew didn't need to hear her voice to know it would sound just like the girl he'd spent that honest, magical, firework-framed New Year's Eve with.

Ari.

13

Ari

Ari's teammates started running around and making plans as soon as confetti began falling to the ground. It was the most exciting night of the year and they wanted to hit the after-parties and late-night dinner spots. They were in the middle of discussing a Team Switzerland cabin party invite when Ari's phone rang. She walked to a quiet spot at the side of the stadium to answer the FaceTime call. It was her mom, sitting in the living room with the TV on. Telling her that she'd already started replaying the live broadcast of the opening ceremony so she could watch Ari walk into the stadium again.

"I'm so proud of you!" Ari's mom cried, wiping away tears as she gushed about how good Ari looked in her uniform, how well she'd carried the flag, and how happy she and her teammates looked on her TV screen.

"I wouldn't be here without you," Ari said, meaning every word. Her mom had pretty much raised Ari and her sister alone.

She'd been the one to pack their lunches, attend parents' evenings, and do hockey practice drop-offs. Ari owed her everything.

"And we can't wait to come and see you on the ice. I've already packed my outfits." She began detailing every dress, sweater, hat, and scarf she was planning to wear in St. Moritz. Her mom was glowing.

"Not until the quarterfinals, remember," Ari said. She loved her family, but they stressed her out. She knew that if they came to watch all her games, they would eventually say or do something that would throw her off. It was never intentional; they just carried their drama with them wherever they went. No matter how hard they tried to be supportive, she always found herself having to defuse arguments and smooth emotions when they were around. So, she'd effectively banned them from traveling to St. Moritz unless she and her team made it to the quarterfinals.

"You've always been so suspicious," her mom said, shaking her head. "It's the one negative thing you got from your father."

Ari sighed. She could tell that while her mom was calling to congratulate her, she had something else on her mind.

"Did you and Anesu figure things out?" Ari asked as she watched the other athletes walking up and down the hallways in excitement, chatting about after-parties and group dinner plans, with a carefree kind of happiness. She wanted to join them, but her mother's response to her question made it pretty clear that her tears weren't just those of a proud parent.

"I still can't believe she would do something like this," her mom said, tearing up again. Even though weeks had passed, her mom and Anesu were still stuck on their Christmas Day argument. The wedding was just a few weeks away, and Anesu hadn't changed her mind about going.

"I moved to another country, raised you girls all by myself, sacrificed everything, and what does she do to thank me for it? Side with a man who did nothing but throw money at her."

"He's still her dad," Ari sighed. "You can understand why she'd want to have a relationship with him." She was trying to get her mom to see it from her sister's side.

"I could understand if he'd actually made an effort to be present. But he just wants to reap the fruits of my labor now that the two of you are grown up and he doesn't have to take care of— Actually, none of that matters because he'll always know that I . . . we did this by ourselves." Her mom smiled from the other end of the phone. "My baby, the Olympian. I've already cleared a space on the fireplace to frame your medal."

Ari laughed. Her mom was adamant that her team would be going home with something. She possessed unflinching belief when it came to her daughters' abilities.

"Remember, you've done hard things before; you can do hard things again. They wouldn't have given you this responsibility if you weren't capable. I know you can do it," her mom said. Ari tried her best to believe it. "Well, I know you're busy, so go and enjoy yourself. Don't forget to send me photos," her mom said before finally letting her go.

Ari hung up and made her way back out into the crowd of athletes, a single question circling in her brain: *Where is he?* While it made absolutely no sense for Drew to be at the Olympics right now, she knew with almost complete certainty that she'd seen him in the crowd. Her friends were still trying to decide whether to go back to GB House and end the night with hot chocolate or join the hockey lads at an after-party hosted by the Swiss curling team. But Ari didn't want to leave until she found Drew, so she told her friends she'd meet them later and walked back in the direction of the stadium.

She maneuvered her way around a huddle of French figure

skaters and walked back to the press pit, but it had emptied out. She scanned the crowd, looking for anyone with a purple photographer lanyard around their neck, but she couldn't spot any. So, after walking around the stadium and taking in the gravity of just how many people were in the Village, she decided to cut her losses and head back to GB House. But when she walked toward the gates, she came face-to-face with the one person she'd been trying to avoid ever since landing in Switzerland: Harrison Cavendish.

It was hard to publicly hate someone that everybody loved. And *everybody loved Harrison*. They either knew him from spending time on the slopes together or admired his gleaming professional reputation. He was a two-time Olympic gold medal–winning snowboarder, and there were thousands of people around the world rooting for him to win his third. He was charming and moved through every room with complete ease. Behind closed doors, Harrison found a million little ways to try to make Ari feel small, but he had the kind of aura that made each person who met him wonder what it was like to be loved by him. In her low moments, Ari missed him. When he turned up the charm, she momentarily forgot that he'd been the worst thing to ever happen to her. But it was true. And she refused to let her heart betray her again.

"Ari, you look beautiful tonight," Harrison said when he finally reached her. He leaned forward and kissed her on the cheek in a way that felt both foreign and familiar. Each encounter with him was a battle between her body and her mind. He ran his hand across her shoulders and down her arm until he reached her wrist.

"You've still got it," he said, smiling down at the birthday gift he'd bought her last year. A black leather and gold watch from Cartier. It was unjustifiably expensive, enough to put down a deposit for a place in the North of England. But Harrison was a Cavendish, so to him it was just pocket change. She'd attempted to give it back after the breakup, but he'd waved it off. She'd lost interest in the giver, but the gift was too nice to lock away.

"And this is gorgeous, you should do it more often," he said, casually running his warm hands over the curls in her hair. She tried not to like it.

"Thanks, Yas helped me do it," she said, recalling the number of flexi rods they'd put in to get her hair in its current form.

"Always more concerned with her hair than her on-ice strategy," he chuckled. She winced a little, taking a step back before he could try to pull her into a hug. Ari was getting impatient. She wanted the conversation to be over. The icy wind was making her eyes water, her ears were numb from the cold, and each moment she spent standing still made it worse. She wanted to be sitting in bed with a mug of chamomile tea, scrolling through all the photos she and her teammates had taken while watching a rerun of the opening ceremony, not talking to her insufferable ex-boyfriend. But Harrison was like a leaky tap, once he started talking, he couldn't stop.

"So, are you heading out to a party? I know your *girls* like setting themselves up for failure by going on big nights out, but surely not you?" He was smiling, but his voice barely concealed the distaste he'd always reserved for her friends. She looked away and over toward the thinning crowd of athletes leaving the stadium to head out to after-parties and late-night dinners and decided it was time for her to leave. She didn't have time to entertain a conversation with him.

"I should head out. I'm going to get an early night."

He winked. "Good. We wouldn't want you getting sloppy, honey."

Once again, Harrison was showing himself for who he really was. She'd ignored it when they were together, but now that they weren't, she could see how repulsive his personality truly was. So, she turned on her heel to leave.

"Let me walk you back since we're heading to the same place. I think you're just one floor below me, actually," he said. It took her a moment to understand what he meant, but then the reality of her situation sank in. The British athletes were staying in a big cabin-themed apartment block: GB House. It was easy to avoid him back home in London. They ran in different social circles and lived on opposite sides of the city. But for the next two weeks, she and Harrison would be living just one floor apart. It was only a matter of time before she bumped into him again at the canteen or outside the gym.

"It's okay, I can get myself home," she said, trying to draw a line between them. But she knew Harrison thrived in the gray areas. He wouldn't give up as long as he thought there was still a shot, but she didn't have the energy to spend two weeks avoiding whole chunks of the Village to steer clear of him. So, she stepped out into the wintry night, spotting the tall coniferous trees cloaked in white blankets, the icicles hanging off nearby buildings. There was a bitterly cold breeze circling the air.

"No, I can't let you go alone. It's dark, and I don't trust that ice," he said, looking down at the well-salted walking paths. He was acting as if he could see something she couldn't, like her safety was his number-one priority. But she knew he was just trying to creep his way into her plans for the night.

"I'm walking back with my friends, actually, so it's alright," she said.

"Which friends?" he asked, looking around.

She searched the crowd, but she couldn't see any of her teammates. She scanned the sea of athletes for a familiar face, but everyone was preoccupied. But then, just as she was about to give up, she saw a face she immediately recognized.

Drew. He had a camera in his hands, a press pass hanging around his neck, and looked just as surprised as she was. There were so many questions she wanted to ask him, but she didn't have time to catch up. She needed an excuse to leave, and she needed one fast.

Ari looked back at Harrison, and then she looked toward Drew.

A light bulb lit up in her mind.

Harrison didn't respect her enough to listen when she said she wanted nothing to do with him. But Harrison respected other men. Her feminism disagreed with the logic of what she was considering, but her instincts told her it was the best option. So, in a split-second decision, she decided to make herself unavailable, or at least make it seem like she was. A perfect, albeit messed-up, solution came to her in an instant.

"Actually, my . . . *boyfriend* is over there. So, I'm going to bounce," she said in a rush as she walked away.

She could feel Harrison's eyes burning holes in the back of her head as she left. But it was too late to change her mind. She walked across the snow toward Drew.

There was a shadow of stubble on his chin that made him seem older, but when she saw the way his eyes twinkled under the light of the lamppost he was standing under, she knew he was still the same man she'd met on the roof. For a moment, it felt like New Year's Eve again. Time stood still as they gazed into each other's eyes. A flood of memories came back to her: their late-night confessions, a sky full of fireworks, the remnants of a perfect midnight kiss.

"Ari?" he asked. Her name sounded like a song on his lips.

"Drew," she said, taking in the way his face softened as she walked closer. It felt like minutes since she'd last seen him, not months.

"What happened to *never* seeing each other again?" he said with a soft laugh. That laugh sounded like sunlight, warm enough to make a Swiss winter night feel like spring. She was about to ask him why he was in the Village, but then she remembered she'd walked toward him for a reason.

"It's a long story for another time, but can you do me a quick favor?" she asked, glancing over at Harrison, who was still watching her. Drew followed her eyes and glanced over with curiosity.

"Shoot," he said gamely.

"Can you pretend to be my boyfriend for two seconds so I can get away from *him*?" The words tumbled out of her mouth before she could think them through.

Drew's eyebrows shot up in surprise. He looked over at Harrison, then back at Ari. Once he put the pieces together, he acted fast.

He put his hand out, and she grasped it. His hand was warm, and the contact of his skin on hers felt so natural that it was as if they'd stood like this a dozen times before.

"What do you need me to do?" he said.

Harrison was still looking over at them.

"Um, do something boyfriendy, I guess?" Ari hadn't thought this far ahead.

"Boyfriendy?" he asked, confused.

"I don't know, you could kiss me?" she wondered aloud, regretting the words as soon as they came out of her mouth.

What a weird thing to ask an almost total stranger, she thought, opening her mouth to take it back. But Drew just nodded. He let go of her hand and slowly leaned closer. She could feel her heart beating a little faster as he looked into her eyes and smiled at her like they were in on a secret together. He wrapped his arms around her shoulder, and she leaned into the comfort of his embrace. He smelled like clean skin, aftershave, and firewood. Like coming home after a long day and settling into someone's arms.

"Is this okay?" he whispered, his voice sending a tingle around her neck. She just nodded, holding his gaze as he ran his finger against her cheek, tracing a line from her eyes down to her lips. His touch was gentle, but she could feel the trail of heat it left across her skin. The way it spread out across her face and down her body as he cupped her chin, brought her closer, and closed his eyes. Everything went quiet for a moment, and then he kissed her. His soft lips meeting hers as she wrapped her arms around his neck and sank into the delicious taste of him. Their bodies moving in a slow, smooth rhythm as he leaned in and pulled her closer. She gently parted his lips, feeling the hot, smooth sensation of his tongue as they deepened the kiss into a heady, slightly dizzying intensity. Soon her reasons for kissing him were forgotten. Because this felt *way* too good to just be pretend.

14

Drew

Drew hadn't left his hotel room that morning expecting to end the day kissing Ari. He hadn't planned to end the day kissing anybody. And he certainly couldn't have predicted that the girl he'd told his secrets to at a random party in another country would now be at the Olympics. Or that he'd be kissing her outside the Olympic Stadium. If it wasn't for the fact that she'd clearly only approached him to get out of a sticky situation, he would have kept his arms around her waist and kissed her the way he'd really wanted to on New Year's Eve. But as good as it felt, it was just for show, and Drew knew when to bow out.

When he pulled away, Ari's eyes were still closed. Maybe it was just the layers of fleece and the big winter coat she was wearing, but she seemed peaceful wrapped up in his arms. Content even. As if they were somewhere warm and cozy, not outside in the snow on one of the coldest days of the year. It had been dark on the roof that night; but now that they were standing under the glow of a lamppost, he could see how beautiful she really was, her curls gently framing her face, her warm brown skin smooth to touch, her eyelashes curling softly from her eyelids.

"Ari," he said gently. Her eyes were still closed.

"Hmm," she replied.

"You can open your eyes now," he whispered.

Her eyes flew open as if waking from a dream. She looked up at him, shook her head, and glanced away. They let go of each other, then both took a very purposeful step back. He tried not to think too much about how empty his arms already felt without her. Or linger on the way she'd glanced down at his mouth and bit her lip the second they'd parted. For a moment, they stood in silence, looking everywhere but at each other. It was a good kiss. So good that he was almost embarrassed to have enjoyed it so much.

Drew cleared his throat and glanced over at the guy Ari seemed to be avoiding. He was a tall, athletic man wearing a huge red bomber jacket emblazoned with the words TEAM GB. Drew had spent years analyzing people from behind his lens. He'd learned how to read the obvious and not-so-obvious cues that gave him insights into who a person was. And while nothing about the guy or the group of athletes now surrounding him suggested he was a bad person, something in his eyes told Drew everything he needed to know. The guy stared Drew down for a second, then nodded at him. But Drew didn't nod back. Instead, he cast his eyes toward Ari, suddenly feeling protective.

"Is he giving you problems?" Drew said, hunching his shoulders and glaring at the guy. Ari rolled her eyes and shook her head. The slightly startled look she'd come to him with was replaced by a mixture of irritation and amusement.

"I'm not a damsel in distress, Drew. I don't need you to save me," she said firmly, before softening. "But that kiss should be enough to get him to back off, so thank you."

"I hate creepy random men," Drew said, thinking of all the times Thandie and her friends had told him about their weird encounters with strangers.

"Harrison's not creepy or random."

"Oh, *Harrison*. As in your ex-boyfriend?"

"How do you—oh, New Year's," she said with a grimace.

"Want to talk about it?"

"And spill my secrets like we're on the roof again? Absolutely not."

"Why not? I'm a good listener, and I have nowhere else to be tonight." Drew knew full well that there was a whole SD card of photos to send to Zeus before the end of the day.

"I only told you *all of that* because I thought I'd never see you again."

"Yet here we are." Drew tilted his head and met her gaze.

She shook her head. "No more confessions, Drew."

"In case we see each other again?"

"We're *not* going to see each other again," she said firmly as they locked eyes. He could feel the tension, and he was sure she could, too. "We shouldn't."

She was right, but that didn't stop Drew from wanting to pick up where they'd left off the last time they'd seen each other. Her phone alarm rang before he could say anything else.

"That's my cue to go to bed," she said, tying a scarf around her neck and reaching into her pockets to put on her gloves.

"But it's only eleven. Aren't you going out?" he asked.

Thandie had told him about at least ten different after-parties happening across the Village that night. And Drew couldn't help but wonder if getting some behind-the-scenes photos would win him the approval of the Zeus Athletics socials team he so desperately wanted to impress. But Ari just shook her head and turned to leave.

"Only mediocre athletes and overconfident medal winners party on the first night," she said as she started walking toward the athletes' quarters. "Champions *and* people flying by the seat of their pants go to bed early."

"And which one are you?" he called out.

"A champion, of course," she said, shooting him a brilliantly confident smile.

"See you later, *Ari*," he said, testing her resolve. She shook her head and walked away.

15

Ari

It was six a.m., and the sun hadn't risen yet. But Ari was already outside walking in the snow with her headphones on, listening to her self-assigned weekly audiobook and trying to look past its corny sports clichés. "Make sure to highlight your teammates' strengths before you address their weaknesses," said the voice of Valentina Ross-Rodriguez, a gold medal–winning gymnast. "Resist the temptation to take on other people's doubts," she said as Ari looked at her own footprints in the snow.

The stress of managing the team's emotions while trying to bring out the best in them on the ice was so overwhelming that Ari had developed a mild case of insomnia during the first three weeks of boot camp. She'd considered calling Gracie for advice—after all, she'd been the first person to text her when her new role as captain went public. But she couldn't. She knew that Gracie would pick up and say something helpful and encouraging. But it felt selfish to interrupt Gracie's recovery with worries about the job Gracie had spent her life working toward. Slipping away for an hour in the morning to listen to someone else's advice felt like the least-complicated alternative.

But Ari couldn't focus on what she was listening to, because she'd woken up that morning thinking about Drew. She would have never predicted seeing him again, and the last place she expected to find him was under a lamppost in the middle of the Winter Village. But to her surprise, she'd felt as comfortable with him as she had on New Year's Eve. Maybe it was because she'd told him so much that first night that it felt like seeing a friend who'd been in the trenches with her. But what really surprised her was how much more attractive he was up close with the lights on. How handsome he looked with stubble. The small spark she'd felt as he gently grazed her skin.

Deep in her thoughts, she lost track of the chapter she was listening to and reminded herself that she hadn't come all the way to Switzerland to spend the first day of the Games thinking about a boy she barely knew. The next ten days were going to be a marathon. They needed to win at least two of their four preliminary games to have a good shot at making it to the quarterfinals. After that came the semifinals and then the actual finals, when the best teams at the Games would compete for gold. Ari had much more important things to worry about than the boy she'd kissed last night. So, she finished her walk at seven, grabbed breakfast with her teammates at eight, and headed over to the other side of the Village to get ready for her first-ever Olympic match.

Ari imagined that in every other area of his life, Coach McLaughlin walked into rooms with a certain air of authority. He'd been coaching hockey for the past thirty years, leading a bunch of the men's teams to victory. But because the women's team had been through so many coaches who'd only stuck around for a few months, they were much harder to impress. Coach liked to empower each team captain he worked with to take on the role of leading and inspiring their team. And one of the ways he did that was by asking them to start each locker room session with a short speech. Gracie's speeches were always memorable. Sometimes she began with a joke about something she'd noticed in training, and other times she started with an anecdote that she would spin into some meaningful lesson or rally cry. Gracie knew how to energize her teammates, but Ari was still just trying to figure it out.

"Let's get started," she said as she walked to the front of the locker room.

But nobody was listening. They were all plotting, panicking, and celebrating the fact that in less than fifteen minutes, they'd be up against the Czech Republic for the first time since their disastrous loss at the start of the last international hockey season.

"Shall we begin?" she asked, trying to get their attention.

But Izzy was teaching her teammates on defense a TikTok dance, Sienna was sitting in a corner with her noise-canceling headphones on, and Yasmeen was chatting in a circle with the girls in reserve, sharing gossip about one of the after-parties. If Gracie had been here, the room would have quieted in an instant. Her very presence inspired focus. But Ari's voice wasn't very loud, and they weren't used to hearing her speak as any sort of authority.

"Okay guys, it's time to get ready. Huddle up!" she said with no success. They carried on milling around the locker room, paying her no attention. She stood there for a moment, trying to find the right words, until Coach McLaughlin finally glanced over and shot her a sympathetic look.

"*She said* listen up!" Coach shouted, commanding the room. Everyone stopped talking and looked over, surprised.

"Captain?" said Yasmeen. A few of the other girls laughed. They'd taken to lightheartedly calling her that whenever she stepped into her role and, while she knew they were just playing around, it still freaked her out. Coach McLaughlin looked over at her and put his hand out, not so subtly telling her to take the reins.

"I've heard you talking about today's match, and I know you're worried," she began. "But if there's one thing we can't afford to do today, it is to go in scared. Yes, the Czech team is brilliant. And yes, they defeated us last time . . ."

"Thanks for the vote of confidence, Captain," said Sienna, who'd never scored a goal against the Czech team. Ari knew she was dreading their upcoming match.

"What I meant to say is that our last game against the Czech team is history now. So, when you go out onto the rink, look at it as a fresh start," Ari said, trying to sound confident enough to convince her teammates that she knew what she was doing.

"Defense?" she said, looking over at Yasmeen and her part of the team. "We have a weak spot when it comes to the right side of the rink, so be mindful of that today. Goaltenders?" she said, looking over at Izzy. "Look alive. I've noticed that you don't get alert until a few minutes into the first third, and we can't afford that today. And centers?" she said, looking over at Sienna and the rest of their teammates. "Stop trying to control what's going on behind you. It's not your job to manage the rest of the team. Focus on getting those pucks into the goal."

Becoming captain made her hyperaware of everything that was going on around her. At boot camp, she'd spent more time trying to lead the team than playing her position. But now it was time to focus on what she'd originally been put on the team to do: score goals. Ari nodded and gave one final line of encouragement.

"Okay, let's get ready, skate to the rink, and play the best match of our lives," she said. The cheers from her teammates temporarily settled her nerves. When she reached over to put her phone in her locker, it flashed with a message from a familiar name:

Gracie: Good luck today!!! Cheering you on from my couch!!

The message came with a photo of Gracie sitting in front of her TV in full Team GB regalia. Patriotic to the point where the plaster cast around her broken leg was decorated with Union Jacks. Ari smiled, sent her a team photo from the locker room, and then joined the girls as they got ready.

Izzy, who was in charge of the playlist that day, pressed PLAY as they separated from their groups and put aside their distractions. It was time to get into match mode. Ari watched her teammates pick up their helmets, lace up their skates, and do their final individual prematch rituals. Izzy danced around the room, hyping herself up as she got ready to leave. Yasmeen sprayed her favorite perfume on the sleeves of her jersey, saying it smelled like good luck. And Sienna closed her eyes, trying to center herself amid the chaos. As the players made the final adjustments to their uniforms, Ari sent out a silent prayer to a God she only believed in on the rink, and then she and the other girls did one final team huddle before they made their way out into the hockey stadium.

The match they played felt straight out of a dream.

From the minute the first puck landed in the center of the rink, Ari realized they had the advantage of being underestimated. The Czech team had beaten Team GB last time, so Ari could tell that they'd come into the match certain they would win again. However, that assumption had made them less alert when it came to preventing the British from scoring. Plus, they'd made the mistake of underestimating just how determined Ari and her teammates were. The girls had something to prove. Going home early wasn't an option.

Izzy had never looked more alert in her life. Ari watched in awe as her friend prevented their opponents from scoring goals, as if she already knew where the puck would land. But the puck rarely reached her because Yasmeen and the other girls on defense took Ari's January training session advice and built a rock-solid wall between the center and the goal. Sienna, who had spent all six weeks of boot camp worrying, skated around the ice with laser focus, and Ari smiled beneath her helmet as she watched her shoot goal after goal with an uncharacteristic level of confidence. The combination of it all inspired Ari to play in what felt like the best form of her life. She scored goals and batted pucks away from the opposition with fierce determination. That morning, the girls commanded the ice rink as if it were their own, and, for the first time that year, their team played in complete harmony.

By the time the final buzzer rang, the score was 6–2. Ari couldn't believe it, they'd won their first preliminary match and had gotten further than the pundits and cynics back home had predicted. And despite all Ari's worries, her first match as captain hadn't been a total mess. She was overwhelmed with relief as her teammates skated to their side of the rink, pulled themselves into a group hug, and cheered in delight.

"I know it's the first game, and we shouldn't get ahead of ourselves, but . . ." began Ari, excited to celebrate but afraid of jinxing it.

"We killed it," said Sienna as she squeezed her tight.

It was definitely too early to celebrate; this was just the first of the four group-stage matches they were playing. But Ari couldn't help but feel a small, tentative wave of hope.

She looked out into the crowd, trying to see if any of her

other athlete friends were there to watch the game. She waved when she saw a Polish speed skater and a Chilean skier she knew cheering in the crowd. But her eyes stopped when they reached the middle of the stands. Because there, amid her friends, was one unwelcome guest.

Harrison.

She hadn't invited him, of course, but he'd still shown up. She hadn't messaged him, but he was only ever a matter of minutes away. The men's snowboarding team was staying just one floor below her in GB House, and the Village was too small to avoid him. So she needed to devise a Harrison-proof plan to stop him from trying to claw his way back into her life.

Harrison didn't really do boundaries, but there was one she knew he wouldn't cross. By the time she and the girls skated out of the rink and headed over to the locker room to debrief, she was already hatching a plan. It was a long shot, and there were a hundred ways it could go wrong, but as she started to map it all out in her head, she realized it might be ridiculous enough to work.

She just needed to figure out where the press office was and find out if Drew was willing to play *one more game.*

16

Drew

DAY ONE OF THE 2026 OLYMPICS

MESSAGE FROM: Zeus BTS team

Key people: Lukas Horvath

Key sports: Freestyle skiing and ski jump

Assignment: Photograph the highs and lows of today's competition. Try to capture the behind-the-scenes moments our followers won't see on the screen.

Drew was pretty sure he was going to throw up. He could feel the cereal he'd eaten for breakfast churning in his stomach and the coffee he'd washed it down with threatening to come back up. It was fourteen degrees Fahrenheit outside, but small, stressed-out droplets of sweat were crawling down his face as he stood in the snow. Drew had woken up early that morning to take a shuttle to the top of the mountain and watch people fly over eight hundred feet through the air in the name of sport.

The ski jump was one of the most dangerous winter sports, but it was also one of the most compelling. The jumpers put their lives at risk each time they left the slope. Drew and the other photographers in the press pit couldn't look away. It felt like watching someone else's life flashing before his eyes, but he had an assignment to complete, so he positioned his camera to get the perfect midair shot. That morning's sunshine made the white snow on the mountains look too bright, so he switched to shooting in manual, lowered the ISO, and walked around to find a spot that didn't have him positioned in front of the sun. As he walked back and forth across the snow taking photos of the skiers, he wondered what it would be like to fly without knowing where he'd land.

When the final jump was over, he rushed over to the athletes standing in the press circle. Zeus Athletics had assigned him to take photos of Lukas Horvath, one of the Slovakian ski jumpers they were sponsoring that year. But when Drew reached him, he realized just how deflated the skier looked. The strangest thing about professional sports was how quickly athletes were expected to go from a devastating loss straight into an interview. Lukas had come last in the ski jump due to a mixture of nerves and a sprain he hadn't quite recovered from. It felt weird to be standing there and documenting him at his lowest point, but Drew was on assignment. So, he got his camera out and took a photo of Lukas's downcast expression, his gloved hands carrying his skis, and the team of coaches surrounding him with reassurance.

At first, Drew felt guilty. As if he was imposing on a private moment. But then he remembered how a person's low points often made for the most memorable and meaningful photos. His sister's devastating ice hockey injury had landed just a few days before her eighteenth birthday. But their grandparents insisted on celebrating anyway. Drew could still remember the photo he'd taken of

Thandie holding a slice of birthday cake with a pained expression. Four years later, she'd used it on the invite for the party she'd thrown to celebrate her twenty-first birthday. One that almost perfectly coincided with her getting an invite to join the Olympic team. He hoped that one day Lukas would find the photo he'd taken and reframe it in his mind.

His official assignment at the Games was to get photos of the Zeus-sponsored athletes in action. But he wanted to impress them, so he'd pitched them a photo diary of candid behind-the-scenes moments. Primarily photos of athletes but also ordinary people, too. Spectators, volunteers, family members, and other people experiencing the Games in their unique ways. So, as he headed over to the line for the chairlift, he tried to come up with a list of people he'd met who might be willing to let him take a portrait of them.

When he got to the front of the line and saw the downhill chairlift, he was overcome by a sinking feeling. Drew wasn't scared of heights, but riding a Ferris wheel or sitting on a residential rooftop was a lot different than sitting in an open-air chairlift a few dozen feet above the ground. However, he needed to get to the bottom of the mountain, so he took a seat and winced as the operator locked him in. At the last second, another passenger came running over. They had their hood up and a woolly scarf obscuring most of their face. Drew watched as they took their place on the other side of the chairlift and checked that the safety bar was secure. The lift began moving, and before Drew could truly understand what he was getting himself into, they were on their way.

The chairlift was over a hundred feet above the ground. Drew's feet were dangling over the mountains with only a flimsy-looking metal bar between him and a deadly drop. The sense of vertigo was becoming overwhelming, Drew didn't realize he was whispering *no no no* until the guy on the other end of the chairlift started laughing.

The man pulled down his hood, unwrapped his scarf, and got comfortable. Drew immediately recognized him. It was Hans Leitner. Drew had spotted him and his film crew gathering footage at the top of the mountain and figured they would wait for the shuttle like the rest of the media crews. But he and Hans were casual travel companions on what felt like the least stable mode of transport in the Village.

"First time on a chairlift?" Hans asked good-naturedly.

Drew had one chance to make a good impression, but as he made the mistake of looking down and seeing how high up they were, he realized there was no chance he'd be able to play it cool.

"Does it show?" he said, trying not to sound as rattled as he felt.

"You look like you're about to throw up," Hans chuckled.

He was, but Drew couldn't throw up next to one of the most legendary documentarians in the world. It was the kind of embarrassment he'd be thinking about at two a.m. for the rest of his life. So, he closed his eyes to try to dull the vertigo.

"Talking is a good enough distraction to stop you from thinking about the height," Hans said.

Maybe it was the fact that he was hundreds of feet above the ground and the altitude was messing with his head, but as soon as Hans mentioned talking, Drew came up with an idea. He and Luiz had talked about the danger of meeting your heroes before having something to talk to them about, but what if he could show Hans his work instead? So, before he could come to his senses or convince himself he was about to make a terrible decision, he opened his mouth.

"Can I take a photo of you?"

Drew had been taking photos of strangers for years, and with an assignment from Zeus to get behind-the-scenes photos of interesting people, Hans seemed like the perfect candidate.

"Why?"

Drew explained his assignment as Hans nodded along.

"We've still got five minutes to go," Hans said, looking down at the slope and shrugging. "Go ahead."

After forcing himself to ignore the height they were at and double-checking that his camera strap was tightly secured around his neck, Drew pulled out his phone. It was much easier to capture a person's personality when they were telling a story, and he figured that a few quotes from Hans would make his photo diary feel extra special. So, Drew tapped RECORD on the voice memo app and framed the shot. There was something extremely daunting about holding a camera up to a man with several Oscars under his belt. But it was too late to back down.

One of the things Drew had learned about Hans from watching his documentaries was that he hadn't picked up his first professional camera until his mid-thirties. Hans had begun his life as an alpine skier. He'd competed in the 1972, 1976, and 1980 Winter Olympics and won two gold medals for Team Austria before making his first documentary. So, rather than asking him about his career in film, Drew decided to ask about the life he'd left behind.

"Tell me about your final Olympics. How did you feel on the slopes?"

Hans stopped and thought about it for a moment. He turned his head, looked out at the snowy mountains, and smiled a little. "When I was at my peak, I loved the feeling of the snow beneath my skis. Some of the best moments of my life were on the slopes. But things started to change at the end of the seventies." Drew took photos as Hans spoke, double-checking that his phone was still recording. Hans's face was framed by a brilliant blue sky, glittering snow, and the warm early-afternoon light.

"I was halfway down the mountain, flying through the air knowing that I was on track to win another medal. But then

I realized with complete clarity . . . that I hate the cold," Hans said, laughing. "I told my coach that I was retiring because I'd achieved everything I'd set out to. But the real reason I left the sport was because I couldn't bear the thought of putting on seven layers of thermals again or feeling my toes freeze midair. So, guess what I did as soon as I went home with my gold medal?" Hans paused and smiled at the camera. "Booked a holiday to the Bahamas."

Drew couldn't believe he'd finally gotten an answer to the question people had been asking Hans for years. They were just a few yards away from the bottom of the mountain. But he figured there was enough time to ask one more question.

"So, what brought you back to the mountains today? Besides working on your next film?"

Hans's expression dropped a little as he looked out at the snow. A ray of light hit the side of his cheek, and for a moment, everything felt still. So, Drew took a photo. He didn't need to search through his camera to know that this was the best one he'd taken all day. When Hans answered this time, he kept his gaze on the mountains.

"When I was your age, I thought that all the good in my life would come back around again. That the magical winters and people I'd met in the snow would always be a part of my life. But they're not, and I'm starting to realize that some chapters are closed for good," said Hans, who was still looking out at the sky. Drew immediately started thinking about his grandma and how right he'd been to move back home. But in the same breath, he thought about USC and the life he'd left behind in California. Hans continued speaking.

"I hear the kids say 'what's for you won't miss you,' and I like the sentiment, but it's not always true. Some things only come around once or twice in a lifetime, so I've decided to stop missing chances to go back up into the mountains." Hans turned his head away from the view and looked back at the camera. "Also, I heard rumors about a secret hot chocolate bar in this year's Village, so I had no choice but to book a flight." He chuckled as the chairlift came to the end of its route.

When they arrived at the bottom of the mountain, Drew and Hans parted ways. Hans went to lunch with his film crew and Drew ran to the nearest café. He knew a good story when he saw one and, while this probably wasn't what Zeus meant by behind-the-scenes content, nobody in their right mind would pass up an interview with a legend like Hans Leitner. So, Drew opened his laptop and began to edit. He needed to get it all over to the team at Zeus while the skiing competitions were still in full swing. But his laptop kept getting stuck at 11 percent when he tried to up-load and send the photos.

Drew looked around at the sea of journalists in the café; they were all on their laptops and phones. No wonder the internet was so slow here. So, he packed his bag, left the café, and sprinted to the press office, almost slipping on the ice. His internet connec-tion got stronger as soon as he reached the front door. By the time he'd walked through the reception and showed the security guards his credentials, his upload increased to 29 percent. He walked past a pair of France 24 presenters, and the upload went up to 42 percent. He waved at an NDTV journalist he'd chatted with during the opening ceremony as it rose to 72 percent. And then, just as he was about to turn the corner and head over to Luiz's desk, it got to 100 percent and finally concluded.

"Yes!" he said, pumping his fist into the air. He walked over to Luiz's desk to tell him about it. But when he looked up from his lap-top, he realized that it wasn't Luiz sitting at the desk watching him.

"I knew you'd be happy to see me," Ari said with a smile, "but not *that* happy."

Drew's fist was still frozen midair. He brought it down and tried to shake off his embarrassment as he closed his laptop. His mind wandered back to the kiss they'd shared last night.

"So, what happened to *never again*?" he said, trying his best to play it cool.

"I changed my mind," she said, spinning around in the chair as if to avoid his eyes. She seemed just as nervous as she'd been after their kiss last night. It was cute.

"How did you find me?" he asked, curious.

"I saw your press pass yesterday and figured that somebody in the press office would be able to help me find you. Then, when I got here, I started chatting to a very charming Brazilian man."

"Luiz?"

"Yes! He told me that you'd probably be back at his desk by lunchtime, so I figured I'd wait until you came back," she said with a shrug.

"Why?"

Ari kept spinning around in Luiz's desk chair. Either trying to avoid his gaze or avoid his answer. But after a moment, she stopped and looked up at him. She scanned his face as if searching for something and then planted her feet firmly on the ground.

"I came to ask . . . will you be my boyfriend?"

17

Ari

Ari's best ideas only ever felt like good ideas in her head. On her walk to the press office, she'd been pretty proud of the plan she'd concocted in the hour after her team's first win. It seemed totally logical, the perfect solution to both her and Drew's problems. But now that she was standing face-to-face with Drew, she realized that the combination of postmatch adrenaline and the optimism of a bright blue day had deluded her into thinking a ridiculous plan made sense. But it didn't. If she'd watched this scene play out in a movie, she would have called it unrealistic. If one of her friends had told her they were going to do it, she would have looked them dead in the eye and asked if everything was okay at home. But the more she thought about it, the more she believed it was crazy enough to work.

"Your . . . boyfriend?" he asked in confusion.

"Wait, that didn't come out right," she said. "I'll explain. But first, can we go somewhere quiet? Private." There were hundreds of journalists scattered around the building and, while she was pretty sure they were all too caught up in their work to notice her, she couldn't afford the risk.

Drew glanced around the press office, then nodded, gesturing for her to follow him. They walked past a TV crew carrying cameras through the hallway and navigated their way around a reporter having a heated phone call next to the coffee machine. The whole building was abuzz with activity, but as they got further into the building, things gradually got quieter. She followed Drew through the maze of corridors until he opened a door and switched on the light.

It was a tiny room stacked floor to ceiling with camera equipment. Tripods, lenses, battery packs, and memory cards. Ari didn't know that much about cameras, but she could tell it was a pretty impressive collection. Drew must have noticed her curiosity because he pulled one down to show her.

"This is my favorite, it's a Nikon F3," he said, opening a camera bag to reveal a chunky black camera with a single red line on its side. He handed it over to her like a proud father. Ari held it in her hand for a moment, slowly examining it.

"What do you like about it?"

"I almost never get to use them for work, but I *love* film cameras." She noticed the way his eyes lit up as he spoke. "You just get this instant sense of nostalgia when you look at the photos they take. I'm trying to convince the company I'm with to let me do a photo diary with the F3, but I haven't found the right story for it yet." He put the camera away and looked over at her, leaning back against a shelf. He seemed comfortable in here, as if he'd just welcomed her into his home. "I could show you a few of the others, but I'm guessing you didn't come here for a tour."

He was right. The door was still ajar, so Ari pulled the handle and shut it tight so they could talk freely, away from prying ears. It wasn't until she turned back around to face him that she realized just how small the room was. There couldn't have been more than a yard between them. And with the door closed, it was quiet enough to hear her own heartbeat, notice the way he tapped his foot when he stood still, and smell the subtle scent of whatever cologne he was wearing. While someone like Yasmeen could have given a detailed description of the formula, Ari couldn't even identify the top notes. All she knew was that Drew's cologne reminded her of winter evenings and made her want to lean in.

They stood in silence for a moment, until she finally plucked up the courage to say what she'd come here for. "Are you secretly an athlete?" she asked.

"Unless carrying four cameras up the stairs counts as lifting, no," he said with pride.

"Did you get back together with your ex-girlfriend?" she asked, trying to sound casual despite the fact that standing in a tiny low-lit room with a man she barely knew made her mind wander back to kissing boys at teenage house parties.

"No."

"Are you seeing someone new?"

"Also, no," he said.

"Is there a girl somewhere else in the world who *thinks* you're her boyfriend?" Ari asked. She wanted to cover all bases to be sure.

"No . . . at least, I don't think so," he said, tilting his head. He smiled when he saw the skeptical expression on her face. "I'm kidding. I don't have a girlfriend. I'm not talking to anybody, and there's no one on the roster right now."

She raised an eyebrow. "There was a roster?"

"No. I've been too busy thinking about this girl I met on New Year's to speak to anyone else," he said, looking into her eyes.

"You're so full of shit," she laughed, relaxing a little as she leaned against a shelf and he rested an arm against a different shelf.

"That's true." He nodded. "And so is the fact that I don't have a secret girlfriend hiding elsewhere. Unless you've been pining after me since December?"

"Oh, I get it now," she said, nodding.

"Get what?"

"Why you're single. Fine boy, no game. It's a tragedy."

"I'm holding back," he said, his lips twitching up, as if she'd just pressed a switch.

"Is that so?"

"Trust me, it's for your own good." He leaned a little closer and lowered his voice, the depth of it sending a tingle down her spine. Suddenly, the distance between them felt shorter, the air warmer.

"If I tried to flirt with you, and I mean really tried? You would want to see me again, and we already know that's a *bad* idea," Drew added.

He was right. As they stood face-to-face in the tiny, unseasonably warm storage room, she couldn't help but wonder what would have happened if she'd gone to an after-party with him last night. The thought was so enticing that it made her want to open the door, leave the press office, and get as far away from Drew as she possibly could. She was on a long streak of good decision-making, and he posed a threat to the progress she'd made. But he could also be the perfect solution to a more pressing problem. So, she decided to outline her plan.

"Remember how we told each other all of those secrets on New Year's?"

His expression turned uneasy. "How could I forget?"

"And remember how we concluded that because we're both

messed up in our own specific ways, there's no way the two of us could ever work out?"

"Which is why you ran away."

"I didn't run away. Well, maybe I did run. But that's not the point," she said, slightly embarrassed.

"So, what *is* the point?" Drew asked. His eyes were searching for something. He leaned forward a little, the space between them shrinking. "Or did you just lure me into a closet because you wanted to see me?"

Under any other circumstances, she would have enjoyed this banter. Ari liked flirting. It felt like playing a game. Tossing the conversation back and forth until someone made the perfect move. But she couldn't let herself flirt with Drew, not like this. Because she'd come to the press office with a serious proposal. She was determined to lay it out without letting herself get distracted by the tension between them. So, she took a breath, reminded herself to stay focused, and cut to the chase.

"What I came to ask you is, Drew . . . will you be my *fake* boyfriend?"

She regretted it the moment the words left her mouth.

"Your . . . *fake boyfriend*?" he asked, looking just as confused as he'd been the first time she'd asked.

"You know, *Pretty Woman*, *The Proposal*, *To All the Boys I've Loved Before*."

He nodded, but she could tell he had no idea what she was talking about. "Okay, let me rephrase that. Why do you *need* a fake boyfriend?"

Ari sighed. She wanted to sugarcoat it, but there was no point in pretending.

"It's messed up, but basically . . . my ex-boyfriend is kind of intense, and I know he'll keep finding reasons to 'bump into me' for as long as we're both in the Village. Guys like that only accept that someone is unavailable if they're in a new relationship. So, I figured the best way to keep him out of my hair for the next two weeks would be to have a fake boyfriend."

"That . . . is kind of messed up," Drew said, looking concerned. But Ari didn't need his worry, so she shrugged it off.

"I'm a woman living in a patriarchal society; everything's kind of messed up." She shrugged again and forced a chuckle. "It goes against all of my feminist beliefs, but I spent the whole morning trying to come up with a solution, and this feels like my best bet," she admitted.

"Me?"

"Yes, you."

"Why?"

"Because he doesn't know you and neither do my friends. So, it would be much easier to paint a picture of a secret whirlwind romance with someone who's a complete stranger to them."

"But I thought you said you'd sworn off men?"

"I had—I mean, I have," she said, surprised he'd remembered. "It's just that my time in the Village would be a lot smoother if everyone knew for certain that me and Harrison weren't going to get back together." She knew how ridiculous it sounded when she said it out loud. Ari absentmindedly spun the watch Harrison had bought her around her wrist. A part of her wanted to give it back to him or give it away completely. But it was almost like a reminder. Her way of never allowing herself to forget that, while the best parts of Harrison would always appeal to her, he wasn't the man she wanted him to be below the surface.

"Do you want to get back together with him?" he asked, curious.

"No. Never again," she said quickly. "But I've said *never again* before and then done it, so they don't believe me anymore."

"Why does it matter what they think?"

"It's . . . complicated," Ari said. She had no desire to explain the last two years or their effect on her friendships. So, she began the second part of her pitch to get Drew onboard. "You should know that this would actually be a mutually beneficial proposal."

"Ari, if you want to ask me out, you can just ask me out. I don't need a pitch deck to take you on a date." She could hear the flirtation in his voice but she had to keep things straightforward. So, she stood upright and reminded herself that she'd come here for a reason.

"I'm not asking you out, Drew. This is *purely* business . . . as per the terms of the conclusion we reached on New Year's Eve," she said. He shook his head and smiled at her. It was a dazzling smile, but she needed to stay focused. "You want to impress the people you're working with, right? Get some behind-the-scenes photos none of the other photographers could get?"

"Yeah," he said cautiously.

"Well, I can be your film camera project," she said, gesturing at the camera he'd been holding just moments ago. "I'm on the British women's ice hockey team and this is our first Olympics. We're hardly underdogs in the grand scheme of things, but I could sneak you into places none of the other photographers could get into. We could capture something good enough to build up a case to get Zeus to hire you for another gig."

"You play ice hockey?" he asked, completely missing the point.

"Do I not look like a hockey player?" she asked, defensively. She hoped he wasn't the kind of guy who'd be weird about that.

"No, I just . . ." He shook his head. "Nothing. But is that a fair trade? Pretending to be your boyfriend for a couple of days is pretty easy, but having a photographer follow you around seems like more of an intrusion."

Ari thought about how nice it would be to have a friend outside of her teammates for the next two weeks. "Trust me, you would be doing me a huge favor. A few mini photo shoots in my downtime won't get in the way of training. In fact, it could be a lot of fun."

"But at the end of this, wouldn't I just seem like a guy who pretended to like you to get ahead in his career? Doing that once was a mistake. Twice would feel kind of toxic," he said, suddenly self-conscious. She put her hand on his shoulder to reassure him.

"Drew, I'm the one planning to lie to everyone I know for two weeks. If anyone's toxic here, it's probably me." She shrugged.

"Well, I do need to do something to stand out if I'm going to try and get a job after this," Drew said, mulling it over.

"Two weeks, all access. I could even get my teammates to join in," she said, knowing they would need no convincing. They loved taking photos and speaking to the press. They would do whatever it took to put Team GB ice hockey on the map. But Drew still looked hesitant.

"And you're convinced this would work?" he said, skeptical.

"Yes," she said plainly. "You're working at the Olympics. You're obviously good at what you do, so the photos are going to come out great. And that kiss? We have enough chemistry to convince my friends that we're dating."

"So, we just need to make sure nobody finds out and neither of us catches feelings," he said. She hadn't even factored in the second part, but she quickly convinced herself there was no risk.

"Exactly. Best-case scenario, we both get what we want . . . if that's what you want?"

18

Drew

Drew wasn't sure he knew what he wanted. But he did know that he needed to impress the team at Zeus Athletics. They were happy with the photos he'd taken so far, but none of them had come close to his photos from New Year's Eve. He knew an obvious solution to getting behind-the-scenes photos would be to ask Thandie, but he had no interest in following his sister around for two weeks. So, he spent the rest of the day mulling over Ari's proposal.

He'd done a quick Google search of her and found some interesting results. She wasn't particularly famous; it was her team's first time at the Olympics, after all. But the few articles he did find intrigued him. The stories that so often caught people's attention were those of people who stepped into action in a moment of crisis, like Ari. There had been almost no mention of her in the sports press besides a few lines in articles recounting past tournaments. But being thrust into the position of captain just weeks before the Games felt like it would make for a pretty interesting behind-the-scenes story. They'd swapped numbers in the storage room, so after texting back and forth last last night, they'd agreed agreed to meet up for breakfast.

When he arrived at the canteen, Ari was standing outside in a huge blue puffer coat, wearing headphones and looking out into the distance. A light snowfall was beginning and when a few flakes landed on her gloves, she raised her hand and examined them as if it was her very first time. Her skin glowed in the early-morning light, almost ethereal in the haze of glittering snowflakes falling all around them. He paused midstep. But then she noticed him, took off her headphones, and waved.

"You're early," she said, looking surprised.

"If I'm going to do something, I'm going to commit," he said, taking a closer look at her uniform. Underneath the coat was a fluffy white fleece, waterproof trousers, and chunky black snow boots.

"Are you checking me out, Drew?" she said, raising an eyebrow.

"You're wearing, like, seven layers of clothing."

"That doesn't mean you're not checking me out," she teased. "I don't blame you. I would want to know what's under this fleece and turtleneck, too."

"Nothing gets me going like a thermal base layer," he joked as he reached toward her. She examined his hand in confusion.

"Do you want me to shake it?" she asked, perplexed.

"No, I thought you would hold it," he said.

The look on her face told him that she still didn't get it.

"If I were your boyfriend, we'd probably hold hands, right?" he said. He watched her expression change from confusion to amusement. She reached forward and took his hand.

"So, you'll do it?" she asked, seemingly hopeful.

"We just need to iron out the details," he said as their fingers intertwined. The security at the door stopped them for a moment, but then Ari showed them her credentials and explained that she was with Drew. They scanned his press lanyard and then let them walk into a large building styled to look like a cozy cabin resort. The Olympic Village canteens were known for their legendary selection of food. Drew could smell the aromas of baked goods, savory meats, and fresh fruit wafting around the room. While Ari and the other athletes were on strict diets and preplanned meals, he had no such restrictions. So, when they got to the food station, he loaded up his tray with crispy maple bacon, cinnamon-flavored French toast, creamy vanilla yogurt, a pot of freshly sliced mango, and a piping-hot cup of coffee. Ari glanced over at his plate, looked down at her meal plan, then begrudgingly picked up a strangely colored smoothie, a bowl of high-protein porridge, two boiled eggs, and sliced avocados on seeded whole-grain bread.

"Does this happen a lot?" Drew asked as they walked across the canteen to find a seat. He could spot at least seven people at different tables watching their every move.

"The eagle-eyed athletes looking for gossip? They're always paying attention. It's like being in the school canteen," Ari said. "Everyone knows each other here, so they know that you're not on our team."

She was right. He scanned the room and realized that while the canteen was a mixture of athletes from different countries, most of them were European, with a significant chunk of them wearing the Team GB uniform.

"I'm guessing the American accent doesn't help?"

"It just makes them more curious to figure out who you are. *And* what's going on between us," she said. They put their trays down. "Speaking of, what *is* going on between us?"

"Well, I spent the night thinking."

"About me?" she said, a glint in her eyes.

"About your proposal. It's the first time a girl has ever locked me in a closet and asked me to be her man," he teased.

"Don't let it get to your head. I just need an excuse to avoid Harrison," she said, scrunching her face as she ate a spoonful of porridge.

"That bad?"

"The porridge, or Harrison?"

"Both."

"Equally gross," she said, and smiled. But it didn't reach her eyes.

"In what way?" he asked. She took another spoon of her breakfast, seemingly hesitant to give him an answer. Drew wanted to know why she was so desperate to convince Harrison she was seeing someone new. Especially if he was going to be the one to take on that role. But he didn't want to pry, so he thought back to New Year's Eve.

"Imagine you were never going to see me again. No consequences, no judgment," he said. "What would you tell me then?"

"You know how guys are always doing big romantic gestures in films? Like standing outside someone's house with a boombox or running through the airport to stop a flight?"

"Yeah, I asked my first girlfriend to go to prom with me by singing 'Can't Take My Eyes Off You' because she loved *10 Things I Hate About You*," he admitted.

Ari smiled. "That's actually very cute. I used to love things like that, and then I met Harrison, who did all of those things but then also . . . I don't know, wasn't a good guy. So, we broke up, but now he thinks he can try and still do all of those things to reel me back in."

"Like what?"

"Waiting around after the opening ceremony just to try and see me. Randomly showing up in the audience at one of my games to surprise me. Asking to be allocated one floor below me in GB House. It would be cute and romantic if I wanted us to get back together, but . . ."

"You don't, so it's borderline creepy." He nodded.

"It's past borderline. But because he's been doing it ever since we broke up, everyone around me thinks I like it. Even my best friends, who are supposed to know me really well, think we're going to get back together. Everyone we know thinks that." She stared at the steam above her porridge, her expression downcast.

"And does everyone else know that Harrison's an asshole?" he said, then corrected himself. "Sorry, you dated him. I shouldn't call him that."

"No, he is an asshole, a gold medal–winning asshole," Ari said, looking down at her watch, and readjusting it around her wrist. "But *everyone loves* Harry."

Drew studied her face. Her voice was upbeat, but he could hear an undertone of sadness. He wanted to ask more but could see it was affecting her, so he tried to lighten things up.

"So, how would it work, the fake-dating slash photo diary exchange?" he asked.

"Well, what do you need for your assignment?" she asked, not so subtly glancing down at the bacon on his plate. He smiled and pushed the plate over to her as she cast her porridge aside and took a bite. Drew paused and thought about it for a moment. His original plan had been to capture a wide array of behind-the-scenes photos of all the athletes he came in contact with, but Ari provided an opportunity to focus on one specific story.

"I never get to use my film camera for work. It's too risky to rely on images I can't see until I've processed the film. But the photos I take with it always turn out better," said Drew, putting a plan together in real time. "So, I could document your journey on film. I already have the New Year's photos from the day you found out you were becoming captain. I could make it a whole full-circle thing. From being a relatively low-key player in London, to the underdog captain everyone's rooting for in St. Moritz."

"I don't think everyone's rooting for me," she said, shaking her head.

"But they will, that's the power of a good story. And I know I can tell one through photos. Let me come to training with you, take photos of you out and about in the Village, ask you questions about each step of the journey. I have no idea what I'm going to do when I go home to Wisconsin, but I've always wanted to be a photojournalist. This could either be the final thing I do before I start fresh back home, or it could be the project that impresses Zeus enough to hire me again."

"So, we would both get something out of this arrangement," she said, nodding.

"Exactly. We just need to figure out the terms," he said. He pulled out his phone and typed FAKE-DATING PLAN.

"Are you making notes?" she asked, amused.

"I was a star student before I dropped out. Of course I'm taking notes," he laughed. "We should probably get our story straight. If your friends or teammates ask, how did we meet?"

"That's easy, we met on the roof of Zeus's New Year's Eve party. We spent the night talking, kissed at midnight, exchanged numbers, and the rest is history."

"So, in this version of events, you stayed?" he asked, trying to sound nonchalant. But when he looked up from his phone, she was looking at him. She glanced down at his lips for a second.

"It's what I wanted to do, I just . . . couldn't."

Drew studied her for a moment. Noticed the way she held his

gaze without flinching, even when she couldn't finish putting her explanations into words.

"I understand," he said. They'd both been in a vulnerable place that night. "So, if your friends or teammates ask, is this a casual situationship, the start of a long-distance relationship, or are we in love?"

"*In love?* That feels like a bit of a stretch," she said, teasing him. "Didn't you lie about being in love with your ex? I'm not sure you'd fall for me that fast."

Drew cringed, remembering just how much he'd divulged that night.

"Can we impose a no-bringing-up-rooftop-confessions rule?" he asked, uneasy.

"No takebacks." She smiled.

"Damn," he said in mock defeat. "So, what you're saying is that given my track record, I couldn't possibly fall in love with you?"

"Given *my* track record, you definitely could."

"So, to make it believable, in *our story*, I have to be the one who says 'I love you' first."

"Why?"

"Because if I told *you* I love you first, I would mean it," he said plainly. She rolled her eyes, seeing right through him.

"I bet you tell all your fake girlfriends that."

"Just my favorites."

"Right, we need some ground rules," she said, trying to put an end to the flirtation. "Rule number one. We're both busy, so we only have to commit to three fake dates on my end and three photo ops on yours." Drew nodded. They felt like reasonable terms.

"Rule number two. We need an expiration date," he said. "At

the end of the Olympics, I'm flying back to Wisconsin, and you're flying back to London. But we should decide on a clear end point to stop things from getting complicated."

"How about we start tomorrow and end things on the day of my final match?" she suggested.

"And when's that?"

"It could be a preliminary game in a couple of days, or the finals. Either way, less than two weeks."

He nodded. That was long enough for him to get all the photos he needed, but not long enough for them to get too attached.

"And rule number three," she said, serious for a moment. "We've got to be honest with each other. You don't have to tell me anything else about your life. In fact, we shared enough on the roof. But whatever happens next, all honesty, no judgment."

"I can't help but be honest around you," he admitted.

But before things could get too earnest, Ari spotted something out of the corner of her eye that made her smile drop. Drew turned his head around to see what she was looking at. A crowd of people in Team GB uniforms had just walked in. It was a mixture of men and women with the easy rapport of people who'd known each other for years. But at the center of them was Harrison, Ari's ex-boyfriend. When Drew turned back to face Ari, she looked exhausted, so he instinctively reached his hand across the table. She took it and their fingers intertwined. It felt strange but familiar.

He watched as Ari tracked Harrison from the front door and through the canteen. Harrison was making his way to their table. As he approached, he flashed Ari a smile and raised an eyebrow at Drew. He opened his mouth as if to say something but then shut it as he noticed their hands on the table. His easygoing demeanor disappeared for a second. But he picked it up as fast as he'd put it down, then carried on walking. Ari relaxed once he was out of sight, but she didn't let go of Drew's hand. They lingered in silence for a moment.

"That's another thing," she said. "Rule number four. PDA."

He nodded. They were practically strangers, after all.

"Is this okay?" he asked, looking down at their hands.

"It's perfect. . . . I mean, it's fine. It works," she said, tripping over her words before letting go. She took a long sip of her smoothie, sat up in her chair, and spoke with an air of formality.

"Holding hands, kissing on the cheek, that's all fair game," she said. He nodded and typed that into his phone. "But kissing on the lips?" she pondered.

"We probably shouldn't—"

"Only in emergencies," she said.

There was a moment of silence as they compared their responses. Then Drew spoke up.

"So, by emergencies, you mean life-or-death situations, right? Like resuscitation?"

"Life-and-death situations, but also . . . fake boyfriend girlfriend emergencies."

"And what is a *fake boyfriend girlfriend* emergency?" he teased, watching her face scrunch up in concentration.

"I'm not sure," she said as she glanced down at his notes. "We'll . . . cross that bridge when we get there."

"Right, I'll be on standby," he said, adding a final bullet point to his list. When he put his phone down, she was looking over at him. "Anything else?" he asked, noting the slight concern in her expression. She paused for a moment and then shrugged.

"We've just got to do everything we can to make sure nobody gets hurt and this doesn't become a complicated mess."

"Noted."

"So, we're on the same page?" she asked. "Two weeks of fake dates in exchange for a two-week, exclusive photo diary."

"Deal," he said with a nod. "But aren't you forgetting the most important rule?" he asked, his lips curving up.

"What?" she asked, as if she had no idea what he was alluding to. So, he leaned forward and lowered his voice.

"Rule number five. Don't fall in love with me," he whispered.

She smiled and shook her head.

"I think you're the one in danger."

19

Ari

Ari was doing a pretty bad job of convincing herself everything was going to be fine. It was eleven a.m., three hours before the Great Britain vs. Japan ice hockey match, the second of four games that would decide whether or not Ari's team would make it to the quarterfinals. If she'd paid any attention to the way the sports journalists back home were reporting on it, Ari would have agreed that the goal of making it this far without Gracie was a pipe dream. Nobody expected anything of them. But Ari had spent her whole life learning to bet on herself. So, when she got to the locker room, she sat on the floor, unpacked her bag, and laid out her toolkit of sticky notes, open-capped highlighters, and scribbled paper.

Ever since becoming captain, Ari had made a point of being the first person in the locker room every morning. Arriving early gave her the chance to get ready, scope out the rink, and spend time alone strategizing before her teammates arrived. She'd been writing detailed recaps of each game since boot camp and using them to make a list of each of her twenty-two teammates' most significant strengths and weaknesses. She'd made it her personal responsibility to spot their blind spots, notice what threw them off, and figure out the hidden skills they could use to their advantage. She was in the middle of making notes about how Sienna and the other girls in defense could tighten their formation when her phone buzzed with a text message. It was Drew. He'd texted to arrange a good time and location for them to take their first batch of photos. But what had started as a back-and-forth about logistics quickly devolved into Drew sending her live updates about each development in his quest to befriend the other journalists in the press office.

Drew: Hans Leitner nodded at me. I think that means we're friends now.

Ari laughed. Drew had spent the rest of breakfast telling her about the retired athlete turned filmmaker.

Drew: False alarm, he was nodding at the photographer behind me.
Drew: But I smiled and waved, so now he's looking at me like I'm crazy.
Ari: Maybe because you're fangirling over a 72-year-old man?
Drew: All my favorite people are over the age of 65.

Ari read his message and shook her head. He was corny as hell, but there she was, smiling on the locker room floor. At breakfast, she'd come to the comforting realization that Drew was still the same person she'd remembered him being on New Year's Eve, which was a relief because she'd spent more than her fair share of time thinking about that night. Usually, it just came back to her in short flashes when she saw or heard something that reminded her of him. She'd listen to a song and try to imagine how he'd spent the first hours of the new year. Scroll through her phone and wonder if she'd ever get to see the photos he'd taken of her. But that had been during boot camp, when she'd thought she was never going to see him again. Back when there was no harm in daydreaming. But things were different now, and she couldn't risk thinking about her fake boyfriend in any way other than as a *fake boyfriend,* especially when she was supposed to be focused on the next game in the preliminary round of the most important tournament of her life.

"Who's got you smiling like that?" asked Izzy with a knowing glance as she walked into the locker room. Her deep red hair was in an ornate fishtail braid—Izzy always put in extra effort.

"And is it the guy you skipped out on team breakfast to take pictures with?" Yasmeen asked, raising her eyebrow as she walked into the locker room carrying her hockey stick and kit bag.

Ari was about to tell them about Drew, but then the entire team walked in together, a few of them carrying matching cups of coffee.

"I didn't know everyone was going to breakfast together," Ari said. A few of them were already deep in conversation, talking about a famous ice skater they'd seen in the line to get smoothies.

"We sent a message in the group ch—" said Hannah, who played on defense. She stopped speaking as soon as she noticed the others glancing over at her. *The group chat?* Ari hadn't seen anything beyond schedule reminders in the group chat for weeks. But as she saw the flash of guilt in Izzy's eyes and noticed how they were all suddenly very preoccupied with unpacking their kit bags, she put the pieces together. Her teammates had made another group chat, without her.

"It's not a big deal," Izzy said in a rush. "We knew you were busy and didn't want to give you another thing to have to deal with," she continued, trying so hard to reassure her that it had the opposite effect.

Ari opened her mouth, then shut it. She'd been in a separate, unofficial group chat with the rest of the team last year. They loved Gracie, but sometimes it was easier to have conversations without their captain in the room. Ari would have never suspected that she'd become the one her friends and teammates wanted to keep their distance from. But then she began to remember the small moments that had gone over her head. The early-January night she'd walked past Yasmeen's room in boot camp to see almost all of them congregated without her. All the conversations that not so subtly came to an end when she walked by. They were her friends, she told herself, her new role wouldn't change that. But as they shuffled around the locker room, she couldn't help but wonder if this was how Gracie had felt.

"But the boy with a camera, who is he?" Izzy asked, changing the conversation as she took out her shin pads and began to put on her protective layers.

Ari paused for a moment. She wanted her friends to believe she was seeing someone new, but she didn't want them to think she liked him enough to distract her from what she'd come to Switzerland to do.

"The guy I met on New Year's," she said to a sea of surprised expressions.

"No way," Yasmeen said, wide eyed.

"Nothing's happening," Ari said with a shrug, knowing that being coy about it would only make the whole thing more believable. "He works for Zeus, so he's taking photos of me that might end up in a campaign they're doing."

"Wait, does that mean you're finally going to agree to do some PR?" Yasmeen said with a grin. She'd been trying to get Ari and the rest of the team to get more active on social media for years. The most important part of being a professional athlete was being excellent at your sport. But an online presence was the key to getting the kind of sponsorships, brand deals, and online fandom you needed to fund and sustain a career.

"A cute guy following you around, that isn't Harrison. *And* some Zeus promo?" Yasmeen said, sounding impressed. "I was not familiar with your game, Ari."

"But let's focus on the actual game we came to play," said Sienna, as she put her hair in a ponytail and fitted her shoulder pads. The rest of the room followed along as they changed into their hockey kits and got ready.

Fortunately, their surprise win against the Czech Republic yesterday had given the girls the confidence boost they'd needed to start the day of their second match on a high. The atmosphere in the locker room that morning was one of excitement, not fear. Sienna, who'd treated the last month like an anxiety dream, was joking around with the goaltenders. Yasmeen, who channeled her worry into plotting out alternate careers, was comparing notes with the other girls on defense. And instead of exchanging Village gossip, Izzy was rewatching their last game and making notes about what she needed to do to get ahead. Once Coach Mc-Laughlin gave them a pep talk, the girls skated onto the ice like people who deserved to be there.

But as soon as the starting horn blew and the puck dropped, Ari realized that this was going to be nothing like their win against the Czech Republic. Because this year, the Japanese team was on top of their game. Their opponents immediately seized the puck and took control of the match. Before Ari and her teammates could even make sense of what was going on, the Japanese team zigzagged across the rink and scored their first goal. They weren't even a minute into the game.

Sienna shot Ari a worried look; they were both startled by how quickly the game was moving. But Ari was the captain now; she wasn't allowed to look worried. So, she gave Sienna a thumbs-up to reassure her and then glided across the ice with fake confidence to show the rest of the team that if she wasn't worried, they shouldn't be, either. It was way too early to panic. But Ari had spent hours rewatching Team GB games and noticed a pattern. As soon as the girls started to worry that the other team was better than them, they stopped playing to win and redirected all their energy into softening the blow of a loss.

Ari could sense it in the cautious way they skated across the rink, how their eyes darted from side to side. The girls weren't focused on scoring goals anymore, they were focused on blocking them. However, defensive play wasn't a strong enough strategy to win. The Japanese team didn't score another goal, but the British team didn't even get close enough to the goal to try. When the first break horn blared and the girls skated back to their side of the rink, Coach McLaughlin gave them practical tips. Told them about weaknesses he'd spotted in the other team and talked about how they could use them to their advantage. When it was Ari's turn to speak, she tried to summon the most pumped-up Gracie-like pep talk she possibly could. But it didn't come out the way she'd wanted it to.

"If we play like we've already lost, we're going to lose!" she said, immediately regretting it. The phrase sounded a lot more inspiring in her head. She tried to backtrack, but panic was infectious.

"Don't say *we're going to lose*! It's not going to happen!" said Yasmeen in horror.

"Why are you talking about losing?" exclaimed Sienna. "You're going to jinx it!"

"What are we supposed to do?" asked Izzy. The team shifted

their attention back to Ari. They were looking to her for reassurance, like they used to look to Gracie. But she knew they could see the fear in her eyes. She tried to remember one of the motivational quotes she'd heard in her audiobooks, but her mind went blank. After a few seconds of silence, the horn blared, and their break ended. When her teammates skated back into their positions, they looked even more nervous than they had a few minutes ago. Ari's misspoken pep talk had thrown them further off-balance. Things only got shakier as the game carried on.

Half of the team played like they had something to lose, and the other half played like they were *going to* lose. They were completely out of sync, and the Japanese players could sense it. Within moments, their opponents navigated their way around the disjointed nature of the British team and scored a goal. They spotted the panic, the lack of harmony, and used it to their advantage to score another goal. And then another. Gracie would have been able to fix this. She would have brought them into a huddle and calmed it down. But when Ari tried to fix things in the second break, she only made it worse.

"It's not too late to turn things around! Remember, we didn't come this far just to come this far," she said, repeating a quote she'd heard in an audiobook.

Her second attempt at a pep talk was met with an audible series of groans.

"Why would you say that?" said Yasmeen, shaking her head.

"Please, don't ever try to give a pep talk again," said Izzy.

"You're not great at this, are you?" said Sienna without thinking.

No. No, I'm not.

20

Drew

DAY THREE OF THE 2026 OLYMPICS

Drew didn't have imposter syndrome. The trepidation he felt when he walked into the press office wasn't a belief rooted in self-doubt, nor was it the nagging feeling that he didn't fit into his surroundings. Drew *was* an imposter in the Village.

He was surrounded by photographers who'd spent decades building up their careers and young hotshots whose careers had ascended at record speed. And while he knew that Zeus wouldn't have hired him if he was completely talentless, he couldn't shake the feeling that he needed to do something spectacular to prove himself every day. Which was why he'd walked into the Village that morning in such a good mood. The content team at Zeus had sent a message saying they loved the photos he'd taken so far. Especially the photos of Lukas, the ski jumper who'd unexpectedly finished in last place. The photos Drew had taken of him after his race had a devastating but alluring quality to them. So, the social media managers at Zeus took his photo and posted it alongside a quote from Drew's conversation with Lukas. One about how, despite his disappointment, he was never more motivated than he was when a competition brought him to his lowest. A bunch of other high-profile athletes reshared his post and the photo made its way into a bunch of news articles reporting on the first day of the Olympics. But he still had a long way to go.

"Are you sure this is safe?" Ari asked as she placed a tentative skate on the ice.

"Trust me," said Drew as he took his camera out of its case and looped the strap around his neck.

"Trust you, based on what? The three days and twentyish minutes we've known each other? For some reason, I trust you with my secrets. But that doesn't mean I'm going to trust you with my life," Ari said uneasily.

She reached down to tap the ice below her with her thick hockey gloves. When the sound made it clear that it was rock solid, she finally relented and placed both of her feet on the ice. After a moment she pushed forward and began to skate, gliding across the ice in the low early-morning light.

Drew had spent the day before scoping out potential photo shoot locations for his and Ari's photo diary. He knew the obvious spots with the backgrounds that would make for the biggest impact. The main stadium, the competition venues, and the various Olympic rings dotted across the Village. But he wanted to find a quieter location, somewhere away from the crowds and TV cameras. He'd spent hours walking through the cold until he'd stumbled across an unexpected spot. At first, he'd thought it was just a frozen lake. It was on the outskirts of the Village, in the quieter section that housed the athletes' accommodation blocks. And it was surrounded by enough trees to obscure it from people walking by. But it wasn't a lake. Luiz told him that it was an outdoor practice rink in the shape of a lake specifically built for athletes who wanted to blow off steam on a rink that didn't resemble their training grounds. So, he'd suggested it to Ari as the location for their first shoot. She had a packed schedule, so they'd agreed to meet up at 6:30 a.m., just in time to see the dawn turn to sunrise. It proved to be the perfect location. The lake rink was lit up by warm bulb-shaped fairy lights that brought a gentle glow to the perimeter, an ethereal contrast to the deep blue early-dawn sky.

As Ari glided across the ice, Drew played around with the settings on his equipment, adjusting the shutter so he could capture sharp stills on his digital camera and dreamlike blurs on his film camera.

"Is this the kind of movement you want?" Ari asked as she zigzagged in precise, straight lines. "Or do you want something more dramatic?" she said, speeding across the ice, leaping up into the sky and landing into a twirl as Drew raced to capture it all. He hit RECORD on his voice memos app to make sure he captured their conversation, too.

"Where did you learn to do that?" he asked, carefully walking across the ice to capture her hockey-uniformed pirouette.

"My mom wanted me to be a figure skater. She said, and I quote, 'You'll scare boys off if you're always walking around with a hockey stick.'" Ari grinned.

"Did her warning work?"

"No, it had the opposite effect. I started going to hockey practice every day, instead of just twice a week. But I *did* convince an older girl who practiced at my local rink to teach me how to twirl. It's fun. You should have a go."

"I can't skate," Drew admitted.

"You've never tried?" she asked, eagerly gliding back toward him. "I could teach you."

"Oh, I tried. But I think I did six months' worth of lessons before my grandparents agreed the injuries weren't worth it." He smiled as he recalled the memory.

Thandie was graceful like their grandmother, so she had taken to it like a duck to water. But Drew was kind of clumsy like his grandfather and never quite found his feet. He was at his best in stillness, he preferred to *capture* the moment than to be in it. The mention of his childhood made him wonder whether he should bring up the topic of his sister to Ari. While they played the same sport, he actually wasn't sure if they knew each other. There were hundreds of national and professional teams and, by virtue of living on other sides of the world, he knew that Thandie and Ari spent most of the year competing in completely different tournaments. He considered mentioning it but ultimately decided against it. His sister's team was the current reigning champions, and he didn't want to throw Ari off by mentioning the competition. So instead, he asked about her.

"I think I have enough skating shots, but we need some candids," he said as she skated off the rink.

"I could pretend to tie up my laces? Act the way I would if I was getting ready for a match?" She walked over to a bench covered in snow, and Drew took a photo of the way her bright blue hockey uniform stood out against the brilliant white snow. The sun was slowly coming up now, a warm light rising from the horizon.

"Quickfire questions?" he said as he replaced the battery in his camera and tried to find the right angle to capture her from.

"Shoot."

"When do you usually wake up on a competition day?"

"Six a.m."

"What song do you listen to when you're heading to training?" he asked, taking a photo of her gloved hands intertwined with the laces of her hockey skates.

"Something like 'Airplane' by Cleo Sol if I need to calm down, or an upbeat Tyla song like 'SHAKE AH' if I want to get myself hyped up."

"And what stresses you out on game days?"

"The answer I would give to a journalist, or the answer I would give to a friend?" she asked, looking over at him as she tied her knot. Drew didn't quite know where he stood on that spectrum.

"The answer you would give to your fake boyfriend."

She smiled at that.

"My teammates. I love them, they're like my sisters. But they stress me out just as much as my family does." She looked out into the distance for a moment, noticing the way the early-morning sun gently shaded the sky with a lilac haze. The color dusted the snow-coated mountains. Drew swapped out his digital camera for his film, silently framed Ari on the left side of his viewfinder, then pressed the shutter. More focused on her than the photo he was trying to take.

"Do you ever get the feeling that you're not cut out for the thing you always wanted?" Ari asked. "As if it's all been placed at your feet but you have no idea what to do with it?"

"Is that how you feel about becoming captain?"

"Oh, I'm asking you. You've been tossing questions over all morning, so it's my turn," she said, relaxing against the bench. Drew had been crouched down on the ice to get a good photo, but his knees were getting tired, so he walked over, brushed some snow off the bench, and sat beside her.

"I felt that way all through college," he admitted, thinking back to California. All the best photojournalists knew that one of the easiest ways to get someone to open up was to do the same, so he told her the truth. "Classic case of big fish small pond as a teenager in Wisconsin, you know? I got it into my head that I could go all the way and take photos like the greats. So, I applied to USC. And at first, I loved it."

"But . . ." she nudged.

"I went to college in Los Angeles, where pretty much everyone is on their way to becoming somebody. My second-year roommate did an internship at CNN, a girl I met on the first day of my freshman year got a book deal at nineteen. Everyone I met at USC was extraordinary in some way and I was just . . . Drew." He shrugged.

"But you still got in," she reasoned.

"I did, but it felt like a fluke. And while I would ace an assignment every once in a while, or land a really good freelance gig from speaking to interesting people at parties, as time went on, I began to realize that I was average at best. So, it didn't make sense to stick it out on the other side of the country if all I was ever going to be was just okay." He shrugged.

"Drew, you're working at the Olympics. You have to be more than just okay," she said. Drew appreciated the compliment, but he knew it wasn't true. It was just a case of being in the right place at the right time. Pure luck. But if he could get this photo diary right, he might be able to ride the wave a little longer.

As they sat there, he noticed the sky getting lighter, the purplish haze becoming a light blue streaked with wisps of rose and lavender. The bulb lights were still on, rivaling the sun with their brightness in a way that he knew would make for the perfect backdrop. So, he got up from the bench, walked into a thicket of snow, and took a photo of Ari looking out at the sky, the GB on the back of her jersey glowing as the sunlight touched the shimmery white fabric.

"Your last name, Shumba, what does that mean?" he asked as she stood up to let him get photos of her uniform against the snow. He made sure to capture the embroidery of the badges and the delicate silver-threaded outlines.

"The best translation is 'lion.' The women's football team back home are called The Lionesses, and I loved watching them when I was younger. It's the main reason I decided to keep his name instead of taking my mother's," she said. Drew opened his mouth to voice a question, then decided against it. But Ari must have sensed his curiosity.

"My dad's not a bad guy, he's just disappointing in the usual ways. Unfaithful husband, mostly absent father." She shrugged like it was nothing, but for the first time since he'd spoken to her, she sounded detached. "It could have been worse."

Drew knew a smarter journalist would have pushed. The unwritten rule was to press until you either got to the root of the story or your interviewee shut it down. But he wasn't sure where he stood on the spectrum of photojournalist or friend. So, he tried to stay on the topic without digging too hard.

"So, is the rest of your family coming to St. Moritz for the Games?" he asked, thinking about how his grandparents had flown in for the occasion.

"They wish." Ari smiled. "They wanted to, but I don't let them come to games. I get distracted looking for them in the crowd, so the deal is they can only come if I make it to the quarters."

"Well, I can be your cheerleader until then."

"Only if you get a T-shirt with my face on it. A Team GB cap and jacket while you're at it, too."

"If I were your real boyfriend, I'd paint your initials on my face, dye my hair red, and learn the British national anthem," he joked.

"But would you learn how to skate? I can't imagine myself with a guy who slips on the ice," she teased.

"I'd take lessons. You like grand gestures, right?"

"Only if I actually like the guy."

"Then I would learn how to skate and glide onto the ice after a big game, holding a bouquet of flowers."

Ari laughed. "Not roses, though."

"Oh, never that, I'm not basic. I'm a real lover. I already know you favorite flowers are . . . dee . . . taa . . ."

"Raa . . . nun . . ." she laughed.

"Ranunthur . . . eo . . . sie . . . remind me again?" he joked.

"Ranunculus."

"That sounds fake, but for you, I'll make them real."

"Good, because I'm definitely getting to the quarterfinals," she said, sounding self-assured. But then her face scrunched up. "Did that sound believable?"

"I hear that if you keep telling yourself something, you can trick your mind into believing it."

"Well, in that case, I'm definitely going to make it to the quarterfinals. And you're going to realize you're cut out for this," she said. This time she sounded certain. Drew tried to let her belief rub off on him.

She picked up her hockey stick and flashed him a smile the second he went to press the shutter on his film camera. They locked eyes the moment he put it down. By that point, dawn had broken to reveal a bright blue sky, golden rays of light touching every surface, including the dark brown curves of her cheek. He'd taken the photo, but she was still smiling.

"Your mom was wrong," he said after a moment. She tilted her head to the side.

"About what?'

"The stick. Nothing about you would scare me away."

21

Ari

LATER THAT MORNING, DAY THREE OF THE 2026 OLYMPICS

Ari and her teammates knew they were doomed the second the Swedish team glided onto the ice rink. They were a pack of tall, athletic players with perfectly shiny ponytails and impeccably strategic game. They blocked every goal Ari's team tried to score and knocked down every defense they'd so diligently tried to build. They needed to rank within the top four teams to advance to the quarterfinals, but after losing to Team Sweden, they'd already lost two of the three games they'd played so far. There was still some hope, but things seemed pretty bleak. By the end of the game, Team GB was five goals down, and, after their loss to Japan, it felt as if their Olympic dream was about to ride out into the sunset without them.

When Ari walked into the locker room after their game, all the girls were muted. Some were wearing headphones and listening to music to try to shake off the disappointment, and others were staring blankly into the distance, having made no attempts yet to change out of their uniforms. All wore dejected expressions. So, Ari sat on a bench and played the game back in her mind to figure out what they could have done differently.

"We actually have to win next time; there is no other option," said Sienna, tugging her headphones off and looking at the other girls.

Ari just nodded. The last time she'd tried to give a pep talk, she'd failed so miserably that she'd destroyed the team's morale. So, attempting one now, when everyone was already feeling so low, would probably make things even worse.

"I knew I should have gotten a better backup degree. I had the grades to become an engineer," said Izzy, staring out into the distance.

"We haven't even filmed enough content to pivot to sports influencers," sighed Yasmeen.

"And it's so unfair because the Swedish team got more rink time than us," said Sienna.

"So did the Japanese team," said Izzy.

Ari's ears pricked up; this was news to her.

"Yeah, I guess they just have a better rink schedule," said Yasmeen as the rest of the girls nodded solemnly.

"What do you mean, a better rink schedule?" Ari asked, walking over to her teammates' circle of dread. She, Coach, and Gracie had gone to a post-qualification meeting with Team GB and listened to the Olympic officials pledge to direct more money into the women's team and ensure there was equality around their coaching and equipment. So, this didn't make any sense.

"You know how all the national teams get the same amount of practice time on the ice rinks?" asked Sienna. Ari nodded. Each country was allocated slots and got to decide how they scheduled out their training day. Ari and Coach had sat together in early

January and plotted out how best to use the two hours a day they'd been allocated and avoid wasting even a second of time.

"Well, I was chatting to one of the British hockey guys at a dinner last night and he let slip that they get three hours a day."

"Three?" Ari said, in shock.

"I don't think he was supposed to tell me. He seemed a little panicked after," Izzy added as if trying to get him out of trouble. But Ari was already lacing her trainers and getting fired up.

Ari had always known there was a disparity between how the men's and women's teams were treated. She'd once spent three hours at a party talking to a woman on Team England's football team about all the part-time jobs and side hustles she worked to compete for the national team. Meanwhile, her male counterparts earned enough in a month to fund a small country. But she and Gracie had fought to make sure the Olympics were different. They'd been promised things would be different.

"We get less funding, lower-quality uniforms, and less investment all year long. This is not okay."

"I don't think it's personal. I guess the coaches just think that the guys have a better chance of—" began Yasmeen.

"Bullshit," Ari said, shaking her head as she tossed her jersey into her kit bag and collected her stuff. "Coach is supposed to advocate for us, and management is supposed to set us up for success. We're not going to keep settling for scraps and thanking them for the bare minimum."

Had something like this happened six months ago, she would have let it go. She'd spent so many years hearing how lucky she was to be playing for the team that she'd bit her tongue in gratitude instead of calling things out. But this tournament was different. She was the captain, and she would do everything she could to fight for her team.

"Right, everyone head to lunch. We have physio in the afternoon and then we need to break down our last match to figure out how to get ready for the next," she said, slinging her bag over her shoulder.

"Aren't you coming with us?" Izzy asked, a flicker of disappointment turning her lips down. Ari wanted to eat lunch with her teammates, but her duties as their captain came first.

"No, I'm going to find out who screwed us over," she said, heading toward the door.

"Shouldn't you just tell Coach?" Sienna asked.

"There's no way he didn't know," she said, disappointed. Ari had spent enough time studying the inner workings of the management team to know what was up. "He either accepted it because even he thinks the men's team deserves more time, or tried to fight for us and lost. Either way, we have less time than we need. So, *I'm* going to fix this." She stalked down the corridor, out of the hockey building, and straight into the snow.

Izzy and the others stayed in the social world of winter sports all throughout the year. It helped them get intel on the politics of each team, predict which athletes were about to take a break, and gather information they could use to their advantage when it came to getting ahead on the rink. Their friendships with the guys on the men's ice hockey team meant that they could quickly spot inequalities and use what they knew to advocate for themselves in the offices of the big Team GB officials. So, that's what they'd spent the last year doing. Izzy fought for higher-quality uniforms, Sienna lobbied for better gym facilities, and Yasmeen networked her way into having them at the forefront of Team GB's winter marketing campaign. But Ari's strength was diplomacy. She was a people pleaser by nature, and all the years of managing complicated family and teammate dynamics had taught her the delicate art of getting what she wanted without damaging a relationship.

Because as avoidant as she could be in her personal life, she didn't believe in excuses when it came to hockey. She could lose a game or miss a goal, but she refused to let the status quo get in the way of her dreams. So, she scanned each door until she found the one with the nameplate COACH CLEMENT CLARKE— HEAD OF GB ATHLETICS.

She knocked and walked straight in as soon as she heard him say, "Come in."

Coach Clarke was a polished man in his late fifties who'd begun his life as a professional athlete before making a career of managing sports teams, athletics organizations, and now Team GB. But he was the kind of guy who spoke with one eye on the person in front of him while the other scanned the room for the next big thing.

"Arikoishe," he said, glancing up from his laptop, "it's nice to see you. How can I help?" His tone made it clear that he wanted to wrap their conversation up as soon as possible. So, she cut straight to the chase.

"Coach, I know that we're new to this and haven't gotten you all the medals that the men's hockey team has. They're your priority, and I get that," Ari said, predicting his reasons before he could say them out loud. "But giving us less rink time than the men's team is *so* unfair. That's setting us up for failure."

It wasn't the first time they'd had a conversation like this. Ari and Gracie had been the ones to ambush him into allocating more funding to their travel budget after finding out that one of their teammates couldn't afford the train journey it would take to get to an important exhibition game. But it was the same spiel each time they approached him with something new.

"Ari, I get it, but your teammates are the *underdogs* this year," he said, which was a more polite way of saying that nobody believed they were going to make it. "The whole country is behind you. That should be enough to spur you on." He shrugged, glancing down at his laptop.

"We don't need the whole country rooting for us, we just need more rink time," Ari sighed. While she appreciated cute drawings from little kids, encouragement from the fans at home didn't compare to having an extra hour to train. Video messages from opportunistic politicians put them into the spotlight, but they didn't increase her team's chances of success. They needed concrete support in the form of resources, but Coach Clarke didn't seem to care.

"I know it's been a tricky couple of days, but we're all really proud of you girls for getting this far—"

"We're not girls," she snapped. "We're women. Competitive athletes. Not just *girls* giving it a go."

Coach Clarke raised an eyebrow, then sat back in his seat.

When women called one another *girls*, it was loving and sisterly. But powerful men like him calling them *girls* while trying to explain why she should be okay with settling for less was infuriating. Ari had spent the better part of her hockey career listening to men like him talk down to her. Coaches who'd acted like they were doing some grand act of service by coaching a women's team, and guys she'd dated whose actions always made it clear they thought she was just "good for a girl." She knew dozens of men like Coach Clarke, and for years she'd just sat back and gritted her teeth through their empty platitudes. But not now, the stakes were too high.

"Qualifying for the Olympics is a real achievement," he said in the tone of voice reserved for speaking to children. "And I truly congratulate you for getting this far. I know it hasn't been easy. But you've got to be realistic, sweetheart. It doesn't make sense to penalize the men's team when we all know that your team doesn't have the best, shall we say, track record."

Ari was so shocked that it took her a second to register what he'd just said. *Penalize the men? Your team doesn't have the best track record? Be realistic, sweetheart?* Be. Realistic. *Sweetheart.* Just as Ari was trying to devise the most elegant, scathing response she could muster without ending her career, a knock rapped on the door.

Coach Clarke told them to come in, drawing his attention to the door as if he and Ari weren't midconversation. In came Harrison. Ari's stomach sank. Things were going from bad to worse. Harrison was Team GB's golden boy; of course he was popping in to have a chat with his buddy Coach Clarke.

"Oh, sorry, Coach, I didn't realize you were in the middle of something," Harrison said, shooting Ari a smile that made her feel nauseous.

"It's alright. We're just finishing up, aren't we?" Coach said with an air of finality.

Ari knew that the smart thing would be to leave. Coach Clarke was infamously dismissive, and if there was one person she couldn't afford to have rooting against her, it was the team's head coach. But then she thought back to the locker room and the dejected looks on her teammates' faces. They'd worked so hard to get here, pinned all their dreams on the Olympics, and for better or for worse, they'd accepted Ari as their captain. She *had* to fight for them.

"No. We're not done." Her voice was firm.

"Are you alright, Ari?" Harrison was using the warm, personable voice he used to get whatever he wanted. It was one of the things that had initially drawn her in. The whole knight in shining armor shtick. It had been charming, at first; there was something nice about a man who took initiative and wanted to protect her. It wasn't a feeling she was used to, it made her feel special. But Harrison used those moments to guilt-trip her into forgiving his wrongdoings. Constantly reminding her of all the things he'd done for her. Controlling her life and making her think the suffocating sensation she felt whenever she was around him was just the price she paid to show her gratitude. But as much as her body tried to forget, her brain could still remember how awful he'd made her feel. Harrison was a good-looking guy who was going to age into an ugly man. His hair would fall out, his eyes would droop, and once he couldn't win medals anymore, his athletic body would sag and wither. The more a person knew him, the faster his charm faded. Without his appearances, he would have nothing left. So, she reinstated her boundary.

"I've got this, Harrison. You can leave," she said bluntly. He put his arms up in defense and backed out of the room, raising his eyebrows at Coach Clarke in the universal gesture of.

After Harrison closed the door behind himself, she turned her attention back to the man on the other side of the desk.

"I'm only asking for an extra twenty minutes," she proposed. She wasn't even asking for equal rink time, just enough to practice for one extra period.

"My hands are tied," he said. But they both knew he had the power to call up the other coaches and get them to change the schedule.

"Just twenty minutes, *please*." The word felt like acid on her tongue. "If we're as mid as you implied, I'll be out of your hair by the end of the week. Then, the men's team can have *all* the time they want," she said, trying to reason with him without getting herself into trouble.

"Sorry, there's nothing I can do, and I think we should end it here because I have to head over to another meeting," he said, getting ready to stand up. Ari could feel herself losing him. She only had a few moments left to change his mind, so she tried a different strategy. A strategy that she hated but knew was effective.

"Coach, you have daughters, right?"

As the words came out of her mouth, Ari got annoyed with herself. She hated the idea of having to bring up the women a man loved to get him to respect women he didn't care about. She felt bile rise in her throat every time she read one of those "imagine she was your sister/daughter/mother/wife" analogies. But she knew Coach Clarke. She'd spent her whole life dealing with men like him. She didn't want to demean herself, but she knew this was the only way to get him to budge.

"You have daughters and granddaughters, Coach. Imagine how inspired they'd feel if they got to see the British women's ice hockey team make it to the Olympic quarterfinals for the first time?" She prayed that the hopeful expression on her face would get him to believe the dream she was selling. "No matter what comes next, we've got the chance to make history and inspire a new generation of girls. We just need *your* help."

Reasoning like this was beneath her, but she was the captain now. She had to play the game if she was going to get the team what they needed. Coach looked at her and then glanced over at a framed picture of his daughters on his desk. He was so predictable.

"Twenty minutes," he said. But Ari wanted to see how far she could push.

"Coach, our last group-stage game is in just a couple of days. A few hours of extra ice time would mean everything to us."

The sweeter and smilier her expression got, the more she felt like a fraud. But she wasn't leaving without a better deal for her team. They stood in silence for a moment as Coach Clarke thought it through.

"Alright, an hour. I'll speak to the men's coach. Make us proud," he said with a nod, finally relenting.

She knew he would go home tonight feeling like the male

feminist hero of the story. Pat himself on the back for being such a good ally and congratulate himself for doing the bare minimum. But Ari decided that she didn't care about what had changed his mind, or how low she'd sunk to get him there. The team had an extra hour of rink time, the same amount as the men's team. That's all that mattered. So, she nodded, thanked him, and left the room.

The fake smile on her face faded as she stepped out of the office, then disappeared completely when she spotted Harrison loitering in the corridor.

"Were you listening to our conversation?"

The expression on his face told her everything she needed to know.

"I just wanted to make sure you were alright so I could jump in if anything went wrong," he said without an ounce of self-consciousness. Because to Harrison, it wasn't an invasion of privacy, it was just a regular Monday.

"Well, everything went well, so you can go," she said, trying to escape the conversation she could tell he wanted to pull her into.

"I'm still really proud of you, you know," he said. But she knew it wasn't true.

Once the charm of their honeymoon period had faded, Harrison belittled her, criticized her teammates, and talked down on her dreams. And she let him. They'd started dating at a point in her life when she didn't feel secure about any of those things, and his words had felt like a reflection of how she already felt about herself. But she'd outgrown those thoughts, then outgrown him.

"I always knew you'd make it this far," he lied through his teeth.

"Harrison. I thought you said I '*play in a middling team full of girls more concerned with their hair than their strategy*' and that us getting into the Olympics was a '*pipe dream*,'" she said, echoing the words from the conversation that had finally pushed her to end things.

"You know I only ever said that to motivate you, honey."

"Is that what you call it? Motivation?" she asked, doing nothing to hide her disgust.

Usually, she did with Harrison what she'd done with Coach Clarke. Stayed pleasant, made things easier for the men around her, pretended not to be annoyed. But she didn't have it in her to pretend that day. Whatever this lingering thing between them was, it needed to end.

"I'm your biggest fan, I always will be," he said. Ari laughed at his audacity, but he kept on going. "I get it, you're stressed out and emotional. Two losses is a lot, but don't take it out on me. I'm just trying to help, babe."

"Don't you have something better to be doing, like training?" she asked. The smile on his face immediately faded away.

"So, you think you're better than me?" he said, the mask slipping right off as he took a step toward her. "Well, I hate to break it to you, but you're not. A girls team getting this far is pretty cool, but don't let it get to your head."

There it was. Painfully predictable. Ari felt nothing but contempt. She'd spent so much of her life, and their relationship, tiptoeing. Choosing her words in a way that ensured nobody got upset with her. But she'd done enough of that for one day. The more she thought about it, the clearer it became that she wasn't going to get what she wanted or repel what she didn't if she kept trying to manage other people's perceptions of her. So, she stopped.

"Why don't you redirect your energy out of my business and into upping your game?" she said. "Word in the Village is, *you're* on a losing streak." She watched thunder cloud his expression and tried not to flinch.

"Fuck you," he said. "You're never going to be anything more than just a novelty."

Ari sighed. This was who he'd been all along. She'd just been too caught up to realize.

"Lose my number. Leave me alone. For good this time," she said, turning around, walking out of the office building, and stepping back out into the snow. She was never going to look back.

22

Drew

DAY THREE OF THE 2026 OLYMPICS

Drew usually spent a few hours a day trailing Luiz around the Village. Luiz always knew where to find the most stunning wintry backdrops for Drew's photo shoots and had intel on almost every team in the Village. But while Drew's assignment was to work through the list of Zeus-sponsored athletes and take photos of them in the lead-up to and aftermath of their competitions, starting the photo diary of Ari had inspired him to make one of Luiz, too.

MESSAGE FROM: Zeus BTS team

Key people: Athletes at their second or third Winter Games

Key sports: Emphasis on indoor sports

Assignment: We have plenty of content showcasing first-timers and multimedalists, so we want to hear stories from those who've been to multiple Winter Games and know the culture inside out.

When he'd broached the idea of following Luiz around with a camera for the day, he'd expected to be met with resistance. Luiz was always busy fighting fires, hunting down tech equipment, and handling every minor emergency and major complaint the journalists in the press office directed his way. But it turned out that the only thing Luiz liked more than helping the people who spent their days working behind the camera was being in front of the camera.

"I'm a multihyphenate, really," Luiz said as he leaned against the doorframe and tried to strike a casual pose as Drew recorded their conversation. "Press liaison officer, Olympic superfan, future world leader," he continued as they took photos of his tour around the press office. "Remember, I don't have a good side. They all are," he joked. Drew shot candids of Luiz grabbing coffee for a team of journalists working at *The Korea Herald*, caught a photo of him running to deliver extension cords for the producers of a CBC Sports special, and then captured a stop-motion of him reorganizing the infamously messy spare tech room.

Once they had enough photos, Drew found an empty desk next to a group of broadcast news runners, opened Photoshop, and got to work editing hundreds of photos for the editorial team at Zeus. There were a bunch of sports-specific photos he was proud of. Skiers midair and ice skaters elegantly gliding across the ice. But the photos he liked the most were those of the invisible moving parts that went into making sure the Olympics ran smoothly. The facilities team that woke up early to grit the paths, the ice makers who meticulously maintained the ice rinks in each venue, the bus drivers who shuttled spectators back and forth between competitions. People who the average viewer would either never see or notice onscreen. But those were the people Drew kept finding himself drawn to. He'd always been interested in taking photos of people on the margins of greatness. The ones whose work behind the scenes made spectacles seem effortless. In college, he'd taken a photo of one of the men who cut the grass at Dodgers Stadium and gotten a small story about him published in the back pages of the *Los Angeles Times*. One of his favorite sophomore-year assignments was a photoset of ballet instructors holding flowers while they waited for their students in the wings.

He knew the team at Zeus probably wouldn't want the photos he was taking of the random people he'd met across the Village. But taking photos of them was the closest he'd felt to the excitement of carrying his camera across LA back in college. He'd left it for good now, but he still missed the feeling of being in a busy city with stories at every turn. So, he decided there was no harm in capturing the people who caught his eye between assignments. He'd done it the night of the opening ceremony with some of the photographers in the press pit. All their cameras had been pointed out at the stadium, but Drew's had been directed straight at them. Without putting too much thought into taking the photos, he'd managed to perfectly capture the atmosphere of the press pit. The focus, sheer determination, and quiet thrill each journalist got from capturing something that would one day become history. So, he'd made a habit of it. Each time he went to a competition or walked through a crowd in the Village and spotted someone interesting working behind the scenes, Drew quickly took a photo of them. Promising himself that he would find a life for them outside of his camera roll.

He was checking his inbox to see if he'd gotten any feedback from the team at Zeus about the last photos he'd sent them when he saw an unexpected contact at the top of his inbox. He read the subject line: SUSPENDING YOUR STUDIES—SUMMER SEMESTER. Drew sat up in his chair, his eyes widening with each new line of the email.

"Why do you look like you've just seen a ghost?" asked Luiz

as he walked past the desk Drew was sitting at. "Has Zeus asked you to find twenty reindeer for a photo shoot with a snowboarder or something?" Luiz joked, well aware of the errands Drew had spent the past few days going on in pursuit of a good photo. But Drew just shook his head and angled the laptop so that Luiz could read it for himself.

"I thought you dropped out?" said Luiz in confusion.

"I did, at least that's what I thought," Drew said as he read and then reread the first line of the email.

We have processed your request to suspend your studies for the spring semester due to extenuating family/health circumstances. To reenroll for the summer semester, beginning May 18, please complete this form by the deadline stated above.

"You suspended your studies instead of ending them?" Luiz asked. Drew nodded and stared at his screen, perplexed. He was so sure he'd dropped out. He could still remember filling in the form and explaining his reasons. But as he read through the email, it became pretty clear that, according to USC's records, he'd just taken the spring semester off. To them, he wasn't a dropout, he was a student taking a break.

"Are you going to go back?" Luiz asked, curious.

"Of course not," Drew said. It came out more defensively than he'd planned it to.

"So why did you click on the form?"

Drew looked over at Luiz and then back at his screen. He paused for a moment as he imagined taking a flight back to California. Moving back into a dorm and feeling the warm sunshine on his arms again. By May 18, summer would have begun. His days would be filled with talks from lecturers who saw the world in fascinating ways. Afternoons on the grass working with his classmates. Weekend barbecues and late-night library sessions with friends he'd barely spoken to since leaving. The memories of his time in college, and the vision of what life would look like if he went back, was alluring. The daydream pulled him in for a moment. But then he snapped back to reality. There was no way he could go back. Not now after spending enough time at home to know his grandma's condition was getting worse. It would be selfish; he would regret it. But the idea of what could be stayed with him as he edited the rest of his photos, then took a shuttle bus with Luiz to get lunch. When they got to the restaurant they'd decided on, his sister was waiting for him at the front door.

"I think I'm going to die if I don't eat a steaming hot bowl of pasta, some ribs, and a slice of cake in the next three minutes," said Thandie, who he knew wasn't going to order a single one of those things. Like all the other athletes, she was sticking to a strict Team USA–approved meal plan.

"Thandie Dlamini, lovely to meet you," she said, smiling, as she reached over to shake Luiz's hand.

"Luiz Souza, the pleasure is all mine," said Luiz. He was all charm but reserved the best of it for his boyfriend, who worked on the anti-doping team.

"So *you're* Drew's press office bestie? You know he talks about you every time I call him, right?"

"I don't talk about him that much," Drew said.

But Thandie liked to make her brother squirm. Her favorite sport, after ice hockey, was teasing him.

"'Thandie, Luiz is the best, he helped me find a spare set of batteries,'" she mimicked. "'Thandie, Luiz is so nice and helped me get into the bobsledding quarterfinals,'" she said with a grin. "'Thandie, Luiz is going to help me become best friends with—'"

"Hans Leitner," finished Luiz, and the two of them started laughing, immediately bonded. He'd known they were going to get along.

As they ate lunch, Thandie talked about hockey practice and what life was like in the athletes' side of the Village. Luiz spoke about his childhood in Brazil and going to university in Canada. And Drew talked about the photos he'd taken for Zeus and wanting to travel through the Alps on the Glacier Express. But then, just when everything was going well, Luiz asked a casual question that turned things around.

"Thandie, I'm helping a BBC journalist with an interview she's doing later with another ice hockey player, and I was wondering if you knew her," Luiz said. Drew had told Luiz about Ari, and he'd been gently teasing him for the smile that crossed his face each time her name came up. But Drew hadn't mentioned her to his sister yet. They'd barely spent any time together since their last family dinner and Drew didn't feel the need to tell her about a relationship that wasn't even real. But Luiz was curious to find out if they knew each other.

"Oh, I know everyone. What's her name?" asked Thandie as she put her cutlery down.

"Ari Shumba?" Luiz asked innocently.

Drew glanced over at his sister, watching as her face screwed up.

"Arikoishe Shumba?" she asked in a venomous tone. "The girl who almost ruined my life?"

"What?" Drew asked, confused.

"She's the one who tackled me and broke my leg," Thandie said, shaking her head.

And in that moment, everything clicked. Drew hadn't seen anything about that match when he'd googled Ari. She wasn't that well known, so none of the articles about Thandie's injury included her name. But Drew had been at the game his sister was talking about. He could still remember watching in horror as his then seventeen-year-old sister was carried off the ice rink. He'd been so focused on her that he hadn't paid attention to the person she'd interacted with. But as the pieces came together, it all began to make sense. On New Year's, Ari had told him about the guilt she felt for a mysterious event that had ruined one person's life and improved hers. Now he realized that ruined person was his sister.

"She's a sorry excuse for a team captain and an even worse player," said Thandie. "Wait, that's not fair. She's a brilliant player, she's just a terrible person."

"What happened?" Luiz asked, glancing between them.

"You know how people sometimes trash-talk before a big game? Try to get into their opponent's head and mess with them a little? It's part of the culture, especially when we were kids. So, when we competed against each other growing up we'd always toss small digs at each other, go back and forth a little. It was harmless fun. But I knew all the other players in the league were a little jealous of my team, and who wouldn't be? We're the reigning champions." Thandie shrugged.

"After Canada," Luiz teased. He'd spent four years in Toronto and was still patriotic about his temporary home.

"Give it a few years and we'll outpace them." She smiled. "Anyway, back to the story. Team GB was doing well in 2021, much better than anybody expected. And, for a season, they seemed like they could become genuine competitors. And you know how sports media gets, *everybody loves an underdog*, but a good story isn't enough. At the end of the day it's about who wins."

"And your team was killing it that year," said Luiz with a nod. He followed all the winter sports in the lead-up to Olympic qualifications.

"Until Arikoishe turned up." Thandie took a dramatic sip of her water, before putting it down and telling a story that Drew had forgotten a crucial detail of. "It was a few months before the 2022 Games, and we had one of our final matches of the year. Right before it started, she skated past me, winked, and said, 'Break a leg.' Half an hour later in the middle of the game, she tackled me and pushed me into the wall with so much force that I . . . broke my leg."

"Oh no," said Luiz.

"So, because of her, I missed out on what was supposed to be my first Olympics."

"Do you think she did it on purpose?" Luiz asked as Drew kicked himself for not connecting the dots sooner.

"No," she admitted. "But I'm pretty sure she's glad it happened."

"So, are you and Ari *friendly* now?" asked Drew, hoping five years had been long enough to thaw the ice.

"Friendly?" Thandie said with a joyless laugh as she shook her head. "I *hate* that girl."

Drew's stomach dropped. He knew the depths of his sister's grudges. Once her mind was set, there was no way to persuade her otherwise.

"But none of that matters," she said.

"Why?" he asked cautiously.

"Because if I play against her, I know I'm going to win." She shrugged. "Me and the girls have been training and strategizing for months. So, I know all my competitors' flaws. Especially hers. I know the weaknesses I can attack and the strengths I can use against her on the rink."

Drew knew what she was saying was pretty standard. All team-sport training included studying your opponents. But this felt different. This wasn't just a match, it was Thandie's way of righting a wrong.

"Revenge?" Luiz asked.

"No, I'm not that petty," Thandie said. "I'm just a better player. So, if her team is unfortunate enough to make it to the quarter-finals and play against mine? I'll make sure she regrets the day she tackled me," Thandie said, her eyes twinkling.

Drew just took a sip of water and glanced over at Luiz. Neither of them needed to say a word to confirm what they both already knew.

Drew was completely and utterly screwed.

23

Ari

"She's acting like I killed someone," Anesu said from the other end of the phone.

"Well, betrayal is kind of like a mini death," Ari joked as she walked across the Village through the snow. The call started with her sister giving her a ring to check in after her last match, but it quickly devolved, as most conversations with her sister did, into a conversation about their parents.

"He's still my dad. You got to spend your childhood with him, so why can't I take a two-week trip to see him?" Anesu said, disappointed. Ari wanted to say that her childhood hadn't been a particularly happy one since their parents had spent the entire time fighting, but she quickly decided against it. Because Anesu idolized their father. He never called her first and rarely spent more than half a day with her when he came to London for work, but Anesu refused to read between the lines. She believed that if she tried hard enough, she could have the kind of father-daughter relationship that her friends did. Because despite all the ways he'd disappointed her, Anesu still really loved their dad.

"You're the only one she listens to. Can you at least try to reason with her?" Anesu asked.

Ari was in the middle of the most important tournament of her life. Mediating a family drama unfolding eight hundred miles away wasn't even close to the top of her priorities that day. But she wanted to have both her mom's and sister's backs.

"Alright, I'll talk to her," Ari promised, adding it to her mental to-do list before saying goodbye and making her way over to the training building.

The one thing that surprised people when Ari talked about her schedule for the Olympics was how little time she and her teammates actually spent on the ice. While they'd dedicated the months leading up to the Games to intense, practical preparation, they were only on the ice for a couple of hours a day. They needed to preserve their energy for their matches and couldn't risk injuring or overexerting themselves in the middle of a tournament. So, the rest of their time was spent doing light sessions at the gym, going to physio appointments, and making sure their bodies were in perfect shape.

Their priority off the ice was mental sharpness and making sure that, as a team, they were mentally in sync. Which was why Ari tried to be the first to arrive to all their locker room and meeting room sessions. As the captain, she set the tone. But after taking photos earlier with Drew, she'd made a stop at a café to grab one of the vitamin-rich teas she'd heard about from her teammates. They were spending hours each day breathing in winter air, and she knew the worst thing she could do was catch a cold. So, she ordered a lemon-and-ginger immune-system-boosting tea and let herself drink it in the café while looking out at the snow. They had a team practice that morning and she wanted a moment to think before preparing for their next game. The detour didn't make her late, but instead of arriving her usual fifteen minutes early, she got to the meeting room at 8:57. Just three minutes before they were scheduled to start. It was a decision she immediately recognized as a mistake, because the scene she walked in on that morning was pure chaos.

"Face it, Yasmeen," said Izzy, "it's your fault all the pucks keep getting past the line!" Izzy, who was usually the most cheerful of them all, was practically shouting at Yasmeen as they stood face-to-face in the locker room.

"Oh, of course," said Yasmeen, rolling her eyes. "Everybody blames defense when we lose, but nobody blames the forwards for barely scoring!"

"We're killing it on the rink!" shouted Sienna, getting up from her seat. "I scored three times in the last game, but why did we lose? Because you didn't save *any* of the goals Sweden scored," she said, pointing over at the screen on the wall, set up for them to review their last match. Ari stood still in the doorframe as she watched it all unfold.

"Maybe if you were a little quicker and got control of the puck from the start, you would have scored more," said Izzy. Pointing to a flipchart on the other side of the room that listed all their game statistics.

"Well, maybe if *you* applied more energy to practice than your social calendar, you'd actually be able to do your job," said Sienna with the kind of shrug that invited an escalation.

Ari had seen this play out before. Since Izzy was the goaltender and Yasmeen played on defense, in moments like this they quickly went from arguing with each other to forming a tight team against anyone who attacked their side of the team, which in this case was Sienna.

"You're so predictable," said Yasmeen with the terrifyingly

calm voice she used when she was ready to dress someone down. "You blame everybody but yourself. But we're supposed to walk on eggshells and ignore the fact that you missed that penalty."

"That's bullshit," said Sienna defensively. "You don't have to tiptoe around me."

Izzy replied by mocking her.

"Yes, we do. All we do is tiptoe around you so we don't hurt your delicate little feelings. 'Oh, Sienna is so stressed, be nice to her.' 'Oh, Sienna is worried, so don't tell her the truth.' 'Oh, Sienna is listening to white noise because she's overwhelmed.' Who cares?" said Izzy with an uncharacteristic amount of venom. Ari had never heard her so angry or mean.

The women on the team had known each other for over a decade. They'd met in their early teens and gone through many stages of life together. Awkward hairstyles, first dates, stressful exam prep, and hundreds of ice hockey games. They knew one another inside out and felt more like cousins or sisters than friends. But knowing each other that well meant that they knew exactly what to say to hurt one another for the sake of making a point. At first, Ari stood back and allowed them to go back and forth. Arguments were a natural part of being on a team in a fiercely competitive sport. But things had been off with them ever since Gracie's injury. The fractures from boot camp were getting deeper. So, Ari tried to step in before things could get any worse.

"How about we stop blaming each other and focus on what we need to do to get better?" said Ari, trying to defuse the tension. But in ending one argument, she made herself the target for the next.

"Ari, be honest. You know we're screwed." Yasmeen shook her head.

"Let's face it, compared to the other teams, we're just not that good," Izzy said, defeated.

"I told you. We should have never gotten our hopes up," said Sienna. "Which is why I always say expect the worst. That way, you're never disappointed."

All the other girls began to groan.

"Why do you have to be so depressing *all the time*?" Yasmeen said.

"I'm realistic, the only realistic one here! We did a good job to get here, but we might just have to accept that this is the end," answered Sienna, but Ari wasn't having it.

"I swear, if you keep talking like that, I'm getting Coach to bench you," said Ari. "Actually, I'll bench all three of you if you keep at this."

The room went silent.

She'd never made a game-based threat before. In fact, beyond a few failed pep talks, Ari had never really put her foot down in a way that reminded them that she was their captain. There were twenty-two other girls on the team, and most of them hadn't given her any problems. But the dynamics between Ari and her three best friends on the team were much more complicated. Izzy was the fun one, Sienna was the honest one, Yasmeen was the chilled-out one, and Ari was the confidante. The person who subtly worked behind the scenes to fix things, the friend you could talk to without judgment. But they didn't talk to her as much now that she was their captain. Not because they liked her any less, but because they couldn't confide in the person whose new job it was to keep them in line. So, Ari had been trying her best not to say or do anything that caused any further divides between her and her friends. But that caution was starting to get in the way of their chances of success.

"You know you're not our *actual* captain, right?" said Sienna. She rarely got mean, but she was staring into Ari's eyes with an intense glare. "Gracie is our captain. Coach *only* gave you the role because—" Sienna stopped herself midsentence, knowing she'd gone too far.

"Because what?" said Ari. The room went silent as they faced each other. They'd been friends since they were kids and fought like sisters when things got tough, so nobody dared get in the middle of things. "If you're going to start something, finish it."

"Because I'm the best player on the team," said Sienna, steely eyed. "I can't be captain because I have to focus all of *my* energy on scoring goals."

It stung a little, because she was right. But Sienna's willingness to say something like that made it clear why their roles hadn't been reversed.

"You might score more goals than me, Sienna, but the real reason you're not captain is because you don't have the temperament to lead a team. Even now. Why are you picking a fight?" Ari asked.

"Because you don't know how to!" said Sienna.

Ari's heart sank. The room stilled. The flash of regret in Sienna's eyes and their teammates' nervous glances made it clear they'd all been thinking the same thing. Izzy stared at the ground. Yasmeen picked up her kit bag and walked across the room.

The room stayed quiet as Ari let the words sink in. The rest of her teammates took their seats, but she and Sienna stayed standing. The words exchanged still hanging in the air.

"Is that what you really think?" Ari asked, trying not to sound as deflated as she felt.

"Ari," Sienna said with a sigh, her voice almost apologetic. "It's not working. Everyone walks all over you . . . and you just let them."

Ari could feel the pinpricks in her eyes. She opened her mouth and tried to voice a response, but the words wouldn't come out. Coach McLaughlin walked in a few seconds later. He looked around, bewildered by the silence, then walked to the front of the room to commence their team meeting. He started talking about strategy and execution, but Ari couldn't take any of it in. Sienna's words were still ringing in her head. They'd had dozens of arguments over the years, but this one felt different because the most painful thing Sienna had said was the truth. And as she glanced around room, it became painfully apparent. Something needed to change, because as she'd learned a long time ago, nobody was coming to save her.

24

Drew

"When are we going to stop lying to her?" Drew said as he and his grandpa stood inside the Village gift shop, examining postcards while his grandma flitted around looking for souvenirs. It was the question that had been circling his mind all day. After taking photos of Ari, he'd headed over to the skeleton track to photograph an athlete on the Latvian team named Andris. Andris's brother was also his coach, so he and Drew struck up a conversation about all the stress their siblings endured. A conversation that reminded him of the secrets he was keeping from *his* sister.

"After the Olympics," his grandpa said firmly.

"Of course." That was one thing they were in complete agreement about. "But when?"

"You're stressing me out, Andrew," his grandpa said as he tied and then retied his scarf, looking out at the snow instead of meeting his eye. It was the conversation they'd been having ever since Drew had moved back home. His grandparents had done a pretty good job of hiding the worst of his grandma's symptoms when he'd FaceTimed them from college. But it was impossible not to notice her worsening condition when he'd moved back home. It was still mostly small things: losing her keys, getting overwhelmed at the grocery store, and calling old friends by the wrong name. But the more time Drew spent with her, the more aware he became of her deterioration.

She'd called him in tears a few days before Christmas, after getting lost while driving to the grocery store. By the time Drew had arrived to pick her up, she'd dusted herself off. Greeting him with a joke and telling him she was overreacting because she hadn't had her morning coffee yet. But back at the house, the three of them sat down and decided that it wasn't safe for her to drive anymore.

In January, Drew had decided to make himself useful by cleaning out the attic and updating a few family albums. But when he'd shown her a handful of photos from the trip they'd taken to Canada, she'd stared blankly at them, unable to recall a single thing they'd done on a trip just two years ago.

So, Drew insisted he accompany his grandma to her next doctor's appointment, which confirmed his fears. Things *were* progressing faster than expected. To the average person, his grandma seemed completely fine, if not slightly scatterbrained. But it took only a full week together to see it was more serious than that.

"I'm just saying we can try to hide it, but eventually Thandie's gonna find out. And then, it won't matter that we were trying to protect her. It will just feel like a betrayal."

"What will feel like a betrayal?" his grandma asked as she walked toward them.

"Getting to her game late. Let's speed up," Drew said, slapping on a cheerful expression and walking to the exit of the gift shop.

As Drew stepped outside, he noticed it was beginning to

snow. He hated the cold, which was one of the main reasons he'd decided to go to college in California—a college he could reenroll in, he reminded himself. Drew lived for the West Coast's endless blue skies and proximity to the ocean. There was always something to do in LA, and the people he met there provided him with endless sources of inspiration. He could lie to himself about many things—he did it all the time. But there was no denying that he missed California. He was trying his best to live in the moment though, so he forced himself to push those memories aside and focus on the present. He was about to see if his grandparents were following him when he heard the sound of an alarm. He turned around. His grandma walked through the gift shop exit, nonchalant. But a security guard immediately followed her out.

"Ma'am, you have to pay for that," he said, sounding nervous. The guard was staring directly at his grandma. He was trying to look tough, but there was a nervousness in his eyes.

"Excuse me?" his grandma said. "Young man, do I look like a person that would steal?" she asked. She didn't. She was the kind of woman who displayed her wealth in her appearance: designer handbags, tailored coats, and decadent brooches. She wasn't a rulebreaker, so she handed the security guard her shopping bag and receipt. But she made sure to give him the kind of glare that would make even the most confident person feel like they were being scolded by their grandmother. The guard looked at her receipt and apprehensively searched her bag. Then he sighed, as if he didn't want to say anything but knew he had to.

"Your pocket," he said reluctantly.

"Yes?" she said incisively, smoothing down the fabric of her coat.

"The left pocket," the security guard sighed.

She reached down, indignant. But her expression fell as her

hand went into the pocket and came out holding an ornate snow globe.

"I . . . I don't know how that got there," she said, looking around, embarrassed. A few tourists who'd been leaving the gift shop glanced over and then immediately looked away. Drew's heart sank a little as he watched his grandpa's face fall, too. He reached for his wallet, gently took the snow globe from his wife's hands, and walked straight back into the shop. Muttering an apology and explanation to the security guard.

Drew immediately went over to put his arm around his grandma's shoulders. She hated sympathy as much as she hated talking about her illness. So, Drew did what he did best.

"That's where Thandie gets it from. Sweeping things up before anyone can notice? If you played hockey, I bet you'd steal a puck as soon as you got on the ice," he teased. His grandma gave him a short look of gratitude, then smiled, playing along.

"I taught her everything she knows," she laughed, though they both knew full well that she'd never stepped foot on a skating rink. But humor was their shared strategy for getting through this. So, they spent the entire walk to Thandie's ice hockey match tossing jokes back and forth until the globe was almost entirely forgotten. When they got to the stadium, Drew cheered for his sister and tried to focus on the game. But he couldn't shake the nagging feeling that his and his grandpa's strategy—to ensure that Grandma and Thandie didn't spend too much time alone together—wasn't a lasting solution. Eventually, Thandie would find out. Drew just hoped he could stop that from happening during the two most important weeks of her life.

After the first period of the game ended, he left his grandparents to head over to his next assignment. As much as he wanted to watch his sister's entire match, he was at the Olympics to work. So, he took a shuttle to the speed-skating rink to photograph a

Swedish athlete who was at the Olympics for the first time and ask him about his journey to the Games. Then he walked to one of the athletes' gyms to do a mini photo shoot with the Nigerian bobsled team Ari had introduced him to. They showed him their training routines and joked about how, in their sport, every day at the gym was arm day. Once he'd completed his list of athletes for the day, he took a chairlift to the top of the Village.

After a series of scattered texts between Ari's training sessions and Drew's assignments, they'd decided on a location for their second fake date: Schokoladenzeit, the glamorous hot chocolate bar up in the mountains.

When he walked inside, Drew immediately understood why it had become the most-talked-about venue in that year's Village. Schokoladenzeit wasn't a regular café with a broad selection of flavors, or even just a specialty hot chocolate shop with Olympic-themed decorations. It was the Willy Wonka's workshop of hot chocolate bars. As soon as he stepped in, he was hit by the delicious smell of chocolate and the warm scents of hazelnut, vanilla, coffee beans, caramel, and cinnamon. The bar was designed like a luxurious log cabin with armchairs covered in thick blankets and fluffy pillows at every turn. There was a fireplace at the center of the room and warm candles twinkling all around them. Drew settled into a cozy corner visible enough to meet Ari's requirement for a very public date.

He was leafing through the menu and browsing the thirty-plus types of hot chocolate they had on offer when he saw a bright blue puffer coat cross the bar. He wanted to tell Ari about Thandie right away, but the first thing he noticed when she walked toward him was the expression on her face. She looked worn out. Her shoulders slumped and her lips turned down. When they made eye contact, she gave him a half-hearted wave.

"Bad day?" he asked as she plopped herself on the opposite

side of the couch he was sitting on. She dropped her bag and sighed.

"Let's just say that if I didn't have two more games this week, I'd be drinking something a lot stronger than hot chocolate," she said, unbuttoning her coat.

Drew hadn't known Ari very long, but he'd spent enough time taking photos of people to figure out how they were feeling. She was joking around as she studied the menu, pointing out all the sports-inspired drink names. But she kept tapping her foot against the floor and had rolled and unrolled the sleeves of her red sweater at least three times in the last minute. He wanted to ask her about it but let her warm up first. They went back and forth on the menu until she ordered the Alpine Ski Almond, and he ordered the Bobsled Banoffee Pie. Their hot chocolates arrived in tall glass mugs on a tray dusted to look like a thin layer of snow. She told him that she was supposed to be on a processed sugar ban as part of her training diet, but this was too delicious to refuse. It wasn't until she had her hands wrapped around her mug that she finally looked content.

"So, what happened today?" he asked casually.

"Nothing," she said, sipping her chocolate.

"We won't know each other anymore in two weeks, remember?"

"So, this is a safe space?" she laughed.

"Exactly. Just listening, no judgment."

She shook her head and smiled, dipping her spoon into the mug to taste the almond flakes scattered across the top before opening up.

"The team bombed at our game yesterday, so all the girls hate me. Well, they don't hate me, they just think I have no idea how to be a good captain," she admitted, putting her cup down and holding her head in her hands. "And honestly, they're right. I just don't think I'm cut out for this."

He wanted to reassure her, but from what he knew about Ari, his words wouldn't be enough. She was the type of person who needed to believe something for herself.

"What makes you think that?" he asked instead.

"Don't get me wrong," she said, putting up her hands. "Being captain, especially at the Olympics, is a life-changing opportunity. I'm grateful that Coach picked me for the job. But since taking it, *everything's* changed. My friends are hanging out without me; and instead of trying to do my best, I feel like I'm constantly trying to prove myself. And I think they're starting to realize that I'm not going to become the person they need me to be," she said, slightly panicked.

"Have they said that?" Drew asked gently, hating how much of an effect it was having on her.

"No, but I can feel it."

Ari paused for a moment and looked up at the wooden beams on the ceiling, closing her hands around her hot chocolate. He'd noticed her doing that a lot. Zoning out of their conversations for a moment and silently thinking things through by herself. Drew recognized it because he did it all the time. Processed his thoughts and emotions alone. He watched as she fidgeted in her chair for a moment and stretched her legs out, trying to get comfortable.

"My legs ache. I think the cold is getting to my bones," she said, fidgeting around.

"Come over here," he said. "There's plenty of space." She let him take her calves into his hands so they could rest on his lap, then smiled as she got comfortable against the side of the couch.

"Ari, they're your friends. Do you really think they'll be disappointed that you can't do everything perfectly all the time?" he asked, returning to their conversation as he rested his hands on her knees. It felt comfortable and familiar. Like they'd done this a dozen times before.

"Kind of, but more than that, *I'll* be disappointed," she said, looking over at him, her voice soft. "It was so hard for us to get to the Olympics that I don't know if I'll be able to forgive myself if I become the reason why we don't make it. Plus, my friend Yasmeen's trying to book us into a spa day the weekend after the finals, so they'll be gutted if we end up having to catch an early flight home," she said wryly. She was trying to lighten things up, but Drew stayed right there.

"You put a lot of pressure on yourself." It was an observation, not a question.

"You don't become great by treating yourself with kid gloves," she said. There was a slight note of defensiveness in her voice. "I wouldn't have gotten this far *without* that pressure."

"But?" he asked, leaving the door open for her to keep going. She looked over at him, studying his face for a moment, a response on the tip of her tongue. But then she glanced over at the door. Something she saw there made her shake her head. Drew glanced over and saw a group of Team GB athletes who'd just walked into the bar. Ari slid her legs off his lap and shuffled over to his side of the couch, moving closer until they were seated shoulder to shoulder. Drew sat up, remembering why they were there.

"Snowboarders?" he asked, scanning the group for Harrison.

"No, bobsledders. But everyone knows each other. I saw him earlier, actually," she admitted. Drew raised an eyebrow. "Nothing interesting, just Harrison being Harrison." She shrugged. The look on her face made it clear there was more to it than that, but she'd moved on, redirecting her energy to shuffling over toward him. He instinctively put his hand against the back of the sofa and smiled when she wrapped his arm around her shoulders.

"Fake boyfriend, remember?" she said, reminding him why they'd come to Schokoladenzeit in the first place. One of the bobsledders glanced over. Ari took it as a cue to move even closer to him. Inching forward until their legs touched.

"Actually, I was looking into the science behind romance yesterday. For the sake of our fake relationship," she said, like it was a regular thing to do. "And I saw this video talking about why seats are arranged side by side outside old French restaurants instead of across from each other."

"And why is that?" he asked, amused to hear her findings.

"Well, according to the video, it's more romantic," she explained, casually placing a hand on his leg. "Apparently, people hold back on being themselves when they're seated face-to-face with somebody, because it feels like being on display. But when you're sitting *next to* someone, you're quicker to break that barrier and more likely to open up."

"That explains New Year's," he said, recalling how quick he'd been to relax around her.

"The shots my teammates convinced me to drink probably helped."

"And the premidnight dread sealed the deal." He smiled. "What else did your video say?"

"That this seating arrangement is perfect for making us look like we're really together. Because sitting side by side makes a date feel more intimate." She shrugged.

"Oh, really?" he asked, looking over at her.

"Well, there isn't a table standing between us." She said it as if she was telling him a secret. "So, there's nothing in the way of you casually leaning over to hold my hand, stroke my leg, or kiss me."

They held each other's gaze.

"Not that I want you to touch my leg, hold my hand, or kiss me," she backtracked.

"I could if you wanted me to."

"Just to test out the research." She smiled.

"Anything in the name of science." He nodded. "I aced my AP Chemistry classes, so I take these things very seriously."

"So, in your *scientific opinion*, how would we make it absolutely clear to the rest of the room that we're together?" she said, looking over at the athletes in matching uniforms.

"Well, I could lean over," he said, until their heads were just a few inches apart.

"You could." She didn't flinch.

"And whisper something in your ear," he said, doing exactly that, smiling as he noticed her bite her lip and then quickly regain her composure.

"Then what?" she asked, daring him to go on.

"I could tuck your hair back," he said, wrapping a curl around his fingers, slowly sliding it behind her ear, and tracing his finger down the side of her face before gently stroking the tip of her chin. The tension between them thickened into a hum. He glanced down at her lips, wanting to close the space between them. But he knew he couldn't.

"If we wanted to make it absolutely clear," she said casually, "I could put my hand on your leg." She gently laid her palm on his thigh and drew a tiny circle with her thumb. The touch sent a shiver up his spine.

"And then I could run my fingers over the stubble on your chin," she said, gently tracing the tips of her fingers across his skin and casually setting a trail of nerve endings alight as her fingers swept over his cheeks and then up to his bottom lip. "Then what?" she asked. There was a twinkle in her eyes; she enjoyed the game as much as he did.

"I could kiss you."

He let the answer float in the air for a second. Felt his heartbeat quicken. Noticed her attention flicker down to his lips for a moment before returning his gaze. Their faces were just a few centimeters apart. Close enough to touch.

"But we're not outside a French restaurant," she whispered.

"And this isn't a *real* date."

Yet there they were, sitting thigh to thigh on the sofa, an unmistakable spark threatening to take them past the point of no return. But they couldn't go against the rules. So, Drew leaned back, reached for a menu, and broke the spell. This couldn't go anywhere, so there was no point in letting it start. Right?

25

Ari

DAY FIVE OF THE 2026 OLYMPICS

Everyone walks all over you . . . and you just let them. Sienna's words had been echoing around Ari's mind all morning. It was a harsh thing to say, especially in front of all their teammates. But as painful as it was, Sienna was right. Being a chronic people pleaser was getting in the way of becoming the person she needed to be.

So when she got to the meeting room that morning, she unrolled a page of flipchart paper and uncapped a new marker, the sharp chemical smell of it filling her with a sense of purpose. She wrote out a list of strategies: ones that had worked well and ones it was time to retire. Then she printed out the personalized feedback notes she'd been compiling over the course of the past few months. When her teammates began walking into the room, she started handing them out.

"What's all of this?" Yasmeen asked as she glanced through the notes. Nodding at some in agreement.

"A fresh slate," Ari said, trying to sound firm as she addressed the rest of the team. "Yesterday's meeting was a disaster, and I dropped the ball. But we have a lot of work to do if we're going to try and make it to the quarterfinals."

"So that's why you left early? I thought you'd snuck away to hook up with that boy you told us about, not do all of this," Izzy teased, pointing at Ari's presentation, notes, and strategy meeting.

She knew Izzy was just messing with her. And even if she wasn't, Izzy was a hopeless romantic. A statement like that would have never been a dig. But it still cut a little. Not because of Izzy's intentions, but because of Ari's past. She'd been in a near-constant state of distraction during her years with Harrison. Their relationship had preoccupied her in all the worst ways. She'd been a confident teenager, but he'd drawn out her insecurities and made her question everything. To the point where she stumbled her way through every game she played after hanging out with him. It had taken her ages to unlearn the lies he'd made her believe, and she'd come a long way since their breakup. But her teammates didn't think she was there yet. So, she had to show them.

Sienna was right, Ari *had* failed to truly take on the authority that came with being the captain of her team. Gracie was good at doing both because her reputation had led the team to respect her immediately. But Ari had known these girls all her life, and she didn't know how to say no to them. Her inability to do that with her best friends made it nearly impossible to portray any sense of authority over the rest of the team. But that ended today.

Ari squared her shoulders. "Okay, first of all, let's address the elephant in the room. The arguments we had the other day in the locker room? We're better than that. A team doesn't work without honesty and harmony, but *this*," she said, waving her hands in a circle, "is a strategy meeting, not our group chat."

It was a little harsh, but she needed to stand her ground. They couldn't allow their friendships to get in the way of the reality that for the rest of the month, they were, first and most importantly, teammates.

"You're right," Sienna admitted, putting up her hands. "I'm sorry."

Coach McLaughlin walked in. He looked over at Ari, waiting to see how she would respond.

"It's alright," Ari said, brushing it off even though Sienna's words from yesterday still stung. "The past couple of months have been intense, but it's only because it matters to us. So let's stay focused on the end goal. Getting to the semifinals."

Coach raised an eyebrow at her statement. It felt like everyone did.

"I thought it was the quarterfinals?" said Yasmeen. "I don't want to sound like a downer, but that feels a little unrealistic."

Ari nodded; of course it was. "It only feels that way because we haven't done it before. But I think we can, we just need to make some adjustments. Right, Coach?" she said as they all turned to him. She knew that they, like her, were still disappointed in him for not fixing the rink time situation sooner.

"Your captain is right. You've put in the time and effort you needed to get here. We just need to push that a little bit harder to stay in the game," he said, giving Ari a small nod of approval before the two of them went around the room, giving each of her teammates detailed feedback.

Ari gave Mia, a player on the left wing of the offense, advice on how to improve her speed. Then, she told a right wing player named Alexis how to get better at blocking. She gave the backup goaltenders, Melissa and Kayley, guidance on how to improve their predictions, then went around the whole team until she finally reached her friends.

"Yasmeen, you *do* keep getting distracted when the puck is coming toward you," Ari began. Yasmeen opened her mouth to object, but Ari just put her hand up to signal that she wasn't done yet. "You panic and get distracted; I can see it in your eyes. You never used to do that back home. So, when you get on the ice, remind yourself that you're excellent in defense. Then focus all your energy into tracking the puck so you can block it in time."

Yasmeen nodded. Ari moved on.

"Izzy. In an ideal world, the puck should never get close enough for you to have to save it," she began. Izzy opened her mouth as if to agree and berate the girls in defense, but Ari had more to say. "However, this is a real-life game. There are no perfect scenarios, just what happens on the rink. So, when the puck comes, be enthusiastic about the fact that you get to do what you've been training your whole life for. You're good at what you do, so focus on how lucky you are to get to do that instead of the fact that the pucks are coming your way." Izzy looked shocked, but instead of reacting, she closed her eyes and muttered a quiet "whatever" because she, like the rest of the team, knew Ari was right.

"And Sienna," Ari said to her oldest friend, who was an excellent player but lived in a near-permanent state of doom.

"Arikoishe," she replied, mirroring her seriousness.

Ari smiled because, in that moment, she could see Sienna as both the sweet and scrappy eleven-year-old who'd invited her to her first ice hockey game and the brilliant but terrified twenty-one-year-old having a crisis of confidence.

"You know I love you. But I don't care if you're the best player we've got. If you're a negative force in the changing room, I won't hesitate to keep you on the bench," Ari said, being firm for what felt like the first time in their long friendship. Sienna's eyes widened a little, but if Ari knew her as well as she thought she did, there was a hint of approval in her expression, too. Sienna had been trying to get Ari to stand up for herself more ever since they'd met. "We're *all* here because we're good at what we do. So, for the love of God, put a little bit more faith in your teammates and start imagining some best-case scenarios. We need all the belief we can get."

A few of the other girls began to mutter, but Ari wasn't having it. She shot them daggers with her eyes and waited until the locker room returned to silence before she addressed them as a team.

"Maybe it was a fluke, blind luck, or the godsend that is Gracie Walters. But how we got here doesn't matter anymore. We're at the Olympics now, we made it. So, what we're not going to do is squander this opportunity by bickering and fighting about petty little things, alright?" she said. A few of the girls muttered.

"I said, alright?" To that, the girls replied with "Okay." She gave them what she hoped was a deeply unnerving, no-nonsense look.

"We have less than two weeks left in the Village and only one more game to get us to the quarterfinals. We can't afford to waste another second. Like it or not, *I am* your captain. So, get dressed, get your shit together, and get on that rink ready to train for your lives. Because I did not get this far just to get this far. And neither did you."

"Okay, Captain," said Sienna with a nod. Ari smiled.

"Good. For the next week, how we feel about one another shouldn't matter. Let's go back to being friends after the Games. Team before everything, okay?" Ari was relieved when everyone seemed to agree.

Yasmeen went over to the speaker and pressed PLAY. The new Little Simz album flooded through the speakers as the team got ready to train on the rink. Ari took a deep breath, turned around, and did the same.

This time around, their training session went brilliantly. Her teammates applied the feedback they'd been given, and the extra hour they had on the ice that day was so productive that they decided to treat themselves.

"This is not what I thought you meant by a team field trip," Yasmeen said as she went around painting matching flags onto her teammates' cheeks. They'd debated going back to their rooms to change into casual clothes. But instead they headed straight to the arena to rifle through the merch shop. There they found colorful wigs, T-shirts, and face paint to cheer on their Team GB friends on the curling team.

Ari's teammates had all been hyper-focused on games and training and hadn't explored the Village. And while she knew that they needed to put their dynamic as a team above everything else, she also knew they needed something to bring them together and remind them why they'd become friends in the first place. So, she'd sweet-talked the woman who worked in the Athletes Liaison office into getting the entire team tickets to that night's curling competition.

They immediately got swept up in the excitement of the crowd as they bought Olympic merch, convinced themselves that foam fingers were essential to the viewing experience, and laughed their way toward their seats.

"I think we should start a wave. If I stand up, will you join in?" asked Izzy. Ari opened her mouth to reply but it turned out that Izzy didn't need much convincing. She was having the time of her life. Izzy just stood up, threw her hands in the air, and watched with glee as the rest of their row followed along and sent a wave of arms and cheers circling around the arena.

Ari was having a good time until she glanced over and caught sight of the one person she didn't want to see. Harrison. He hadn't noticed her, but seeing him made her feel uneasy. So, she stood up, looking for an excuse to change seats so that she wouldn't be in his direct line of sight for the rest of the game.

"Does anyone want a snack?" Ari asked, performing cheerfulness. She'd made it her responsibility to make sure everyone was fed, hydrated, and happy.

"A healthy snack, or a *thank you for working so hard today yes you can have a cheat meal* snack?" Izzy asked with a conspiratorial smile. The team looked over at Ari. She'd been all business all day, trying her best to be firm with them. But when she saw the hopeful expressions on their faces, she relented. One cone of fries wasn't going to make everything fall apart. Being captain, she decided, was about balancing discipline with morale, so she nodded and agreed. Everyone immediately headed over to the food stalls.

Ari was looking through the smoothie options when she saw a familiar figure weaving his way through the crowds with a camera around his neck. She liked seeing Drew in his natural habitat. He seemed completely at ease when he was talking to people and taking photos. She watched from a distance as he photographed a group of athletes warming up on the ice, then smiled as she saw them laughing at some joke he'd told them that she couldn't hear. She could understand why each person he interacted with seemed so comfortable around him. In a world where photographers and journalists could be intrusive and push too hard, Drew had a way of making everyone feel like they were already friends. He was safe, personable, and open. The complete opposite of the type of guy Ari usually went for. But every time she saw him, she wanted to lean in.

So, when he walked over and pulled her into a hug, she did. Relaxing as she settled into his arms. There it was again, that combination of firewood, fresh laundry, and warm, musky cologne. She held on until he let go.

"I thought you were spending the day doing an *extreme team bonding* session."

"Oh, I am. Hot dogs and slushies are essential to making sure the rest of the team doesn't turn against me," she joked.

"So you and your friends fixed things?"

Ari looked over at the group of girls congregated next to the hot dog stand. They'd been deep in conversation the last time she'd seen them, but now they were looking over at her and Drew with curious eyes. Ari watched as Izzy gave her a knowing look, and all of her friends began to walk over. She needed to act fast.

"I told them about you, well, the fake version. Can you . . ." but she didn't need to ask. Drew was already draping his arm around her shoulders. Ari tried not to like it too much.

"You must be Drew." Izzy was carrying an unnaturally blue slushie that would never pass the nutrition test. Ari let it slide.

"The one who's had her smiling down at her phone all week?" Yasmeen asked. Ari *wanted* to object. While she definitely did light up each time she saw a message from Drew, she didn't want him to think that she had a crush on him or anything. But then she remembered the arm around her shoulders. Making this seem convincing was the whole point.

"You're cute together." Yasmeen was being friendly, but Ari could see the long, hard look she was giving Drew. She was the one who tried to get a read on the guys her friends were dating. And after Harrison, she knew that it was going to take a lot to convince her friends that the next guy she'd chosen was good for her, but Drew made it easy.

"*She's* cute, I'm just happy to be here," he joked. Yasmeen cracked a smile, a real one this time.

"Let me guess: Izzy, Yasmeen, and Sienna?" he said, correctly matching the descriptions she'd given him of each of her friends. "She's told me so much about you," he said with that friendly, golden retriever smile. "Let me get a photo of all of you, something for the photo diary."

Ari got into the frame and posed with her friends as Drew took photos. But she couldn't focus on the lens because her attention kept drifting back to him. To how focused he looked with a camera in front of his face and the light-hearted jokes he made with her teammates. He slipped into her life with ease, as if he'd known her friends for years, not seconds.

"Are you working the rest of the game?" Izzy asked once he was done.

"No, but I was going to edit some photos," he said, looping his camera strap back around his neck.

"Come and sit with us," Izzy said as the other girls nodded along. "There's a spare seat at the end of our row, and I know she's not saying anything but it's obvious Ari wants to hang out with you," Izzy continued, throwing her a knowing glance.

"I don't want to gate-crash," Drew said, looking over at Ari, scanning her expression for an answer.

"You wanted candids with Ari and the rest of us, right?" Yasmeen asked, never one to miss an opportunity. "What's more candid than a spontaneous team trip? And actually, come to think of it, I have a couple of questions for you," she said before asking Drew a dozen questions about how to draw enough attention to their teammates to get the brand deals and sponsorships they needed for their next season.

Drew was game, answering all her questions, giving her contact details for the people he knew at Zeus, and taking a bunch of photos of the team as they walked from the food stalls back into the arena. Ari watched on with a smile as her friends invited

Drew into their conversations, peppered him with questions, and occasionally glanced over at Ari in approval. As the rest of them took their seats, Drew put his arm around Ari's shoulders.

"Sorry for the ambush," Ari said, quiet enough that only the two of them could hear.

"Don't be. Anyway, aren't we due for our third fake date?"

26

Drew

Drew was under investigation. Ari's teammates had been peppering him with direct, if not slightly intrusive, questions ever since they'd sat down to watch the rest of the curling match. *What's your relationship like with the women in your life? How did your last relationship end? Where do you see yourself in five years?* He took them in stride because he knew how important it was to make sure a girl's friends liked him. Even if he was just her two-week fake boyfriend. So, he expertly maneuvered their questions and skated his way out of any answers that would force him to mention Thandie. He hadn't told his sister about Ari yet, or told Ari about his sister. It was a necessary conversation, but now wasn't the time to complicate things, so he decided to wait until they were alone.

"When you said you and your teammates were having a big night out, this is not what I thought you meant," Drew said as they watched players sweeping brooms across the ice.

"I will not tolerate any curling slander. It's a slow burn, but it's beautiful," she said before whispering excited commentaries and tossing out witty observations about every second of the game.

"You're going to kill it at the nursing home in sixty years," he joked.

"Oh, no doubt, I'm going to be the eighty-year-old who runs the annual curling tournament like the navy," she laughed.

"And I'll be the old man who spends hours telling everyone the stories behind his photo albums," he said as she pulled her eyes away from the ice and looked over at him.

"Will I be the long-lost love of your life whose photos make you tear up?" she asked.

"No, you'll be my gray-haired love of my life. Walking around the common room wearing your gold Olympic medals while telling some random man named Gerald you saw him cheating in the bingo game," he said, picturing it in his mind.

"I think I'll be your glamorous ex-wife by then," she said, absentmindedly glancing down at the toffee popcorn box on his lap.

"We're breaking up?" he joked as he handed her the box. She'd insisted on sticking to healthy snacks, but he knew she couldn't resist a sweet treat.

"Yeah, I think we'll get married, divorced, and remarried. Maybe twice actually," she said as she popped a few kernels in her mouth.

"Like true romantics." He nodded.

"You'll be the Burton to my Taylor," she said. He didn't understand the reference, but the smile on her face told him it was a good thing. "Speaking of love, did you tell your grandparents about USC?" she asked, the competition unfolding on the ice long forgotten.

"That's at the top of the long list of things I'm trying to avoid right now," he admitted.

"Oh, sorry, we don't have to talk about it," she backtracked.

"No, I want to," he reassured her, surprising himself. Ari had so much distance from his real life that she felt like the easiest person to open up to about it.

There was a long list of reasons for him not to even consider going back to California. As much as Grandpa insisted he could look after his wife alone, Drew knew that eventually her condition would deteriorate to the point where she would need more support. They were both in their seventies, and while they were more active than the average forty-year-old, it would be irresponsible to let them handle it alone. And then there were the financial reasons. While his grandparents had done pretty well for themselves and spent years building up his college fund, he couldn't justify going back to school when he knew they could spend that money helping Grandma get the very best medical treatment. Plus, Thandie was a full-time professional athlete, and female athletes especially were infamously underpaid. He couldn't bear the idea of her moving back home or reallocating any of her earnings to help out with the care he knew he was better positioned to contribute to. Which is what he told Ari, careful not to let slip what exactly his sister did for work. He'd cross that bridge when he needed to.

"But don't you feel like she'd want to know?" Ari asked. "I'd be pretty disappointed if I knew my sister was going to miss out on college to protect me."

She was right. But Thandie was his younger sister, it was on him to make the sacrifice.

"I know. She's definitely going to be hurt when she finds out that I kept it a secret. But I'd rather postpone the conversation than have it before I can control the outcome."

He refused to add stress to the two most important weeks of her life—he and Grandpa had agreed to that. But Ari shook her head in disagreement. Her gaze was going back and forth be-tween him and the competition as the players swept their brooms across the ice with an intense level of focus.

"You can't postpone things forever to control— Yes!" she said, getting up to cheer as Team GB hit the target. She and her team-mates clapped and high-fived one another as if it was them on the ice. They were just spectators today, but their enthusiasm made him realize just how excited they probably got in the aftermath of their games. Most of Drew's assignments clashed with Ari's games, but the joy on her face as she sat down made him resolve to find a way to watch at least one of her matches in the next couple of days. He wanted to see her doing what she loved.

"So, what I was saying, before that beautiful moment, was that secrets have a way of blowing up in your face," she said, taking a cheery sip of her smoothie as the teams on the ice switched sides. He knew she was talking about his grandmother's diagnosis, but he couldn't help but wonder if that's what would happen when he eventually explained to her that his sister was her archrival.

"Is that from experience?" he asked, nervous.

"Yep. Remember how I told you about my family drama?"

"Your mom and sister's fight?"

She nodded.

"My dad called to tell me about his engagement months ago. He sent both of us an invite. But we kept it a secret from our mom until my sister announced that Dad had already booked her flight. It was the secretiveness that hurt her."

"But if your sister *hadn't* accepted the invite, don't you think keeping the secret would have protected your mom's feelings?"

She shrugged. "That's what I tried to convince myself, but finding out once we'd already made our decisions made her feel like we'd betrayed her." She turned in her seat to face him. "I get wanting to protect someone's feelings. I do it all the time. But people have a right to know the secrets that will affect them, even if it leads to an uncomfortable conversation," she said before returning her attention to the curling match.

Her words made it clear to him that the longer he kept Thandie's identity a secret, the more likely Ari was to be upset when she found out the truth. So, he made a mental note to tell her before they left the stadium. Then he sat back and watched the second half of the game with Ari and her teammates. But before he could focus his attention on the ice, or the odd rules that governed the game, a horn blared and the match came to a sudden pause.

"What's going on?" asked Ari, looking around and trying to figure out what was interrupting the competition.

"I have no idea," said Drew, as they scanned the ice and audience for some sort of sign. After a moment they noticed a bunch of staff reaching for their walkie-talkies and a group of officials huddling into a hushed discussion. After overhearing a few conversations and checking his phone, Drew figured out what was going on. It turned out that there was a tech issue with the live broadcast feed streaming the competition out to the rest of the world, so the competition had come to a halt. The officials looked stressed out and the camera crews were glancing over at each other in despair. Millions of viewers tuned in to watch the Olympics, and each minute of lost time cost the broadcasters millions of dollars. Drew could only imagine how chaotic things probably were behind the scenes as they worked to fix the issue. The audience watching the competition at home from their TV screens had probably been taken from a live feed of the game to a studio recording of commentators making small talk to avoid an empty screen. But that wasn't an option inside the arena. So instead, the speakers around them started playing music. At first, Drew thought they were just filling the silence. That it would be a short musical interlude to kill time, but then he heard the opening beats of Stevie Wonder's "As." A wave of excitement filled the room as colorful lights started flashing. A camera began to scan the audience and project people's faces onto the screen.

"Is that . . . ?" said Drew.

"The kiss cam?" said Ari, looking at him wide eyed. "I love the kiss cam!" she said, grinning as she pointed up at the TV monitor.

The screen filled up with hearts as the camera quickly flashed across audience members around the room. First, it landed on a sweet-looking older couple who laughed and then kissed on the cheek. Then it landed on two people wearing matching New Zealand fan T-shirts who immediately went in for a full-on make-out session. It panned to a toddler who blew a kiss, making the whole audience say *aww* in response. And then, Drew saw his own face up on the screen. Ari was beaming, but she froze when she realized what was happening. They quickly turned toward each other with startled expressions. Harrison sat in their direct eyeline, looking on and shooting them daggers. Her teammates were excitedly cheering her on. They needed to act fast.

"Ari," he whispered as they locked eyes.

"Drew," she replied, her expression something he couldn't quite place.

"Is this . . ."

"An emergency? Yes," she said without hesitation.

"I thought so." He smiled.

"But . . . kiss me like you mean it," she whispered.

Drew leaned in closer, brushed a curl away, and traced a finger down the side of her face, from her hair to her cheek, to her lips and then down to her chin. He slowly tilted her face up until they were just a breath away, and then his lips softly landed on hers. He instantly felt a spark. One that made its way across the entire length of his body. Her lips were soft and gentle against his, as if asking him a question. So, he answered it by placing a hand on her face, pulling her in, and meeting her with a slow, tender-but-firm kiss. Drew felt like he'd just touched a live wire. His whole being set alight as she traced a trail along the stubble on his chin and then down to his neck before wrapping her arms around it. Their lips melding together and moving in harmony as if they'd known each other longer than their minds had. It was the same feeling he'd felt on New Year's Eve, the same tension in the air when he'd seen her after the opening ceremony, and the heady, electrifying feeling at Schokoladenzeit.

Drew was kissing her like he meant it . . . because he did.

27

Ari

DAY FIVE OF THE 2026 OLYMPICS

When their lips finally parted, three things became abundantly clear:

1. Drew was an excellent kisser.
2. "As" by Stevie Wonder was one of the greatest love songs of all time.
3. Ari was in big trouble.

The kiss cam had left them long ago, but her hand was still tracing the stubble around Drew's mouth. Her lips were still tingling from the intoxicating effect of his lips, and as they held each other's gaze, she realized that there was nothing she could do to stop her feelings for him from multiplying. The arena was filled with music and conversation, but they sat in what felt like silence. Looking at each other as they adjusted to the clear distinction between who they'd been before the kiss and what might become of them after it. But then a horn blared to mark the start of the next round, breaking the spell. Ari and Drew pulled apart, looked away, and redirected their attention back to the ice rink.

Ari tried her best to focus on watching the curling competition and letting the slow progression of the game bring her back down to earth. During the breaks, she encouraged Drew to use her teammates all being in one place as an opportunity to get some more photos for his behind-the-scenes photo diaries. She watched as he asked them questions and captured them in one of the rarer moments of the Games when everyone genuinely seemed to be having a good time. But as much as she enjoyed cheering with her teammates and watching the curlers sweep, the game wasn't enough to distract her from the fact that she and Drew were still leaning against each other, their shoulders side by side.

She was supposed to be watching the competition, but her mind kept replaying the kiss. She'd told him to kiss her like he meant it, but all she'd meant by that was to make it look convincing enough for her teammates, and Harrison, who was still in her eyeline, to think they were in a real relationship. Not to kiss her in a way that made *her* feel like it was real. But it had felt real. Like a genuine, tender, and romantic moment. A natural culmination of the tension that had been lingering between them since New Year's Eve.

Every time she reached for her drink and they brushed hands, she felt a pleasant tingle run down her arm. When she explained a convoluted curling rule and he looked at her with those gorgeous, intent brown eyes, she felt like placing her hand on his cheek and kissing him again. Her teammates must have sensed the fact that she wanted to be alone with him because, when the game ended and he put his coat back on, Izzy winked at her, Yasmeen smiled, and Sienna gave her a knowing look. They made excuses to speed ahead and told her they'd meet her at GB House at the end of the day.

"Do you have anywhere to be tonight?" Drew asked once they left.

"No, I'm done with training for the day. Do you want to take more photos?" she asked, grateful for an excuse to keep hanging out with him.

"Yeah, we could do something in the arena?" he said, looking out at their surroundings. The arena was littered with half-empty cups, discarded flags, and scattered decorations. The seats were emptying out and the lights were down. It was like the moment you realized the party was over—the strange, euphoric but slightly melancholic limbo between one moment and the next. Ari and Drew walked around the arena taking photos and talking about all the other times they'd experienced similar feelings. Ari told him about some of the best and worst postmatch moments she'd had in the last few years, and he told her about some of the strangest things he'd witnessed while taking photos at parties back in California.

"Can you look to the left for a sec? As if you're watching that screen?"

"Why, is this my best side?" she said, turning.

"They're all your best side. I just want to get a shot of your jacket."

So, she posed in the middle of the bleachers and smiled as she watched him climb up and down the stairs, switching between cameras and lenses to get the perfect shot. She could tell how much he loved what he did. It was evident in how much care and attention he put into framing things just right. It was her favorite trait in a person: loving something enough to go all in.

When they took their final photo, left the stadium, and stepped outside, the sky was deep dark blue. The air carried a crisp chill. Ari could see the snow-capped mountains in the distance, hear the crunch of gritting salt beneath her boots, and feel the icy chill in the air coating her skin. It was February in Switzerland, and the Olympics was experiencing one of the coldest Winter Games in years. But she instantly felt warmer when Drew put his arm around her shoulders. Like she would brave the harshest of winters if she could just find a way to stay in the gap between his arm and chest. She looked up at him, but he was looking in the distance. She followed his gaze until they landed on the same sight: a group of Team GB snowboarders on Harrison's team who had just walked out of the arena and onto the same path. When one of them glanced over, Drew pulled her in closer and kissed her cheek. She knew that this, like the kiss cam performance, was only for their benefit. He was just playing the role of the romantic interest in her two-week charade. But she couldn't help but imagine what it would be like for him to do it just because he wanted to. Just because he liked her. She wanted to extricate herself from the early onset of complicated feelings, but she couldn't help but lean into his shoulder. She told herself that she was just doing it to play along. But the wave of butterflies she felt each time he glanced down at her didn't make it feel like they were *just playing along*.

As they walked past a bar, Ari spotted a TV screen broadcasting the other competitions unfolding across the Village and sighed a little as she remembered that the Games would be over soon. She and Drew would be on different sides of the Atlantic in less than two weeks. Each yard they walked took them one step closer to the end of what they'd barely begun. It was a fake relationship with real parameters and a clear expiration date. But while she knew that there were a dozen reasons why she and Drew wouldn't last past the closing ceremony, she couldn't help but want to stay in this moment with him for a little while longer.

They walked away from the arena, out into the Village, and down a long, icy path. Talking about everything except the lingering tension in the air.

"My teammates like you," Ari said. "Which is pretty high praise, because they don't like anyone." She smiled as she thought back to all the questions he'd gotten right in their interrogation.

"I'm glad. I get why you're friends with them. They seem tough but loyal, funny, too. The right people to have in your corner."

Things had been so tense between them since January that sometimes Ari forgot that their friendship was ten years deep. They only called her out because they loved her, but it was hard to know she wasn't living up to their expectations.

"Well, thank you for stepping in back there, with Harrison watching and everything."

"Have you spoken to him since you saw him outside the office?" he asked curiously.

"No. To be honest, I think I've fixed it. He hasn't tried to call or come up to me. I think the combination of confronting him and being seen with you sent the message."

"So, I guess my work here is done." His eyes were searching for a response. Ari didn't want their arrangement to be over. She knew that they probably didn't need to go on any more fake dates or play things up for Harrison's sake. But she liked spending time with him.

"Do you have everything you need for the photo diary already?" she asked, trying and failing to sound nonchalant.

"Oh, you're not getting rid of me that fast. We've got a contract to fulfill, remember?" He smiled.

"Good, I don't want this to end yet," she said without thinking.

"Me neither," he said softly as Ari glanced away from him for a moment and looked up. It was snowing. Tiny crystals were falling so gently that they were almost imperceptible. But as Ari and Drew walked down the path, the snowfall got heavier. A rush of snowflakes floated down from the sky and danced around them. The glow from the streetlights made the flakes glisten as they settled on treetops and coated the Village in bright, white dust. Ari looked up in delight. Thinking that sudden winter snowfalls were the closest thing to magic.

"We're still doing no consequences, no judgment, right?" he asked.

"Always." She nodded. He paused for a moment, then looked down at her reluctantly and began to speak.

"If we were going home to the same city after this, would this still end with your final game?"

"This?"

"Us."

"You'd want to keep on fake-dating after the Olympics?" she asked, knowing that's not what he meant.

"*Dating* dating. For real this time," he said, looking down at her. As she watched a snowflake melt on his skin, she felt a short pang of hope.

"If we were going back to the same city, yes. But we're going to be on opposite sides of the ocean in a couple of weeks," she said, reaching out to hold his hand anyway. "So, I guess this will have to be enough."

It was a beautiful night. The path was lit with streetlights, and the sky was sprinkled with stars. But nothing above them came close to rivaling the moon. It covered everything with a silver, shimmery glow, making an ordinary night dreamlike. Ari was wearing a bunch of layers and thermal gloves. But she'd accidentally left her scarf in the locker room that morning. She spent her whole life on the ice, so she was used to the cold, but there was a particularly sharp chill in the air that night, and as much as she loved the snow, she could feel herself starting to shiver. Drew must have noticed because he unwrapped his arm from around her shoulders, stopped in the middle of the path, and wordlessly took off his scarf.

"It's okay, I'm not that cold," she began. But Drew gently traced his finger against her cheek and looked her in the eye, the sides of his lips curving up.

"Goosebumps," he said, tracing a small circle at the bottom of her chin.

Ari wasn't sure if they'd been caused by the snow or the lightness of his touch. So, she stood still as Drew draped his huge blue scarf across her shoulders, lightly grazing her skin as he wrapped it around. The scarf was soft and woolly with the texture of something well loved. It smelled like fresh laundry, firewood, and hot chocolate. When he was done wrapping her up in it, he started walking again. His footsteps left gentle marks in the snow.

For a moment, Ari just stood there and watched him, struck by how much that small gesture had affected her. But then Drew turned around, realizing they'd fallen out of step. He smiled at her, reaching his arm out as if to offer her his hand. The side of his face was highlighted by the moon, and his silhouette was framed by a thousand tiny snowflakes. Against the backdrop of the night sky, he looked exactly the same way he had on New Year's Eve. Like the boy she'd met on a whim and told all her secrets. She knew there were at least a dozen reasons not to make a move, differences that would make for a rocky journey, and truths she would hold close to protect herself from hurt and hurting. But she decided that if she was only going to know Drew for another eleven days, she was going to do everything she could to stretch them out into the kind of memory she could spend the rest of her life replaying. So, she ran across the icy path before she could change her mind.

She put a hand on either side of his face and pressed her lips to his. Fast and urgent, as if he'd disappear like the snowflakes on her skin if she dared to hesitate. She kissed him like she meant it, and he quickly reciprocated. Leaning in and parting. One of his hands slowly slid around her waist, clutched her side, and drew her near with a grip that brought their bodies closer and made her feel a deep pang of longing. His other hand cupped her chin, gently tilted it up, and traced small, delicate circles against her skin as he kissed her, deep and slow. Taking his time, as if she was something to be savored. They were outside in the middle of a snowfall, and she was wearing seven layers of clothing, eight if she counted his scarf. But the way he held her made her body think it was summer, a searingly hot wave of desire washing over her as his teeth met her bottom lip. The delicious dizziness pulling them even closer together.

If the first kiss had been a question, this kiss was a series of answers.

Yes, I like you. No, I don't think this is a good idea. But yeah . . . we're definitely going to do this again.

28

Drew

DAY SIX OF THE 2026 OLYMPICS

Drew almost dropped his phone in the middle of the café when he saw the message that had just popped up in his emails. The team at Zeus had been sending him on assignments to photograph the athletes they sponsored all week. And when those emails arrived, he picked up his camera bag, walked out into the snow, and immediately went to find and photograph the next athlete on their list. But this assignment was different. This athlete was different.

MESSAGE FROM: Zeus BTS team

Key people: Harrison Cavendish

Key sports: Snowboarding

Assignment: Harrison was the lead ambassador for our AW 25 campaign. He's taken a few losses this week, but he's still a fan favorite. So can you get a few shots of him at practice?

Drew was standing by the pickup counter of the coffee shop, racking his brain to find an excuse to get out of his next assignment. He stared at his phone, wondering if he could find a loophole to avoid having to see Harrison in person. But he knew he couldn't avoid this, not when his career depended on acing each assignment.

"Double shot espresso?" asked the barista with the tone of someone on their third or fourth time repeating themselves. Drew looked up. He couldn't figure out how long he'd been waiting there. But from the slightly irritated looks of the other customers, his drink had been called out more than just a few times.

"Thank you, and quick question. How well do you know the Village?"

The barista, who according to his name badge was Jørgen, gave him a knowing look. "I've been brewing coffee here since they started building it."

"So, can you tell me the fastest way to get to the snowboard training center?" Drew asked. He was dreading the assignment that lay ahead of him, but he was in St. Moritz for work. So, he took Jørgen's directions and rode a shuttle bus to the southwest side of the Village where the training centers were.

He had a brief panic at the security gates when he couldn't find his press credentials, but he quickly recovered when he realized his lanyard had just found its way to the bottom of his camera bag. He was handing it over to the security guard when he finally spotted the subject of that morning's assignment.

Harrison was dressed in his Team GB uniform and standing in the middle of a group of people who seemed entertained by whatever story he was telling. In any other circumstance, Drew might have thought he seemed like a nice guy. He had an easy, carefree demeanor about him. The vibe of the kind of person who breezed his way in and out of every room he entered. However,

Drew had gleaned enough from his conversations with Ari to know better than to take Harrison at face value. But he still had a job to do, so he walked across the reception toward the group of athletes. He was about to introduce himself to Harrison when he spotted a familiar face in the crowd.

"Thandie?" he asked, startled as he saw his sister among the group of athletes wearing training uniforms and carrying their kit bags. He noticed a few of her other teammates, too. When Thandie spotted him, she shot him the subtle *don't embarrass me* look she'd been giving him ever since she was a little girl.

"Drew, you know the girls. But this is Harrison, he's a snowboarder on Team GB," she said, gesturing over to Harrison, introducing him as if she thought Drew would be excited to meet him.

"You know each other?" Drew asked, glancing over at Harrison, who was giving him a curious look.

"Yeah," Thandie said, her eyes lighting up. "Me and Harrison might be doing a campaign together after the Olympics."

Her voice was full of hope, and Drew understood why. At twenty-one, his sister was already an incredibly successful athlete. She was one of the best players in North America and skated for one of the country's top professional teams during tournament season. But that success had never translated to the kind of brand deals and sponsorships that the high-profile men in winter sports got. He'd had a bunch of conversations with her over the years about how hard it was to build a financially viable career in sports. She'd concluded that she would need to get a huge deal to sustain her career the way she wanted to.

"It's still being confirmed, so don't tell anyone, but it could be a game changer." She smiled. "Wait, do you know Harrison?"

Harrison and Drew locked eyes. Drew could tell he recognized him. But to explain how they knew of each other would mean having to explain that he knew Ari, which was a conversation he didn't want to have yet. So, he made sure to speak up before Harrison did.

"No, I'm just here on assignment. I'm Drew, I'm here to take photos for Zeus," Drew said, pointing to his camera bag. "Shall we head out?" he asked, trying to remove his sister from the situation as soon as possible.

"Sure, let me just grab this," Harrison said, picking his kit bag up from the ground but then gesturing between Drew and Thandie. "Wait, I forgot to ask, how do you know each other?"

"He's my older brother, only by like eleven months, though. We're kind of like twins, but I got all the athleticism," Thandie teased before waving them off and heading over to her training session.

When she left, the two men stood in silence for a moment before Drew began to walk in the direction of the practice slopes. Drew did his best to keep their conversation to a minimum as he begrudgingly took photos of Harrison walking through the snow and then directed Harrison to reposition his board so he could capture him in different types of motion.

"Your sister, huh?" Harrison said after Drew had gotten a few shots of him at the edge of a slope.

"Yes," he said, hoping short answers would kill the conversation.

Drew took his second camera out of its bag and attached it to a special wide-angle lens. He wanted to ask Harrison to take a chairlift up the mountain so he could capture him snowboarding again, but Harrison kept pushing.

"Are you close?" Harrison asked, undeterred.

"Mm-hmm."

"And she's okay with you dating the girl who broke her leg?"

Harrison asked, giving him a long, hard look. Drew had done his best to avoid the topic, but it was inevitable.

"Who told you that? Thandie or Ari?" Drew asked, trying not to give himself away.

"Your sister. We've been spending *a lot* of time together, you know," Harrison said. The emphasis made Drew tense up and glare at him. Harrison put his hands in the air in surrender, but his mouth turned up into a smirk.

"For the campaign, of course. The sponsorship team wanted to see if we have enough in common to go on a PR tour together after the Games. And it turns out, we get along *really* well," Harrison said.

Drew knew he was being weird and suggestive to rile him up. And he might have been successful if Drew didn't know his sister so well. Thandie could generally only tolerate a few people, and guys like Harrison were the type she avoided at all costs. She had zero patience for golden boys and false prophets. So, if they were getting along as well as Harrison claimed they were, his sister was either just keeping it cute and cordial to secure the brand deal she wanted, or the two of them had hit upon a genuine shared interest.

"We realized we have Ari in common," Harrison said, confirming Drew's second theory. "She kind of screwed us both over."

"Ari didn't screw you over, you were just a shitty boyfriend," Drew said without thinking. Harrison raised an eyebrow.

"Oh, so you've discussed me." He looked pleased with himself. "Sorry, it probably sucks to be the rebound. But don't take it personally, she just doesn't know how to get over me."

"Can you put your ski goggles on? The team at Zeus wants more photos of you in the merch," Drew said, deciding to skirt the conversation Harrison was trying to pull him into. But the distraction only made Harrison more curious. He stopped and examined Drew for a moment. He must have sensed his evasive body language, because his eyebrows raised and his eyes widened.

"Ohhh," Harrison said knowingly. "Thandie doesn't know, does she? That you're seeing Ari."

"It's not—"

"Wow, they hate each other. You know that, right?" Harrison almost looked impressed. "I'll hand it to you, even I wouldn't hook up with someone my sister hates."

"We're not . . . Ari doesn't . . ." Drew stammered. He couldn't explain himself, especially not to Harrison. "I'm going to tell her later."

Telling the truth proved to be a mistake, because as soon as the words left his mouth, a sly smirk crept up onto Harrison's face.

"So neither of them knows?" Harrison asked, searching his expression.

"Neither of them *needs* to know," Drew said firmly.

"So what are you willing to do to make sure they don't find out, huh?"

"I'm not doing this with you. Could you hold your snowboard up?" he asked, trying to redirect the conversation back to the photo shoot. But Harrison wasn't going to let it go. In fact, he seemed pretty pleased with this new information.

"I'm sure she's probably told you all sorts of exaggerated stories about me. But me and Ari always end up getting back together. So cut your losses and break up," Harrison said with the casual tone of someone used to getting what he wanted.

"Why would I do that?" Drew asked, irritated.

"Because if you don't break up, I'll tell your sister," Harrison said. Drew shook his head as he took a photo of Harrison leaning against his bright red snowboard. He didn't want to be here, but there was no way he would let this guy stop him from fulfilling an assignment.

"What are you, a twelve-year-old boy who thinks he can blackmail me by . . . reporting me to my little sister? Grow up," Drew said, surprised that Harrison thought he could manipulate him so easily.

"Okay then, break up or I'll make sure your sister doesn't get the deal," Harrison said, staring him down.

"You can't do that," Drew said, unaffected. "You don't have that kind of power."

"Yes, I do," said Harrison with an ominously level voice. "I'm the lead winter ambassador. I have sway at Zeus. If I tell them that the girl they had in mind for the next campaign isn't the right pick because she's *difficult to work with*, they'll believe me."

"You wouldn't," Drew said. He liked to think of himself as a good judge of character and could tell that Harrison was used to throwing around empty threats.

"Oh, but you see, I definitely would." Harrison smirked. "Don't get me wrong, your sister is good at what does. But there are dozens of other female athletes. Why do you think Thandie got the offer in the first place? You think I just picked some girl my ex hated by *accident*?"

Drew stood still. Startled by Harrison's calculations. He'd picked Thandie to get back at Ari?

"You would be that petty?"

"Not petty. Strategic." Harrison shrugged. "What better way of showing her what she's missing out on than by making it clear how quickly I can replace her?" Harrison smiled. It was ominous. The type of smile Drew could tell he used in equal parts to charm and disarm. But Drew didn't bow down to bullies, so he removed the lens from his camera, switched it off, and packed it away.

"I think we're done here," Drew said with an air of finality.

Zeus wanted photos, but Drew didn't need to endure another moment with this guy to fulfill his assignment.

"Be careful, it's icy out there. Wouldn't want you to slip," Harrison said, his voice dripping insincerity. "I mean it, Drew. Break up."

"Or what? You'll try and *ruin my life*?" Drew mocked.

"Fuck around and find out."

29

Ari

"If I tell you something, will you promise not to get mad?" Izzy asked from the other end of the phone. Ari was in her Village bedroom, packing her kit bag before heading out for training.

"Okay, but why would I be mad?" Ari said, pausing as she folded her jersey.

"No reason . . . but could you come to the medical center?" Izzy asked sheepishly. Ari closed her eyes and took a deep breath.

When she got to the medical center, she saw her teammates crowded around Natalie, a defense player. They all looked over at her with guilty facial expressions. Now Ari understood why Izzy had made her promise not to get mad.

"She sprained her ankle doing *what*?" Ari asked in disbelief as she approached them.

"It was just supposed to be a bit of fun," Izzy said, grimacing.

"Iz, why are you always at the scene of the crime?" Ari said, dropping her bag as she walked over to Natalie, who was trying and failing to hold back tears.

"Are you in a lot of pain?" Ari asked, taking her teammate's hand. Natalie just nodded, her cheeks damp and her eyes red. Ari wanted to be mad at her, but she'd promised not to. So instead, she leaned forward and gave Natalie a hug. She didn't need to berate her, the injury itself was enough to remind her that she'd messed up. That they'd all messed up.

One of the most loved Olympic traditions was the ritual of swapping pins. The athletes were all given official pins by their home country, and a few of the more famous sporting figures made their own custom badges. So, Izzy and a few of their other teammates had made it their mission to collect a pin from every single competing country. Their lanyards were covered in metallic souvenirs from the countries that had sent the biggest delegations to St. Moritz. But there were a few rare pins from smaller nations that they were desperate to track down. So, when they'd bumped into an Emirati skier, they'd immediately tried to convince him to swap pins. It was his country's first time competing at the Olympics, which made his pins the rarest of them all. But he'd only brought a handful of pins and could only offer the group one. So, Izzy had come up with a grand idea. She and her teammates would do a good old-fashioned race to decide who got to keep his pin. But instead of finding a running track or postponing it to *after* they'd finished the most important tournament of their lives, they'd decided to start the morning by lacing up their skates and racing across the ice. Natalie brushed her hair aside to reveal the red-and-green pin on her lanyard.

"I won, but at what cost?" Natalie laughed through her tears. The race had ended with a painful fall. But luckily, she'd escaped with an ankle sprain instead of a break. Their team medic had reassured her that she'd be able to play safely, though painfully, in a couple of days. But her injury meant that the team would lose one of their best defenders two days before their fourth preliminary game.

Ari reassured Natalie that everything would be okay, promised to go back and visit her after the game, and then ushered the rest of her teammates out of the medical center.

"Coach is going to kill me when he finds out," Izzy said, looking panicked as they all walked down the corridor. Coach McLaughlin had zero tolerance for foolish decisions, and Izzy's race suggestion would be enough to have her and the rest of the team banned from doing anything but training for the rest of the Games. But Ari wasn't going to let that happen.

"He's not going to kill you, because he's not going to find out," she said, pausing in the middle of the corridor. Izzy looked over at her in surprise, and so did the rest of the girls who'd been involved in the misguided race.

"You're not going to tell him?" asked a girl named Emily.

"No. He doesn't need to know. If it comes up, tell him that she hurt herself because I asked everyone to do laps around the ice rink."

"But why would you take the blame? It was my stupid suggestion," Izzy said.

"Because team above everything, right? Natalie's injured, and you'll all have to live with that. But beating yourselves up isn't going to make you play any better," Ari said. She'd happily take one for the team if it meant they wouldn't spend the rest of the day worrying. But she realized she was going to have to put her foot down. Again.

"Okay, listen up," Ari said, raising her voice to get the rest of the team's attention as they stood in the hallway of the medical center. "What you did this morning? Unacceptable." Internally, she flinched. She hated putting on her captain voice, but she had to take a stand.

"We're not the men's team, who can fool around, make dumb decisions, and still be given grace," she said. Their male counterparts had been caught at a cabin party in the mountains last night and gotten away with a slap on their wrists, but there were different standards for the women's team. "We can't afford to make any silly mistakes. I get it, you want to have fun. Take the edge off a little. But this isn't a regional tournament, this is the Olympics. I need you all to get it together and start treating this more seriously."

Izzy nodded, looking down at her shoes. She seemed embarrassed, but Ari didn't have time to try to make her feel better. They were friends, but she was going to have to deal with the consequences of her actions by herself.

"Jasmine?" she said, looking over at one of her teammates who played defense. "I need you to step up and take Natalie's place. You're ready to be on the ice." Jasmine looked nervous but just nodded and gripped the kit bag on her shoulder.

"Soha? I heard you came in last." Soha opened her mouth as if to protest the allegation, but then she clamped it shut, realizing that wasn't going to help her. "Well, I spoke to Coach after our last game. Today you're going to be on the starting line." Soha nodded. It would be her first game of the week, and Ari knew that being selected would boost her confidence for the rest of the tournament.

"Izzy, you're going on the bench."

"What? You can't be serious."

"Serious as death, which is what could have happened this morning if your *race* had ended differently."

Izzy grimaced, looked down at her kit bag, and then gave her a nod. "Okay, *Captain*," Izzy said, but Ari could hear the note of annoyance in her voice. She would have usually let it slide, but not today.

"Do we have a problem?"

"No," Izzy said quickly.

"Good. Because there's no way I'm letting *this* be the reason we go home."

30

Drew

Thandie: Are you friends with Harrison now?

Drew: No? Why?

Thandie: I just saw him.

Thandie: He told me to pass on a message, so I thought you'd bonded over photos or something?

Drew: What was the message?

Thandie: It's a photo. Wait, let me send it.

Drew nervously watched the three dots until a photo arrived. He opened it to reveal a photo of Harrison at a party. He was posing with Klaus Lindberg, the guy whose dad owned Zeus. As Drew examined the photo, he realized it had been taken at the New Year's Eve party they'd all gone to. He didn't know what rattled him more: the fact that Harrison might actually be able to leverage his apparent friendship with Klaus to get what he wanted, or the fact that he'd sent the message through his sister to try to intimidate him.

It was unnerving, but he refused to let Harrison's taunts get to his head. So, he told his sister it was just an inside joke and tried to hatch a plan to deal with all of his problems without anybody getting hurt.

He knew he needed to talk to Thandie about Ari and make sure Harrison didn't get in the way of his sister's shot at a big brand deal. But the problem his mind kept wandering back to was the email burning a hole in his pocket. There was no denying it anymore: Drew wanted to go back to college. The email had unlocked a wave of feelings he'd spent the past three months doing his best to repress. But the more time he spent running back and forth across the Village, the more he missed doing this kind of work in LA.

After photographing a pair of figure skaters at practice that morning, he'd gone to the camera shop to get his first few rolls of film developed. He was pleasantly surprised by how well they'd turned out. The photos of Luiz showing him around the press office. The shot of Hans Leitner telling him stories in the chairlift. And the stills of Ari looking out at the sunrise and then smiling over at him. He knew he could take his camera anywhere in the world and still get to do what he loved. But as he leafed through the photos, he realized that he was probably never going to get the opportunity to capture photos like this, or the ones he'd taken at college, if he stayed in Wisconsin.

"Can I get these scanned and digitized?" asked the familiar voice of a man who'd just walked into the shop. Drew looked up; it was Hans Leitner carrying a whole bag of film rolls. He looked stressed out.

"Busy week?" Drew said as he looked at the rolls of film the woman behind the desk was starting to organize. Hans shook his head and let out a heavy sigh.

"Midproduction chaos, you know how it is."

Drew *did not* know how it was. The only documentary he'd ever worked on was a student film. But he was curious, so he asked Hans about it.

"My unit photographer quit yesterday," Hans explained. "He got booked onto a big streamer gig and fled to their studios overnight. Left me for a Hollywood check and some C-minus A-listers, but what can you do?" Hans shrugged as if something like this wasn't that unusual.

It made sense. Hans had one of those deeply respected careers that translated to Academy Awards, not box office hits. His productions had gotten the reputation of being like apprenticeships for people on their way to greatness. Aspiring filmmakers worked with Hans for two years, learned a lot, got introduced to a variety of interesting people, and then left to become the next big thing.

"So, are you flying someone new in to finish the job?" Drew asked, intrigued.

"No, one of my ADs is going to do it for the rest of the week. But we still have three months before we wrap production. After this we go to New York, Toronto, and London. So now I have to go through the entire hiring process again." Drew was about to ask more, but Hans's attention shifted.

"Are these yours?" Hans asked, spotting the photos Drew had laid out on the table.

"Yeah, wait, let me show you my favorites," Drew said, eagerly shuffling them around. He wasn't one of those people who hated showing his work, because he'd learned to detach himself from the final product. Drew saw himself as a messenger, someone who noticed beautiful things and had made it his responsibility to capture them. So, whenever a photo came out well, he put it down to the subject, not him. Hans leafed through the photos and then pushed three forward. One of Ari seated in the middle of the curling arena surrounded by a sea of leftover flags and paper cups. Another of his grandparents jumping up to cheer Thandie on at one of her games. And then, to his disappointment, a photo of Harrison glaring into the camera as he lifted his snowboard.

"These ones are very good," Hans said, his voice neutral. "What are you doing when the Olympics end?"

"I . . . I don't know," Drew admitted, wishing he had a better answer for the man he so desperately wanted to impress. Hans just nodded and walked back over to the front of the store.

Drew wanted to ask him questions, seek out advice, but Hans had moved on, already deep in conversation with the woman behind the desk. So instead, he unlocked his phone and looked up the website for Hans's production company. Just as he'd hoped. The job ad was already up. Junior unit photographer, six weeks, in New York, Toronto, and London. The contract was due to start at the start of March and end in the middle of April. Just two weeks before the start of the spring term Drew knew he couldn't reenroll for.

Working on a Leitner documentary would give him more experience than a whole year at college. But as soon as the idea came up, Drew's brain began to list the reasons why he shouldn't even apply. A lot could change with his grandma's health in six weeks, and it felt irresponsible to be traveling back and forth when they already had medical appointments booked back home. But even that was getting ahead of himself. Drew had taken three, in Hans's words, good photos. That wasn't enough to get a job on the set of a big documentary. So, Drew closed the tab, waved Hans goodbye, and left the camera shop. Because he had a date to get ready for.

It was two days before Valentine's Day. But Ari's final preliminary game was on the fourteenth, so they'd agreed to make this pre-Valentine's dinner their final date. Her plan was to post a photo of them online after the date, as an official hard launch to seal the coffin on her and Harrison's relationship. When she'd brought it up, Drew had agreed to avoid sparking suspicion. But he knew he needed to do whatever he could to prevent Ari from posting them as a couple that night. Thandie couldn't find out that way; she would burn him at the stake if she learned about it on Instagram. Plus, Harrison's threat still loomed over him. Drew didn't believe he would actually follow through; he seemed like a pretty spineless guy. The knowledge that Harrison *could* sabotage things made Drew nervous, but not nervous enough to risk telling either of the women in his life the truth in the middle of their competitions. The conversation would end badly no matter when he spoke to them. So, he decided that the smartest plan would be to postpone them both until the closing ceremony. That way, everybody could be mad at him *after* the most important games of their lives.

So, after getting through that day's list of photo shoots, he returned to his hotel room and changed into a date-night shirt and blazer. He splashed on some cologne and then grabbed his oversized, waterproof extreme-winter coat. It was still six degrees Fahrenheit outside, after all.

The restaurant they were going to was one of Luiz's recommendations, and when Drew walked in, he could immediately tell why he'd had to sweet-talk the maître d' to get a table that night. Verliebt was a beautiful, exclusive restaurant full of elegantly laid tables and Michelin-starred chefs. With modern chandeliers hanging from the ceilings and ambient lighting setting the mood, it oozed luxury. But the most eye-catching feature of the restaurant was the view. It was on the thirtieth floor of a building in the middle of the Olympic Park, and one of its walls was a floor-to-ceiling window that looked out at a breathtaking mountain-lined view of the Village. Verliebt was fancy as hell, but it had a warmth to it that made him feel at ease. The tables were filled with couples having romantic date nights and old friends seated around meals bustling with laughter and conversation. It was both laid-back and romantic, the perfect place for a first date. Or in Drew and Ari's case, a final fake date. It was also, conveniently, full of athletes. He knew Ari wanted to put the final nail in the coffin of the rumors about her and her ex, and this looked like the perfect place to do it. While most of the athletes were out of uniform, wearing nice dinner outfits, the dietitian-approved meals and competition talk gave them away. Drew was playing a game of guessing what sport each athlete played when Ari walked in.

He sensed the shift in the room before he saw her. A few people seated at the tables around him were glancing up and looking at the front door. A couple next to him, one of whom was wearing a Team GB snowboarding jacket, whispered between themselves. Drew lifted his eyes up and then glanced in the direction they were looking at. And as he did, he felt his breath catch. Ari had just walked in through the front door and undone the zip of her winter coat to reveal a long, purple dress that shimmered under the dim lights of the restaurant. Her curly hair bounced against her shoulders as she walked in, and the light from the candles on each table hit her crystal earrings, making them look like tiny mirror balls reflecting across the restaurant. She looked beautiful. But it wasn't the dress or the earrings or the hair, it was her face that lit up the room. All she was doing was smiling, but the way her eyes shone made Drew feel like they were the only two people in the room. As if there was nowhere in the world he'd rather be than under her gaze.

"Congratulations!" he said as he walked over to give her a hug. He'd seen the news that based on Team GB's current rankings, relative to the other teams in their group, they had a pretty solid chance of staying in the top three and advancing to the quarterfinals.

"We still have one more game to play," Ari said cautiously, but he could tell by the way her eyes lit up that she knew the odds were in her favor.

He walked over to the other side of the table to pull out her chair.

"Drew, I can get my own chair," she said, shaking her head.

"And if I were your friend, I would let you. But—"

"But you're my boyfriend," she said as she remembered. He glanced over at her and smiled as she nodded and sat down. The tension between them was flickering as if they'd already had a drink or two and were beginning to loosen up. There was a sense of anticipation in the air, the early sparks of possibility. It felt like a real date.

Drew and Ari were seated right next to the window that looked out on a night sky full of stars. There was a quietly magical playlist of contemporary jazz music playing above them, and the main source of light came from candles that filled the room with a gentle, romantic glow. The dark sky, low lights, and feeling of being alone together just feet away from a crowd reminded Drew of the night they'd first met.

"You look nervous," he said, noticing the way her eyes flickered around the room.

"I am. I just saw a few people I recognized on the way in. I can feel them watching us."

"I thought that was the whole idea," he said softly.

"Yeah, it just makes me . . . self-conscious," she said with a gentle exhale. Without thinking, he reached his arm across the table and stretched out his hand. She grasped it like a life preserver.

"It's weird," she began, "I always feel so assured on the rink. I'm the most confident version of myself on the ice. But no matter how hard I've been trying to play up the role of the confident captain, I'm just not there yet."

"I thought the plan was to just fake it till you make it?" he asked.

"I tried that, it doesn't work," she sighed, stirring her straw around her glass. "You know when you watch a film and get to the point where you can feel everything about to go on a downward spiral?"

Drew nodded; he was way more familiar with that feeling than he wanted to be.

"I've felt that way ever since New Year's Eve. I'm keeping it together for the sake of the team, and I would never admit it to them, but I have no idea if we're going to win our next game, or any other game."

"Isn't that part of the fun, though? Not knowing how it will end?" he wondered, thinking about how he felt whenever he took a photo with a film camera. It was an act of blind hope.

"Maybe it would be if it was just about me. But it's the whole team, you know? I don't know what I'll do if we don't make it to the quarterfinals. How I'll even be able to look them in the eye."

"But is it really your responsibility to figure everything out?"

"Yes," she said without hesitation.

"Why?"

"Because . . . I'm the captain, and the girls look up to me. It's my responsibility to make sure we win."

"But it's their responsibility, too. Have you tried talking to them about how you feel? It seems like you're carrying it all by yourself," he said.

"I can carry it by myself," she said with a touch of defensiveness. "I know how to handle things. I've been doing it my whole life."

"That doesn't mean you have to."

Drew absentmindedly ran his thumb up and down the side of her hand before glancing down. He began to pull away, but she drew him back. This time she was the one tracing her fingers against his skin. He glanced down at their intertwined hands and then up at her.

"If your teammates are the way you describe them, you have people in your life that love you. You don't have to do it all alone to prove a point."

"Do you take your own advice?" she asked.

"What would be the fun in that?" He smiled, thinking of all the truths he held back from those he loved. "Why tell my family the truth when I can share my secrets with strange girls on rooftops in the middle of parties?"

"Ugh, I regret that," she laughed.

"Why?" he said, trying to sound casual. She looked up at the ceiling and then at him.

"Because . . . in normal circumstances, I would never tell a guy I liked all my secrets within minutes of meeting him."

"Really?" he asked, deciding not to latch on to the "guy I liked" part of the sentence.

"If I'd known I'd see you again, I would have played it cool." She shrugged.

"Okay, so what would you do differently if this was our very first date?"

She took a sip of her drink and carefully studied his face. She did that a lot, but he couldn't work out what she was looking for.

"I would have leaned over and told you all my best stories. Acted like we were in on the same jokes, given you a few conspiratorial smiles," she said, aiming one at him. "I should have just flirted a little and kept it cute. Simple and fun. But instead, I let myself be messy and honest. Who wants *that* on a first date?"

"I do," he said. She shook her head.

"No. If I'd told you all of that on a real first date, you would have run away."

"Like you did?"

"When did I run . . . Oh, yeah," she said, no doubt remembering the sound of footsteps and fireworks.

"I don't blame you for leaving, though. I wouldn't have told you all my real red flags on a first date either . . . or the specific ways I'd end up disappointing you."

"If you could redo that night, what would you do differently?" she asked, tilting her head.

"I would have just tried to make you laugh." He shrugged. "Turned on the charm to try and get you to like me, flirted without coming on too strong. Talked enough to show I have a personality, but given all your stories my full attention," he said with a nod. "I probably would have kissed you sooner, too."

"I wanted you to kiss me sooner."

They sat in silence for a moment, as if they'd been transported back to the roof to start again. But as Drew looked into Ari's eyes and thought about the past few days they'd spent together, he realized he had no regrets.

"I'm glad it didn't play out that way. Not the kissing part—I definitely should have kissed you sooner." He smiled, taking a sip of his drink. "I mean that I'm glad we didn't pretend with each other. That we were completely ourselves from the start."

All that either of them had ever wanted was to be with someone who knew their flaws and liked them anyway. Someone who didn't require perfection but for whom they wanted to become the best version of themselves.

"Imagine if everyone was like that from the get-go?" he said. "Messy and honest."

"Nobody would get a second date," she laughed.

"Yet here we are."

"I realized something while I was on my way here," she said.

"What?"

She lifted her glass, took a sip, and looked over at him.

"We had breakfast, went to the hot chocolate bar, and saw the curling competition. That's three dates. We were only supposed to go on three fake dates."

He looked her in the eye. They both refused to break. He could feel the tension in the air. Everything unsaid, but felt, between them.

"Well, I guess that means this is real."

31

Ari

Ari knew they should have never gone on a fourth date. The restaurant was too romantic, she was still holding Drew's hand, and the way he was looking at her made her feel light and heady. It was a pull she couldn't quite explain or disentangle herself from. She'd been attracted to Drew ever since the night they'd met. He was handsome and funny and made her feel completely at ease. And at first, that had felt harmless. There was nothing wrong with admiring the face of a good-looking man, laughing at his jokes, or feeling a quiet thrill whenever she caught his eye. But she was starting to realize that it wasn't just a girlish crush on a guy she knew she couldn't have. Ari *liked him.* They'd quickly become friends, told each other way too much, and there was a strange untouched intimacy between them that made it feel like she'd known him a lot longer than eight days. Had it only been eight days? He was wearing a small smile, the candlelight was casting a golden glow onto his face, and he was looking at her with a warm, gentle gaze that made her want to lean over toward him and cuddle up in his arms. It was becoming a lot harder to convince herself that this was all pretend. She needed to reroute the conversation before she got too starry eyed.

"So, I know why you take photos, and I know why you moved back home, but I could never figure out why you decided to completely leave college. How come you didn't transfer to a school closer to home?" she asked, hoping the new topic would kill the romance in the air.

"Because I wanted my full attention to be back home with my family," he said unconvincingly.

"I don't want to sound insensitive but . . . that kind of sounds like a cop-out."

She knew she was pushing too hard, but the story didn't entirely add up. His grandmother was ill and he wanted to spend more time with her, which Ari completely understood. But he had other options and, while he'd been game to play along with her, she didn't get the sense that Drew was a particularly impulsive person. He chose his words carefully and assessed it all. Dropping out of a college course he'd clearly loved seemed incompatible with who she now knew him to be.

"What I mean is, was that Thanksgiving trip back home a split-second decision or the final push?" she asked curiously. He looked at her for a moment as if trying to figure out how much to tell her, but then he took a sip of his drink and sighed.

"You know how hockey means everything to you, so you want to be the best at it?" he asked. She nodded.

"I got it into my head I would never truly excel as a photographer. Not in the way everyone I went to college with would. Typical self-doubt stuff. I thought I was okay but not brilliant enough to make it all the way."

"You've almost got to be a bit delusional to believe you'll be the one who makes it," she said, thinking of how many years she had spent trying to convince herself she could.

"Exactly, so when I found out my grandma was sick, I decided to cut my losses and go back home. That way I wouldn't have to put myself through the slow torture of giving it my all in LA just to find out that I was only ever going to be *just okay*."

"So you opted out to stop yourself from getting hurt?"

"Yeah, and it's the biggest mistake I think I've ever made. But I'm going to fix it."

"You're going back?" she asked, surprised.

"No, worse. I think I'm going to try to go all in with this," he said, tapping his camera. "Try and make it on my own. There's this job I'm going to apply for using the portfolio I've been building up," he said, sounding excited as he explained the conversation he'd had with Hans Leitner and listed all the opportunities he was going to go for when he went back home to the States.

"I think speaking to you kind of inspired me," he admitted.

"How?" she asked, surprised. "All I've done since meeting you is divulge my secrets and fears."

"But you *did it*." He smiled, squeezing her hand. "In spite of all the reasons you've been trying to count yourself out, you made it to the Olympics."

Ari let it sink in. He was right. She'd been so focused on what came next that she hadn't really stopped to appreciate how far she'd come.

"Speaking to you has made me realize that I'd rather put my all into something at the risk of failing than keep playing it safe to avoid disappointment. I love what I do so much that I'd rather spend the next ten years being below average for the shot at maybe, one day, getting good."

Ari knew what he meant; pouring all her time and energy into hockey was a risk. She had trained every day and dedicated years of her life to strict routine. But wanting something and working hard for it didn't entitle her to success, even now. She was at the Olympics, but that didn't mean she would play well enough for the next four years to come back. There would always be someone who could skate faster or hit the puck sooner than her. There was no guarantee that she would even score another goal again. But she did it anyway, foolishly faced the odds and decided that she loved what she did enough to risk the real likelihood of failure. They both did.

"This could all fail, miserably. There's a significant chance that I'm going to become one of those failed artists who spends the rest of his life talking about how he peaked at twenty-two," said Drew. He was joking, but she could hear the undertone of fear.

"And I could become a jaded former hockey star who spends the rest of my life talking about how I went to the Olympics once but got so in my head that I didn't enjoy a single match," she said, feeling the fear, too.

"One day, we might look back on our lives and wish we'd made smarter, safer decisions. Because you know what? It might not work out," said Drew.

"But I'd rather be able to say I tried." She nodded.

She knew that they were both thinking the same thing. The truth hung between them. Unspoken but deeply felt.

"So why are we wasting time?" Drew asked, sitting back in his chair and really looking at her.

She was going to ask him what he meant, but it became crystal clear as soon as she saw his eyes. They *were* wasting time. Drew and Ari seemed to go against the odds in every other aspect of their lives, so why did their relationship feel like a bigger risk?

"Because we know too much about each other," she said, gripping on to flimsy reasons.

"Some people spend months trying to get to know someone as well as we do," he said.

"Exactly, it's not supposed to be like that. In a normal relationship, you'd start to spot the potential problems over weeks, months, or years."

"Isn't it better that we already know, then?" he asked.

"No."

"Why?"

She thought about it for a moment.

"It's like buying a used car."

"And am *I* the used car in this situation?" he asked, amused.

"We both are." She smiled, knowing how unromantic she sounded. "If you buy a new car, you expect it to be perfect, so you get disappointed when a problem comes up on the road. But if you buy an old car, you expect it to have issues. So, when the radio breaks, the engine fails, or the wheels fall off, you're just grateful it lasted longer than you thought it would," she said.

"I never thought a girl would liken me to a faulty old car on the fourth date," he laughed. It was a ridiculous metaphor.

"I don't mean it in a bad way. I mean that I'm not talking to you and looking for reasons why it won't work out like I would on a regular date. We both already know why it might not work out. So, I guess my worry is, what if . . ." She paused midsentence, opened her mouth, then closed it. She couldn't bring herself to say what she was silently thinking out loud.

"But what if it does work out?" he said.

"Exactly."

"That's what you're worried about?" he asked softly. She just nodded. He gently took her hand from the other side of the table. "I like you, and I'm pretty sure you like me, too. Isn't that a good enough reason to try?"

"I don't know. . . ." she began, because a hundred thoughts were swirling in her mind all at once.

"Can you give me one good reason why we should leave this date and never see each other again?"

"We have less than ten days before the Games end."

"That's more time than we had on New Year's."

"When it ends—" she began.

"*If* it ends," he interrupted.

"*When* it ends, Drew, we're going home to opposite sides of the ocean, remember?" she said. His smile wavered for a moment but then it lifted.

"Okay, fair. But a lot of really great, life-changing things end. That's no reason not to start."

"It could get messy," she said.

"Let's be honest," he laughed. "It already is."

She racked her head for more reasons, but they all seemed weak. As Drew looked over at her with that soft, gentle smile, her mind listed reasons to stay. They sat in silence for a moment before he nodded, quietly let go of her hand, and sat up in his chair.

"We should take that photo you wanted," he said. "But not for the internet, just for us. It will either be a good story one day, or something to remember each other by."

As Drew asked a waiter walking past if he could take a photo of them, Ari quieted the voices in her head telling her not to get her hopes up. She shuffled her chair closer to Drew's, and he did the same until they were side by side. He wrapped an arm around her shoulders, and they turned toward each other at the same time, their cheeks brushing for a fraction of a second before they both gently pulled back. Ari heard the click of the shutter and felt the pace of her heartbeat go up. The waiter gave the camera back, but neither of them moved.

"Do you remember those photos you took of me on New Year's?" she asked, giving in to the pull.

"Yeah, I printed them this morning so I could give them to you."

"Where are they?"

"Back at my hotel."

"Can we go and see them?" she asked.

He looked over at her. Up close, she could see the tiny flecks of gray in his bright brown eyes and the way the skin around them softened as his expression settled into understanding. He nodded and paid the bill. Then they stood up, grabbed their coats, and headed out into the snow together. Ari knew it was a bad idea. But surely it couldn't hurt if she'd already accounted for the ending?

32

Ari

DAY SIX OF THE 2026 OLYMPICS

When Ari and Drew stepped outside, the sky was clear. Their surroundings were bathed in moonlight. The early-evening clouds had left behind a fresh white blanket of snow, and although they were in the center of the Village, it was surprisingly quiet. All she could hear were the gentle sounds of her and Drew's footsteps crunching in the snow as they slowly walked along the pavement. This time he gave her his scarf without question, wrapped his arm around her shoulders, and kissed her, sweet and slow.

Sometimes Ari could feel herself forming a memory in real time. Experiencing a moment knowing she'd return to it in the future. So, she focused on all the details she knew she would one day remember. The warm streetlamps that lit up the path, the stars bright enough to map out constellations, the trees dusted with a light layer of snow. She knew that one day, she'd get lost in a daydream and remember the song playing in the lobby as they walked into Drew's hotel. Her mind would latch on to the longing glances exchanged as they rode the elevator and the tension in the air as they walked across the landing. The sound of Drew's door clicking shut and the quiet rustle of coats and scarves coming off.

It looked just how she imagined Drew's hotel room would look. It was clean and cozy. There were cameras, hard drives, and freshly printed film photos laid out on his desk. A wardrobe full of sweaters bearing his university logo. Polaroids scattered across the top of his dresser. Most of the photos were of the athletes he'd been assigned to, but she noticed a set of photos of an older couple. The woman had Drew's eyes, and the man had his smile. Ari realized they were probably his grandparents. Drew had been in the Village for only a week but he'd somehow already made the place feel like home.

"And here's what I took on New Year's," Drew said as he walked over to his desk and picked up an envelope labeled FOR ARI.

Ari approached him, moving closer until they were only a few inches apart. He handed her the envelope, and she pulled out three photographs. The memory of that night came back to her with startling clarity. The photos were dimly lit, but she could see every detail. First a frame of her looking out at the London skyline, her hair blowing in the wind as her silhouette broke up a sea of city lights. She was surrounded by skyscrapers and distant cars speeding across a bridge, but she looked serene. She turned to the next photo. This time, she could see the faraway look on her face. An expression filled with both wonder and worry as she stared out at the last night of the year. In the third photo, she was directly facing Drew. Her face was lit up by the fairy lights on the roof, and her expression was one of amusement and curiosity as she looked beyond the lens and up at the man holding the camera.

He'd somehow managed to capture her exactly as she'd felt that night: a little bit lost and overwhelmed but hopeful too.

"You're good at this," she said as she landed on the final photo.

"You're easy to photograph."

"In what way?"

"You're beautiful," he said with a shrug. Ari rolled her eyes, while trying to hold back a smile.

"Does that line actually work?"

"I don't know. Is it working on you?"

She paused. "Only time will tell."

"What's your line?" he asked.

"I don't need one," she said, taking his Polaroid camera from his desk, switching it on, and taking a photo before he could figure out what was happening. Capturing him in the low hotel light, his eyes bright as he looked past the lens and over at her. They stood in silence for a few moments as the photo developed, then she gave the camera back to him. The image showed the stunned expression on his face, and the smile curving up his lips. As she watched him looking down at it, she gently stroked his cheek and spoke softly.

"See, look at you. You're already falling. Don't blame yourself. I just have that effect on people," she said, making him laugh.

Then he paused, stood back, and took a Polaroid of her. When it came out, she took the photo from his hands and slid it into his blazer pocket before she could look at it. He raised his eyebrows questioningly.

"Something to remember me by," she said quietly, letting her hand linger on the chest of his blazer. Things got quiet again. Neither of them was laughing anymore. Instead, they were standing in the tension. Waiting to see who would break it.

"We're not strangers anymore. And we *will* see each other again," Drew said as they locked eyes.

"So, *this* would objectively be a bad idea," she agreed as he stepped closer.

"Exactly," he said, gently taking the photos from her hand and placing them on the dresser.

He walked back over to her until their faces were inches apart. Then he gently ran a finger across her arm, stroking her bare skin. There were those goosebumps again. He traced her skin from her wrist up her arm, to her elbow and higher up, until he reached her shoulder. It felt like every single nerve in her body stood on end. Something about the gentleness of his touch felt electrifying.

"It probably won't work out," she said quietly.

"And we both already know how it could end," he said, breaking eye contact to lean forward and kiss her shoulder, neck, and the tender area under her jaw.

His hand snaked around her waist, sending a pulse of desire down her body. In response, she placed her hands on his shoulders, first over his blazer and then sliding underneath to slowly ease it off, not looking down as it hit the floor.

"I broke a rule," she said plainly.

"Which one?" he whispered.

They were face-to-face. She could hear her heart beating and feel his beneath her hands. Time stood still for a moment as they looked into each other's eyes. It all felt so vivid. The taste of the drink she'd left behind. The distant sound of the music played in the lobby. The touch of his hands. The smell of his cologne.

"I lied," she said quietly. "I don't regret a single thing I said or did on New Year's."

"Me neither . . . except I do wish I'd kissed you sooner," he said, his voice low and raspy.

"Well, don't make the same mistake tw—" she said, but before she could finish her sentence, he cupped her chin, looked into her eyes, and took the breath right out of her. The world went silent as she closed her eyes and felt their lips brush. It was so gentle that she could have mistaken it for not happening. But the tingle on her lips let her know it was real. They pulled back for a second as if giving each other one last chance to change their minds. But then, like gravity, their lips collided. This time, there was no hesitation.

His hand, which was already wrapped around her waist, pulled her closer as she gripped on to his shoulders and leaned into the kiss. She used the palm of her hand to caress his face, his neck, and the fabric of his shirt. He ran a finger down the bare back of her dress and sent a lightning bolt of heat down her spine. She put her hands in his hair and sighed as he eased one of the stiff straps of her dress to the side and began to place a quick hot trail of kisses across her neck, shoulders, and the smooth skin above the neckline of her dress.

She was ready to ease the other strap off, take the whole thing off. But instead, he went back up, took her face into his hands again, and kissed her with a kind of passion that made her legs weak. But then his hands were holding her up, his fingers firm against her back, tracing lines up and down her skin as she wrapped her arms around his neck and sighed at the small, intense ripples of pleasure she felt with each touch. Her hands found their way down his chest, clutched at the hem of his shirt, and slowly eased it up and off. She looked straight into his eyes as she traced each muscle across his chest, noticing which parts he was sensitive to. Using the tips of her nails to gently graze his skin until he shook his head, used one arm to lift her under the knees, and laid her on the bed.

He kissed her deep and slow. Each nerve ending across her skin seemed to respond to him as all the unnecessary fabric left their skin. They became a tangle of smooth curves, moving limbs, and desire. Words whispered between two bodies making sense of each other in the dark. It felt like holding a hand up to a flame. A wave of heat strong enough to melt the ice outside and ensure that, by the time the sun came up, neither of them would be the same.

33

Drew

Drew woke up to the sight of the early-morning light pouring through a gap in the curtain and the sensation of Ari's breath against his chest. She was fast asleep and looked more peaceful than he'd ever seen her. A ray of sunlight landed on the side of her face, coating her skin with a soft, golden glow and bringing out all the shades of brown in her hair. They were both wrapped up in a thick, white wintery duvet, and although Drew's eyes were still relaxed enough to let him go back to sleep, the sight of her made him feel wide awake.

Ari, he thought, sounding out the letters of her name in his head. It felt like liquid gold. Every part of her did. The sound of her laugh. The way her presence lit up a room. The look she gave him when she was trying to figure him out. Looking down at her peaceful, sleeping face, he could imagine that in a world in which they had more time, it would be pretty easy to fall in love with her.

The thought should have startled him, but it came so immediately and without question that he knew there was no point in fighting it. His life was too much of a mess for her, and he knew she was too bright to let herself pretend that this thing between them could be anything more than just a moment. It was a winter romance that seemed magical under the moonlight but wouldn't make sense once spring began and the impossibilities of a relationship were exposed to the light. But that didn't stop him from wondering what life would look like if they were going home to the same city.

He absentmindedly ran his finger over her cheek, tracing the shadows that a distant tree left on her skin as the early-morning light shone in.

"Are you watching me sleep, Drew?" she said softly, her eyes still closed. Her voice was sweet in the morning, soft and gentle.

"I didn't want to wake you up," he said softly as he watched her eyes open. Her head was still comfortably tucked between his shoulder and chest. He wondered how long they could stay like that, how much longer they could live in the moment before it had to end. He got his answer when Ari's alarm began to ring. Upon hearing it, she opened her eyes, left his embrace, and sat up. His chest felt much colder without her.

"Is that your alarm to go to training?" he asked as she rolled over to the bedside table to turn it off.

"No," she said, wearing an embarrassed smile. It was cute, he wanted to kiss it.

"What is it?" he asked, smiling back at her, amused by her refusal to make eye contact with him then.

"Don't judge me," she said.

"I would never," he said as she shuffled to his side of the bed. He stretched his arm out, an open invitation, and she rolled back over to him, getting comfortable in the space between his shoulder and chest that felt like it had been created just for her.

She looked up at him and smiled.

"I get up every morning at six a.m. to take a walk and listen to a self-help book. But not in a listening to *Rich Dad Poor Dad* and *The Law of Attraction* kind of way," she insisted.

"I'd still like you if you listened to *Rich Dad Poor Dad* every morning," he said.

"It's sports biographies to help me become a good captain. It's corny, but I'm trying to be the best I can for the team, you know?" she said, her eyes wide and earnest. How she looked when she started talking about the things she loved made his heart swell. As she explained what she was reading, that early-morning thought came back to him. And this time, he was certain. Drew could definitely imagine himself falling in love with Ari one day.

"Why are you looking at me like that?" she whispered suspiciously.

"You know why," he said.

"I'm going to need you to spell it out." She smiled.

"Because I like you," he said plainly. Her eyes lit up as she looked over at him.

"I think I like you, too," she said with a small smile.

"But? There's always a *but*," he said, sensing her hesitance but trying to keep it light.

"There's no *but*. This is all that matters right now," she said, resting her head on his chest. The two of them lay in bed and looked up at the ceiling in quiet contentment. Skin to skin in the early-morning light. After a moment, she turned around to face him, tilted her head until they were looking straight into each other's eyes. She used her fingers to trace the lines and contours of his face before settling on his lips and kissing him until he felt deliciously dizzy. When they pulled apart, he felt words he couldn't say rise to the tip of his tongue. *Stay, we could make it work, I've wanted this since the night we met.* He wanted to run his fingers through her hair, sleep in late, and spend all the time he possibly could with her. But after a few seconds, she pulled away, got out of bed, and headed to the bathroom.

When he heard the sound of the shower turn on, he rolled out of bed and put on some clothes. He walked across the room, and opened the curtains, letting the golden early-morning light fill the room. Drew knew he was in trouble. There was no going back from a feeling this real. He wanted to honor the rules of their arrangement and convince himself he could still play pretend. But there was nothing fake about the way he felt about her anymore. He wasn't sure his feelings for her had ever been anything less than completely real. He was trying to find the words to tell her he couldn't pretend to be her boyfriend anymore when the bathroom door opened, releasing a cloud of minty shower gel–scented steam and Ari wrapped in a teeny-tiny towel. She looked perfect. Like *what were they doing getting dressed up to start the day when she looked that good* perfect. He'd seen her body only once, but it would probably be imprinted on his mind for the rest of his life. By the time his gaze returned to her eyes, there was a little smirk on her face. She could tell he'd been checking her out. But then her face turned serious.

"We have a problem," she said. He was slightly alarmed by her tone.

"Are you okay?" he asked, his mind immediately running to worst-case scenarios. But she shook her head and smiled.

"Wearing last night's dress while trekking through the snow the morning after isn't my vibe. Especially in a hotel full of journalists. Do you have anything I can borrow?" she asked.

He got up and walked over to his wardrobe.

"I could lend you a Team USA hoodie," he said with a smile as he walked to his wardrobe and pulled a hanger.

"The girls would kick me off of the team if I showed up to practice in that," she said, shaking her head.

"A Team USA *T-shirt*?" he joked.

"They would revoke my citizenship," Ari said, laughing as she walked over to search the wardrobe with him. She was still so fresh out of the shower that he could see the steam evaporating off her skin and small droplets of water rolling down her shoulders.

"How about this?" she asked, pulling out one of his old USC sweaters.

"You can take this too," he said, handing her a fresh pair of tracksuit bottoms before going to the bathroom to brush his teeth for four minutes longer than he needed to give her space to change.

"Okay, I'm ready. Ta-da!" she said when Drew knocked on the door and came back out. He was greeted by the sight of her spinning around and waving her hands in the air while wearing his clothes. Everything was too big, but it suited her perfectly. For a moment, he imagined what would have become of them if she'd gone to college in California. If he'd met her for the first time on campus wearing that same red hoodie. All the alternate realities flashed in his mind for a moment. All the lives in which they'd met sooner and didn't live on different sides of the world. She was still here, just a few yards away from him, but he could already imagine how much he would miss her once this all ended.

"Are you okay?" she asked in amusement, no doubt catching the faraway expression on his face. He wasn't okay, but he nodded anyway. It was a violation of their most important rule, but he couldn't tell her the truth without the risk of coming on too strong. She gave him a funny look, as if she didn't quite believe him, and then began to walk around the room, picking up her scattered belongings.

"I've got to dash. I need to listen to two chapters of this book before training," she said as she collected the clothes that had gotten lost last night and put them in her bag.

"I could come. We could get breakfast," he began. He could hear the earnestness in his voice. It had been about a week, and he was already down bad.

"Drew," she said softly, looking over at him. She didn't need to say anything else for him to know she wanted to just let things stay as they were. He nodded. It would be foolish to try and make it last.

"I'll see you around," she said, putting on her shoes and coat. She left the room before either of them could change their minds.

Drew flopped back on his bed and stared at the ceiling, realizing he was in trouble. Because Drew was falling for a woman he would know for only a few more days. Someone his sister hated who lived a whole ocean away. It was supposed to be a relationship with a clear expiration date, doomed to end before it could begin. But as he sat up, looked through the window, and watched the golden early-morning light cast its rays against the snow, he couldn't help but smile. He shook his head and laughed. This was definitely going to hurt.

34

Drew

"Let me guess, you and Hans have progressed from a subtle head nod to an actual 'hi'?" asked Luiz, studying the slightly lovestruck expression on Drew's face as he walked into the press office that afternoon.

"How do you know if you like someone, for real?" asked Drew.

"Hans?" asked Luiz. "I'm pretty sure having a seventy-two-year-old sugar daddy is frowned upon in most communities," he joked.

Drew shook his head. "Ari," he admitted.

Drew wasn't delusional. Despite all the risks he'd taken in his professional life, when it came to relationships, he didn't rush into things. He'd met Ari two months ago, and they'd only spent a week together. So, Drew knew that he wasn't *in love* with her. But after she'd left his room that morning, he'd paced around the Village taking photos and wondering what it would *be like* to fall in love with her. He didn't believe in love at first sight, but he did believe in meeting someone for the first time and knowing they would play an important role in his life, and he'd felt that way about Ari since the very first night.

"When you know, you just know." Luiz shrugged.

"That's super helpful and not at all cliché," said Drew, shaking his head.

"It's true, ask anyone," said Luiz, scanning the room for someone to back him up. As Hans Leitner walked past them, Luiz smiled. "Mr. Leitner, how do you know if you're falling in love?" Luiz asked. Drew's eyes widened as he wondered how Luiz felt comfortable casually asking Hans Leitner such a personal question. Hans paused midstep and looked at the two of them with a little sparkle in his eyes.

"You stop asking yourself, 'Am I falling in love?' and start thinking, 'Oh, I'm falling in love,'" said Hans with a firm nod as he walked toward their table. "Luiz, where did you put that spare battery charger?" he asked. Luiz grabbed a charger out of his top drawer and handed it over to Hans, who nodded at the two of them and then walked away. Drew immediately swiveled his head.

"You know him?"

"I worked at the 2022 Winter Games and 2024 Summer Games. I know everyone," he said nonchalantly. "But on to the more pressing matter: What does Ari think of the whole dating-her-rival's-brother situation?" Luiz asked. Drew had divulged his secret to Luiz after his odd encounter with Harrison the other day, but he still hadn't done anything about it.

"Drew?" Luiz raised his eyebrows as Drew rifled through a drawer of charging cables to avoid his gaze.

"You've got to be kidding me," said Luiz, shaking his head.

"I'm going to tell her," Drew said despite having no idea how to.

"You're digging yourself a bigger hole every day you don't tell her, trust me."

Drew knew that. It felt like every single path in the Village was littered with holes he'd dug for himself. Not telling Ari about Thandie. Keeping his grandma's illness a secret from his sister. Entertaining the idea of going back to college. Developing real feelings for his fake girlfriend. It was only a matter of time before he fell into a trap of his own creation.

As Drew left the press office to photograph that afternoon's speed-skating competition, he examined all the secrets and half-truths he was keeping from the people he loved. The elaborately interconnected nature of each of the secrets he was keeping meant that he didn't even know where to start when it came to fixing things.

So, he did what he did best: distracted himself. He took photos of athletes at a cross-country skiing final, did a behind-the-scenes shoot of figure skaters preparing for that evening's competition, and convinced a journalist from *Forbes* to let him take a portrait of her and her colleagues for the photo collection he was building on his laptop.

He and Ari had been texting back and forth in between her training sessions and, while it wasn't enough to distract Drew from all the explaining he had to do, it was light and fun enough to convince him that everything would be fine once he did. So, he made plans to see Ari at the café near GB House after her practice match. Drew hoped that walking there would give him time to figure out how to approach the conversation he knew they needed to have. But halfway down the path, he was greeted by a six-foot-seven, Team GB–uniformed, slyly smiling problem.

Harrison.

"I was starting to think the message I sent Thandie didn't get through to you," Harrison said with an unmasked air of contempt. The feeling was mutual.

"Oh, it did, but you can't threaten me or my sister into getting what you want," Drew said. "Thandie's the best in the game. She would have gotten the deal without you. So, spreading rumors won't stop her from being one of the best contenders for that sponsorship contract."

Drew believed every word he said, but he had no idea if the second sentence was true.

"You really want to put your sister's career on the line like that?" Harrison said, trying to maintain a kind of menace Drew knew people only used for empty threats.

"What are you going to do? Call Zeus? I dare you," Drew said, holding Harrison's gaze. He had no idea if Harrison actually had that kind of power, but he figured that if he sounded confident enough, Harrison would back down.

"I'm giving you until the closing ceremony. Break up, or I'll call them," Harrison said. But Drew could tell he was bluffing. His unwavering eye contact was the giveaway. It's what people did when they were trying really hard to appear to be honest. Drew knew because he was doing it, too.

"Give it up," Drew said, trying to sound dismissive. "We're not ending things to soothe your insecurities, so just move on. Ari has."

"Here's the thing, *Drew*. I know Ari. I know what she needs. We've broken up before, but we always get back together. So, enjoy your time with her . . . but try not to add too many miles. She knows where home is," said Harrison with a smirk.

Drew could feel the anger spreading across his body as he sized him up. Drew had met dozens of guys like Harrison before. People who'd built their entire identity on one thing and assumed that everyone respected them because of it. Guys who used their stature to try to intimidate and saw women as objects to spar over. Drew hated guys like Harrison, and he was disgusted that the poor excuse for a man standing in front of him had the gall to talk about anybody like that, never mind Ari.

"Don't speak about her like that," Drew said firmly. His voice was level, but the threat in his tone was clear.

"Or what?" said Harrison, taking a step closer. Drew did the same. Boys like Harrison didn't intimidate him. He knew the person standing in front of him was all talk. Drew knew how to fight, and he wouldn't hesitate to show Harrison his answer to "or what?" if he needed to. But before things could escalate, Drew heard footsteps approaching them. He turned around and saw Ari.

"I don't know what *this* is, but it's an immediate no from me," she said, shaking her head as she looked between Drew and Harrison. Drew wasn't one to back down, but when Ari shot him a questioning look and he noticed the hint of irritation in her tone, he took a step away from Harrison and toward her.

"I can look after myself, remember?" she muttered so only he could hear her.

He nodded; he didn't want to let his desire to shut Harrison down eclipse the fact that she clearly didn't want him to intervene. Still, he made sure to pin Harrison down with a glare.

"We're just chatting, no need to worry," said Harrison with a wink that made Drew tense up. It was a sleazy smile and a seedy wink, worn by a man that Drew immediately hated more than anyone he'd ever met.

"Wait, is he carrying my watch?" Harrison asked, looking over at the black leather and gold watch in Drew's hands. Ari had left it behind last night, so he'd brought it with him to return to her. But something about the look she and Harrison exchanged made it clear that it was more than just an accessory.

"Drew, let's go before the line gets too long," she said, reaching for his hand. But Harrison wasn't done.

"Ari, I knew you were strategic, but I didn't think you'd go this far," said Harrison, right as they were about to leave.

Drew's first impulse was to tell Harrison to keep his fake girlfriend's name out of his mouth. But then he noticed the way Ari paused midstep. He scanned her expression, but she was wearing a poker face.

"What are you talking about?" she asked with an indifferent tone that masked the fact that she was holding Drew's hand tighter than before.

"Keep your enemies close . . . but keep your *enemies' families* closer, I guess?" Harrison said, looking between the two of them.

Drew's heart sank. He glanced over at Ari. Her poker face had dropped and in its place was confusion. It was all happening so quickly that Drew didn't have time to reroute the conversation.

Harrison looked at Ari, then at Drew. He must have sensed the fact that the two of them were still on completely different pages, because he smiled, raised his eyebrow, and nodded in thinly veiled glee.

"You're dating your rival's brother, right? I didn't think you'd sink *that* low to try and win a game," said Harrison, clearly delighted at the opportunity to drag out the reveal.

"What?" said Ari, whose confused glance moved from Harrison to Drew. Drew opened his mouth to start explaining. But Harrison had other plans.

"Ari, your *boyfriend* is Andrew Dlamini, right? Thandie Dlamini's brother. Wait, he didn't tell you?" said Harrison, tilting his head in mock confusion and then shooting Drew a *gotcha* glare.

Drew could feel his chest tightening and his whole body flooding with dread. But it wasn't Harrison's reveal that he cared about, it was how Ari would react. He looked over at her face, searching for the anger and betrayal he was expecting. But she'd reprised her poker face. Her expression so unreadable that it terrified him. The three of them were silent for a moment, and then she nodded.

"Of course I knew," said Ari with a calm, collected voice. She shrugged and then squeezed Drew's hand so tightly that he wondered if she had the strength to cut off his blood flow. Still, her face revealed nothing. "Right, I need that cup of coffee. Let's go, Drew," she said, turning around and practically dragging him through the snow and over to the café.

As soon as the door shut behind them, Ari dropped his hand and turned around to face him. The light had left her eyes. Drew knew he was in trouble. Big trouble. He'd dug himself a hole and was falling straight into it.

35

Ari

Ari was too stunned to speak. The combination of "Dating your rival's brother" and "Wait, he didn't tell you?" had completely thrown her off. The information was laid out before her, but the pieces didn't fit. She'd noticed the stacks of Team USA merch in Drew's wardrobe, but she'd assumed he was just patriotic in the way everyone was during Olympic season. She knew Drew had a younger sister, but he hadn't mentioned the fact that she was an athlete, never mind that she was one of the world's most successful ice hockey players. And while she'd been the one to suggest the fake-dating, she'd assumed that he'd gone into it without any personal conflicts.

A part of her wanted to believe that it was all just a coincidence, that Drew had been just as blindsided by Harrison's statement as she had been. But the guilty expression on his face said otherwise. She looked him in the eye, and he immediately averted his gaze to the ground, to the ceiling, and then to the busy café.

Innocent people didn't feel the need to avoid eye contact, so her mind put the pieces together in the shape of a mental spiral. If Drew was Thandie's brother, then he knew about the injury. If he knew about the injury, then he knew that Ari had been responsible for the accident. And if he knew that Ari was responsible for the accident that had almost ruined Thandie's life, then he knew that his sister, who was known for holding grudges, hated Ari.

"Tell me that you didn't know," she said softly, clinging on to one final moment of hope.

"Ari . . ." he said, his face a mix of guilt, nerves, and panic. Her stomach sank as she realized that he'd held back the truth. Alarm bells began ringing in her head. She didn't want to jump to conclusions, but if Drew had known all along, how many lies had he told to get them this far? Had his sister been in on it the whole time? Had their entire relationship been some strange attempt at sabotaging her Olympic chances as a shot at revenge? Had he purposefully instigated the whole mess on New Year's Eve? Each piece of the puzzle forming in her mind was jagged and distorted now. Their first rule had been no lies, and to her, a lie of omission was just as bad. If he could lie about something that so directly involved her, what else was he capable of? The thought threw her so off-center that she couldn't bring herself to finish it. So, she turned around and redirected her energy into ordering a golden matcha latte. She didn't want to look at Drew, but as soon as she finished her order, he walked right into her eyeline, tapped his card against the reader, and paid. She knew he probably meant well, but the gesture irritated her. He wasn't getting out of this by buying her a drink she'd intended to get for herself.

"I can explain," he said as he put his card back in his wallet.

"You have until my drink is ready," she said, her voice detached and emotionless.

Drew glanced over at the barista and gave him a nervous smile.

"Hey Jørgen. Sorry to ask, but could you make her drink extra slowly?"

Drew's coffee runs had put him in touch with all the baristas in the Village. But he wasn't the only one with friends in highly caffeinated places. Ari had been getting all her drinks from this café from the start.

"Jørgen," she said, turning to the barista with a sweet smile. "Sorry, but could you please ignore him and actually make it as fast as you can . . . because if Drew needs that much time to explain himself, this conversation might as well already be over."

Jørgen glanced between the two of them with a slightly startled expression.

"It takes four minutes to make a golden matcha latte, that's the fastest and slowest I can do it," Jørgen said, holding up a milk frother to defend himself.

So, Ari began to count down.

"Three minutes fifty-nine, three minutes fifty-eight, three minutes fifty-seven . . ." she began.

"I'm so sorry, I promise I didn't know who you were on New Year's Eve," he protested. "I didn't even know your full name. Seeing you at the opening ceremony was the first time I even realized you were an athlete."

"But then I told you I was. You took photos of me playing hockey and met my teammates. You can't tell me that the thought that me and your sister were competitors didn't cross your mind?"

He opened his mouth, and then he closed it. The silence was all she needed to know that she'd hit the nail right on the head.

"Drew, you can't be serious right now," she said, rubbing her temples.

"I didn't know until after we agreed to do the fake-dating," he said, scratching his head.

"Excuse me," said a man standing a few paces away from them, "you're holding up the queue." Ari looked around and realized they were, so she and Drew shuffled away and toward the end of the counter to resume their conversation. This time in hushed whispers, because there were way too many prying ears to have a conversation like this in public.

"So, when did you find out?" Ari asked, leaning against the counter, willing it to give her strength.

"The day after Schokoladenzeit. And I wanted to tell you, but I couldn't find the right time to mention it. You weren't supposed to find out this way."

Ari's eyes widened. They'd only been together for a week and in any other circumstance, it wouldn't have been a big deal. But each week in the Village felt like a month in the real world, and so their friendship—relationship, situationship, whatever it was— had accelerated pretty quickly. They'd gone on dates, shared secrets, and slept together. He'd had plenty of time to tell her the truth, and from the look on his face, he knew that, too. She wasn't even angry, she was disappointed.

"How was I *supposed* to find out, then, Drew?" she asked, looking him in the eye. "On the internet? When you popped up in the US supporters' box at one of my games? Or was your unhinged little sister planning on whispering it in my ear at the start of a game to mess with my head?"

"She's not unhinged. . . . She's just passionate," Drew said, avoiding her eyes.

"The last time she crossed paths with a player she hated, the girl left the game with a broken arm."

"She didn't *break* anyone's arm," he said defensively. Thandie was his sister, after all. "The girl tried too hard to tackle her and crashed into a wall. That's not her fault."

Ari would have respected his commitment to having his sister's back in any other situation. But this wasn't any other situation. A part of her didn't believe that Drew could have gone out of his way to deceive her like this. From what she knew of him, he was kind, honest, and sincere. But then she thought back to the party.

Ari was used to people who lied and hid the darkest parts of who they were. So, when Drew had shared all those truths about himself on New Year's Eve, she'd implicitly trusted him. She'd reasoned that there was nothing to be suspicious of if his cards were already on the table. But now, she was beginning to wonder if he'd intentionally divulged all those secrets to get him to trust her. Lulled her into a false sense of security so he could spot her weaknesses and use them to his advantage. After all, his sister was Thandie Dlamini, and Ari knew that, like her, Drew would do anything for his family. He seemed like a good guy, but she couldn't put it past him to have strategically gotten into her head to destabilize and distract her on behalf of his sister. And while Drew had seemed startled when Harrison revealed the truth, all of this coming together now seemed a little *too* convenient. What better way to throw her off her game than to drop a bomb right in the middle of the most important tournament of her life?

"Did you . . . plan this? New Year's, agreeing to the fake-dating thing, spending all this time with me?" she asked, stumbling over her words as her mind formed worst-case scenarios. Ari had known Thandie for almost ten years. She was definitely capable of using mind games to mess with an opponent.

"Ari, no. I promise none of this happened on purpose," he said firmly. "I would never do anything like that."

His expression was sincere. But Ari didn't know what to

believe anymore. She glanced around the café, trying to think it through. If he'd been the one to reveal the truth, she would have believed him. But finding out through Harrison, of all people? She shook her head and let herself be pulled in by everything going on around her. The smell of coffee beans, the sound of spoons clinking against glasses. She wanted to float away and watch this scene play out as an objective observer. Her instincts had allowed her to spend years with Harrison, so when it came to men, she didn't trust her gut anymore. Taking Drew at his word felt like risking all the progress she'd made.

"Was this all just a game for you?" she asked plainly.

"The fake-dating? No. I agreed because I wanted to spend time with you." His face softened. "And then everything else that happened between me and you? It was real. *It is real.*"

"Don't get ahead of yourself. It's a fake relationship," she said, trying her best to protect her feelings.

"So, that first kiss was fake?" he asked, raising an eyebrow.

"It was an emergency. I was just playing it up for the kiss cam," she said, crossing her arms though nothing about that moment had felt like acting.

"That wasn't our first kiss," he said.

"The opening ceremony? I was trying to get away from my insane ex-boyfriend."

"No, Ari. New Year's. There was nothing fake about that," he said. Her mind wandered back to that night. To the instant familiarity, the tenderness in their eyes, the kiss so good she'd run away from it.

"There wasn't," she admitted. "But everything since then has just been pretend."

Drew shook his head, refusing to accept her answer.

"The dates, the *obvious* chemistry, the way you look at me and how I look at you? That was all fake, too?" he challenged, taking a step closer. She was mad at him, but that didn't make him or the low, slow tone of his voice any less attractive.

"It was just an act to fool Harrison and my friends," she said coldly, determined not to fold.

"And last night . . . was *that* all pretend?" he asked with a look that made her feel completely exposed. No, nothing about last night had been fake. What use was there in pretending when there was nobody else around? How could she ever convince herself that the way she'd kissed him had been pretend? That the ways their bodies had moved in perfect, synchronized motion had been just for show? The way they'd touched each other and the things he'd made her feel had been more real than anything before. She didn't want to believe that it was all a casual extension of something that had never been real to start with.

But she had to, for her own good. So, she put on her most unbothered expression.

"Drew, it was just sex," she said. A woman standing nearby waiting for her coffee looked over, intrigued. Ari felt a little embarrassed but stood her ground.

"We both know it wasn't *just* sex," he said, looking her in the eye. It sent a tingle down her spine.

"Okay, fine." She shrugged. "But it was a mistake," she said. She saw him flinch as soon as the words came out of her mouth, but she needed to keep going. "I knew it would be a mistake when I walked into your hotel room last night, and you probably knew it was a mistake this morning when I left," she said plainly.

The silence lasted too long. She didn't realize how much she'd wanted him to object until he didn't. It stung. The woman stood beside them, eavesdropping on their conversation, giving her a sympathetic look she couldn't bear. She needed to leave the café as soon as she could, so she asked Jørgen, who was clearly listening to their conversation, too, if he could put her drink into a take-away cup. But Drew followed her to the counter.

"I was going to tell you," he said.

"But you didn't," she sighed, suddenly exhausted. Ari didn't have the patience for shoulda woulda couldas.

"I just didn't want to do anything that could risk making you worry or throw you off your game. Once I realized how you and Thandie knew each other, I figured you would be better off not knowing."

He sounded sincere, and she could understand the logic. But he'd hit upon the one thing she couldn't look past in a *real* relationship: dishonesty.

"I don't want to be a girl you lie to, to protect their feelings. I don't think you lied to protect your ex-girlfriend's feelings, and I don't think you held back the truth to protect mine. I think you did it because you're too much of a coward to face having a difficult conversation," she said. Her words had stung him. She could tell by the look on his face. But Ari needed to tell the truth. A part of her wanted him to defend himself, or even throw a painful truth back at her or take something she'd told him up on the roof and use it as ammunition. But when he spoke again, his tone was calm and even.

"You're right. It was cowardly to avoid telling you the truth. I should have told you sooner. But as flawed as I am—and my god, do I have a long list of issues—I'm not one of the guys you've dated in the past, Ari. You can push me away all you like, you're entitled to it. But I'm not the kind of person who's going to go back and forth with low blows," he said, holding her gaze before reaching behind her. He took the cup of matcha the barista had left on the counter and handed it over to her.

"You should drink it before it gets cold," Drew said.

She was too shocked to do anything but take the cup. She'd

become so accustomed to chaos in every other part of her life that she didn't know how to respond when someone was calm and measured instead of letting a conflict become a fight.

She took the cup and let him gently ease her away from the counter. When she looked back, she realized that they'd been holding up the line. At least seven other customers were looking at them, some with annoyance, clearly desperate for their coffee. Others were curious, trying to eavesdrop on their conversation and connect the dots. Ari was still trying to make sense of it all.

"I should have told you about Thandie, and for that, I'm sorry. I'm really sorry. But Ari, I like you, and I think you feel the same. I don't want to throw away what we have because of my mistake."

"Drew . . ." she said, trying to stop him from carrying on. She wanted to end the conversation before it could further complicate her feelings for him, but Drew wasn't done.

"When I listened to you talking about your teammates, your family, and your friends, I listened because I cared. I wasn't trying to strategically get information about you. When we went on those dates, I went because I genuinely wanted to get to know you. I wasn't trying to trick you," he said. Ari could tell from the look in his eyes that he was telling the truth, which was somehow more terrifying than a complicated lie. "I didn't tell you about Thandie because I didn't want you to think that *anything* that had passed between us was insincere," he said.

She believed Drew. But she also knew Thandie. She couldn't convince herself that Thandie wouldn't try to use this against her. They were both highly competitive athletes who would use every piece of information available to them to play the game to their advantage.

"But you knew this whole thing would make her more determined to crush me, right? The villain in her life dating her *brother?*" Ari shook her head as she thought about the implications. "How many times has she asked you about me to try and figure out the weak spots she can use against me on the rink?"

"Thandie doesn't know."

Ari could feel time standing still.

"What?" she asked in confusion.

"Thandie doesn't know that we're together . . . that we're *fake together*. She doesn't even know that I know you," he admitted.

Ari's jaw dropped. Somehow, it was even worse than she'd thought. That was the moment she truly began to spiral.

Ari had known Thandie Dlamini since she was fourteen years old, and if there was one thing she knew about her, it was that she lashed out the moment she felt like she was out of control. She played her very best when she was slighted. And if Ari and her teammates won their match against Team Finland, they might end up playing a quarter or semifinal game against Team USA. The team Thandie had been fiercely captaining for the past year.

Ari suddenly felt lightheaded. So, she walked over to a nearby table, sat on a stool, and sipped her matcha. She stared into the distance, thinking of all the poor decisions that had led her to this moment. Drew took the stool across the table from her. His face did not reflect the seriousness of their predicament.

"She's going to murder me," Ari said, nodding in acceptance as she took another sip.

"She's not going to murder you," Drew said, slightly amused.

"Do you know your sister? I'm a feminist, and I wholeheartedly support women's wrongs. In fact, I love women's wrongs! But Thandie is capable of doing wild things in the name of revenge."

"No, she's not like that. She's just . . . she's a very . . . the thing with Thandie is . . ." began Drew, who had clearly just remembered who his sister was.

"Your sister is one of the best players in the world," Ari said, because even she could give credit where it was due. "She's incredible on the rink, especially when she's got something to prove. But when she's been slighted—and I mean this with all the respect in the world—your sister terrifies me."

"Come on. Thandie?" he scoffed. "She's harmless."

"When a Canadian player said something bad about her in an interview, she and Team USA made sure to demolish Team Canada in the next game. When someone on the Danish team got her in trouble for unsportsmanlike conduct, she spent the rest of the season strategically stopping them from even touching the puck," Ari recalled. "If that's how she reacts to small things, can you imagine what she'll do to me if she thinks I'm dating her brother to mess with her head?"

"Shit," he said.

"Shit, indeed. We are in some major shit."

"What are we going to do?" he said, resting his arm on the table. She sat up in her chair.

"We? *We?*" She shook her head in astonishment. "There is no *we*, Andrew Dlamini! *You* got us into this mess by letting this keep going when you realized that me and your sister were connected. You *knew* it was a bad idea."

"It takes two to make a bad idea work, though, doesn't it?" he said, a slow smile curving up across his face. He was so attractive it was annoying her. She was supposed to be mad at him, not laughing at his jokes. So, she tucked in her stool and got ready to leave. As terrified as she was of Thandie, Ari wouldn't even get the chance to play against Team USA if she and her teammates didn't nail their next game.

"I don't have time for this," Ari said, shaking her head. "I have one of the most important games of my life in less than twenty-four hours, and I have no idea what I'm doing," she continued, the panic beginning to rise.

"Hey," Drew said, gently laying a hand on her shoulder. She was still mad at him, but something about the warmth of his hand and the softness beneath his eyes calmed her down a little. "You do know what you're doing. You're an excellent player, your teammates love you, and you're going to do a brilliant job, like you always do. Okay?" he said with a kind, reassuring smile. It worked; she immediately felt more relaxed. But she forced herself to turn around and leave him. It was that damned smile that had landed them in this situation in the first place.

36

Ari

Despite all her usual doubts and insecurities, Ari knew they were going to win the moment she stepped into the locker room. Her rational brain wanted to find things to worry about, but there was no denying the gut feeling she got as her teammates huddled into a circle, counted down from three, and skated onto the ice. Thanks to all the conversations she'd had with them individually and as a team, they were finally in sync. And it showed.

Natalie sat on the sidelines, watching as she rested her ankle, and Izzy cheered on from the bench, taking the consequences like a grown woman. The rest of the team zoomed around the ice, playing in the best form they'd been in since the Olympics had begun. Yasmeen defended Team Finland's attempts at scoring by staying intensely focused on the game, and Sienna won them a series of glorious goals within the first twenty minutes. Ari commanded the team's attention in the intervals in a way that had them step onto the ice with a sense of determination she hadn't witnessed since they'd last played with Gracie. When the final buzzer blared, all twenty-three of them skated off the ice and into a huge team hug. Then they ran to the locker room.

"Don't do it," said Sienna, but she couldn't hold back her excitement.

"It's basically the national anthem. You have to play it," said Yasmeen as Izzy picked up her phone, connected it to the speaker, and grinned.

"Izzy," warned Sienna, but even she was smiling.

"*Izzy . . .*" said Yasmeen, spurring her on.

"Izzy!" laughed Ari as she let herself experience the joy around her.

She heard the opening beats to a song they hadn't played in the locker room since their last major win at the Ice Hockey World Championship. The trumpets began to play, the drumbeat kicked in, and, to everyone's surprise, Sienna jumped onto the bench. She used her hairbrush as a microphone and sang along to the Neil Diamond song.

Ari, holding her hockey stick like a mic stand as the whole team began to sing the chorus of "Sweet Caroline." The entire locker room was up on their feet chanting and the joy in their voices was infectious.

Though they'd landed in Switzerland with hope, and Ari had spent all their pregame moments trying to drill in some level of optimism, nobody, least of all themselves, believed they would get this far. When they returned to the rink, Coach McLaughlin shed a tear, the supporters' section erupted into cheers, and all of their friends and family back home started calling to congratulate them and book tickets to fly to the quarterfinals and celebrate their historic win. Because, even though Gracie wasn't here and Team Finland was better than them in almost every single way . . . they'd won and were advancing to the quarterfinals. It was no wonder they felt on top of the world.

Ari and the rest of the girls wanted to transform their GB House corridor into a party. But Coach McLaughlin quickly put a stop to that idea by reminding them they had practice first thing the next morning. So instead, the team transformed the locker room into a club and spent an hour singing, dancing, and celebrating. They were about to head to the canteen for a celebratory dinner when Ari's phone rang. She told her teammates that she would meet them there.

The call was from her mom and sister. Her family had tried to book tickets to be with her from the very start of the Olympics, but she'd insisted that having them there would distract her, so she'd convinced them not to come over unless she qualified for the quarterfinals. And now she had. Ari *thought* they were calling to celebrate her win and confirm their travel plans. But when she picked up her phone, excited to bask in their excitement for her, she realized she'd been mistaken.

"Ari, you need to speak to your sister," her mom said from her end of the phone call.

Her mom wasn't calling to celebrate her win, she was calling to get her to mediate the family drama unfolding eight hundred miles away.

Again.

"She thinks she can just fly away to go and spend a week with a man she barely knows," her mom said, exasperated.

"Well maybe if you'd let me have a real relationship with him growing up, wanting to spend *two weeks* with him wouldn't be such a big deal now," said Anesu.

Once again, Ari was being brought in to act as the second parent her dad had failed to be. She wanted to go and celebrate with her friends, but family came first. So, she sighed and jumped in.

"Anesu, I get what you mean, but don't you think—"

Her mother immediately, unsurprisingly, took it the wrong way.

"You get what she means? Arikoishe, who took you to school and after-school clubs? Me. Who helped you with homework and went to your parents' evenings? Me. Only me. Your dad could have gotten on a flight to actually be a father if he wanted to. But he didn't." Her mom's voice was shaking.

"Maybe he would have if you weren't so . . ." Anesu paused midsentence. Ari held her breath.

"If I wasn't so . . . what?" Their mom's voice was steely and quiet.

Ari needed to intervene before things got worse, that's why she'd been called, after all. The two of them couldn't have a conversation that didn't descend into chaos.

"Anesu, I think Mom's hurt because she feels like you didn't consider her feelings before agreeing to go to the wedding," Ari began, glancing out the window and watching as her teammates laughed and messed around in the snow.

"Why is it my job to tiptoe around Mom's feelings?" said Anesu. "She's the mother, and I'm the child."

"Exactly!" shouted their mom. "That's what you need to remember. I am your mother, you are my child. And because you are my child, I will not let you fly to Zimbabwe to celebrate the man who left us."

"He left *you*," muttered Anesu.

Ari froze. It felt like all the oxygen was being sucked out of the call. She turned away from the window and back in the direction of the locker room. She walked over to a bench and sat down as she listened to the silence on the other end of the line. Ari didn't need to be in the room to imagine her sister's regret and picture her mother's hurt. She wanted to say something to defuse the tension. Smooth things over and deescalate the situation before things got worse. But her mother was the next one to speak, and the hurt that had been in her voice for the first half of the conversation shifted into something calmer and more honest.

"Anesu, your father left you, too," their mom said, her tone almost pitying. Their mom got sad and angry, but she almost never got mean. "In his sudden desire to spend time with you, did he ever mention the fact that I got full custody because he didn't once, for a second, want a joint arrangement?"

"He . . ." said Anesu, her voice deflating. Gone was the stubbornness and determination. Now she just sounded like a young girl being forced to hear the truth.

"No, of course he didn't mention that," their mother said plainly. "Why would he? He's this superhero dad in your head because he's not around enough for you to see him for who he is. But I am your mother. I will protect you even when you don't realize that's what I'm trying to do. I'll be the strict one, the parent with rules, the punching bag you get angry at. And one day, you'll thank me for it. But until then, you're not going anywhere," she said, a sense of finality in her tone as she hung up and left the group call.

"I knew you wouldn't do anything," said Anesu, the deflation in her voice familiar. It was the same tone of voice Ari remembered from all her childhood birthdays. From the moment when the parties ended, her friends went home, and there was still no birthday card at the front door. From the school talent shows and end-of-term plays when she looked out at the audience hoping, despite all evidence to the contrary, that he was in the crowd. It was the voice that came to Anesu when her disappointment turned inward. Ari hated knowing that this time she was the cause. If Ari had been there, she would have hugged her sister, but she was eight hundred miles away.

"You *always* take her side, but this hurts my feelings too. Couldn't you have just backed me up this one time?"

"I was going to—" Ari began.

But Anesu had already hung up.

Ari held her silent phone and stared out at the falling snow. She'd seen a text from her sister that morning. A message saying that her mom was threatening to hide her passport so she couldn't go to the wedding at the end of the month. Ari had intended to reply, but she'd spent the morning with Drew, and once she'd left his hotel, there'd been no time to check her phone, text back, or think about anything other than the game. She knew being focused on the biggest match of her career was a perfectly justified reason not to reply to every single text her family sent her. But she couldn't help but feel guilty for not fixing the situation before it got this bad.

Ari's childhood had revolved around trying to mediate conflicts within her family. First between her parents and now between her mom and sister. She'd spent years of her life fighting for the people she loved, defending them when they were wrong, and pouring her energy into fixing things. It was her role as the eldest daughter, and she took it in her stride. But this time felt different. She'd just won the most important game of her life, and instead of calling to congratulate her, her family had called to get her to resolve their issues.

As Ari sat in the locker room, on her own, she began to trace that pattern through from her childhood to her current situation. She was there for everyone, but it felt like nobody she loved was willing to sacrifice their time and energy to be there for her. Then, just as she was about to pack up her things and call it an early night, a text came through.

Drew: SHE SHOOTS, SHE SCORES, SHE QUALIFIES FOR
THE QUARTERFINALS. . . . Should I start learning the British
national anthem?

Ari smiled. Drew had messed up, but despite her better judgment, she was still happy to see his name lighting up her phone.
She tried her best to stand her ground.

Drew: Meetup at 5 to celebrate/apologize/return the watch
I forgot to give you yesterday?

She didn't even realize it wasn't on her wrist anymore. Hmmm.
Maybe that's why she'd woken up feeling lighter. A part of her
wanted to be rid of it for good. But for some reason, there was no
one in her life that she wanted to see more that day than Drew.

Ari: Let's meet at 5 p.m., but just to get the watch.
Drew: 5 p.m.? It's a date.

37

Drew

Drew watched Ari's final heats game with Luiz and the rest of the journalists in the press office, cheering for Ari and her teammates the entire time. He jumped out of his seat when she scored the winning goal and clapped as the commentators announced that, in doing so, Ari had just secured Team GB's place in the quarter-finals at their first Olympics. A few of the CNN journalists he'd been sitting with had given him a funny look, no doubt confused as to why an American photographer was cheering so loudly for a British team, but Drew was way too proud not to celebrate Ari's win as if it were his own.

He left the press office and went straight to the Village gift shop, impulsively buying the biggest, brightest bouquet of flowers he could find before heading toward GB House.

Drew walked across the Village trying to figure out how to make things right with Ari. They'd both done a pretty good job of complicating things on Thursday night, but she'd been certain to remind him that this ended with the closing ceremony. She'd even gone as far as to call it all a mistake, so he had to respect her wishes. It was supposed to be a fake two-week relationship, and they only had a few more days left until that contract expired. But knowing that didn't change how Drew's face lit up when he spotted a figure in a huge blue coat walking toward him, carrying a gym bag.

"Do you have my watch?" she asked. He could tell she was trying to stay mad at him, but the sparkle in her eyes betrayed her. He reached into his bag and handed over the watch, as well as the earrings and scarf she'd left behind.

"This is *your* scarf."

"It looks better on you."

They stood in silence for a moment. She gave him a hard stare, then let her shoulders drop.

"I'm still mad at you," she said as she wrapped the scarf around her neck.

"I know, you're right to be," he admitted. After a moment she glanced down at the bouquet in his hands.

"Are you getting into floristry? Interesting choice for a side hustle."

"Before you ask, they're not *I'm sorry* flowers. They're *I watched your game today and you were incredible. It's Valentine's Day, so I was thinking of you and also . . . I'm sorry* flowers," he said.

She examined the bouquet and then she studied him. A small smile appeared on her face. She tried to straighten it out, but then she gave in.

"Ranunculus, you remembered," she said, taking the flowers, bringing them closer to her face, and then smelling them.

"I knew you'd make it to the quarterfinals, and I'm proud of you."

"Thanks, pal," she said, elbowing him.

"Pal?" he asked, tilting his head. She had never called him that before.

"Pal. Buddy. Temporary fake boyfriend. Heavy on the *friend*," she said, feigning nonchalance.

"Ari."

"Drew."

"We're not just friends," he said, shaking his head.

"Yes, we are," she said firmly. "We are friends in a contractual relationship that ends in a couple days."

"That's in a couple days, though. What does that make us until then?" he asked. She looked around and thought about it.

"Friends." She shrugged, then paused. "Okay, *friends* who are occasionally more than friends but are committed to only doing what's right."

"What's right or what *feels* right?"

She shook her head, but the air between them had just gotten incredibly thick.

"Do you regularly kiss your friends?" he asked, tilting his head.

"I've been known to kiss a forehead when we win," she said, nodding.

"And you *sleep* with your friends?" he asked.

"The dorm room has four bunk beds, so technically, yes."

"But do your friends know the way you taste?" he asked, and her eyes widened. "Do you let your friends go down on you until—" he began, but she threw her hand over his mouth and clamped it shut. He laughed, but he could see how startled she was. She was looking at something behind him with an alarmed expression that quickly turned into embarrassment and then a practiced smile.

"Mr. and Mrs. Dlamini?" Ari said, widening her eyes at Drew as she took her hand off his mouth. Drew's stomach dropped. *Mr. and Mrs. Dlamini?*

He turned around, and to his horror, there stood his grandparents. His grandpa was shaking his head and his grandma's face was a mixture of horror and amusement. His grandparents were obviously in the Village to watch Thandie's games, and he'd already met up with them a couple of times that week. But he hadn't factored in the possibility that he might bump into them when he wasn't expecting it. Never mind that he might spot them while he was with Ari. Drew ran through his options and decided the best option was to stick to the story Ari had been telling her friends.

"Grandma, Grandpa, this is Ari, my . . . girlfriend," he said, immediately questioning whether he'd made the right decision.

"It's so nice to meet you, sweetheart. I thought Drew might be seeing someone, but he's always been so secretive," said his grandma, reaching out to hug her. Ari hugged her back, looking over at Drew with wide eyes as if trying to figure out his plan.

"It's nice to meet you too. I've heard so much about you," Ari said, quickly composing herself when they pulled apart. Drew did his best to send her a *please, let's go with it* look. She gave him a gentle nod, letting him know she was going to play along.

"And these flowers are beautiful, honey. Valentine's Day? I didn't think you were a romantic, Drew," his grandma said, raising her eyebrow. He scrambled to come up with an explanation.

"I'm a romantic when I'm with the right person," he said, reaching for the first thing that came into his head, but when he glanced over at Ari, he realized it was true. "And yes, it's Valentine's Day, but the *real* celebration is that Ari and her team just won a big game. She's incredible."

He looked over and caught her eye. She smiled, and for a moment, they were back in their own little world.

"Arikoishe Shumba, right?" his grandpa asked, his face flashing with recognition. His grandpa was a Team USA women's ice hockey fan to his very core. His blood bled red, white, and blue. But he wasn't just a supportive grandpa, he was a genuine fan of the sport. Of course he knew who she was.

"Yes, but all my friends call me Ari," she said, extending her hand to shake his.

"Congratulations on your win," his grandpa said. From the tone of his voice, Drew knew it was a genuine compliment. The four of them stood in silence for a moment before Ari tried to find a quick escape.

"Well, it's almost six, so I've got to leave and grab dinner now," Ari said, looking down at her watch.

"Yeah, I'll walk you there," Drew said, nodding along. He wanted to escape this conversation just as much as she did.

"Wait, *we're* going for dinner too. Why don't you join us? It would be lovely to get to know you," his grandma said eagerly. Drew couldn't possibly think of a worse idea.

"I'm sure Ari has other plans," Drew began. But before he could get out of the invitation, his grandma was locking arms with Ari and asking her questions about her life. Ari glanced over for second, as if looking for a way out, but his grandma was a charmer, and soon enough, Ari was smiling and laughing along, the two of them lost in their own conversation.

"Drew never introduces us to his friends, and I know the food you're eating in those canteens isn't good," his grandma said. Drew watched as a set of mental calculations flashed across Ari's face. His grandma was looking over at her with a warm smile, and Drew recognized it as the one she wore when she was up to no good. But Ari must have received it as that of a sweet older lady extending a kind invitation.

"I don't want to intrude," Ari said.

"Oh darling, I insist," his grandma said, whisking her away before she could protest. And soon enough, all four of them were off to dinner together. When his grandparents started talking about what they wanted to eat that evening, Drew took it as an opportunity to step back, reach for Ari's hand, and walk a few spaces behind.

"Lying to my grandparents was definitely not part of the plan. Sorry to reel you in to that. I panicked," he whispered, quiet enough that only she could hear him.

"It's okay, they seem really sweet."

"Don't let them fool you," Drew joked. "But seriously, you don't have to come. I can tell them you're busy or need to go and meet up with your teammates. Dinner with my grandparents wasn't part of the agreement."

"Do you want me to come?" Ari asked, looking over at him. Drew paused, thinking about it for a moment.

"If this was real? Yes. Absolutely. I know they'll like you."

"So I'll come, but what's the plan? What's our story?" she asked.

"The same one we gave your friends?" He figured that maintaining the same lie they'd been telling everyone else would be easier than trying to come up with a good reason for why Drew was giving his sister's rival a bouquet of flowers. Saying they met on New Year's Eve felt like the least complicated explanation.

"Okay, I'll play it up. But your sister can't find out. So after tonight, tell them we've broken up. Because this? Me and you? It's over."

38

Ari

Ari was trying her hardest not to enjoy herself. But she couldn't stop herself from feeling like she was meeting her *real* boyfriend's family for the first time. There was a warmth to Drew's grandparents that she immediately fell for. The four of them were seated at a round dinner table, and Drew's grandparents kept finishing each other's sentences and giving each other soft, loving looks. As if they were just as in love with each other as they'd been from the start. They ordered different drinks, he an Old-Fashioned and she a vintage white wine, sharing them with a casual familiarity and laughing like schoolchildren as they teased their grandson in front of who they thought was his new girlfriend.

"And then he showed up to the school dance wearing a full-body space suit." His grandpa laughed as he told Ari a story about one of Drew's childhood obsessions. Each time Drew tried to steer the topic of conversation away from something embarrassing and toward the menu, Ari leaned forward and asked more questions.

"When he turned fifteen, I accepted that Drew was probably going to end up living with us for the rest of his life," his grandma said with a chuckle.

"Please, stop," Drew said. He looked mortified, but Ari could tell he didn't really mind. He looked more comfortable around his grandparents than she'd seen him anywhere else but behind his camera. They seemed like the kind of tight-knit family that genuinely enjoyed spending time together. Which was more than she could say for hers.

"Are we embarrassing you, honey?" his grandma asked sweetly, giving Ari a conspiratorial wink, as if she was already part of the family. Her heart swelled a little before she reminded herself that this wasn't built to last.

"Andrew, you were a strange kid. There's nothing to be embarrassed about," his grandpa said with a chuckle.

They were in a cozy, rustic barn-themed restaurant that specialized in warm, homey Swiss comfort food. The server kept coming over to ask for their order, but Drew's grandparents were so invested in telling stories that they kept apologizing and promising to be ready the next time she came around. After twenty minutes, she smiled and handed them some more plates of warm, freshly baked bread, telling them to take all the time they needed. The bread was a permission slip for Drew's grandparents to quiz Ari and Drew about how they'd met, how long they'd been dating, and why Drew had been hiding her.

Drew had a sweet relationship with his grandpa. He expected a lot from him, but he doted on him, too. And it was immediately apparent just how much Drew loved his grandma. He was constantly glancing over at her and checking if she was okay. As they interacted, she imagined the child he must have been when his grandma told him stories, and she got glimpses of how much like his grandpa he might become. Drew kept shooting her *please make this stop* looks as she and his grandparents joked around at Drew's expense. But despite his embarrassment, he seemed comfortable—happy, in fact. They'd held hands on the walk there to play up the whole dating thing, and at some point, he'd put his arm around her shoulders. But she reminded herself that as natural as it felt, it was all for show.

"So, what are you ordering, Arikoishe?" Drew's grandma asked. Ari liked how older people committed to saying her full name; it made her feel like they were really paying attention. Ari already liked Drew's grandparents. They were warm and easygoing and made her feel at home in ways she didn't always feel when she was in her own home. She knew she would never see them again, but still she wanted them to like her.

"What would you recommend?" she asked, smiling over at his grandma.

"Don't get her started on the menu." Drew's grandpa chuckled warmly as he glanced over at his wife with affection.

"I spent a summer in Switzerland in my twenties. Did Drew tell you that? I lived a vivid, exciting life before I married this old man," Drew's grandma said with a twinkle in her eye. "Trust me, all of the food on the menu is incredible. But we've got to get the cheese fondue, some schnitzel, a bowl of Älplermagronen, Rösti, a little bit of raclette, more bread, and maybe—ooh, there's so many options," she said, pointing to various dishes as she talked to Ari about her favorite travel adventures.

"What if we just order one of everything and share it?" Drew's grandpa said, to everyone's agreement. They were handing their menus back to the waitress when Ari noticed an abrupt shift in the room.

Everybody cast their gaze away from their menus and over at Ari.

No, they were looking behind Ari.

She glanced over at Drew. He looked startled.

His grandpa looked nervous, and his grandma cast Ari an apologetic glance. She had no idea what was happening until it was too late to run.

"Sorry I'm late. Practice ran over and—" Ari didn't need to turn around to recognize that voice. But when she did, she was immediately greeted by an oversized red puffer coat emblazoned with the Team USA logo. The familiar face wearing it looked down at her in shock. It was Thandie. Thandie Dlamini.

It felt like the whole room went silent for a moment as everyone at the table watched them, waiting with bated breath to see what would happen next. The moment was so tense that Ari felt like one wrong move would bring everything around her crashing down. Thandie had the same look in her eye that she got in the first second of a competition, the intense focus that overcame her as she waited for the puck to land on the rink. It was the look she got when she was about to scramble to take control of the game. The determination of a person ready to tackle whoever she needed to in order to win. Ari had seen that look dozens of times before. But this was different. They weren't on the rink, they weren't playing hockey, and they weren't with their teams. In fact, Ari was seated with three people who, on any other day, would have been wearing supporters' jerseys for the opposition.

"What are you doing here?" Thandie said, so calmly it terrified her. But Ari still wanted the Dlamini grandparents to like her, so she tried to sound upbeat.

"Hey, Thandie, it's nice to see you," Ari said, nervous.

"No, it's not," said Thandie, shaking her head.

"Thandie, be nice," said her grandma.

Ari felt like she was stepping out onto a wobbly tightrope.

"What's going on here?" asked Thandie, shooting her family

confused looks. But nobody answered her, they all just looked at Drew.

Drew opened his mouth, then clamped it shut. Ari leaned back in her chair and closed her eyes. It was like sitting in a nightmare. The kind of anxiety dream she got before a big match where none of the scenes or characters made sense. When she opened her eyes and looked at Drew, she saw the blood draining from his face.

"Drew? What is *she* doing here?" asked Thandie, who, from the look in her eyes, had figured out that her brother was at the center of this mess.

"You didn't tell your sister?" said Drew's grandpa in a too-loud whisper. Thandie's eyes widened. She looked at Drew, and then she looked at Ari. The missing pieces in the puzzle clicked.

"I'm going to need someone to explain what's going on *right now*," said Thandie.

But something dangerous was taking over Ari. She was usually a measured person. She thought things through, kept the peace, and tried to de-escalate situations before anything could go wrong. She'd spent her whole life doing that with her family and the past three months doing that with her teammates. But something about Thandie brought out her teenage self. Maybe Drew hadn't planned this whole thing to throw Ari off her game, but that didn't mean that Ari wouldn't use it to rile Thandie up a little, to get her back for all the years she'd spent doing the same. All was fair in love and competitive sports. So, she found Drew's hand, held it, and made a show of pressing them together until their fingers were intertwined.

"Thandie, me and your brother . . . we're in *love*," she said, blinking shyly as if she couldn't help but tell the truth. Thandie looked horrified.

It was petty, childish, but Thandie had spent years messing with her head on the ice rink in retaliation for that accident all those years ago. Ari had apologized countless times, but each *sorry* landed on deaf ears. In fact, the more Ari tried to make amends, the more Thandie doubled down on trying to get into her head and throw her off her game. Ari could write pages of accounts of all the times Thandie had purposefully tried to get her back, of sly moves on the ice, subtly cutting comments behind the scenes, and all the people whose perception of her was shaped by the image Thandie had painted in their heads. So, it was only fair that she give Thandie a small taste of her own medicine.

"Ari," said Drew, tilting his head and looking at her with a weary expression. She could tell that he knew what she was doing and why she was doing it. But at the end of the day, he was the one who'd gotten them into this mess. She was just playing along.

"You can't choose who you love," said Ari with a shrug as she patted Drew on the cheek.

"This isn't happening," said Thandie with a blank expression.

"Honey, take a seat," Mrs. Dlamini cooed.

"You," Thandie said, glaring at Ari.

"Me?" said Ari, feigning innocence. She wasn't being mean-spirited, she just liked having a rival to bounce off. It was fun. Feuds had existed since the dawn of creation, and knowing someone was praying for her downfall gave her a reason to work harder. The animosity between them made them both play better. The fabled rivalry raised the stakes of every game.

"What kind of fucked-up psychological warfare is this?" Thandie asked, narrowing her eyes.

"Language, honey," her grandpa warned.

"Do you really think I would go to all of this effort just to throw you off your game?" said Ari.

"Actually, I don't care why you did it, because I'm going to enjoy every single minute of destroying your team on the rink regardless," said Thandie, glaring at Ari as she pointed a dessert spoon in her direction.

"Okay, here's the cheese fond—oh," said the waitress, who'd just arrived at their table with a trolley topped by a large copper-colored fondue pot.

"Don't worry, sweetie, you can go ahead," Drew's grandma said, shooting an intense *behave* glare at all three of them. The whole table sat in silence as the waitress laid out their food, the tension palpable. When she was done, they all gave her polite, slightly embarrassed thank-yous before going back to where they'd left off with Thandie, directing her annoyance at her brother.

"Of *all the people* in the world, *her*? When did you even meet each other?" asked Thandie, annoyed but curious.

"New Year's Eve, at Klaus's party," Drew said, speaking up at last. Ari looked over at him. He had a strange look in his eyes. She wondered if he was thinking about the same moment up on the roof that she was thinking about. That kiss at midnight and everything that had happened since.

"Why didn't you tell me?" Thandie asked.

"It's complicated," Drew said.

"Oh, I'm sure it is," Thandie said, forcing her fork into a chunk of bread, dipping it into the fondue, and taking an angry bite.

"Well, for the record, I approve," his grandma said, patting Ari on the shoulder and giving her a kind, reassuring smile. "If you make Drew happy, you're perfect. Right, honey?" she said, looking over at her husband, who was having a lovely time dipping different vegetables into the fondue pot. He took a bite of cheese-coated potato and looked up, nodding in agreement.

"Absolutely. You look better than you have for months, kid," their grandpa said, examining Drew with what looked like relief. "I know you've had a tough year. You deserve to be happy."

Ari's heart sank. Drew's family was so sweet that she felt bad lying to them. They were already going through so much. His grandma's illness, Drew's abrupt life changes, and having to keep secrets from Thandie. She didn't want to be responsible for bringing another lie into the picture if it had the potential to hurt someone. So, she looked over at Drew, trying to communicate the fact that they needed to give it up, but he looked just as conflicted as she was.

"Are you actually happy, Drew?" asked Thandie, her tone genuine for a moment. "Don't get me wrong, I'm still going to crush your little leg-breaking girlfriend at the quarterfinals," Thandie said, glaring at Ari before turning her head back to her brother. "But, Drew, if you're genuinely happy . . ." There was a searching look in her eyes as she examined her brother's face.

Their grandparents were looking over at her with hopeful expressions, as if Ari was the solution to their grandson's problems. And as she realized that Thandie might be willing to put aside her long-held grudge for the sake of her brother's happiness, Ari realized that they'd gone too far. She couldn't bear the thought of lying to his grandparents when they'd been nothing but kind to her. So, she slowly detangled her hand from Drew's. He looked down and then over at her. He looked guilty, too. As if he'd just realized that their game of pretend wasn't as harmless as he'd hoped it would be.

"Drew," she said quietly as they looked over at each other. They didn't need to say anything to know they were going through the same thought process. They had to end this before anyone got hurt.

"It's not . . . it's not real," he admitted. "We were just pretending to date."

"What?" said his grandparents in unison.

"Drew. I hope you're lying, because if you made this up as some sort of dumb joke, I am going to disown you," said Thandie, getting annoyed again. She hadn't changed one bit since she was fourteen years old, Ari thought. It was kind of endearing.

"Andrew, what are you talking about?" his grandpa asked, more seriously. Ari stopped smiling. She looked over at Drew; his whole body had deflated.

"We're not actually dating, it was just . . . mutually beneficial to pretend we were," he admitted.

"But you told us you met a girl you liked on New Year's Eve all the way back in January," his grandma said, confused. "Have you been pretending all this time?" she asked, looking at Ari, whose face no doubt betrayed her surprise.

He'd told his grandparents about her back in January? She caught his eye, and then he looked away. She'd been thinking about him ever since then, too.

"This is the girl you met on the roof, right?" his grandpa asked, looking between them.

"She is," Drew said, lost for words. "But it's complicated. I mean—"

"You don't have to pretend that you don't like each other for Thandie's sake," said Drew's grandpa as he looked at Thandie with a fond, loving smile.

"Et tu, Brute?" she asked, looking at her grandpa in mock betrayal.

"We're not really together," said Drew, finally admitting the lie. "It was all just pretend." Drew glanced over at Ari. She held his gaze for a moment and then looked away. The table was silent.

"You don't look at each other like it's all just pretend," his grandma said with a curious eye.

"You're right. It looks pretty real to me." Drew's grandpa nodded.

Ari and Drew locked eyes for a moment. It did feel pretty real. But that didn't mean anything.

"Well . . ." said Ari, not sure what to say, "Drew and I are just friends. It wouldn't—"

"It wouldn't work out," Drew finished, not looking her in the eyes. Which was good, because she could feel hers starting to sting.

"There are at least a dozen reasons why it wouldn't end well, right?" she said, trying too hard to sound chipper as she leaned back and began to pull her chair out.

"Ari," Drew said as she stood up and plastered on a smile.

"I've got to go to . . . training," she lied. She and the team didn't have anything else scheduled for the day except resting after the afternoon's big game. But it had been a long day, and this wasn't how she wanted to spend her evening. "I'm sorry for intruding on your family dinner. It was lovely to meet you," she said, looking over at his grandparents. Then she glanced over at Thandie.

"See you on the rink," Thandie said, but there wasn't an ounce of venom in her words this time. It seemed like she was just as exhausted as Ari was.

"Let me walk you out," said Drew, standing up. But Ari's eyes continued to sting, so she shook her head.

"No, I'm good. I can take care of myself," she said, tucking her chair in and rapidly blinking away the tears that were just a few seconds away from falling. "We're not together, remember?" She watched a wave of disappointment wash over his face, but his feelings weren't hers to worry about anymore.

So, she put on her coat, picked up the bag, and began to reach for the scarf she'd walked in wearing. But as she looked at the embroidered name on the scarf, she realized that while it fit perfectly, kept her warm, and smelled like home, the scarf wasn't hers to keep. And neither was Drew.

39

Drew

Ari could probably come up with a whole list of reasons why Drew wasn't boyfriend material. He smoothed things over instead of dealing with uncomfortable conversations, allowed things to pile up instead of handling them right away, and waited for things to unfold instead of chasing after what he wanted. But even though he knew he couldn't be the perfect boyfriend she needed, he wanted to find Ari and tell her that the only thing he really regretted about New Year's was playing along with the whole *this could never work out* thing in the first place. Because even though the part of him that doubted himself thought it was true, the braver, more important parts of him wanted to believe otherwise—wanted to believe that the way they talked, kissed, and looked into each other's eyes when no one else was around meant that there was something there worth trying for.

Drew wanted to tell her how he really felt and try to convince her to stay. But the determination with which she left the restaurant made it clear that this was where things ended. Staying apart was probably for the best. Their situation had parameters, and because of his mistakes, it had reached an early expiration date. So, he stared at the restaurant exit until his family dragged him back to reality.

"Andrew, sit down," his grandma said softly, reminding him that he was standing in the middle of the restaurant, frozen in the state Ari had left him. So, he sat down, tucked his chair in, and dipped a sad, not-so-toasty piece of bread into the fondue while trying to ignore his sister's glare and his grandparents' concern. After a few moments of silence, his grandpa cleared his throat and spoke up.

"If you like her, you should tell her, kid," he said softly, taking a sip of his Old-Fashioned.

"Wait a minute, is no one going to address the elephant in the room?" Thandie said, refusing to let them glaze over the facts of the situation. "Drew is dating—sorry, is fake-dating, sorry *was* fake-dating—*Arikoishe Shumba*. The girl who almost ruined my career. Can we address that first?"

"I didn't know that when I met her," he said, though he knew it wasn't a good enough answer. If anything, the admission made things even worse.

"So, you're saying that in all these years of talking about the defining moment of my adult life, you haven't been listening to anything I've said?" asked Thandie, her annoyance turning to hurt. Thandie stared at him long and hard before telling him exactly how she felt.

"Do you know what, Drew? I'm sick of your shit."

"Thandie," warned their grandpa, shaking his head as he cut himself a forkful of schnitzel. The poor guy was just trying to have dinner.

"Why are we acting like my language is a bigger issue than the fact that Drew's been in self-destruct mode for months?"

"What are you trying to say?" Drew asked, confused by the shift in the conversation. He thought she was annoyed about Ari, but now it just seemed like she was mad at him.

"That you've become such a *quitter*. You used to be this person I looked up to, but you've spent the past year getting in your own way, skipping out on all of your commitments, and self-sabotaging everything you care about," she said. Drew felt like she'd just slapped him.

When Thandie wanted to hurt someone's feelings, you could hear it in her tone. But as she spoke to Drew at the dining room table, she was calm and to the point. It made her words sting even more.

"You're smart and talented and could make something of your life, but every time something is about to get good, you do everything in your power to stop it from working out," she said plainly.

"No, I don't."

But Drew knew she had hit on something true. Thandie spooned some Älplermagronen onto her plate, ate a bite, and then ran through her brother's self-sabotage highlights reel.

"The degree? The minute you realized you weren't going to be at the top of the class, you dropped out. Living in California? You didn't have the grit to stick it out, but I'm sure you just convinced yourself you were leaving because Grandma's sick."

Drew froze. His grandma's face crumpled, and his grandpa reached out for her hand. The mood in the room fell to a new low as the illness took the seat at the table that Ari had left behind.

"You know?" Drew asked, in shock.

"Of course I know," Thandie said. There was a mixture of sadness and hurt in her eyes.

"Oh, sweetheart, you weren't supposed to find out yet," their grandma said, her eyes tearing up.

"How long have you known?" their grandpa asked, his expression troubled.

"Since the summer," Thandie said, looking down at the table. His sister had always been good at hiding her emotions, but Drew couldn't believe she'd been able to go this long without talking to him about it. If she'd known since the summer and he'd only found out in November, she'd successfully carried it alone for almost half a year without showing any noticeable trace of distress. Meanwhile, he'd uprooted his life and embarked on a three-month crash-out.

"How did you find out?" Drew asked, leaning forward so he could study his sister's face and figure out if she was actually okay.

"I noticed grandma was acting off, so I . . . read through her emails," she admitted with a grimace as she used her fork to move food around her plate. She always fidgeted when she was worried.

"Thandie! That's an invasion of privacy," their grandma scolded.

"You kept asking me to go into your inbox to reset passwords." She shrugged.

"Which password was I looking for?" their grandma asked, as if it was a crucial detail.

"That bingo website you were obsessed—"

"Alright, alright, we can move on," their grandma cut in, looking slightly embarrassed. She didn't have a gambling problem as such, she just spent such an unreasonable amount of money on a bingo site she and her friends loved that it had become an inside joke. But that wasn't the point of the story. Thandie told them about how she'd spotted an email at the top of their grandma's inbox with the subject line: URGENT, YOUR LAST APPOINTMENT WITH DR. KHAN. She'd been too curious not to look but had kept her discovery a secret, thinking Drew didn't know, either, until he started making erratic enough decisions for her to tell that something major must be throwing him off. She could guess why her family had kept it a secret, but she was still disappointed in them for hiding the truth.

"We didn't want to upset you or give you something to worry about in the lead-up to the Olympics," said their grandpa, his eyes watering. He only ever cried tears of joy, so it was painful watching him like this. Watching them all like this.

"You were going through a lot last year, and we didn't want to add to that, sweetie," their grandma said, putting an arm around Thandie's shoulder and pulling her into a hug. When they pulled apart, he saw an expression on his sister's face that he hadn't seen since they were kids: She was scared. But when she spotted him looking at her, she shook it off and redirected the conversation.

"If there's anyone you should have been worried about, it was Drew. He's the one who's been spinning out for the past six months," Thandie said.

Drew had always considered himself to be the older, more responsible sibling. The unflappable, confident son his grandparents confided in. So, Thandie's words took him by surprise.

"Don't tell me that's the real reason why you dropped out?" his grandma said, disappointed. "You love what you do. You always did. And you only had two more weeks until graduation."

Drew sighed and noticed his sister's shoulders sag as she heard their grandma's mistake.

"I was in my junior year, Grandma. I still had a year and a half to go," he said gently.

"Oh, I just— That doesn't matter," his grandma said, sitting upright. She looked a little embarrassed. Drew didn't like to correct her—the doctor had told them it would only just upset her—but she was illustrating his point. Things were changing, and he couldn't waste a year and a half at college when things had changed so fast. But Grandma was insistent, telling them that even though she hadn't grown up with the same options as they had, she'd made the most of her youth. Traveling, taking risks, falling in love, and finding herself.

"So, I don't want either of you to put your lives on hold for me. It would break my heart. I'm not going to get better with time, so you can't just wait it out."

"Don't say that," Drew said reflexively, looking over at the sad expression on his sister's face.

"It's true. There's no use in pressing pause. Some people get worse over months or years or decades." She said it casually, as if she was talking about the warranty on an electrical appliance, not her life. Drew flinched. His grandma had always been pretty forthright, but this level of honesty was too much for dinner.

"She's right," his grandpa said, speaking up. Drew looked over at him, noticing the ways the past year had aged him. "We've made a decision. We love you and like having you at home. But you're not allowed to move back in with us."

Drew's eyes widened.

"You're kicking me out?" he said in shock, looking over to Thandie for backup. But she put her hands in the air as if this conversation was none of her business.

"Don't be dramatic, honey. You can stay for a few weeks. Two months at most. But then you've got to come up with a plan. You can't walk around Wisconsin feeling sad for the rest of your life," his grandma said.

"With all the love in the world, you're not math-minded enough to join the firm," his grandpa added. Thandie laughed at that, then caught Drew's eye and pantomimed zipping her lips as she dipped some asparagus into the cheese fondue—a dinner combination that didn't quite follow her Team USA nutrition plan.

Drew's mind immediately began laying out options. Reenrolling and moving back to California, putting together a portfolio to apply for the Hans Leitner job. But no, he thought. He'd made his decision, and he couldn't just waver. He was older and knew they needed help.

"I'm staying at home," he said firmly.

"No, you're not," his grandma replied. "Life isn't as long as you think it's going to be." She gently patted him on the shoulder.

Her words sent a chill down his spine. He looked over at his grandma. Her gray hair, her frail skin, her shrinking stature: He could feel her missing herself while she was still here.

"Things *are* going to change, Drew. But it's not your responsibility to throw your future away. Plus, I'm turning your room into my home library. You're not allowed to move back in," his grandpa said with a hint of a smile.

"But—"

"He's scared," Thandie said, taking a bite of her schnitzel. He hated to admit it, but she was right. They'd known each other all their lives. "Going home means that if he doesn't end up with the life he wants, he can blame it on Wisconsin."

"That's so cynical," Drew protested.

"But she's right. You quit while you're ahead so you don't have to risk it not working out," his grandpa said as he took a bite of his Älplermagronen, which was essentially just Swiss mac and cheese.

Drew sat and watched as his family ate their food, casually moving on from the confrontation-turned-intervention. He looked at all the cheese on the table, the wooden paneling on the walls, and the low lights of the room. Their house back home in Wisconsin looked nothing like this, but the scene before him reminded him of every family dinner he'd ever had. Aside from the silence about Grandma's health, his family was deeply honest. They loved each other too much not to say the truth and call each other out. So, Drew took his first bite of food and thought about everything they'd said. Maybe he did default to quitting before he had the chance to fail. They were probably right about his moving back home to escape the imposter syndrome he'd felt in California. Spending his life running away from what he loved to avoid failure wasn't the path to feeling fulfilled. Thandie noticed his empty glass and passed the jug of water over to him. He could tell that she was still annoyed with him. It was written all over her face, so he went to apologize.

"I'm sorry about Ari. If I'd known who she was from the start . . ."

"You don't need to explain yourself. I'll take my apology in the form of a lifetime's worth of favors," she said with a smile that promised she would find uniquely bizarre requests for him to fulfill as payback. "But seriously, Drew. Get your shit together. If you're not careful, you're going to miss out on the best that life has to offer you. Like Ari."

"You'd be okay with that?" he asked, surprised.

"No. But you *do* actually like her, don't you?"

Drew nodded as he watched his sister's face soften. "Yeah," he admitted. His grandparents looked back and forth at them, then Thandie sighed and gave him a long, hard look.

"So . . . what are you going to do about it?"

40

Ari

Ari was supposed to be heading to a celebratory team breakfast but instead she was sitting at the edge of her bed, replaying each scene from last night. The sight of Drew holding flowers for her, the comfort she'd felt around his grandparents and how, for a moment, she'd allowed herself to forget that this was all just pretend.

But then she thought about how tense things had gotten when Thandie arrived. The moment Drew had said this would never work out, and how she'd run out of the restaurant before she could let him say goodbye. She'd made the mistake of allowing herself to imagine an unlikely world in which she and Drew did make it work. She'd found whispers of it in the carefree laughter that came out whenever she was around him. In the way he reached out for her hand at the exact moment she needed it most. And in how many times she'd glanced over to find him smiling at her with those bright, kind, warm eyes. Because Drew wasn't like the boys she'd dated before. As she got ready to leave her room, she thought back to all the guys in her past.

Ari had a type: athletic, charming, and a little too intense. She'd spent so much of her life managing every situation around her that she'd found herself drawn to men who did the managing, who took care of things, made plans, and made sure everything was under control. But Drew was different. He never tried to change or direct her. She didn't feel like she was auditioning to be the other half of some sports power couple, nor did she feel like she had to curate an image of perfection to seamlessly fit into his world. With Drew, she felt lighter, more girlish, almost entirely unburdened.

Usually, when she started seeing someone new, her brain went on high alert. She was always looking for red flags and listening for alarm bells. But Drew had put all his cards on the table that very first night. So, instead of looking for signs that it wouldn't work, she'd absentmindedly started looking for reasons why it might. However, thoughts like that went against the terms and conditions of their arrangement. She and Drew had always had an expiration date, and now it was over. She wanted to go back in time, walk back into the restaurant, and tell him that she liked him for real. But she couldn't. So, instead, she put on her coat and left GB House to join her teammates for their quarterfinal-qualification breakfast.

Her phone started ringing as she opened the front door, so she patted herself down, trying to figure out which of the eight pockets in her puffer coat she'd put it in. When she pulled it out and saw that it was her mom, she answered immediately.

"Arikoishe, congratulations!" her mom said. She was on the other end of the phone, singing and ululating. So, her mom *had* heard about their win. Her congratulations were coming a day late, but Ari had always been quick to forgive.

"Thanks, Mama!" she said, stepping out into the snow. Excited to FaceTime with her mom and give her a play-by-play of the game. But she quickly realized that her mom hadn't just called to congratulate her.

"Well done, but I wanted to call you to talk about your sister. She's becoming a serious problem now, very unruly," her mom said with irritation.

Ari felt deflated. She loved her mom. When Ari was a teenager, she, her mom, and her sister had spent every night snuggled up on the sofa watching TV, and every weekend walking around the shops. Without their father in the picture, they were a tight unit. A solid three-rope bond. And because of that, Ari had always been her mother's closest confidante. It had started in small ways, with her mom telling her about how stressful work was or telling her about the latest extended-family drama. Then Ari became the first person her mom called whenever anything bad happened. Her mom told her about her money worries, the relatives back home who blamed her for the divorce, and all the arguments she had with Ari and Anesu's dad. Her mom spent hours confiding in her, and on more than one occasion, her mom ended the night weeping in her arms.

At first, Ari had seen it as a sign that her mother trusted her and thought she was responsible enough to talk to about grown-up things. But as she'd gotten into her later teenage years and started trying to build a life for herself, it became a burden. She knew that she was the only person her mother truly trusted, but that responsibility had started to weigh down on her. Her mom had so much going on that there was only enough air in their conversations for *her* issues. Now Ari was tired of it.

"Mom, when is my quarterfinal game?" Ari asked softly, coming to a pause in the middle of the path that led out of GB

House. She sat in the silence that confirmed her mom didn't know.

"Why did I break up with Harrison?" she asked, her eyes beginning to water as the silence continued.

"Arikoishe," her mom said gently. "We can talk about that when you come home, but first we need to fix the wedding dilemma." As Ari walked in the snow that morning, listening to her mother talk about how betrayed she felt by the situation, she realized she couldn't go on like this. She didn't want to. So, she shook her head and took her gloves off to better handle her phone. Getting her contacts up and tapping on the screen until she connected another call.

"Girl, I can't talk for long. I have to head out in ten minutes," her sister said as she appeared on her screen. She had half a face of makeup on, the lines of her contour still standing out against her neck and cheekbones.

"I think it's going to take you more than ten minutes." Ari smiled, then remembered that she wasn't just calling to chat. She tapped a few more buttons until a third face appeared on the screen.

"Arikoishe, is everything alright?" said her dad, sounding panicked. Ari rarely called him, and never without prior warning. It was strange to hear his voice on the other end of the phone. He still had a full head of hair, but it was speckled with strands of gray, highlighted by the sun pouring through the windows of his house in Harare, Zimbabwe. She'd never visited him and had no intention of going to his wedding. But on the two or three occasions a year when she called her dad, she always imagined what his home looked like. She wondered whether he had any framed photos of his daughters, if he'd kept any of the clothes she remembered from her childhood, or if he ever walked the halls of his new place and thought about his family.

But instead of asking him that, she tapped a few more buttons on her screen until the call merged and all four of them were on the line.

"Mom, Dad, Anesu. I love you, but I'm gonna say this for the first and last time: You're all draining the life out of me."

"You're being a bit dramatic," said Anesu.

"What is he doing here?" asked her mom.

"Is everything okay?" questioned her dad.

No. Everything wasn't okay. With them, or with her. But as snow fell in St. Moritz that morning, she realized that only the latter was her responsibility. They hadn't all sat on a call together like this in years, but desperate times called for desperate measures.

"Is this an attempt to get me to change my mind? Because I'm not doing that," began her sister.

Ari wasn't there to change anybody's mind. Or manage anybody's feelings. Not anymore. She needed to say her piece and leave them to sort things out for themselves.

"Dad, you shouldn't have left Mom to raise us by ourselves, and you shouldn't have left Anesu or me trying to figure out how to get you to be involved," she said bluntly. She heard her sister gasp. "You can't fix a decade-long absence with plane tickets and a wedding invite."

He looked startled by her words, but he didn't have anything to say in his defense.

"Arikoishe, don't speak to your father like that," began her mom, who loathed her dad in private but tried to keep up appearances in public. However, Ari wasn't done.

"Anesu, I'm not going to the wedding with you. But nobody should make you feel guilty for wanting to spend time with Dad. Going behind Mom's back wasn't fair, but it's up to you whether you go or not," she said softly.

Ari had given up on her relationship with her father a long time ago, but she hoped things would be different for her sister.

"And Mom, I love you," she said, her voice faltering. "But you're the mom. I'm your child, not your best friend. I don't want to take on all your burdens and I can't keep figuring everything out."

Ari felt guilty, but she needed to admit the truth. She'd been the fixer for so long that she didn't know how to operate in her family in any other way. But it wasn't her responsibility to always ensure everyone around her was okay, especially when they seemed incapable of doing the same for her. She needed to cut the umbilical cord and get them to figure out their own problems for once.

"Okay? Okay. I've got to go now, bye," she said, leaving the call before anyone could draw her back in.

She expected the group call to drop, but the minutes ticked by, and the call continued without her. The people pleaser in her was aching. She wanted to rejoin the call and stay on until everything was resolved. But she was starting to realize that each time she fixed something, she stopped the people around her from learning how to do it for themselves. Maybe her dad would stop inviting her sister to his gatherings after the wedding. Maybe her mom would feel so betrayed that every family dinner for the rest of their lives would be met with dread. Maybe her sister would get to know their dad enough to realize why Ari had tried so hard to keep her from disappointment. Anything could happen. It could all crumble and fall apart. But it wasn't Ari's job to be the glue that held her family together anymore. She had to focus on being everything to herself, not to everyone else. She didn't know who she would become if she closed the tap, but she wanted to find out.

With that problem out of her hands, she couldn't help but wonder what might happen if she took another leap. If she found her way back to one of the few people in her life who had never needed anything from her. The man who'd borne witness to her mess and complications. Who'd sat on a roof at the edge of a party and talked to her as they waited out the night. Because that moment had been too precious, too real, too important *not* to risk. So, she put her gloves back on and started walking to the canteen, mentally composing a text message to Drew with each step.

But then, just as she was about to turn the corner, she saw a group of guys wearing white, blue, and red uniforms, donning fleeces, winter coats, and branded kit bags. It was the Team GB snowboarding team and Harrison.

41

Drew

Drew jumped straight out of bed to go looking for Ari. He'd spent the entire night tossing and turning as he thought back through their last few conversations and reckoned with his family's mini intervention. Thandie was right about him. Each time he got close to the life he wanted, he jumped ship to quit on his own terms. His whole life felt driven by his fear of failure. But he didn't want that to be the thing that made him lose Ari. So, he got ready, stepped out into the snow, and searched the Village for the woman who'd been preoccupying his thoughts since New Year's Eve.

He knew that she and her teammates usually went out for breakfast at around 8:30 a.m., so he headed over to their canteen. But when he turned the corner and spotted Ari's bright blue puffer coat, he realized she wasn't alone. She was standing face-to-face with Harrison Cavendish. Drew stopped in his tracks as he watched Harrison wrap his arms around her and pull her into a hug. He tensed up and walked toward them, ready to intervene. But his shoulders dropped as he watched Ari wrap her arms around Harrison and hug him back.

They stood there for what felt like a lifetime. Ari showed no sign of wanting to let go.

Harrison looked up, spotted Drew, and locked eyes with him. Drew couldn't see Ari's face, but Harrison's looked satisfied. There was a clear *I told you so* in his gaze. Drew knew that Harrison was a grade-A asshole. And he knew that Ari had fake-dated him for the specific purpose of getting Harrison off her back.

But maybe there was more to the story than he thought. Ari had known Harrison for years, after all. They played on the same team, knew the same people, and shared the same world. Harrison and Ari made sense. They looked good together, had the same interests, and belonged to the same group of friends. Like Ari, Harrison was athletic, ambitious, and accomplished. Plus, Harrison had been in a *real* relationship with Ari. Which was more than Drew could say.

Maybe the plan had been to make Harrison jealous the whole time, and now that their arrangement was over, Ari was free to spend time with whomever she wanted to. He didn't want it to be true, but the longer he saw them together, the more accurate it seemed. Drew wanted to walk over to them and say something, in the hope that his suspicions weren't true. But Ari had made it clear from the get-go that she didn't want him to interfere. So, he turned around and walked away. After all, Drew hadn't come to Switzerland to chase after her, he'd come to pursue his professional dreams.

He had no idea whether he was going to go back to college or apply for the Leitner Productions job, but he did know that he was still on assignment with Zeus. He needed to edit all the recent photos he'd taken and head to a figure-skating competition that afternoon. So, he did his best to scrub the image of Ari and Harrison from his memory and get through all his tasks for the day. Focusing felt like a nearly impossible task, because while he was supposed to be editing, he kept replaying their conversations in his mind and wondering what she would think of each athlete he'd photographed that day. He walked to the ice rink for that afternoon's competition, hoping it would take his mind off of things. But he quickly realized that thinking it would distract him from Ari had been a mistake. Why? Because ice dance was romantic as hell.

Drew watched from the sidelines as sparkly-costumed skaters glided across the ice with the strength of hardened athletes and elegance of classically trained dancers. He snapped photos of each detail and watched each dance with pained admiration. His breath caught as each athlete skated through the air, and he gritted his teeth as he watched them land spins that were just as beautiful as they were terrifying. But it wasn't the fragile bones and unforgiving moves that wowed him. It was the couples on the ice. The intense stares into each other's eyes, the subtle emotions on their faces, the confidence it took to trust each other with their lives. He knew they were athletic partners, not usually romantic couples. This was all for show. But each dance was a story. A mesmerizing symbol of what it was to love and be loved. Putting oneself on the line, entrusting the most vulnerable parts of oneself to somebody else, jumping with the faith that they would catch your fall.

Or at least believing the dance was worth the risk.

"It's beautiful, isn't it?" said Hans Leitner as the dance ended and the audience took a break. Hans was standing just a few feet away in the press pit. But Drew had been so distracted thinking about Ari that he hadn't even noticed.

"It is," Drew said solemnly as he gazed out at the ice rink. His first impulse was to be embarrassed by his emotion, but Hans seemed to pick up on how Drew was feeling.

"I met my wife on an ice-skating rink. It was the Lake Placid Winter Games in 1980," Hans said, gazing out at the ice rink, his eyes wistful. "It was my first Olympics, and I'd spent the entire first week walking around, all wide eyed. Once my competitions were over, I drove to the next town over. I wanted to get away from the crowds for a moment, and that town has a lake that freezes up every year," Hans said with a faraway look, as if he could see the memory with complete clarity in his mind. Drew put his camera down and looked at Hans. He'd been trying to get some behind-the-scenes photos of the skaters as they awaited their turns, but he was so distracted that he decided he was better off listening to the story Hans had to tell.

"I was skating and taking photos of the scenery when I noticed her. She had one of those smiles that lights up a room, and I could see it from the other side of the lake as she skated around with her friends. But I was a quiet man back then, way too shy to talk to her. Even now, I prefer using my camera to having an actual conversation."

"Me too," said Drew, thinking of how much more comfortable he'd felt around Ari that first night with his camera around his neck. "So, who was the woman on the ice?"

"Eliza," Hans said with a twinkle in his eyes. "While she looked graceful and majestic from a distance, she had never been ice skating before. She was trying her best, but the lake was on a bit of a slope, so once she started skating downhill, she couldn't stop. Next thing you know, she was screaming and skating at full speed down the lake," he chuckled. "Kids were running away, and families were jumping off the ice so as not to get caught in her path. But I didn't, I couldn't. I had my camera out and kept pressing the shutter because she looked so mesmerizing in the early-morning light."

Drew immediately thought of Ari and how beautiful *she'd* looked in the early-morning light.

"Eliza was skating at full momentum, but in my trance, I forgot to move out of the way. So, she crashed right into me. We've been skating side by side ever since," Hans said with a smile, then hefted the camera in his hands and switched his focus back to the ice rink.

"What do you wish you had known about love before you found it?" asked Drew. It had nothing to do with the Olympics, but it was the question he wanted the answer to most. Hans looked to the side for a second as if carefully thinking through the last seventy-two years of his life.

"Love only comes around a few times. So, when it finds you, don't let it pass you by."

With that, the speakers erupted with sound, announcing the start of the next dance. The audience was intently focused on the rink again, and Hans had gone back to taking photos. But Drew was frozen still. He knew that he was supposed to be out in the crowd capturing audience members and taking photos of the skaters Zeus had sponsored. But as the song for the next skate began, Hans's words played back in his mind: *When it finds you, don't let it pass you by.*

Drew knew that there were no guarantees in life, and that lightning rarely struck twice in the same place. He and Ari lived in different cities and on different continents and they occupied completely different worlds. But by some beautiful twist of fate, they'd found each other again. The Winter Olympics would be over in less than a week, and although there was a tiny chance he could end up back in London in the spring, in all likelihood he would never see her again. As he watched the final moments of the next dance, he realized that if he didn't go all in, something that had the potential to be great would pass him by. Again. So, he put his camera into his pocket, walked out of the press pit, and ran out into the snow.

42

Ari

It had all gotten to be a bit too much for Ari.

The pile of things weighing down on her kept getting heavier. So, when she saw Harrison and experienced the dread of being faced with yet another one of her problems, her final dam of self-preservation broke. She'd been holding it together since January, but she couldn't pretend to be stronger than she was anymore. So, she began to cry, an involuntary action that led her into his arms. Harrison was the last person in the world she wanted to see. But a warm body was a warm body. So, she let herself sink into the hug.

"Come here, babe, it's going to be okay," Harrison said, holding her tight. For a moment, she found it comforting, but then she came back to her senses.

"If that guy hurt your feelings, just tell me. I'll deal with him," said Harrison, unnervingly tense.

"It's fine," she said, pulling back from the hug. But Harrison wasn't listening. He never had. The first time she'd seen him like this, jealous and protective, she'd found it attractive. Assurance that he would do anything for her. But that jealousy had extended to every single person in their vicinity, including her friends. She'd desperately wanted to make things work with Harrison, so she'd allowed herself to be gradually pulled away from the people she loved, straining her relationships until she rarely saw her friends outside of hockey games and compulsory team-training sessions.

"You know I love you, I always will. It kills me that you're seeing someone else, but I know in the end, it's you and me," Harrison said, trying to pull her back in. But being around him reminded her of how constricting their relationship had been. So, she pulled back and extricated herself from his arms. Deciding that this time, it was for good.

"Harrison, we're not together. We're never getting back together," she said plainly as she took a step back.

"You don't mean that," he said, taking a step forward.

She'd spent the past six months tiptoeing around this conversation. Avoiding calls, walking to the other side of rooms, fake-dating someone new. Anything to avoid this conversation with him. But it was time to be honest.

"I don't want to see you again," she said firmly, so it was clear that there would be no gray area. "I don't want you to keep conveniently popping up wherever I go, I don't want you lurking in the shadows of my life in case I change my mind," she said, watching his expression grow darker.

"You're being emotional. But it's okay, I know how you really feel," he said, shaking his head. Back to acting like every boundary line she tried to draw was an overreaction.

"No, I'm *telling* you how I really feel."

"You'll change your mind," he said, stepping closer.

"No, I won't," she said, stepping back again.

"You will, because in the end, it's you and me," he said, reaching for her and slowly stroking her hair in a way that sent a haunting chill down her spine.

"I don't like you anymore, Harrison. Let it go," she said, but he had just placed a firm grip on her shoulder. She stood completely still for a moment as she realized what was happening. He was trying to hold her in place. He'd never hurt her, not physically. At least, she didn't think so. But there was a strange look in his eyes, and it made her feel uneasy. In that moment she realized that this was the man Harrison had always been.

"Let go," she said. Her voice didn't come out as loud as she wanted it to.

"Babe," he said, holding on tighter. She shook her shoulder, but he didn't move his hand.

"*She said* let go," came a familiar voice as the sound of footsteps crunched across the snow.

Ari turned around. It was Sienna. And Yasmeen. And Izzy. All three of them were holding their kit bags and hockey sticks. They glared at Harrison with looks so lethal that even the strongest person would have withered.

"Back off, Harrison," said Izzy, brandishing her hockey stick.

"If you don't take your hands off her, I'm calling security," said Yasmeen, her tone laced with venom.

At first, Ari was embarrassed.

I can handle it myself, a small voice in her mind said.

But I don't have to, another, slightly louder voice said.

Harrison took a step back, assessed Ari's friends with barely contained disdain, and looked at Ari as if to say, "Are you going to let them talk to me like this?"

But Ari wasn't the same woman she'd been last year. So, this time, she took a stand.

"I don't want to see you again. And I mean *never*. Don't text, don't call, stay out of my life for good," she said.

And with the four of them looking at him in disgust, Harrison finally relented and walked away. He could be horrible in private, but he was too much of a coward to be his true self when other people were around.

Ari let out a sigh of relief as the surge of adrenaline began to dissipate. Between her family drama, the pressure of becoming a good captain, and dealing with her relationship dilemmas, she felt like she'd been running at full speed for days and was about to crash.

"I hate that guy. I always have and always will," said Sienna quietly. Yasmeen and Izzy nodded along.

"I just feel so tired," Ari said, her voice barely a murmur as she felt tears starting to fall again. But this time, she ended up in the arms of her three favorite girls.

They'd grown up together, lost games, carried each other through heartache, and been there for each other through the best and worst of life. But somewhere along the way, that bond had fractured. And since then, Ari had felt like a swimmer alone at sea. Desperately searching for a buoy, but so far removed from everyone who loved her that it seemed necessary to deal with it all alone.

"I'm sorry I've been so distant," she said, her voice quivering as she sat on a nearby bench.

"It's okay, you know we love you," said Izzy as they went over to sit beside her. But Ari couldn't stop thinking about how alone she'd felt through it all.

"I just feel like I've been on this treadmill all year, carrying everything by myself, and I don't think I can do it anymore," Ari said.

"We can carry it with you," said Yasmeen, giving her arm a squeeze.

"But how am I supposed to keep the team together if I'm falling apart?" she said, her voice breaking. She'd done a pretty good job of holding it together, but the worry that had come over her ever since Gracie's injury was threatening to break her.

"It's not your responsibility to keep us together, Ari, we're grown," said Sienna.

"If we make a mess, we can fix it. You can't take on everybody's burden," said Yasmeen. Ari shook her head. That didn't feel true, it hadn't felt true for a long time. And since she was on a streak of honest conversations, she decided to tell them.

"But whenever an issue comes up, whether it's training, a big game, or friendships, you all look to me. I love you, I love being there for you. But do you know how much responsibility that is right now?" she said, being honest for once. "It's exhausting trying to be everything to everyone without getting anything back. I don't even feel like I can talk to you anymore because I have to maintain this image of having it together," she said.

Her friends had been her safe space, but she'd let a chasm form between them. When she was appointed captain, she began compartmentalizing to try to ensure that her self-doubts didn't affect the team. It had gotten to the point where there was no space left in which to be complicated, messy, and occasionally broken. Except when she was with Drew.

"I just don't want to let you down," she said as tears slid down her cheeks. Her three best friends squeezed her tight.

"You could never let us down. You're an excellent player and an incredible captain. But most importantly, you're our best friend. If anything, we've been letting you down," said Izzy. Sienna nodded.

"The stress of everything made us focus more on winning than making sure we were winning together. We probably put way too much pressure on you to deal with how hard this has been," said Sienna, and the other two nodded.

Ari had put too much pressure on herself, too. She'd spent her whole life hearing pundits say that women weren't strong enough for the game, that they let their emotions get the best of them, and they couldn't handle pressure. So, she'd unintentionally spent her life trying to prove them wrong, taking on more to appear stronger and more effortless than she needed to be.

And the truth was, she could handle a lot.

But a man she'd met on a rooftop had reminded her she didn't have to handle everything alone to prove a point. So, she looked around at her friends, wiped her eyes, and decided it was finally time to let herself lean on them. Because as long as she had her girls, she would never be alone.

"Okay, in the spirit of helping each other, could you do me a favor?" Ari asked, and they all nodded. She reached for her wrist and unclasped gold timepiece and black leather band that had been weighing her down for too long. "Could you help me get rid of this watch?"

43

Drew

Drew knew that calling Ari wasn't enough. There were certain conversations that had to be done in person. Face-to-face, close enough to bare your soul. So, once he'd said goodbye to Hans and left the figure-skating competition, he walked out into the Village and tried to find her. He ran through the snow and over to the skating rink to see if she might be there for practice, but the rink was occupied by the Finnish men's team training for their quarterfinal. As the sun set, he went to Ari's favorite café to ask if she'd ordered a cup of matcha, but they hadn't seen her since that morning. So, he headed to the multibuilding complex known as GB House.

Every team in the Olympic Village had a log cabin–themed team lounge room to hang out in when they weren't training or competing. The lounge rooms were decorated with fireplaces, cozy blankets, and athletes hanging out in loungewear holding steaming mugs of tea as day turned to night. The cabins were where they unwound after a long day of training and competitions. When Drew walked in, the only people inside were the athletes living there. He didn't want to intrude, so he turned around and readied himself to leave. But then someone called his name.

"Drew?" came a voice he vaguely recognized. He turned toward the voice and saw a woman with pale skin and red hair. Izzy. She was one of Ari's teammates he'd met at the curling competition.

"Wait, don't smile at him, Izzy, we don't know why he's here," said Yasmeen, who'd led the courtside interrogation a few days ago.

"Take a seat, *Drew*," said Sienna, beckoning him over. She carefully studied him as if trying to figure out whether to let him stick around. "So, what are your intentions with Ari?"

"Don't make it weird," Izzy said to Sienna.

"Are we supposed to just let him in without doing a background check? *She* likes him, but *we* barely know this man," said Sienna, assessing him with a cold, protective glare.

"Tell us, Drew, why *are* you here?" asked Yasmeen, studying him.

Drew looked at all three women and thought about the question. He realized that if there was anybody he could tell, it was probably the people who cared about Ari the most.

"I don't know how much she's told you about the fake-dating situation. . . ." he began.

"You were fake-dating?" said Izzy, her eyes widening in shock.

"Izzy, it was so obvious," said Yasmeen. "When has Ari ever dated a guy who wasn't a carbon copy of everyone we went to school with?"

"The fact that he takes photos was a dead giveaway. She dates athletes, not . . . artists," said Sienna.

"Well, the way she's been smiling at her phone all week didn't look fake," said Izzy. The other two nodded and cast their eyes back to Drew. So, they'd seen it, too?

"Well, yeah . . . it was complicated. Which is why I'm here. I want to tell her how I feel," he said, watching their expressions soften. The three of them exchanged glances, having a conversation without saying a word. After a few moments of unspoken dialogue, they reached a silent consensus. They were still fixing him with intensely protective looks, making it clear that they wouldn't hesitate to deal with him if they needed to. But eventually, he got a response.

"She's outside, on the lake," said Sienna.

"She skates in circles when she's stressed out," said Yasmeen with a nod, gesturing to the window. The lounge was on the seventh floor of the building, so you could see a good view of the village from its windows. As Drew looked in the direction Yasmeen was pointing toward, he noticed a circle of trees surrounding a frozen lake. The very place he and Ari had visited a few days ago. And sure enough, there was a tiny figure in a blue puffer coat skating in circles in the middle of the frozen lake. Drew immediately stood up.

"Do you have ice skates I can borrow?" he asked, looking over at the ice.

"What's your shoe size?" asked Yasmeen.

"Eleven," he said. Unsurprisingly, Ari's teammates didn't wear the same size shoe as him. So, Izzy got up, stood on the armchair she'd been sitting on, and raised her voice for the whole common room of athletes to hear.

"Does anybody have size eleven skates I can borrow?" she shouted across the room. When no one responded, Izzy raised the stakes. "This man, Drew, is in love!" she shouted.

Drew hadn't said he was in love. But he could imagine a future time when that would be true.

"He's in love and has to tell her right now," Izzy said dramatically. "But he needs to cross the lake to get to her. So again, I'm asking, does anybody have a pair of size eleven skates?"

"I could fit into a twelve, too," Drew said.

"He could fit into size twelve, too!" Izzy shouted. People looked up, but nobody responded.

"Theo, I know you have skates he could borrow," said Sienna, looking over at a guy wearing a speed-skating jersey.

"Theo?" said Yasmeen, looking at Sienna curiously.

"*Theo?*" said Izzy with a teasing voice.

"What happens in the Village stays . . . actually, that's none of your business," Sienna said, crossing her arms as her friends laughed. But Theo came over, gave Sienna a kiss on the cheek, and took a pair of skates from his kit bag. Izzy grinned, Yasmeen smirked, and Sienna focused her eyes on the ground. But Drew just grabbed the skates and thanked them.

When he left the cabin, his feet plunged straight into eight inches of snow. He ignored the cold and ran down the slippery steps toward his destination. As he descended, he looked around at the Village. At the buildings that now lit up the sky and the way the moon reflected onto the icy lake. Tiny flakes of snow were falling all around him, but the night felt still. The world felt quiet. He slowed the pace of his snowy trudge when he reached the bottom of the steps. Only then did he realize how big the lake actually was.

Ari was still skating around it, moving in fast-paced circles along the perimeter. But she occasionally crossed from one side to the other without any pattern or apparent cause. She was wearing headphones, that blue coat, and heavy-duty hockey skates. But she looked as graceful as anything, smoothly moving along the ice like a seabird skimming a quiet ocean. As he watched her and thought of all the moments he'd spent with her, he realized that what Izzy had said was right.

So, he sat on the ground, tied up his laces, and hobbled through the snow until he reached the lake. But as his first skate hit the ice, he remembered one fundamental flaw in his spontaneous plan.

Drew couldn't skate.

44

Ari

At nighttime, the Village always came alive with streetlights, brightly lit venues, and thousands of tiny smartphone screens as people milled in and out of each competition. But things were quieter here down on the frozen lake. Ari had spent so much of her life playing hockey that she'd forgotten she could experience the ice just for fun. So, what had started as a few slow laps around the perimeter to take her mind off things had turned into an hour of gliding across the lake to old romantic jazz songs while watching the snow fall like tiny crystals. Skating and admiring the sky as it went from dusk to nightfall. Nights like this made her think of Drew, took her back to the moment the clock had struck midnight, to kissing him in the snow, and the perennial twinkle in his eyes. She wondered if she could teach herself to be satisfied with the memory of him.

People were complicated, relationships were multilayered, and the more she knew someone, the less she could contain them to just one perfect moment in time. Maybe Drew was better as a perfectly framed memory, a fleeting moment for her future self to remember as a dream. Containing him like that would be the easiest way to protect her heart. But Ari didn't want to protect her heart. She wanted to walk through the snow with him, sit beside him on a rooftop, and wait out the night. She was skating around in circles, trying to change her mind, but for better or for worse, her mind was set on Drew.

She was about to complete her final lap, pick up her phone, and find him. But when she skated around the corner, she saw a small figure in a black coat shuffling across the ice.

The person who'd joined her had no idea what they were doing. They walked across the ice as if they were wearing shoes and slipped a little with each step. Ari watched as they attempted to skate, but they lost momentum after a few feet. Ari had no idea who would be foolish enough to attempt something like this, but they were heading toward her. She took off her headphones to assess the situation. Only then did she realize he was calling her name.

"Ari, it's me!" the man shouted from the other side of the lake. He was slipping and sliding across the ice, but he was persistent. Picking himself up and trying to skate despite the fact that he clearly didn't know how to. Ari's face softened, and her heart picked up the pace. It was Drew.

"What are you doing here?" she shouted across the lake as they began to skate toward each other.

"I had to speak to you!" He was still too far away to talk without shouting, but he was shuffling across the ice with fierce determination.

"But I thought you didn't know how to skate?" she shouted across the lake.

"I don't, but I had to give it my best shot to skate to you!" he shouted as he slipped again. Ari began to laugh, and so did he. He looked ridiculous flailing around in those speed-skating boots, but maybe that's why she liked him.

"You could have just called!" she shouted.

"I had to tell you in person!"

"Tell me what?"

He just looked at her and smiled, shuffling toward her faster than before.

"I lied on New Year's! I take it back. Thinking something will end isn't what makes it feel so romantic. It's the possibility that it *might not end*!" he shouted as his shuffle finally became a skate.

"What are you saying?" she asked, but she already knew. It terrified her as much as it delighted her.

"You watch the last ten minutes of a film first and then go back to the start, which is so bizarre. But you do it because you want to know there's a happy ending, and I think that's beautiful. Your eyes light up whenever you speak about the things you love, which makes me never want to stop asking you questions. In fact, I would watch curling competitions every day if it meant spending more time with you," he said, skating toward her with more confidence.

"Drew, you can't say all of that," she said, raising her hands. He wasn't allowed to tell her things that made her heart swell when they both knew he would be out of her life before the end of the week.

"It's true, though. I mean it. It was a fake relationship, but they were *always* real feelings," he said as he skated closer. She could feel her heart beating a little faster. She wanted to give herself up to how she felt, but reality kept trying to hold her back.

"But I'm not a perfect person," she said.

"Who *is*?"

"I don't have all of my shit together."

"Does it look like *I* do?" he said with a boyish smile as they both looked down at his borrowed skates.

"We could mess each other up," she said, voicing the fear she'd been trying to protect herself from.

"It's always a possibility." He nodded.

"And it could end really, really badly."

"It could." He nodded again. "But maybe it won't." He crossed the final length of ice to stand, precariously, right in front of her.

Ari had spent hours trying to protect herself from heartbreak. But maybe she'd been holding herself back from something good, too. Hope was a delicate, dangerous thing. Falling in love meant giving someone the key to the most vulnerable, sensitive parts of who she was. It was diving in while knowing she could hurt him, and she could get hurt too. On paper, the risk was worth it for the right person. However, she wouldn't know who the right person was until she got to the other side. But as Ari looked at Drew, standing on the ice with a nervous smile and a twinkle in his eye, she decided that he was worth taking the chance.

"Ari, I know there are a dozen reasons why it might not work out, but I would risk them all for the chance to get to know you better. I want to be the one cheering you on from the bleachers, walking with you through the snow, and sneaking out of parties to get to talk to you."

"But Drew . . ." she said, slightly overcome with emotion. He just nodded his head and looked her in the eye.

"I know, I know. But if we're an old, messed-up, well-loved secondhand car, I want to see this thing through until the engine breaks down," he said with a smile. She laughed as she remembered what she'd said the other night.

"Until the radio stops working, and we're just humming to pass the time?" she joked.

"Until the wheels fall off," he said, reaching for her hand. "So, can we please break up? I don't want to be your fake boyfriend anymore, and I don't want to be just your friend. I'm falling for you," he said plainly.

"I think I am, too," she whispered, the knowledge only hitting her as she said it out loud.

"So, who cares about all the reasons it might not work out," he said.

"Because it might," she replied.

"It might."

He leaned forward, wrapped his arm around her waist, and pulled her in. Drew's half-frozen fingers traced a delicate line across her face, putting a sparkle in her eyes. Crystal snowflakes floated down from the night sky and moonlight shimmered against the ice. Time paused as they stood there in each other's arms. This, she realized, was the closest she'd ever come to magic.

45

Ari

Ari had been the first person on her team to wake up every morning since New Year's Day. She'd gotten out of bed at the first chords of her alarm and left the dorm to take a walk while listening to her audiobooks, studying her team's last game, and equipping herself with the knowledge she needed to help them play better than ever. But when Ari woke up on the morning of the quarterfinal, she was surprised to see that everyone else in her room was already up and ready. She immediately panicked and grabbed her phone, thinking she'd somehow slept through her alarm. But when she looked at her screen, it was 5:59 a.m. She rubbed her eyes and looked at her teammates.

"Why are you awake so early?" she asked as Sienna zipped up her fleece.

"It's game day," Yasmeen said as she laced up her shoes.

"But the game isn't until four p.m.," Ari said, sleepy and confused.

"You wake up early every morning, walk alone, and get ready for all our matches by yourself. So today, we're joining you," said Yasmeen as she shrugged on her coat.

Ari paused, smiled, and got dressed before the four of them left their room and walked out into the corridor. When she opened the door, the entire team was waiting in the hallway. All twenty-two of her teammates were wearing thermals and winter coats as they clutched hot flasks of tea and got ready to go outside.

"Let's go, Captain," said Izzy, handing Ari a flask with her favorite golden matcha as they all walked down the stairs of GB House. The sun hadn't risen yet, but the first glimmers of early-morning light would appear on the horizon in an hour. Ari had gotten so used to going outside alone that she'd equated the first hours of the day with silence. All she'd heard was the sound of the snow beneath her feet and the facilities management staff gritting the pathways to melt ice. But as she and her girls walked through the snow that morning, the Village sounded more alive than ever before. The path was filled with laughter, conversation, and the sound of her team's excited feet stepping out onto an untouched layer of snow. They spent the walk sipping from their flasks, talking about the game ahead of them, and catching up on everything they'd missed in each other's lives since arriving in the Village, including the truth behind Ari's new relationship.

"I'm really happy for you," Yasmeen said. "And Drew seems like a nice guy, but . . ."

"Dating Thandie Dlamini's *brother*? Not my best decision," Ari said, rubbing her temple.

"You know what this means, right?" Sierra said, flashing her a wicked smile.

"That Thandie is going to try and destroy us just to get back at me? Yes," said Ari.

That morning marked the day of the ice hockey quarterfinals. Against the odds, they'd made it further than any other GB women's ice hockey team by making it to the quarterfinals. And their prize for making it this far was playing a group of women they'd never won a game against in their lives, Team USA.

"Well, I hope Drew's worth it," Sienna said with a warm smile. Ari just nodded. No matter what happened next, he was.

Coach McLaughlin always sequestered them on the day of a major game, so Ari decided to use her phone to get the behind-the-scenes photos essential to capturing the day of the quarter-final. She and her friends spent the morning getting ready and taking dozens of photos of each step in the process. From grabbing breakfast and packing their kit bags to trudging through the snow as they made their way to the stadium. Upon arriving at the training rink, Ari was in the middle of taking a picture of Yasmeen and Sienna dancing down the halls when she saw a familiar face waiting for them outside the corridor that led to the locker rooms.

"Thandie?" Ari said, looking over at the woman who stood in front of them.

She was dressed in the comfiest version of the Team USA uniform that morning. Sleek, white tracksuit bottoms and a stylish blue sweatshirt with her name embroidered on the sleeves. It was strange to see Thandie like this, fresh faced in the morning light. She seemed younger than usual, her face soft and open.

"Can we talk . . . alone?" Thandie asked, looking over at Ari's teammates.

They cast her curious glances but headed over to the locker room once Ari gave them a nod to go ahead. Once they'd left, Ari and Thandie walked over to a bench in the hallway and sat down. Ari's mind instantly wandered back to dinner the other day, cringing at the memory. They'd both acted out, but Ari could understand why Thandie hated her so much.

"I am really sorry about the accident," Ari said. "Truly, I would have never done something like that on purpose. I was just—"

"I know," Thandie said softly. "You don't have to apologize."

When they were kids on the teenage league, a few of their teammates had been friends. So, they'd ended up at enough of the same sponsor talks, brand events, and post-competition after-parties to become friendly acquaintances. But they hadn't spoken one-on-one like this since the accident. After a few moments of silence, Thandie finally sighed and spoke up.

"If I was on the men's team, people would love me for being competitive, you know," Thandie said. "The way I move on the rink? They would praise me for being strategic. The energy I put into being the best? They would say I'm focused, relentless, an athlete on their way to the hall of fame."

"You are," said Ari, because it was true. Thandie was undeniably one of the best in the game.

"Thank you. But that's not the narrative that people focus on when I'm on the rink. Did you know that a commentator once said live, on air, that I'm 'not a girl's girl'?" Thandie sounded genuinely hurt. It was one of those throwaway insults that cut deep.

"I organize all my teammates' birthday dinners, coach the under-fourteens' team in the breaks between seasons, and would literally go to war for the people I love. But I'm allegedly *not a girl's girl* because I have the audacity to be *and believe* that I'm the best at what I do?"

"It's bullshit." Ari nodded. She'd never really looked at things from Thandie's point of view. But she knew full well that it wasn't easy being a woman in professional sports.

"So, if you know it's bullshit, why do you perpetuate it?" Thandie said, looking directly at her. There was no annoyance in her voice. Just curiosity, and a little bit of hurt. Ari paused for a moment.

"I don't understand."

"I heard you, you know. At the first major game I played when I came back from the injury that almost ruined my life? I walked into the canteen and heard you and your teammates describing me like I was this mean, vicious, unreasonable person just because I didn't want to make small talk and hand out fake smiles."

Ari thought back to the competition Thandie was talking about. She did remember talking about Thandie with her teammates, but she had no idea that she'd overheard them. She would have never said anything if she'd known she was in the room.

"I didn't know," Ari said, but it was a weak excuse. Thandie shook her head.

"It's one thing to hear that from commentators and rival teams, but from you? We don't have to be friends, but a little bit of grace and consideration would have been nice. You know how quick they are to villainize women. *Especially* Black women. Of all the people in the league, I hoped that you would stand up for me when I came back." Thandie shrugged, disappointed.

And suddenly everything clicked into place. Ari was hit with a wave of self-awareness.

"I guess I was just so caught up with my own worries and insecurities that I never stopped to question whether I was projecting them onto you," Ari said, looking over at Thandie. "I'm so sorry."

But words didn't feel like enough, so she lifted her arms and pulled Thandie into a hug. At first Thandie froze, but then she hugged her back. It felt like the end of one chapter and the start of another. When they let go, both women laughed a little.

"Don't think I'm going to go easy on you because we hugged it out." Thandie smiled.

"I would expect nothing less than you at your best." Ari nodded, but she couldn't just leave it there. So, she told her the truth. "You know we all look up to you, right?"

"Flattery doesn't work on me," Thandie said, waving her off and picking up her bag.

"But it's not. It's the truth. Your comeback was the best thing to happen to the sport, seeing you pick yourself up, come back better than before, and be so determined. It inspired us, especially me."

"Really?" Thandie's eyes lit up.

"Yeah, it did. I used to think, *If Thandie can come back like that, there's no excuse for us not to do everything we can to do the same.* The sport is better because you're in it, and it shouldn't have taken all of this for me to tell you that."

"Okay, that's enough sincerity for one day," Thandie said, standing up.

"See you on the rink?" Ari said.

Thandie flashed her a wicked smile.

"May the *best team* win."

46

Drew

"Did you see the news?" Luiz asked as soon as Drew walked into the press office that morning.

"No, what news?"

Drew braced himself a little. He'd grown a bit too accustomed to new information turning his life upside down. But as Luiz spun his laptop around to show him the headline on the screen, Drew couldn't help but smile.

"No way. Is that real?" he asked, seeing the photo of Harrison at the very top of the BBC News website.

As much as Drew disliked Harrison, there was no denying that the man was an excellent snowboarder. But to many people's disappointment, Harrison had just had his gold medal revoked. According to the news article, he'd been met with a surprise drug test that came up hot. Unexpected urine sample tests were a standard part of Olympian life; they came at random and followed people throughout the entirety of their athletic careers. Everyone knew they could be tested at any time, though it was rare to be met with one immediately after a big Olympic-gold celebration party. The urine test hadn't found any steroids or performance-enhancing drugs, but it had found a powdery white substance in his blood more potent than snow.

"Wait, isn't your—" Drew began to ask, knowing full well that Luiz's partner worked on the anti-doping team. But Luiz put his finger over his lips and shook his head before Drew could finish his sentence—they were in the press office, after all. They couldn't risk an overheard conversation getting out.

"What an . . . unfortunate coincidence," Drew said, correcting himself.

"Wasted talent," Luiz said, careful not to implicate himself. "I guess he just let the success get to his head."

"You could say . . . he fucked around and found out." Drew shrugged as the two of them laughed and wordlessly agreed to never talk about it again.

Luiz's desk was cluttered with press credentials, SD cards, charging cables, and notebooks. But he and Drew pushed them all aside to place a wide-screen monitor at the center. They hooked it up to Drew's laptop and called everyone over to see the post that was about to go live.

"It's nine fifty-eight," said Drew, nervously staring at his screen as a crowd of people he'd met over the past two weeks assembled around him. The staff were drinking their morning coffees, the volunteers were chatting about competitions, and the journalists were scrolling through emails from their editors, but they all looked just as excited as he was. Everybody had a hectic day ahead of them, but Luiz had gathered them together for one reason. There was a sense of quiet anticipation in the air as they looked at the screen and then at Drew. A few of them even had their phone cameras out, ready to capture the moment as it happened.

"Nine fifty-nine," said Luiz.

As Drew looked around at the press office, he realized that this was the kind of day he would want to remember. Maybe his future self would trace all the best things in his life back to this moment. Or perhaps he'd refer to it as his peak. Whether it was the start of a new era, or the golden summit of one that was about to end, he wanted to savor it. So, he paused for a second and took it all in. The gentle flutter of snowflakes outside the window, the constant chatter of the press office, the sound of typing keyboards, the smell of filtered coffee, the memory of Ari's face lit up on the lake. And finally, the sense that no matter what came next, it would be worth the risk. If this was as good as things ever got, this morning would be more than enough.

As all the world clocks on the wall ticked to mark the start of a new hour, Drew nodded and faced his screen. He placed a hand over his mouse, moved the cursor, and clicked REFRESH. He held his breath as the shaky Wi-Fi refreshed the home page of the official Olympics website, staring at the screen as it turned white, froze for a second, and then reloaded.

The top headlines were as he expected. A gold medal for a legendary figure skater, an interview with the head of the Olympic Organizing Committee, and a highlights reel of the Games so far. But when he scrolled down, he was greeted by a wide-screen photo collage that made the crowd surrounding him begin to cheer.

A security guard from the accreditation team patted him on the back, a CNN photographer gave him a small nod of respect, and a volunteer took a video as the rest of the crowd urged him to click on the page they'd been waiting to see all morning.

**THE GAMES MAKERS: THE HEROES BEHIND THE SCENES
OF THE WINTER GAMES BY ANDREW DLAMINI**

Since arriving in the Village, Drew had been taking photos of the volunteers, contract workers, and staff members who brought the Games to life. It had started casually, something he just did because his eyes were drawn to the people doing the jobs he aspired to. But then he'd become more intentional with it. The Olympics was as significant a career milestone for the people behind the scenes as it was for the athletes. But because they all spent so much time fielding requests, averting crises, and making sure everyone who stepped into the Village had a smooth experience, they rarely stopped to take photos of themselves. So, Drew had become their unofficial self-appointed photographer. He'd taken photos of the security guards as they checked everyone's credentials, the medics who stood by the side of each match ready to intervene, and the gritters who woke up early each morning to clear the snow and cover the pathways with salt to make sure nobody got hurt. For a while, he'd had no idea what to do with those photos, so he just printed them off and gave them as gifts to the people he'd met and photographed along the way. But then he'd gotten talking to Luiz.

Their easy friendship had led Drew to forget that Luiz worked for the media department of the Olympics. When Drew had shown him the photos and explained that Zeus didn't want them, Luiz had made a few calls and then sent the photos over to one of the online content managers in the press office. A few emails and questions later, they agreed that the photos deserved a home—and thus, his behind-the-scenes photo diary had come to life.

There was a portrait of a broadcast engineer from Colombia accompanied by the story that explained how she'd handled the curling match streaming crisis. There was a group picture of Jørgen and the other baristas talking about the hundreds of coffees they made each day for the coaching teams during the most important weeks of their professional lives. And there was a set of photos of the chief icemaker who spent hours meticulously perfecting the ice rinks in the Village. But the centerpiece of it all was a photo of Luiz on his laptop amid the chaos of the press office: the calm in the storm.

As Drew got up from his chair to show the other volunteers and staff members the photos he'd captured of them, he looked around the press office and thought about how far he'd come. From slipping on the snow between Zeus assignments to somehow plucking up the courage to ask his heroes to let him take photos of them. He was still uncertain about the future, but since last night, a few more things had clicked into place. He'd sat down with his family and had an honest conversation about all the secrets they'd been keeping from each other. He and Thandie had bickered for precisely three minutes before she forgave him for keeping Ari a secret. On the condition that he photographed her entire team's headshots for free. Drew still didn't know if he was going to go back to college or accept his new life in Wisconsin, but he was beginning to find comfort in the uncertainty of just doing the next right thing.

So, once he'd collected his things, he, Luiz, and the friends they'd made in the press office put on their coats and walked out into the snow. It was time to head over to the hockey stadium and sit in the delightfully neutral press box. Because soon the horn would blare and the puck would land in the middle of the rink for what felt like the most important game of the year.

"Which team are you cheering on?" asked Luiz, taking a sip of coffee as they looked out at the ice.

Drew shook his head and smiled. He knew where his loyalties were supposed to lie. But as supporters and fans began to fill the audience, he realized that despite the last twenty-two years of his life, for half of the game at least, he'd be cheering on the other side.

47

Ari

Ari was walking down the corridor toward the locker room when she saw a familiar face coming her way The wheelchair was new though. Ari dropped her plastic cup and headed straight into the arms of the woman who'd unintentionally changed her life.

"Ari, I'm so proud of you!" Gracie said as she squeezed her tight. Ari couldn't hold back her tears, and as it turned out, neither could Gracie.

"You're here? How? When?" Ari asked as she crouched beside her wheelchair.

"I took the first flight I could get as soon as you qualified for the quarterfinals. I knew you could do it," Gracie said, beaming at her.

"Oh, it wasn't me, it was the rest of the team. I just asked myself, 'What would Gracie do?' and then started doing it," Ari said, quickly shrugging it off.

"Don't do that," Gracie said firmly. "*You* did this. You were always capable of doing it, that's why Coach and I decided you were the best fit for the job."

Ari was taken aback. She had no idea that Gracie had been involved in that conversation. In fact, she'd felt so bad about Gracie's accident that she'd pushed the question of why she'd been made captain to the back of her mind. Only sending Gracie a handful of texts and refusing to let herself call for help, even though she knew there was no one better to seek advice from than the woman who'd spent years captaining ice hockey teams.

"You had it in you the whole time. *Enjoy* this moment," Gracie said, squeezing her hand. Ari wanted to ask more, finally get some advice and listen for the magic words she needed to win the match. But Gracie was already wheeling herself away. Ari tried to get her to go to the locker room and give the team a pep talk, but Gracie just shook her head and waved her off.

"This is *your* moment; they're your team now. Just let me be your biggest fan," Gracie said with a grin before making her way to the entrance of the supporters' box. She was right. So, Ari left to join her team.

The energy in the locker room that afternoon was different. It wasn't like the heated tension before their competition against Japan or the terrified dread of their game against Sweden. It didn't match the hopeful playfulness of their first game or the celebration that followed their last game. This was something different altogether. That afternoon felt like the night before a big birthday. It was excitement, mixed with dread, sprinkled with a healthy dose of fear. Izzy was dancing around the room to her pregame playlist, Yasmeen was spraying her favorite perfume onto her jersey sleeves, and Izzy had her eyes closed, trying to center herself amid the chaos. Ari stood still, framing the memory. She and her best friends would never be as young as they were right now, at their first Olympics, about to play the biggest game of their careers.

Ari sent out a silent prayer that she would know her teammates for the rest of her life. That even if they grew up, stopped playing professionally, and moved apart, they'd always come back together on the ice. But she decided that if they didn't, this afternoon would be enough. So, once everyone was ready, she stood up on a bench to make sure they could all see her.

"I know I don't have a great reputation for pregame pep talks, but it's the quarterfinals and I'm feeling sentimental. So, first of all, I just want to say that I really love you all," she said, smiling as they heckled her. They weren't an emotionally earnest team, but Ari wasn't going to back down.

"I've known most of you since we were just teenage girls with acne, aggression issues, and outlandish dreams. But look around, we made it," she said softly, gazing out at her girls. "This is a culmination of all the years we spent on the rink, playing our best *long before* anybody else believed in us. I'm so proud of how far we've come," she said, watching as they nodded and took it in. "I know everyone's terrified of playing Team USA, and if I'm honest, so am I. But if they're going to try and beat us, let's make every single second they spend on that rink a misery," she said to a crowd of faces surprised at the pivot in her tone. But Ari knew what she was doing. She wasn't just there to make them feel good about themselves, she was there to remind them of the huge chip on their shoulders that had carried them through the last decade or so on the ice.

"They have the championship advantage, but we have something to prove. So, I want to see them squirm. For them to be so surprised by how much better we are than when they last played us that they panic on the ice. I want them to remember this as the day they got crushed by a team that was at the bottom of the league two years ago. So, let's go out onto the ice and give them *hell*," said Ari to a round of cheers and applause. Her speech had filled the locker room with so much energy that they lifted her up from the bench and carried her around the room, chanting "Give them hell!" Somehow, it was the most wholesome moment the team had shared since landing in Switzerland. Coach McLaughlin shook his head and laughed, then turned up the music. Ari didn't do pep talks, but she knew how to get the girls fired up.

As they walked into the stadium, they were greeted by a wave of applause. The Team GB supporters' stand was filled to the brim with Union Jacks and hand-painted signs. She knew that her family had bought tickets, but she hadn't spoken to them since leaving them to sort out their issues on the phone. She usually had a strict no-contact rule in the twenty-four hours before a monumental game, restricting her conversations to just her teammates and coach. She did it to avoid being thrown off by an unexpected text, doom scroll, or call; and no matter how much drama was going on back home, her family usually respected it. But since their last conversation had ended on bad terms, she'd almost expected them to stay at home. She'd been pretty harsh with them and hadn't checked in each morning like she usually did. But as she looked out at the supporters' stands, she saw two familiar faces. They were dressed head to toe in Team GB supporters' merch, singing along to each chant the crowd sang. Her sister spotted her first and started jumping up and down with a sign that read TEAM ARI!. Then Ari locked eyes with her mother. She was wearing a big Team GB hoodie, crying tears of joy, and holding the sign up even higher. Ari whipped her phone out to take a photo of them, but when she looked at her screen, there was a message waiting for her.

Mama: We should have been at every game. We love you. I'm sorry.

Ari nodded and waved at her family before putting her phone in the locker and letting out a sigh she'd been holding in for years. The weight she'd been carrying felt lighter now. For once she could channel all of her mental energy onto the ice.

When the girls skated onto the rink this time, their whole demeanor was different. The tension that had been lingering among them had dissipated. The caution with which they'd been playing ever since they'd landed in Switzerland was replaced by a confident yet playful sense of determination. Because today, for the first time, they'd resolved to play like they had nothing to lose.

They took their positions, glanced over at one another one more time, and got ready for the game to begin. Team USA did the same thing, skating across the ice in their blue-and-white jerseys, dripping with confidence.

As Ari made her way to the center, so did Thandie. They made eye contact through the helmets that protected their faces.

"Good luck," Ari said quietly enough that only they could hear. Thandie smiled.

"Break a leg," Thandie whispered with a wink. Ari laughed and then tried to regain her composure as the stadium quieted and everyone on the ice locked in. They gave each other one final nod before positioning themselves for game time. This was it.

The stadium went silent as the referee skated to the center and raised his hand. The world slowed down for a second as he loosened his grip, let go of the puck, and watched it land.

Ari clutched her hockey stick, swept the puck before Thandie could touch it, and in an instant, the game was on her side. Everything happened at full speed after that.

The puck whizzed across the ice from player to player as each team took control of the game, lost it, recovered, slipped up, triumphed, and started again. The first score should have gone to Team USA, but Izzy saved it by just the width of a hair.

After an excellent three-person attack, Sienna scored Team GB's first goal and raised the stakes of each second.

Thandie missed her first attempt, but made up for it by scoring twice before the end of the first period.

But then Yasmeen and the defense built an iron-clad wall between the blue jerseys and the goal, blocking each of their attempts and shooting the puck across the ice each time they got close.

They went back and forth, nonstop. The game was so action-packed that they didn't have a moment to second-guess themselves. Ari scored a goal and then another. For a fraction of a second, she saw what looked like fear in Thandie's eyes, but her teammates immediately picked up the pace with another score just seconds into the third period.

The scoreboard kept going up. Each time one team scored a goal, so did the other. The action was nail-bitingly intense as they skated up and down the rink, chased after each other, and hit precisely angled shots.

But when the game reached its final thirty seconds, something magical happened. Izzy blocked a goal that unintentionally shot the puck to Yasmeen, who sent it flying on the ice to Sienna, who expertly hit it toward Ari, just as their opponents looked to the side.

Without a moment's hesitation, Ari hit it with her hockey stick and watched the puck fly across the ice, skim past a blue-and-white jersey, and hit the net, scoring a majestic goal in the last twenty seconds of the game.

They had never played in such harmony before or executed a play with such skill and precision.

Ari's eyes widened as she realized what they'd done. A goal in the final twenty seconds that tied their score with Team USA.

However, before she could allow herself to smile, the puck

was out in the rink again, the seconds before the game ended counting down in slow motion as the blue jerseys took control of the game and passed the puck back and forth until Thandie Dlamini got ahold of it and scored the winning goal.

Team USA had won the quarterfinals in the very last second.

But when the final buzzer blared, Ari couldn't help but grin as a wave of joy swept across her whole body. She wanted to skate her way into a dance, sing the words of her favorite song, and hug her best friends. Because they'd made it further than anybody could have ever imagined they would. The American team was high-fiving one another and taking photos to mark their qualification to the semifinals. But the Team GB girls were celebrating as if they'd just won gold.

Ari ripped her helmet off her head and skated straight over to Sienna, Yasmeen, and Izzy. The four of them began to dance, cheer, and celebrate like the Olympic champions they were.

"We did it!" shouted Izzy.

"We gave them hell!" declared Sienna.

"We're Olympians!" said Yasmeen, her eyes watering up. Soon they were all a mess of laughter and joyful tears. All twenty-three of them skated to the center of the court and embraced each other as if this was the greatest win of their lives. Someone found a bottle of champagne and popped it. And then, before Ari could even figure out what was happening, the girls lifted her up and skated her around the rink, shouting, "Captain! Captain! Captain!" at the top of their voices as she laughed and cheered along.

She felt happier than she ever had before and freer than she could have ever imagined. They hadn't won the match, but it felt like they had won the Games. She couldn't imagine any other team being as happy as they were right then. It was the pinnacle of all the years they'd spent in locker rooms, ice rinks, and training fields. Pure euphoria. But as the girls put her down and began to skate to the locker room to continue their celebrations, she saw one more face in the crowd, scrambling down the stairs with his camera around his neck and a huge smile on his face.

He climbed over the barrier until he was right there, just outside the ice, waiting for her. She got lost in his big brown eyes, savored the sight of his bright, warm smile, and let the moment sink in. Then she skated out of the rink and straight into his arms.

48

Drew

"O Canada! O Canada! Our home and native land!" sang Luiz at the top of his lungs as they left the press office and walked out into the snow.

"Don't sing that when we get there, or they *will* kill you." Drew smiled.

Team USA had won the quarterfinal match and breezed through the semifinals, but Canada won the final. Thandie and Ari had both spent the past few days lamenting how close they'd been to gold, but the experience of getting this far had bonded them. They would always be rivals on the rink, but things seemed to be thawing between them the more time they spent together off the ice. A few of their teammates had been friends for years, so with their competitions over, they'd started hanging out and going to watch games together around the Village. To Drew's surprise, they'd even gone so far as deciding to celebrate the final night of the Games together.

While most teams made it to the opening ceremony, only a few athletes attended the closing ceremony in person. Unlike the Summer Games, where people lingered in the host city for an extended summer vacation, after two weeks in the snow, most of the winter sports athletes had already gone home. So, Thandie and their remaining teammates had taken over the hot chocolate bar, filled it with their favorite people, and made it the site of their closing ceremony watch party. Drew walked in and smiled at the fairy lights strewn across the room, the cookies iced with world flags, and the big screen playing the winter highlights as they waited for the final broadcast to begin.

"When you said closing ceremony party, I thought you meant a casual hangout," Luiz said. He pointed to the Zeus branding on the tables, goodie bags, and paper cups.

"Well, that's all thanks to you, Luiz," Thandie said as she greeted them at the door wearing a chunky winter sweater and a sparkly silver skirt. "You're the one that got Harrison banned for—"

"I wasn't involved, remember," Luiz said, giving her a firm look as he picked up a drink, but the twinkle in his eyes spoke for itself.

"You're right. What I *meant* to say was Harrison being reckless enough to take drugs at his medal party worked in our favor." Thandie smiled. It wasn't kind to celebrate someone's downfall, but when Drew had explained the entire situation to his sister, she'd happily cut ties with Harrison and decided that she wanted no part in a campaign that included a man who'd been willing to hurt her career to get back at his ex.

And it worked in her favor. Harrison's drug scandal had put his professional sports career on hold. Ruining his reputation when there were already stories floating around about his misconduct behind the scenes had made it pretty easy for Zeus to break their contract with him and award it to Thandie instead. But instead of allowing them to make her the sole ambassador at the heart of their new 2026 campaign, Thandie had called them up and made a deal to split it with several other women who'd been successful at that year's Games.

The result was an awe-inspiring video that featured various women defying the odds, exceeding expectations, and smashing people's preconceptions of them by becoming the greatest athletes in their sport. It had gone live the day after Thandie's silver-medal win and was shaping up to become one of Zeus's most successful campaigns. So, it was no wonder why they'd sponsored Thandie's closing ceremony party and made a commitment to investing more money into training, facilities, and equipment for young women in ice hockey across the world.

"So I'm not saying I forgive you for going behind my back. But I guess it worked out pretty well," Thandie said to her brother as he picked up a cup of hot chocolate and looked out at the party before him, marveling at how his terrible decisions had accidentally worked in his sister's favor. But he'd learned his lesson.

"No secrets next time," Drew said.

"No secrets." His sister nodded, then rattled off a list of images she wanted him to capture. His apology for lying to her was a lifetime of free photographs, so he lifted his camera from his neck and took a picture of Thandie and Luiz against the backdrop of a huge chocolate fountain. The three of them chatted for a while about who else was coming before Thandie made her way out into the crowd to go back to being the social butterfly she was. Drew watched the party unfold, noticing all the people in the room experiencing it from different points of view. The Team GB ice hockey players congregating around the chocolate fountain as they exchanged stories and laughed about something he was too far away to hear. Luiz schmoozing with the social team from Zeus Athletics, no doubt plotting out his next career move. The athletes heading over to the makeshift dance floor that had popped up in the middle of the room, and the family members who'd traveled to St. Moritz sitting on the outskirts as they caught up with the people they loved. Drew's grandparents had invited themselves to the party and were deep in conversation with Thandie's coach, and Ari's sister, Anesu, was having a starstruck conversation with a gold medal–winning figure skater.

Drew had never really loved parties. He'd always felt that he was better suited for the sidelines. But being surrounded by people who, like him, had successfully gotten through the Games felt pretty magical. He lifted his camera and took a photo of the scene that lay before him then went to get a drink. But then, right as he was about to turn a corner, he heard a laugh he would have recognized anywhere. He turned around to walk in the direction of it until he saw her. Ari.

She was wearing a long, white knit dress that folded over at the shoulders and hugged her curves in all the right ways. Her hair was tied back, but a few curls fell forward, gently framing her face. She'd been laughing at something one of her friends said while holding a clear glass mug filled with the spiced apple tea they were serving at the bar. But when she saw him, she cut her conversation short and walked straight over. When she kissed him, he could taste the cinnamon and sugar on her lips. When they parted, she placed a gentle hand on his cheek and looked at him, her eyes soft and sparkly in the dim evening light.

"You know we were supposed to break up after the last game, right?"

"Well, it's a good thing I'm bad at sticking to the plan," Drew said, pulling her into his arms and leaning in to kiss her again. "Want to get out of here?" he asked, pointing over to the balcony on the other side of the room. When she nodded, he took her hand and led her out, feeling all warm inside. As if they'd just met.

When they walked out onto the balcony, they were met by a dark night sky, lit up by a dozen constellations and a curved half-moon. The mountains were coated with snow and the air was chillier than ever. But the balcony was lined with outdoor heaters and blanket-covered outdoor seats, so they found an empty bench and snuggled beside each other.

"I applied for the job with Hans," he said after a while. She was the first person to know.

"Did you get it?" she asked, looking up, her expression full of hope.

Since deciding not to return to USC, he'd opened himself up to the possibility of taking a year to chase opportunities around the world, as long as he could spend most of that year in Wisconsin. His grandparents still disagreed with his choices, but he knew he was doing what felt right for him. He'd sent in his application for the job with Hans only a few days ago, so he still had no idea if it would work out. The logistics of potentially traveling for six weeks put everything up in the air, and he didn't know whether he'd be able to do a good enough job if he did get the position. But Drew had decided it was better to apply than spend the rest of his life wondering what might have happened if he'd been brave enough to take the risk.

"I won't know for a few more weeks. But if I do get it, I'll be in London in April," he said. Her eyes lit up.

"And I'm going to be flying to your side of the ocean to watch the North American playoffs in May," she said, telling him how an eBay bidding war for the vintage Cartier watch she owned had paid for her flights and hotel. "I'll be in Chicago for two weeks."

"Which is practically next door to Wisconsin."

"Really? It doesn't look close on the map."

"It's just a three-hour drive," he said, reaching for one of the blankets and wrapping it around them. Despite the outdoor heaters, it was still pretty chilly outside. When he looked back at her, Ari had a puzzled expression on her face.

"Only an American would say a three-hour drive is just next door," she laughed. But the possibility of extending their time together into the spring was more than enough to keep his hopes up.

"And then after that?" he asked, reaching for her hand and kissing the back of it.

"Well, the last time we parted ways, we found each other, right? I get the feeling it will happen again. Plus, I've been speaking to Thandie. . . ."

"I can't believe you're friends now." He smiled.

"She's a riot, and we should have become friends sooner. Me and the girls went to lunch with her the other day and we got to talking. I love London, but all of the best ice hockey teams are on the other side of the world. So she put me in touch with a few coaches, and who knows, I might be on your side of the pond by the summer," she said.

"Are you serious?" Drew asked, sitting up in excitement and looking at her, seeing the hopeful expression in her eyes.

"It's too soon to know, they might not even want me."

"They'd be fools not to. But what about your family?" He turned around to look through the window and back inside at the party where her mom and sister were tearing it up on the dance floor.

"They'll figure out how to manage without me." She shrugged. Drew heard a bit of guilt in her voice, but they'd talked enough about the push and pull she felt. Detaching a little bit was the best thing she could do for their relationship.

"So, winter in St. Moritz and summer . . ." she said, unsure.

Drew had given up on certainty, but he knew exactly where he wanted to be that night.

"In the summer, we'll be wherever we're meant to be. But tonight? Let's dance." He took her hand, then led her back inside to the dance floor—right in the heart of a room filled with the people they loved.

Maybe Ari and Drew *would* be in the same part of the world again by the summertime. Or maybe they'd take their flights back home in a few days and spend the rest of the year apart. It could all click into place, or fall apart before it even had the chance to begin. A lot could happen in the days they had left together in the mountains. But who knew if they'd be able to cultivate something strong enough to withstand the realities of life beyond the Village? It was all up in the air, but for once, Drew wasn't worried about all the ways it could end. Because there was no worst-case scenario that could eclipse the hope of falling in love.

As an old love song played out of the speakers, she put her hands on his shoulders, and he wrapped his hands around her waist.

"I didn't know you could dance." She smiled.

"I don't skate, but I can definitely dance," he said, holding her close and then spinning her out into a twirl that ended with them face-to-face. The room was packed, but he didn't notice. Outside, snowflakes had begun to dance their way down from the sky. Soon the night would be lit up with fireworks, just like the night they'd first met. It was as if they were figurines in a snow globe, looking into each other's eyes as the world spun around. Everything else faded away until it was just them. Drew realized he wasn't just forming a memory. That thought was a glimpse into a potential future, a whisper of what lay ahead.

He would gravitate toward her at every party. And she would reach for his hand at the edge of every dance floor. They wouldn't need to escape to be themselves, because they could make midnight rooftops of train carriages, bookshop aisles, and kitchen floors. Spend miniature lifetimes telling each other their secrets and making stories of their own. It could last eighty years, seven months, six days, or just a few more hours. But as long as they stayed in each other's arms until the end of the song, this would be more than enough.

Acknowledgments

Writing this book was truly a case of faking it till I made it. I'm infinitely grateful to those who believed in me throughout the entire process and those who fell for the act that I was feeling way more confident about the process than I actually was. The two years that led to releasing this book were full of so much joy, fear, excitement, and dread. I've never felt a stronger desire to go to a party and tell a stranger my secrets, but I'm so grateful for the knowledge that I could, at any point, call the village of people who helped bring this story to life:

Thank you to my family, always. Dad for going to every parents' evening, playing sports in the background of my childhood, and teaching me about the female role models I'll spend my life aspiring to. Mom for taking me to my first ice rink, constantly betting on yourself in a way that inspires me to do the same, and allowing us all to have deeply uncomplicated childhoods. Takomborerwa for checking in on me when I looked disheveled during edits, delivering the meal I needed, and buying me my first camera. I think most people just need one person to loudly and consistently believe in them, and you've always been that for me. Ruvimbo for regularly listening to me spiral about publishing, being deeply nonjudgmental even when I am very obviously crashing out, and taking 24,923 photos/videos to help me document the process. I genuinely couldn't have published this or the last book without you helping me to maintain my sanity. I can't wait for the day you run things and retire me into stay-at-home sisterdom.

Shout out to my agent Jemima for helping me navigate my debut year and all the twists and turns that came with bringing this book to life! Thank you for giving me great advice, encouraging me to be strategic and go with my gut, and coming up with the *perfect* title for this book. Thank you to my editors Kukuwa and Kara for your smart, thoughtful, and encouraging guidance throughout the entire process of editing this book and for bringing Ari and Drew's story to bookshelves in cities I've never visited before. It's such a joy to get to work with people who understand what I'm trying to do while pushing me to become a writer.

Endless thanks to Allison Hunter, Natalie Edwards, and everyone at Trellis for helping me release *another* book in North America, a reality that felt like such a distant dream. And a really big thank-you to Giulia Bernabe, Georgie Smith, and everyone at David Higham for advocating for me and being so encouraging throughout the past three years. Thank you to Soraya for being excited about and believing in Ari and Drew's story; so glad we get to work together! And thank you to everyone at Flatiron and Headline who championed this book in calls and conversations. I only get to see a glimpse of all the work you do, but it's so lovely to know there's been such a brilliant team of people fighting in Ari and Drew's corner, including Marlena, Katherine, Drew, and Emma. A special superthanks to Bria for giving *Let the Games Begin* the perfect summer rollout!

Thank you to all the friends I love deeply who I either mentioned in the *LTGB* acknowledgments or whose names I've hidden in the pages of this book. Writing is delightful and holding the book in your hands is a dream, but the journey from one to the other is just as stressful as it is exciting. So infinitely grateful for Anam for being the first writer friend I met in London, Alexis and Soha for organizing meetups and holding me accountable (when I *really* just want to chat), and the incredible authors in the Black Book Ladies group chat for making publishing feel like a real community. Thank you to Pyae Moe Thet War, Jasmine Burke, Annabelle Slator, Lily Chu, Grace Reilly, and Kanitha P for your incredibly kind blurbs; and the 250 Pages regulars, whose conversations make me want to be a better writer.

A huge thank-you to Simidele Adeagbo for being such an incredibly inspirational athlete *and* for letting me ask you dozens of questions about life as a Black woman in professional sports. Can't wait to cheer you on through my TV screen during Milan 2026! Thank you to Debi Thomas, Vonetta Flowers, and Blake Bolden for being such pioneers in the world of winter sports. And to Denise Lewis, Serena Williams, and Simone Biles for being such ever-present figures in the background of my life that Black women have always been the center of my sporting universe. And finally, a cosmic thank-you to Kenny Ortega and Peter Barsocchini for the films that came out twenty years ago that unintentionally became the biggest inspirations behind my books. I'll be chasing the high of those Friday-night premieres for the rest of my life.

And finally, so much love to you for making it to the end. For being the reader I think about while creating stories. I'll be writing for you until the wheels fall off.